This book must be returned by the date specified at the time of issue as
the DATE DUE FOR RETURN.
The loan may be extended (personally, by post, telephone or online) for
a further period if the book is not required by another reader, by quoting
the above number / author / title.

Enquiries: 01709 336774

www.rotherham.gov.uk/libraries

Also by Dianne Drake

Bachelor Doc, Unexpected Dad
Second Chance with Her Army Doc
Her Secret Miracle
New York Doc, Thailand Proposal

Sinclair Hospital Surgeons miniseries

Reunited with Her Army Doc
Healing Her Boss's Heart

Also by Karin Baine

Reforming the Playboy
Their Mistletoe Baby
From Fling to Wedding Ring
Midwife Under the Mistletoe
The Single Dad's Proposal
Their One-Night Twin Surprise
Their One-Night Christmas Gift

Discover more at millsandboon.co.uk.

FALLING FOR HER ARMY DOC

DIANNE DRAKE

HEALED BY THEIR UNEXPECTED FAMILY

KARIN BAINE

MILLS & BOON

First Published in Great Britain 2020
by Mills & Boon, an imprint of HarperCollins*Publishers*
1 London Bridge Street, London, SE1 9GF

Falling for Her Army Doc © 2020 by Dianne Despain

Healed by Their Unexpected Family © 2020 by Karin Baine

ISBN: 978-0-263-27961-0

MIX
Paper from
responsible sources
FSC® C007454

This book is produced from independently certified FSC™ paper
to ensure responsible forest management.
For more information visit www.harpercollins.co.uk/green.

Printed and bound in Spain
by CPI, Barcelona

FALLING FOR
HER ARMY DOC

DIANNE DRAKE

MILLS & BOON

I dedicate this book to Mr. Kahawaii,
who took me into his amazing world for a little while.

CHAPTER ONE

SHE LOOKED BEAUTIFUL, standing outside in the garden, catching the morning light. He watched her every day about this time. She'd take her walk, sit for a few minutes on the stone retaining wall surrounding the sculpted flowers, then return to the building.

Once, he'd wondered what weighed her down so heavily. She had that look—the one he remembered from many of his patients, and probably even more he didn't remember. She—Lizzie, she'd told him her name was—always smiled and greeted him politely. But there was something behind that smile.

Of course, who was he to analyze? It had taken a photo he'd found among his things to remind him that he'd been engaged. Funny how his memory of her prior to his accident was blurred. Nancy was a barely recognizable face in a world he didn't remember much of. And, truthfully, he couldn't even recall how or why he'd become engaged to her. She didn't seem his type—too flighty, too intrusive. Too greedy.

Yet Lizzie, out there in the garden, seemed perfect. Beautiful. Smart. In tune with everything around her.

So what wasn't he getting here? Had he changed so much that the type of woman who'd used to attract

him didn't now? And taking her place was someone…
more like Lizzie?

Dr. Mateo Sanchez watched from the hospital window until Lizzie left the garden, then he drew the blinds
and went back to bed. He didn't have a lot of options
here, as a patient. Rest, watch the TV, rest some more.
Go to therapy. Which somehow he never quite seemed
to do.

This was his fourth facility since he'd been shipped
from the battlefield to Germany, and nothing was working. Not the therapy. Not his attitude. Not his life. What
he wanted to know they wouldn't tell him. And what he
didn't want to know just seemed to flood back in when
he didn't want it to.

The docs were telling him to be patient, that some
memory would return while some would not. But he
wanted a timeline, a calendar on his wall where he could
tick off the days until he was normal again.

He reached up and felt the tiny scar on his head.
Whatever normal was. Right now, he didn't know. There
was nothing for him to hold on to. No one there to
ground him. Even Nancy hadn't stayed around long
after she'd discovered he didn't really know her.

In fact, his first thought had been that she was a
nurse, tending him at his bedside. She'd been good when
he'd asked for a drink of water, even when he'd asked
for another pillow, and she'd taken his criticism when
she'd told him she couldn't give him a pain pill.

This had gone on for a week before she'd finally confessed that she wasn't his nurse, but his fiancée. And
then, in another week, she'd been gone. She wasn't the
type to do nursing care in the long term, she'd said. And
unfortunately, all she could see ahead of her was nurs-

ing care, a surgeon who could no longer operate, when what she'd wanted was a surgeon who could provide a big home, fancy cars, and everything else he'd promised he'd give her.

So, he knew the what and the when of his accident. What he *didn't* know was the annoying part. As a surgeon he needed to know all aspects of his patients' conditions, even the things that didn't seem to matter. It was called being thorough. But for him…

"Giving you the answers to your life could imprint false memories," his neurologist Randy always said, when he asked. And he was right, of course. That was something he did remember. Along with so many of his basic medical skills—the ones he'd learned early on in his career.

The more specific skills, though… Some of them were still there. Probably most of them. But in pulling them out of his memory he hesitated sometimes. Thought he remembered but wasn't sure of himself.

Wait a minute. Let me consult a textbook before I remove your gall bladder.

Yeah, right. Like *that* was going to work in surgery.

He looked up and saw Lizzie standing in his doorway, simply observing him. Probably trying to figure out what to do with him.

"Hello," he said, not sure what to make of this.

She was the house primary care physician—not his doctor, not even a neurologist. Meaning she had no real reason to be here unless he needed a vaccination or something.

"I've seen you watch me out in the garden. I was wondering if you'd like to come out with me for a while later…breathe some fresh air, take a walk?"

"Who's prescribing that?" he asked suspiciously.

"You are—if that's what you want to do. You're not a prisoner here, you know. And your doctor said it might be a good idea…that it could help your…" She paused.

"Go ahead and say it. My disposition."

"I understand from morning staff meetings that you're quite a handful."

"Nothing else to do around here," he said. "So, I might as well improve upon my obnoxious level. It's getting better. In fact, I think I'll soon be counted amongst the masters."

"To what outcome?"

He shrugged. "See, that's the thing. For me, there *are* no outcomes."

"If that's how you want it. But I'm not your doctor and you're not my problem. So, take that walk with me or not."

"And tomorrow? What happens to me tomorrow?"

"Honestly? I'm a one-day-at-a-time girl. Nothing's ever guaranteed, Mateo. If I get through the day, tomorrow will take care of itself."

"Well, I like seeing ahead. And now, even behind."

"To each his own," she said nonchalantly.

"Which implies what?" he asked, feeling a smile slowly crossing his face. Lizzie was…*fun*. Straight to the point. And challenging.

"You know exactly what it implies, Mateo. In your effort to see 'behind,' as you're calling it, you're driving the staff crazy. They're afraid of you. Not sure what to do with you. And that false smile of yours is beginning to wear thin."

"Does it annoy you?" he asked.

"It's beginning to."

"Then my work here is done," he said, folding his arms across his chest.

He wanted clothes—real clothes. Not these blue and green things that were passed off as hospital gowns. Those were for sick people. He wasn't sick. Just damaged. A blood clot on his brain, which had been removed, and a lingering pest called retrograde amnesia. That kind of damage deserved surfer shorts and a Hawaiian shirt, seeing as how he was in Hawaii now.

"And my work has nothing to do with you. I was just trying to be friendly, but you're too much of a challenge to deal with. And, unfortunately, what should have been a simple yes or no is now preventing me from seeing my patients."

She sure was pretty.

It was something he'd thought over and over about Lizzie. Long, tarnished copper hair. Curly. Soft too, he imagined. Brown eyes that could be as mischievous as a kitten or shoot daggers, depending on the circumstance. And her smile… It didn't happen too often, he'd noticed. And when it did, it didn't light up the proverbial room. But it sure did light up his day.

"And how would I be doing that? I'm here, wearing these lovely clothes, eating your gourmet green slime food, putting up with your hospital's inane therapy."

"And by 'putting up with,' you mean not showing up for?" She took a few more steps into the room, then went to open the blinds.

"In the scheme of my future life, what will it do for me?"

"Maybe nothing. Maybe everything."

"No vagaries here, Lizzie. Be as specific as I have to be every time I answer someone's orientation questions. 'Do you remember your name?' 'Where are you?' 'What's the date?' 'Who's the current President?'"

"Standard protocol, Mateo. You know that." She turned back to face him. "But you make everything more difficult than it has to be."

She brightened his day in a way he'd never expected. "So why me? You're not my doctor, but you've obviously chosen me for some special attention."

"My dad was a military surgeon, like you were. Let's just say I'm giving back a little."

"Did he see combat?"

"Too many times."

"And it changed him," Mateo said, suddenly serious.

"It might have—but if it did it was something he never let me see. And he never talked about it."

"It's a horrible thing to talk about. The injuries. The ones you can fix…the ones you can't. In my unit they were rushed in and out so quickly I never really saw anything but whatever it was I had to fix. Maybe that was a blessing."

He shut his eyes to the endless parade of casualties who were now marching by him. This was a memory he didn't want, but he was stuck with it. And it was so vivid.

"Were you an only child?" he asked.

Lizzie nodded. "My mom couldn't stand the military life. She said it was too lonely. So, by the time I was five she was gone, and then it was just my dad and me."

"Couldn't have been easy being a single parent under his circumstances. I know *I* wouldn't have wanted to drag a kid around with me when I was active. Wouldn't have been fair to the kid."

"He never complained. At least, not to me. And what I had…it seemed normal."

"I complain to everybody."

In Germany, after his first surgery, it hadn't occurred to him that his memory loss might be permanent. He'd been too busy dealing with the actual surgery itself to get any more involved than that. That had happened after he'd been transferred to Boston for brain rehab. Then he'd got involved. Only it hadn't really sunk in the way it should have. But once they'd got him to a facility in California, where the patients had every sort of war-related brain injury, that was when it had occurred to him that he was just another one of the bunch.

How could that be? That was the question he kept asking himself over and over. He had become one of the poor unfortunates he usually treated. A surgeon without his memory. A man without his past.

"You're a survivor who uses what he has at his disposal to regain the bits and pieces of himself he's lost. Or at least that's what you could be if you weren't such a quitter."

"A quitter?"

Maybe he was, since going on was so difficult. But did Lizzie understand what it was like to reach for a memory you assumed would be there and come up with nothing? And he was one of the lucky ones. Physically, he was fine, and his surgery had gone well. He'd healed well, too. But he couldn't get past that one thing that held him back…who was he, *really*?

Suddenly Mateo was tired. It wasn't even noon yet and he needed a nap. Or an escape.

"That walk this evening…maybe. If you can get me some real clothes."

Lizzie chuckled. "I *should* say you'll have to wear your hospital pajamas, but I'll see what I can do."

"No promises, Lizzie. I don't make promises I can't keep, and who knows what side of the pendulum my mood will be swinging on later."

"Whatever suits you," she said, then left the room.

Even though he hated to see her go, what he needed was to be left alone—something he'd told them over and over. He needed time to figure out just how big a failure he was, medically speaking. And what kind of disappointment he was to his mother, who'd worked long and hard to get him through medical school. The arthritis now crippling her hands showed that.

There was probably a long list of other people he'd let down, too, but thankfully he couldn't remember it. Except his own name—right there at the top. He was Dr. Mateo Sanchez—a doctor with retrograde amnesia. And right now that was all he cared to know. Everything else—it didn't matter.

She was not getting involved. It didn't usually work. Didn't make you happy, either. Didn't do a thing. At least in her case it never had.

Lizzie's mom had walked out when she was barely five, so no involvement there. And her dad... Well, he'd loved her. But her father had been a military surgeon, and that had taken up most of his time. While he'd always said he wanted to spend more time with her, it hadn't happened. So no involvement with him, either, for a good part of her life.

Then there had been her husband. Another doctor, but one who wouldn't accept that she didn't want to be a surgeon like him. He was a neurosurgeon and, to him, being a primary care physician meant being... *lesser*. He did surgeries while she did cuts and bruises, he'd always say. Brad had never failed to show his disappointment in her, so she'd failed there, too. Meaning, what was the point?

None, that Lizzie could think of. But that was OK. She got along, designed her life the way she wanted it to be, and lived happily in the middle of it. Living in the middle was good, she decided. It didn't take you far, but it didn't let you down, either.

She wondered about Mateo, though. She knew he watched her in the garden every morning. Knew he'd asked questions about her. But the look on his face... there was no confidence there. Something more like fear. Which was why she'd asked him out for a walk this evening. He needed more than the four walls of his hospital room, the same way her father had needed more.

But her father had been on a downward spiral with Alzheimer's. Mateo was young, healthy, had a lot of years of life ahead of him—except he was getting into the habit of throwing away the days. It was hard seeing that, after watching the way her father had deteriorated.

But to get involved...? They weren't friends. Weren't even doctor-patient. Weren't anything. But she'd been watching the watcher for weeks now, and since she'd be going on holiday shortly what would it hurt to get involved for once? Or, in this case, to take a simple evening walk?

Watching Mateo walk toward her now, she thought he struck her as a man who would have taken charge. His gait was strong, purposeful. And he was a large man—massive muscles on a well-defined body. He'd taken care of himself. You didn't get that physique by chance. Yet now he was stalled, and that didn't fit. To look at him was to think he had his life together—it was in the way he carried himself. But there was nothing together about him, not one little piece. And he was sabotaging himself by not trying.

Many of the staff's morning meetings lately had opened with: *"What should we do about Mateo?"*

The majority wanted him out of there. Even his own doctor didn't care. But Lizzie was his advocate because he deserved this chance. Like her dad had, all those times someone had tried to convince her to put him away. That was exactly what they wanted to do with Mateo, and while neurology wasn't her specialty, she did know that some types of brain trauma took a long time to sort themselves out.

But beds here were at a premium. The waiting list was long, and military veterans always went to the top of the list. There was no guarantee they'd stay there, though, especially if they acted the way Mateo did.

He was never mean. Never outright rude, even though he was always on the edge of it. In fact, he smiled more than anybody she'd ever seen. But he refused to try, and that was ultimately going to get in the way, since there were other veterans who could have his bed and display more cooperation.

The waiting line for each and every bed was eight deep, Janis always reminded her, when she was so often the only one at the meeting table who defended him. His bed could be filled with the snap of her fingers, and that was what she had to impress upon Mateo or he'd be out.

Truthfully, Lizzie was worried about Mateo's progress. Or rather his lack of it. His time was indeed running out, and there was serious talk of transferring him elsewhere. He knew that, and it didn't faze him. Not one little bit. Or if it did, he hid it well. Making her wonder why she tried so hard to advocate for a man who didn't advocate for himself.

"Well, you look good in real clothes," she said as he walked up to the reception hub where she'd been waiting.

He spun around the way a model on a runway would, then took a bow as a couple of passing nurses applauded him. "It's good to feel human again."

"You're allowed out in the garden any time, Mateo. All you have to do is ask and someone will walk along with you."

"But today I scored you." He leaned in toward her and whispered, "Who happens to be the prettiest doctor in this hospital."

"Save the flattery for someone else, Mateo. All I'm doing is trying to chart a doctor's note saying you were cooperative for once. So far there aren't any of those on record."

Staff were tired of sugar-coating what they said about him and had started opting for snarky comments instead. In their defense, they were a highly dedicated lot who were bound to their jobs by the need to make improvements in patients' lives—physically and emotionally. And, while Mateo might make them smile, he also frustrated them by pushing them to the limit.

Lizzie nudged a wheelchair in his direction.

"You know I can walk," he said.

"Of course, you can, but…hospital policy. If I take a patient outside, they must go by wheelchair or else I'll be in trouble. In other words, comply, or give back the clothes and go to bed."

* * *

"Comply? Easier said than done," he said, not budging from where he was standing at the nurses' hub. "Especially when you're treating me like an invalid."

In truth, he'd prefer not to step outside—or in his case, be wheeled. There were too many things reminding him of how much he'd forgotten. Most days he wasn't in the mood to deal with it. Staying in bed, watching TV, playing video games, sleeping…that was about the extent of his life now.

Except Lizzie. She was the bright spot. And she was asking him out…no way he could turn that down.

"Isn't that how you're treating yourself?" she asked. "We've designed a beautiful program for you here—took days going over it and tweaking it. It's a nice balance for what you've got going on, yet have you ever, just once, referred to it? Daily walks in the garden, for instance? It's on there, Mateo. And workouts in the gym. But I'll bet you tossed the program in the trash as soon as you received it.

"Might have. Don't remember."

"Saying you've forgotten has become an easy excuse because retrograde amnesia is about forgetting things in the past. Not in the future, or even now. What you're not retaining right now is left over from your brain surgery, but that will improve in time. With some effort. If you let it. Also, if you don't care about your past you can walk out of here right now—a new man with a clean slate. You're healthy, and with some caution you're basically healed. Your destiny at this point is up to you. You can go, if that's what you want. But I don't think it is, because I believe you still want help with your memory loss, as well as trying to recall as much as you can about your life."

"Oh, you mean I want to remember things like how to repair a hernia?"

"It's all in there," she said, tapping her own head. "Like you've been told. Unless you missed your session that day, procedural things aren't normally lost. Life things are. And, as you already know, you do still have a little bit of head-banging going on after the surgery. But that's not even significant at this point. Your attitude is, though."

"Head-banging would be your professional diagnosis?"

Why the hell did he do this? He didn't like it, but sometimes the belligerence just slipped out anyway. And Lizzie was only trying to help. He'd heard it whispered that she was the only one standing between him and being sent elsewhere.

"It would be the way *you* described your headaches when you were first admitted. But you remember that, Mateo. Which means you're in one of your moods now. You think you can smile your way through it and maybe the staff won't notice that you're not working toward a better recovery? Well, I notice. Every little detail." She smiled back at him. "I'd be remiss in my duties if I didn't."

"So, I'm part of your duty?"

"You're one of the patients here. That's all. Whatever I choose to do, like go for a walk with you, is because I understand where you are right now."

"*Do* you, Lizzie?" he asked, his voice turning dark. "Do you really? I mean, even if I do retain knowledge of the procedural side of the surgeries I used to perform, would you honestly want a surgeon who comes to do your appendectomy and doesn't even remember what kind of suture he prefers?"

Lizzie laughed, giving the wheelchair one more push toward him. This time it bumped his knees, so he could no longer ignore it.

"Sometimes I wonder if someone should change your diagnosis to retrograde amnesia with a secondary symptom of being overly dramatic. You're a challenge, Mateo, that's for sure. And, just between us, an open appendectomy skin closure works best with an absorbable intradermic stitch. Although if you're doing the procedure laparoscopically, all it takes is a couple of dissolvable stitches on the inside and skin glue on the outside."

"And you know this because…?"

"I've done a few stitches in my time. That's part of being a PCP. So quit being so dramatic. It doesn't score points with me, if that's what you're trying to do."

Well, he might have gaps in his memory, including the kind of women he'd been drawn to, but Lizzie certainly held his attention now. Petite, bouncy. Smart. Serious as hell. And that was the part that didn't escape him. Lizzie Peterson was a great big bundle of formidable perfection all tied up in a small package.

Maybe that was what intrigued him the most. He couldn't picture himself with someone like her. Of course, in his recent spotty memory he couldn't picture himself with anybody, including his former fiancée.

"Not overly dramatic. I'm allergic to flowers, which is why I don't want to go to the garden."

"Says who?"

"Says me."

"Then why, just a few minutes ago, did you want to go out?"

"Maybe I wasn't allergic a few minutes ago. Maybe it was a sudden onset aversion."

"Well, it's your choice, Mateo. Your life is out there somewhere. Maybe it's not the one you want, but it's the one you're going to be stuck with. You can make your own choices with it, but what you do now will affect what you do later on. And there is a 'later on' coming up. You can't keep postponing it indefinitely."

She started to walk away but turned back for a final word. She smiled when she saw that he was in the wheelchair, ready to go. Why not? he thought. Nothing else was happening in his life. So why not take a stroll in the garden? Or, in his case, a roll.

He gave Lizzie a deliberate scowl, which turned so quickly into a smile it almost caught her off-guard. "Is there any way I can talk you out of the wheelchair?"

"Nope. I play by the hospital rules and you play by my rules. So, here's the deal. You cooperate."

"Or what?"

"That's all there is to it. You cooperate."

"Isn't a deal supposed to be two-sided?"

"Maybe your deals are, but mine aren't. I like getting my way, Mateo. And when I don't, I'm the one who gets grumpy. Trust me—my grumpy out-grumpys yours any day of the week, so don't try me."

He liked Lizzie. Trusted her. Wanted to impress her even though that was a long way from happening. "OK. Well…if that's all you're offering."

"A walk is a walk, Mateo. Nothing else. So don't go getting ideas."

"You mean this is a pity walk?"

"Something like that. You cooperate and I'll do my best to help you. If you don't cooperate…" She smiled. "I'm sure you can guess the rest."

He could, and he didn't like it. This was a good facility, and as a doctor he recognized that. But as a patient he didn't even recognize himself—and that was the problem. When he looked in the mirror, he didn't know the face that looked back. The eyes, nose and mouth were the same, but there was nothing in his eyes. No sign of who he was or used to be.

And he was just plain scared.

"Big date? You wish," she said on her way out through the door, pushing Mateo in front of her.

Today was Lizzie's thirteenth day on without a break. But she had her nights to herself and found that if she worked hard enough during the day she could sleep through her nighttime demons. So, she worked until she was ready to drop, often stopped by The Shack for something tall and tropical, then went home and slept. So far it was working. Thoughts of her dad's death weren't invading every empty moment as much as they'd used to.

Leaning back to the wall, just outside the door, Mateo extricated himself from his wheelchair—which was totally against the rules.

"Is he getting to you?" Janis Lawton asked, stopping to hand Lizzie a bottle of water.

Janis was chief of surgery at Makalapua Pointe Hospital. The one in charge. The one who made the rules and made sure they weren't broken. And the one who was about to send Mateo to another facility on the mainland if he wasn't careful.

"I know the nurses are having problems with him." Janis leaned against the wall next to Lizzie and fixed her attention on Mateo, who'd rolled his chair off the walkway and seemed to be heading for the reflecting pond. "But the thing is, he's so darned engaging and nice most of the time. Then when he's not cooperative, or when he's refusing therapy… It's hard justifying why he's here when my waiting list is so long."

"Because he needs help. Think about what you'd do if you suddenly couldn't be a surgeon anymore."

"I do, Lizzie. All the time. And that's why Mateo keeps getting the benefit of the doubt. I understand exactly what's happening. The rug is being pulled out from under him." She held up her right hand, showing Lizzie a massive scar. "That was almost me. It took me a year of rehab to get back to operating and in the early days… Let's just say that I was more like Mateo than anyone could probably imagine. But as director of the hospital I have some lines I must draw. And Mateo isn't taking that seriously. Maybe you could…?"

Lizzie held up her hand to stop the older woman. "It's an evening walk. That's all. No agenda. No hospital talk, if I can avoid it."

Like the walks she used to take with her dad, even in the days when he hadn't remembered who she was. It had been cathartic anyway. Had let her breathe all the way down to her soul.

"The way Mateo is happens when you don't know who you are." The way her dad had gotten. The less he'd remembered, the more uncooperative he'd become— and, while Alzheimer's was nothing like amnesia, she was reminded of the look she'd seen so often on her dad's face when she looked at Mateo. The look that said *lost.* And for Mateo, such an esteemed surgeon, to have this happen to him...

"You're not getting him mixed up with your dad, are you?" Janis asked.

Lizzie laughed outright at the suggestion. "No transference going on here! My dad was who he was, Mateo is who he is. And I do know the difference. My dad was lost in his mind. Mateo is lost in his world." She looked out at Mateo, who was now sitting on the stone wall, waiting for her.

"You do realize he's supposed to be in a wheelchair, don't you?" said Janis.

"But do *you* realize how much he doesn't like being treated like an invalid? Why force him across that line with something so trivial as a wheelchair?"

"Well, just so you know, your *friend* isn't on steady footing and he might be best served in another facility."

"This is his fourth facility, Janis. He's running out of options."

"So am I," she said, pushing herself off the wall, her eyes still fixed on Mateo, whose eyes were fixed right back on Janis. "And with you about to take leave for a while..."

That *was* a problem. She'd signed herself off duty for a couple of weeks. There were things in her own life she needed to figure out.

Was this where she wanted to stay, with so many sad memories still fighting their way through? And hospital work—it wasn't what she'd planned to do. She liked the idea of a small local clinic somewhere. Treating patients who might not have the best medical services available to them. Could she actually have something like that? Or was she already where she was meant to be?

Sure, it was an identity crisis mixed in with a professional crisis, but working herself as hard as she did there was no time left to weigh both sides—stay or go? In these two weeks of vacation there would be plenty of time for that—time to clear her mind, time to relax, time to be objective about her own life. It was a lot to sort out, but she was looking forward to it.

Everybody had choices to make, and so far, all her choices had been about other people. What did her husband want? What did her dad need? But the question was: What did Elizabeth Peterson want and need? And what would have happened if she'd chosen differently a year ago?

Well, for starters, her dad might still be alive. That was the obstacle she could never get past. But maybe now, after the tide had washed it all out to sea, that was something she could work on, too. Guilt—the big flashing light that always shone on the fact that her life wasn't in balance. And she had no idea how to restore that balance.

"I thought we were going to walk?" Mateo said, approaching her after Janis had gone inside.

"Did you *have* to break the rule about the wheelchair in front of Janis?" Lizzie asked, taking the hand Mateo offered her when she started to stand up.

"Does it matter? I'm already branded, so does it matter what I do when decisions are being made without my input?"

The soft skin of his hand against hers… It was enough to cause a slight shiver up her spine—and, worse, the realization that maybe she was ready for that aspect of her life to resume. The attraction. The shivers. Everything that came after.

She'd never had that with Brad. Their marriage had turned cold within the first month. Making love in the five spare minutes he had every other Thursday night and no PDA—even though she would have loved holding hands with him in public. Separate bedrooms half the time, because he'd said her sleeping distracted him from working in bed.

But here was Mateo, drop-dead gorgeous, kind, and friendly, even though he tried to hide it. All in all, he was very distracting. How would he be in a relationship? Not like Brad, she supposed. Brad was always in his own space, doing everything on his own terms, and she had become his afterthought. There was certainly no happily-ever-after in being overlooked by the man who was supposed to love you.

Not that it had made much of a difference, as by the time she'd discovered her place in their marriage she'd already been part-way out the door, vowing never to make that mistake again.

But was that what she really wanted? To spend her life alone? Devote herself to her work? Why was it that one mistake should dictate the rest of her life?

This was another thing to think about during her time off. The unexpected question. Could she do it again if the right man came along? And how could she tell who was right?

Perhaps by trusting her heart? With Brad, it had been more of a practical matter. But now maybe it was time to rethink what she really wanted and how to open herself up to it if it happened along.

Shutting her eyes and rubbing her forehead against

the dull headache setting in, it wasn't blackness Lizzie saw. It was Mateo. Which made her head throb a little harder. But also caused her heart to beat a little faster.

CHAPTER TWO

"I'D CLAIM AMNESIA, but I really don't know the names of most flowers. The purple and white ones…

"Orchids," Lizzie filled in.

"I know what orchids are." Mateo reached over the stone wall and picked one, then handed it to Lizzie. "There's probably a rule against picking the flowers, but you need an…*orchid* in your hair."

She took it and tucked it behind her right ear. "Right ear means you're available. Left means you're taken."

"How could someone like you not be taken?" he asked, sitting down next to her on the stone wall surrounding the garden.

Behind them were beautiful flowers in every color imaginable, with a long reflecting pond in the background. One that stretched toward the ocean.

"Because I don't want to be taken. It's one of those been-there-done-that situations, and I can still feel the sting from it, so I don't want to make the wound any worse.

"That bad?"

"Let's just say that on a rating of one through ten, I'd need a few more numbers to describe it. So, you haven't been…?"

"I was engaged briefly—apparently. Don't really have any memory of it other than a few flashes, and those aren't very flattering. Definitely not my type, from the little I recall."

"Maybe with your head injury your type changed. That can happen with brain damage. People are known to come out the other side very different from what they were when they went in. Could be the Fates giving you a second chance."

"You can't just have a normal conversation, can you? You turn everything into work."

"Because that's what I *do*."

"That's *all* you do, Lizzie. You come in early, leave late, and probably sandwich some sleep in there somewhere. I lived that schedule in Afghanistan too often, and it catches up to you."

"But this isn't about me, Mateo."

"First-year Med School. 'Treating a patient is as much about you as it is the patient.' Even though some of my patients came in and out so fast they never even saw me, I worked hard to make every one of them feel that they were in good hands, even if those hands were exhausted. But you… There's a deep-down tiredness behind the facade you put on, and it shows in your eyes. And I don't think it's physical so much as something else."

"It's just an accumulation of things. Tough decisions. My dad's death. Things I've wanted I haven't had. Things I've had I haven't wanted." She gave him a weak smile. "You're very perceptive for a man who claims amnesia at the drop of a hat."

"Straightforward talk, honesty…that's what I was all about, Lizzie. Have to be when you're out on the battlefield making quick decisions and performing life-changing procedures." He sighed. "In the end, when you're all they've got, the only real thing that counts is your word."

"Was it difficult…practicing like that?"

"Isn't it what your dad did?"

She shook her head. "He had rank, which got him assigned to a base hospital. He was the one who took the casualties that people like you had fixed after you sent them on."

"Wouldn't it be crazy if our paths had crossed somewhere? Yours and mine?"

"He kept me pretty isolated from that part of his life. If our paths had crossed it would have been somewhere like that little *bäckerei* on Robsonstrasse in Rhineland-Palatinate. We lived in a little flat about a block from there, and I loved getting up early and going for a Danish, or even a raspberry-filled braid."

"The plum cake there was always my favorite. A little bit sweet, a little bit tart."

"So, you've been there?" Lizzie asked, smiling over the shared memory.

"When I had time. My trips in and out were pretty quick, but I started getting a taste for the plum cake about the same time I stepped on the plane to go there, so that was always my first stop."

"Small world," Lizzie said. "Almost like a fairy tale…where the Princess meets the Prince in the most improbable way, then they have battles to fight to get to each other. You know—the love-conquers-all thing, starting with a fruit Danish and plum cake."

"And the rest of the story in your little world?" he

asked. "Do they ever get to their happily-ever-after, or do they eat their cakes alone forever?"

"Let's see…" she said. "So, their paths crossed at the bakery… His eyes met hers—love at first sight, of course. It always happens that way in a nice romantic story. But since the hero of my story was a soldier prince, their time was fleeting. Passionate, but brief. And the kisses…?"

"Were they good?"

"The best she'd ever known. But she was young, and very inexperienced. Oh, and she'd never kissed a real man before. He was her first. Her other kisses had come from boys in the village…no comparison to the kisses of a man."

It was nice, putting herself in the place of a young village maiden. Yes, Mateo's kisses would definitely be those of a real man. She could almost imagine how they would taste on her own lips.

"Was he her first true love?"

Lizzie nodded. "Of course he was. But, the way as many war stories end, they were separated. He was sent somewhere else and her heart was broken."

"Badly, or would she eventually heal?"

"I don't think you ever heal when you've lost the love of your life. But she went after him. She was strong that way."

"*Then* true love prevailed?"

"In my story, yes."

"And they lived happily ever after?"

"As happily-ever-after as any two lovers could with six children. A house in the country. Maybe a few dairy cows."

"Or just a couple of children, a house on a beach in Hawaii, no cows allowed?"

"Nice dream," she said on a sigh. "And I'd kill for a blueberry Danish right now."

Mateo started to slide his hand across the ledge on which they were seated—not so much to hold her hand, but just to brush against it. But either she saw it coming and didn't want it, or she was still caught up in her fairy tale, because just as he made his approach she stood, then turned toward the beach.

"We used to come here when I was a child. It's grown up a lot. Not much tourism back then."

"Is there any one place you call home, Lizzie?"

She shook her head. "Not really. Home was where we were or where we were going. And you?"

"A small village near Guadalajara, originally. Then wherever my mother could get work after we came to the States."

"Is she…?"

"She's got some health problems…can't travel anymore. But we chat almost every day, and someone at the facility is helping her learn how to video chat."

"Does she know about your injury?"

Mateo shook his head. "Her life was hard enough because of me. Why add to it if I don't have to?"

"After what my dad went through with his Alzheimer's, I think you're doing the right thing."

"Now, about that walk…"

He would have been good doctor. She was sure of that. And she was touched by his caring attitude toward his mother. Even toward *her*. This wasn't the Mateo who refused his treatments or walled himself into his room like a recluse. This was someone entirely different. Someone she hadn't expected but was glad she'd found.

"Well, if we go one way we'll run into a shaved ice concession, and if we go the other way it's The Shack."

"And The Shack is…?"

"Fun, loud, dancing, music, watered-down drinks for the tourists… Pretty much a place I shouldn't be taking you."

"Which is exactly why I'm taking *you*."

"Two-drink limit, Mateo. Beer, preferably. You're not on any prohibitive meds, but…"

"I was wondering when the doctor would return."

"The doctor never left."

"Oh, yes, she did," he said, smiling. "And I was the one who got to see it happen."

It was well into the evening—"her time," as she called it. She really needed to go home and rest. But now that he was out here, she wanted to keep him here. Because while he was here he wasn't inside the hospital, getting into trouble. Even his good looks—which everybody noticed—weren't enough to change their minds, and right now the mindset was not in Mateo's favor. Presently she was too exhausted to deal with it, so this little time out was badly needed. Probably for both of them.

Lizzie took a quick appraisal, even though she knew what he looked like. But she liked his dark look. The muscles. The smooth chest. And his hands…large, but gentle—the hands of a surgeon. How would they be as the hands of a lover? she wondered, as he spotted her amongst the crowd, then came her direction.

"I saw you staring at me," he said, as a couple of

young women from the bar watched him with obvious open invitation.

Who could blame them? Lizzie thought. He was the best-looking man there.

"Not staring. Just watching to make sure you weren't doing something that would embarrass you and cost me my job."

"But you're off duty."

"And you're still a patient of the hospital."

"But not your patient, Lizzie. And therein lies the distinction." He grabbed a cold beer from a passing server and handed it to Lizzie. "Do you ever allow yourself to have fun?"

"Do you ever allow yourself to *not* have fun?" she asked, wondering if, in his previous life, he'd been a party boy.

He held up his bottle to clink with hers, but she stepped back before that could happen.

"You're a beautiful woman, Lizzie. Prettier than anyone else here. And you're smart. But if I were your doctor I'd prescribe more fun in your life—because even when you're standing in the middle of it, you can't see it."

"Then it's a good thing you're not my doctor, isn't it?"

Mateo reached over and took Lizzie's beer, then took a swig of it.

"That's your limit," she warned him.

"Actually, it's one over—but who's counting?"

Lizzie shook her head, caught between smiling and frowning. "I shouldn't have to count. Somewhere in the manual on being adult there's a chapter on responsibility. Maybe you should go back and re-read it."

"You really can't let go, can you?"

"It's not about letting go, Mateo. It's about all the things that are expected of me—not least of which is taking care of you, since I'm the one who brought you here."

He reached over and brushed a stray strand of hair from her face. The feel of his hand was so startling and smooth she caught herself on the verge of recoiling, but stopped when she realized it was an empty gesture. Still, the shivers his touch left behind rattled her.

"I'm not going to let anything hurt you or your reputation," he said, his voice so low it was almost drowned out by the noise level coming from the rest of the people at The Shack. "I know how hard it is to get what you want and keep it, and I wouldn't jeopardize that for you, Lizzie."

This serious side of him…she hadn't seen it before. But she knew, deep down, this was the real Mateo coming through. Not the one who refused treatment, not even the one who partied hard on the beach. Those might be different sides to his personality, but she'd just been touched by the real Mateo Sanchez, and she liked it. Maybe for the first time liked *him*. If only she could see more of him, now.

"I appreciate that," she said.

She toyed with the idea of telling him that her job here might not be everything she wanted, that she was rethinking staying. But he didn't want to hear that. It was her dilemma to solve.

"Just keep it reasonable and we'll both be fine."

"Everything in my life has been reasonable, Lizzie. I may not remember all about that life, but I do recall who

I was in the part I remember, and I was you—always too serious, always too involved."

"And now?" she asked.

"That is the question, isn't it? I have so many different pieces of me rattling around my brain, and I'm not able to put them in order yet."

And she suspected he was afraid of what he might find when he did put them into place. She understood that. Understood Mateo more now than she had.

"Sometimes they don't always come together the way you want or expect."

"Then I'll have a lifetime to adjust to what I'm missing, or what got away from me. And that's not me being pragmatic. That's me trying to deal with *me*, and I'm not easy. I know that."

He reached out and brushed her cheek, this time without the pretense of brushing back her hair. It was simply a stroke of affection or friendship. Maybe an old habit returning. And she didn't mind so much.

Affection had never really been part of her life. Not from her dad, not from her husband. Even if this little gesture from Mateo meant nothing to him, it meant something to her. But she wouldn't allow herself to think beyond that. What was the point? He was a man without a memory; she a woman without clear direction. It wasn't a good combination, no matter how you looked at it.

Still, his touch gave her the shivers again.

"So, moving on to something less philosophical, you wouldn't happen to know if I can swim, would you? I mean, being in the Army, I'm assuming I have basic skills. But enough to get me out there on one of those surfboards?"

"I could always throw you in to find out."

"You're not a very sympathetic doctor, Dr. Peterson."

She laughed. "Well, you're finally catching on."

"What I'm catching on to is that you're a fraud. I know there's a side of Lizzie Peterson she doesn't let out. That's the side I want to see."

"Good luck with that," she said, giving his shoulder a squeeze. "Because what you see with me is what you get."

"Under different circumstances that might not be so bad. But with what I'm going through..." Mateo shrugged. "As they say: timing is everything. Too bad that's the way it's working out."

Which meant what? Was he really interested, or was this only one small aspect of Mateo that had been damaged?

"In my experience, it's not so much about the timing as it is the luck of the draw. Things happen when they happen, and the only thing dictating that is what you're doing in the moment. If I'm the one paddling around in the surf after I've been warned there's a rip current, it should come as no surprise to me that I'm also the one who gets carried out to sea. Things happen because we make them happen—or we choose to ignore what could happen in their place."

"Like my amnesia. It happened because... Well, if I knew the answer to that, I'd tell you. But my doc prefers I make the discovery on my own. 'Vulnerable mind syndrome,' he calls it. Which means my mind is open and susceptible to anything."

"Except doing the things you're supposed to in order to help yourself improve."

"Claiming amnesia on that one," he said, smiling.

"As long as you're just claiming and not believing. And as for swimming... I don't know. But at some point, after I return from my holiday, if you're still here..."

"Ah, the veiled threat."

"Not a threat. An offer to take you out and see how you do in the water."

"That could motivate me to be on my best behavior."

"Or you could motivate yourself. Your choice, Mateo. So, are you up for a wade?" she asked.

"Didn't you just say something about throwing me in?"

"Maybe I did...maybe I didn't," she teased.

Mateo laughed, then suddenly turned serious. "What happens if the real me comes back, Lizzie—all of me— and I don't like who I am?"

"You haven't given yourself enough time. And maybe you underestimate yourself. Whatever the case, you're aware of changes and that's the first step. Always be mindful of that and you'll be fine. I mean, we all lose track of ourselves at one time or another, with or without amnesia. I really believe you're more in touch with who you are than you're ready to admit. So, like I said, there's no rush. Now, if you go in the water with me, it's ankle-deep or nothing."

"I could have been a Navy SEAL...which means I'm an expert swimmer." He kicked off his flip-flops and waded out in the water with her.

"Except you were an Army surgeon, stationed in a field hospital in Afghanistan. No swimming there."

"In my mind I was doing something more glamorous and heroic."

"You *were* doing something heroic. Patching, stitching, amputating..." She took hold of his hand, even though he was in perfect physical condition, and they waded in up to their knees. "Might not have been glamorous, but you were saving lives."

"Only some of which I remember," he said, taking the lead and then pulling Lizzie along until they were in halfway to their hips.

They stood there together for a few minutes, simply looking out over the water. In the distance, a freighter was making its slow way across the horizon—not destined for Oahu, where they were, but perhaps one of the other islands.

Faraway places, she thought, as she reluctantly turned back toward shore. She'd spent her life in faraway places, but she'd never taken the time to notice as she'd been too young, or too involved in trying to get along in yet another new place.

A big pity, that. So many opportunities wasted. Maybe someday she'd go back and have a do-over. Or maybe she wouldn't. Maybe she'd put the past behind her, find her roots, and venture out to see if a little happiness might go with that. Right now, she didn't know what she'd do. Her life was a toss-up.

"You're drunk," Lizzie said, not happy about this at all. Well, maybe not downright drunk so much as a little tipsy. But it would be the same once Janis found out.

After their wade in the ocean Mateo had decided to go back and join the partiers.

"That's why I'm taking you in the back door of Makalapua. Because if we go in the front, I'll lose my job."

Actually, she wouldn't. She was the primary care physician there and that brought some clout with it. And the patients weren't prisoners. Doing what Mateo had done, while not advisable, wasn't illegal, and in the hospital not even punishable. His condition wasn't physical. He was on no medications that had any bearing on the beers he'd consumed. So nothing precluded alcohol.

Lizzie recalled the evenings when her dad had been a patient here, and she'd taken him to The Shack for tropical drink. He'd loved that. When he was lucid, he'd claimed it made him feel normal. But he hadn't been on the verge of being sent elsewhere, the way Mateo was.

Still, there was no reason for Mateo to make a spectacle of himself—which he had done after three craft beers. He'd danced. On a table. With a waitress.

She'd turned her back to order herself another lemonade, and when she'd turned around there he'd been, doing everything a head trauma patient shouldn't do. And he'd refused to stop when she'd asked him to get off the table. It was almost like he was trying to get himself kicked out of his spot at the hospital.

It had taken two strong *wahines he'e nalu*—surfer women—to pull him down for her, and by that time he'd been so unsteady he hadn't even been able to take ten steps back without zigging and zagging. And there she'd been, looking like a total idiot, trying to get the man who'd become the life of the party to quit.

Well, in another day she'd have two whole weeks to sleep, swim, and forget about her patients, her obligations…and Mateo. Except he worried her. After having such a nice chat with him… Well, she wasn't sure what she'd hoped for, but this wasn't it.

"Not drunk. Just pleasantly mellow. And I'll take responsibility for my actions," he said, slumping in the wheelchair one of The Shack patrons had run back to the hospital and retrieved for her.

"You bet you will—because what you did is way out of line and I'm not going to get myself into trouble because you can't control yourself."

"Meaning you're going to report me?

"Meaning I'm going to make a note in your chart. You're already close to the edge, Mateo, and you know that. Depending on what kind of mood Janis is in when she reads what I'm about to write, there's a strong likelihood she'll have you transferred. You know the policy."

"Yeah…one month to show I'm working, eight weeks to show progress. Well, isn't dancing progress?"

"I was trying to be nice by giving you a little time away from the hospital, but you turned it into a mess. And while dancing may show *some* sort of progress… on a table? With a waitress?"

"You're sounding a little jealous, Lizzie. I'd have asked you to dance, but, well…all work, no play. You'd have turned me down."

Yes, she would have. But was he right about her jealousy? Not over the other woman, but over taking the chance to have a little fun. She was all work, wasn't she? Maybe all these years of no play had caught up to her and she didn't know how to have fun. Or maybe "Daddy's little soldier," as he'd used to call her, had never known what fun was.

Lizzie pushed Mateo's wheelchair up a side hall, through the corridor behind the kitchen, then through the physical therapy storage area. Finally, when they came to the hall that led to his room, Lizzie stopped, looked around, then gave his chair a shove and stood there watching him roll away while she did nothing to stop him.

It took Mateo several seconds to realize she wasn't controlling him, and by the time he'd taken hold of the chair wheels he was sitting in the middle of the hall, too woozy to push himself past the two rooms before his.

"Why are you doing this to me?" he asked, managing to move himself along, but very slowly.

"That's the same question I was asking just a little while ago," she said, walking behind him. "Why are you putting me in this position?"

"Maybe there's something wrong with my amygdala or even my anterior cingulate cortex. You know—the areas that affect impulse control and decision-making."

"Your brain is fine. I've seen enough CTs of it to know there's nothing wrong. The blood clot was removed successfully. No other bruising or swelling present. No tumors. No unexplained shadows. So you've got no physical excuse for the way you act."

When they came to the door to his room Mateo maneuvered to turn in, didn't make it, backed away, and tried again, this time scraping the frame as he entered.

"I wasn't aware I was putting you in any kind of bad position," he said, stopping short of the bed and not trying to get out of his chair.

"Seriously? You don't work, you don't cooperate with the nurses, you refuse to go to your cognitive therapy sessions most of the time, and when you do go you don't stay long. You've recovered from a traumatic brain injury and you're battling retrograde amnesia, Mateo, in case you've forgotten. Then you get drunk and dance on a table. All that puts me in a very difficult position."

She had no idea if he was even listening to her. His

eyes were staring out of the window and there was no expression on his face to tell her anything.

"Look, I like you. And I know you're in a tough spot—you look normal, but you're not normal enough to get back to your old life."

"My old life?" he said finally, and his voice was starting to fill with anger. "You mean the one where I was a surgeon one minute and then, in the blink of an eye, a surgeon's patient? Is that what you're calling 'a tough spot?' And don't tell me how I'm working my way through the five stages of grief and I'm stuck on anger, because I damn well *know* that. What I don't know is what happened to me, or why, or what I was doing prior to the accident, or anything I did last year. And I'd say that's a hell of a lot more than *a tough spot*."

He shook his head, but still didn't turn to face her.

"I'm sorry if I got you in trouble. That wasn't my intention. Being a bad patient isn't my intention either. But when you don't know..." He swallowed hard. "When you don't know who you are anymore, strange things happen in your mind. Maybe you were this...maybe you were that. Maybe you're not even close to who you were. I have a lot of memories, Lizzie, and I'm thankful for that. But sometimes, when I'm confronted with something I should know, and it's not there..."

"It scares you?"

"To death."

"My dad... I lived for three years with him, watching him go through that same tough spot and never returning from it. His life was taken from him in bits and pieces until there were more gaps than memories—and he knew that. At least until he didn't know anything anymore. He didn't have the option of moving on, starting over in a life that, while it wasn't his, was still a good life. There's going to come a time when you must move on with whatever you have left and be glad you have that option. Some people don't."

She walked over to him, laid a reassuring hand on his shoulder, and gave him a squeeze.

"You've got to cooperate with your doctors, Mateo, instead of working against them. Right now, working against them is all you do, and I'm willing to bet that's not the way you were before the accident."

"I'd tell you if I knew," he said, his voice more sad now than angry. "I'm sorry about your dad, Lizzie. He deserved better. Anyway, my head is spinning and all I want to do is sleep. But I think I'll need some help out of the chair."

Immediately alert, Lizzie pulled a penlight from her pocket and bent over him to look into his eyes, in case there was something else going on with him other than the beginnings of a hangover.

"Look up," she said. "Now, down…to the right… to the left."

When she saw nothing of note, she tucked away her light, then offered Mateo a hand to help him get up. Which he did—but too fast. He wavered for a moment, then pitched forward into Lizzie's arms.

"Care to dance *now*?" he asked, not even trying to push himself away.

Admittedly, he felt good. And she could smell a faint trace of aftershave, even though he typically sported a three-day-old stubble. Had he splashed on a dash of scent for their walk?

"I think you've already done enough of that," she said, guiding him to the bed.

Once he was sitting, she helped him lift his legs, then removed his flip-flops when he was stretched out on the bed.

"I'll have one of the nurses come in and help you change into your…"

There was no point in continuing. Mateo was already out. Dead to the world. Sleeping like a baby.

And she—well…time to face Janis.

This wasn't how this part of her day was supposed to have gone. Taking a patient out for a walk…him getting drunk…

Thank heavens she had two blissful weeks of sitting on the beach, reading, and swimming coming up. She needed the rest. Needed to be away from her responsibilities. Needed to put her own life in order in so many ways.

CHAPTER THREE

"No, it's not your fault," Janis said, handing Lizzie a tiki cup filled with a Hawaiian Twist—a drink made of banana, pineapple, and coconut milk. And, yes, she'd even put a paper umbrella in it—not that Lizzie needed a tiki cup, a paper umbrella, or even a Hawaiian Twist. But Janis loved to make island favorites for anybody who came to her office, and today this was the favorite.

So Lizzie took a drink and, amazingly, it made her feel a little bit better. It didn't ease the headache, but it gave her a mental boost.

"It's not like I haven't taken a patient out for a walk before."

"Well, that's why we built the hospital here," Janis said, sitting down in a wicker chair across from Lizzie.

They were on the lanai outside Janis's office, as a perfect tropical breeze swept in around them.

"I know—to take advantage of the location. And the gardens. Because we want our patients to experience paradise. And I do truly believe there are curative powers in simply sitting and enjoying the view. And, in the case of some of our patients, when the memory is gone, they can still find beauty in the moment."

"Sometimes you're too soft," Janis said. "It's not necessarily a bad thing, considering most of the patients we treat, but for Mateo I'm not sure it's a good thing. He's a strong man, with a strong will, and right now that will isn't working to his advantage. I think he's trying to find his way around it. Get a foothold somewhere. Honestly, there's something in Mateo that just isn't clicking."

"Do you think he's trying to take advantage of me? Hoping I can do something for him?"

"He could be. It's always a consideration with some of our patients."

"Well, he seems harmless enough to me. And it's not like anything is going to happen between us."

"Just be careful of Mateo. I haven't figured him out yet."

"Nothing's going on," Lizzie stated. "We've crossed paths for weeks, and this evening I just… It was a *walk*, Janis. That's all. Except for the drinking, everything was fine."

"Everything except you gave in to your sentimental side and he used it against you. Be careful, Lizzie. I've seen it happen before and it never turns out well. And you're better than that."

Janis was right. She *was* better than that. But it wasn't showing right now. Yet she wasn't sure that she wouldn't take another walk with Mateo if he suggested it. Why? Because he was attractive? Because when the real man shone through she liked him? Because she was in the middle of her own crisis and Mateo was a distraction?

"Why don't you go ahead and start your holiday early? Get away from here. Forget us, forget your patients, and most of all, forget Mateo."

"There's no one to cover for me."

"The locum arrives in the morning. We'll put him straight to work while you sleep in or sip a mimosa on your lanai. However you choose to spend your days off, Lizzie, they start tomorrow. I need you back at your best and, while I have no complaints about your work, you seem so distant lately. Take the time…get it sorted."

Forget Mateo? Easier said than done. But with any luck, and two weeks of rest ahead of her, she'd get much more sorted than Mateo. Her dad. Her life. Putting things into perspective.

Now, that was something she was looking forward to.

In her life she worked, she slept, and every Saturday morning she went surfing, if conditions were right. That was it. All of it. And even though she owned her house she'd never really settled in, because she had been so up in the air about her dad.

Was this the place for him? Did he have the best caregiver? Did he need more? Should she enroll him in a day program a few times a week even though he wouldn't have a clue what it was about?

She'd taken care of her dad for five years before he died, and all her energies outside work had been devoted to him.

Of course, she'd been contacted about great facilities all over the country that would have taken him in and made his last days meaningful. But what would have been "meaningful" to him? Her voice? The familiarity of his old trinkets and clothes? The chicken and rice she'd fixed him every Saturday night that he'd seemed to enjoy, when his enjoyment of other foods had gone away?

He'd had so little left, and there had been nothing

any of these facilities could have done to make him better, so why deprive him of things he might remember?

Which was why she was here. He'd always wanted to retire to Hawaii and spend his days sitting on the beach, or planting flowers. That was what she'd given him when they'd moved here...the last thing she could recall that he'd ever asked for.

Now, here she still was, not sure whether to stay and live with the memories or go and start over someplace else. She really didn't have a life here. All her time had been taken up by work or her dad. Then, after he'd died, she'd filled in the empty hours with more work. Now it was all she could see for herself, and she wasn't sure she liked what she saw.

So maybe it was finally time to settle down, turn her house into a home, and start working on some of those plans she'd made when she'd moved here.

"I'll call you in a few days and let you know how it's going," she said to Janis as she headed out the door. "And maybe I'll have a party. A vegetarian luau."

"With lots of rum punch, since they won't be getting roast pig?"

Lizzie laughed. "Sounds like a plan. And if you get swamped, let me know. I'll come back."

"I know you will—which is why I'm going to ban you from the hospital until you're back to work full-time. Understand?"

Janis could be hard. In her position she had to be. But, as her former med school professor, and now her friend, she was the best. In fact, she'd been the one who'd offered to take her dad, when his Alzheimer's had been on the verge of becoming unmanageable at home. She'd even come to the mainland to help her make the move.

"Then how about we meet up at The Shack every few days and you can tell me all the gossip?" Lizzie suggested.

"Or maybe you could hang around there by yourself… meet a man…preferably a nice blond surf bum. How long's it been since…?"

"*Too* long," Lizzie said. "For anything. No details necessary."

"Then definitely find yourself a surf bum. A nice one with an older brother for me."

Lizzie was thirty-four, and Janis had twenty years on her, but with her blonde hair, and her teeny-bikini-worthy body, Janis was the one the men looked at while Lizzie was hiding in the shadows, taking mental notes on how to be outgoing.

"I thought you liked them younger these days?" Lizzie teased.

"I like them any way I can have them." She smiled at Lizzie. "Seriously, take care of yourself. And keep in touch."

"OK and OK," she said, then waved backward as she walked away, intending to head back to her office, tidy up, then leave.

But before she got there she took a detour and headed down the wrong hall. Or the right one, if her destination was Mateo's room. Which, this evening, it was.

"Well, the good news is I get to start my holiday early," she said to Matteo, who was sitting in a chair next to the window, simply looking out over the evening shadows of the garden, and not sound asleep in bed, as she'd expected. "So, this is me telling you good-bye and good luck."

"What? No more dates at The Shack?"

"First one was a total bust. With me it's one strike and you're out."

"But you haven't seen the real me. When that Mateo Sanchez emerges, do I get another chance?"

Lizzie laughed. "I'm betting you were a real charmer with the ladies. One look into those dark eyes and…"

"Do *you* like my eyes?" he interrupted.

She did—more than she should—and she'd almost slipped up there.

"Eyes are eyes. They're nice to use to get a clear picture of when you're being played."

"I'm not playing you, Lizzie."

"It doesn't matter if you are or you aren't. I'm off on holiday now, and once I'm outside the hospital door everything here will be forgotten for two whole weeks."

"Including me, Lizzie?"

"Especially you, Mateo. So, if you're not here when I return…have a good life."

He stood, then crossed the room to her before she could get out the door. He pulled her into his arms. He nudged her chin up with his thumb and simply stared into her eyes for a moment. But then sense and logic overtook him and he broke his hold on her and stepped away.

"We can't do this," he whispered. "I want to so badly, but I never should have started this, and I'm sorry."

"So am I," she said, backing all the way out through the door, and trying to walk to the hospital exit without showing off her wobbly knees.

Whatever had just happened couldn't happen again.

She wasn't ready. Her life was in a mess. But it was one more thing to be sorted in her time off.

Was she really beginning to develop feelings for Mateo?

Or was Janis right?

Was he looking for a foothold? Someone to use?

Was he playing her?

She didn't want to believe that, but the thought was there. And so was the idea that she had to shore up her reserves to resist him, because he wasn't going to make it easy.

He wasn't sure what to think. Didn't even know if he cared. Still, what he'd done was stupid. Going against hospital policy. Drinking a little too much, dancing to prove…well, he wasn't sure what he had been trying to prove.

Had he been the doctor of a patient like himself he'd have taken it much worse than Janis and Randy had. In fact, all things considered, they'd been very calm. Or was it the calm before the storm?

Lizzie wasn't here to defend him now, and he missed her. Not just because she'd seemed to take his side, but because he genuinely liked her. Maybe even missed her already. Right now, he didn't have any friends, and she'd turned out to be not only a friend but someone he trusted.

Except she wasn't in the picture now. He was on his own and trying to figure out what would come next in his life.

"None of this is what I planned," he said aloud to himself as he looked out the window.

Five years in the military, then find a good surgical

practice somewhere in a mountainous area. Or maybe near canyons or desert. He wasn't quite sure what he'd wanted, to be honest, but those were the areas that were tugging on his mind, so maybe that was what he'd wanted pre-amnesia. Not that it mattered now.

"You haven't been to your cognitive therapy group," Randy Jenkins said from the doorway.

He was a short man with thick glasses, who wore dress pants and a blue shirt, a tie and a white lab coat. He didn't look like he'd seen the inside of a smile in a decade.

"Haven't even left your room. You're way past the point where your meals should be served to you on a tray in your room. But you're refusing to come to the dining room."

Because he didn't want to. Because nothing here was helping him. Because he wanted his old life back, whatever that was, and he was pretty sure it didn't involve sitting in a group with nine other memory loss patients talking about things they didn't remember.

"And what, exactly, will those prescribed things do for me?" he asked, turning to face the man.

"Give you a sense of where you are now, since you can't go back to where you were before."

"Where I am now is looking out a window at a life that isn't mine."

"Do you *want* to get better, Doctor?"

Mateo shook his head angrily. "What I want is what I can't have. And that's something you can't fix."

"But there are other things you can do besides be a surgeon."

"And how do you think I should address the obvious in my curriculum vitae? *Unemployed surgeon with amnesia looking for work*?"

It wasn't Randy's fault. He knew that. It wasn't anybody's fault. But he was so empty right now. Empty, and afraid to face the future without all his memories of the past.

"Look, sit in on a therapy session this afternoon. Then come for your private session with me. I'll have my assistant look for some training programs that might interest you and—"

"Training programs? Don't you understand? I'm a surgeon."

"No, you're not. Not anymore. I've had to report you to the medical licensing board and—"

"You couldn't have waited until we were a little farther along in this?"

"You're not *in* this, Mateo. And that's the problem. Your license as a surgeon will be provisionally suspended, pending review and recommendations if and when you recover. I had to do it or risk my own medical license."

He'd worked so hard to get that. Spent years and more money than he'd had. Even if he couldn't operate, at least he had the license that proved he'd achieved his lifelong goal. He'd been somebody. But now he didn't even have that.

"I guess we all do what we have to do, don't we?" he said.

"It's nothing personal. And, for what it's worth, you'll probably still have your general license to practice, because at the end of all this there's every likelihood you'll be able to find a place in medicine, somewhere. But you've got to cooperate *now*."

But if he cooperated that meant all this was real. And he wasn't ready for that yet. Which was why he fought so hard against everything. Once he admitted it was real, he was done. Over. Nothing to hope for. Nothing left to hold on to. Not even that thin scrap of resistance.

Two days had gone by and she was already feeling better. She'd boxed up a few of her dad's belongings, which she'd been putting off for too long. Read a book on the history of Kamehameha, which had been sitting dusty on her shelf for two years. Done a bit of surfing and swimming.

Even just two days had done her a world of good, and as she headed off to the little stretch of beach at the front of her house, a guava and passionfruit drink in her hand, she was looking forward to more relaxation, more time to figure out if she should stay here or go somewhere else and start over.

Her plan had always been to go back home to upstate New York, but little by little this tiny patch of land she owned on Oahu had drawn her in. Her house was all glass on the side with the ocean view. It was large, but not too large…comfortable. Her dad had planted flowers that still bloomed in the garden and would for years to come, and the thought of leaving those brought a lump to her throat because he'd loved them so much in the last good days of his memory.

Her job… Well, that was one of those things she needed to rethink. It was good, but she wasn't sure it was where she belonged. She liked working there, loved working with Janis, but the whole fit seemed… *off.* Maybe because her dad was gone now. Maybe because she was alone. Or maybe those thoughts were simply her fatigue taking over. And, since she wasn't one to make rash decisions, she was going to let the job situation ride. Work through to the end of her contract, then see how she was feeling.

Stretching out on a lounger, Lizzie sat her drink on a little table topped with a mosaic of beach shells that her dad had collected and let her gaze drift to the waves lapping her small beach. She owned a *beach*. An honest-to-goodness beach. Even the sound of it impressed her a little, when very little else did these days.

"It's a nice view," came a familiar voice from behind her.

"How did you know where to find me?" she asked, turning to see Mateo standing just a few feet away with a duffle bag slung casually over his shoulder.

"Went to The Shack. Asked. They knew you and pointed me in the right direction."

"So, I'm assuming that since you've got your duffel you're no longer a patient?"

"Randy Jenkins made the recommendation this morning that I be transferred and your friend Janis dropped the axe." He shrugged. "So here I am."

"Then you're on your way to another facility?"

Mateo shook his head. "My transfer is back to California, where I was before I came here. It didn't do me any good then, and nothing's changed so it's not going to do me any good now."

This wasn't good. Too many soldiers returned home with PTSD and other problems and ended up on the street. Suddenly, she feared that for Mateo.

"What are your plans?" she asked, not sure she wanted to hear them.

"Don't have any. When they said they'd arrange a transfer in a couple of days I arranged my own."

"Meaning you're homeless? Or do you have a home somewhere?"

She didn't want to get involved. Shouldn't get involved. But he didn't deserve this, and it wasn't his fault that he'd lost the life he'd known.

"No home. Sold it when I went into the Army and used the proceeds to buy a house for my mother. It's in Mexico, and I'm not a citizen there. To get my veterans' medical benefits I have to live in the States. Meaning until I leave Hawaii I'm a beach bum. But before I take off to…let's call it to 'discover myself,' I wanted to thank you for being so kind to me and trying to help. I appreciate your efforts, Dr. Elizabeth Peterson, even if they were wasted."

"And what now? You walk off into the sunset? Because that's not where you're going to find yourself, Mateo."

He shrugged. "Do you really think I'll find myself if I'm admitted to an eight-bed ward and assigned to therapy to which I won't go, until I'm deemed so uncooperative they put me away in a home, give me drugs, and let me spend the rest of my life shuffling through the halls wearing bedroom slippers and existing in some kind of a stupor?"

"It's not that bad," she argued, even though she knew that in some cases it could be.

But for Mateo…she didn't know. He wanted something he wouldn't get back and he was stuck in the whole denial process. For how long, she had no clue. She was a personal care physician, not a psychiatrist.

"Could you go stay with your mother for a while?"

"I could, but she still doesn't know what happened to me and I'd rather keep it that way as long as I can."

"Well, I admire the reason, but how long do you intend on keeping up the charade?"

"To be honest, I don't know. Haven't thought it through that far, yet."

Everything inside Lizzie was screaming not to get involved, that Mateo wasn't her problem. But she felt involvement creeping up, pulling her toward the edge.

She thought of that day her dad had wandered off, just a year ago. If only someone had found him in time... And while Mateo wasn't at all in the same condition there could be just as many bad consequences for him as well. So, swallowing hard as she pushed aside all the reasons why she shouldn't do it, she did it anyway.

"Look, there's an *ohana* unit on the other side of the house. It's small, but no one's using it, and you're welcome to stay there a couple of days until you get things sorted."

"This is where me and my bad attitude would usually take offense or say something to make you angry or hurt your feelings, but I'm not going to do that. I didn't come here looking for help, but I'm grateful you're offering. So, yes, I'd appreciate staying in your *ohana*. Because I don't want to be out there wandering alone, trying to find something I might not even recognize. I don't like being this way, Lizzie. Don't like being uncooperative...don't like hearing half the things I'm saying. But if I do get to be too much for you to handle, kick me out. You deserve better than what I know I'm capable of doing."

"I don't suppose you can cook?" she asked.

He chuckled. "No clue. But if you're willing to take a chance with an amnesiac surgeon in your kitchen…"

For the past two days there had been nothing incoming, meaning nothing outgoing either. No imposed time limit on life or death. One less death to record, one less chopped-up body to send back was always good.

Passing the time playing cards with his best buddy Freddy wasn't necessarily what he wanted to be doing, but there wasn't anything else. And it was always interesting to see the many ways Freddy cheated at cards. Some Mateo caught. Many he did not. He could see it— Freddy palming one card and trading it for another.

"Cheat," he accused his friend. All in fun, though.

"Prove it," Freddy always said. "Prove it, and when we get back I'll buy you the best steak dinner you'll ever eat."

Problem was Mateo couldn't prove it. Freddy was just as slick in his card-playing skills as he was at being a medic. The plan was that after they returned home Freddy would finish medical school and eventually end up as Mateo's partner.

But tonight, there was no plan, and Freddy was pacing the hall the way he did when he got notice that someone was on their way in. In those tense minutes just before everything changed. Activity doubled. The less injured soldiers stepped aside for the more injured.

Sometimes they lined up in tribute, saluting as the medical team rushed through the door, pushing a gurney carrying the latest casualty.

"Stop it!" Mateo shouted at his friend. "Don't do that! Because if you do they'll come. Stop it. Do you hear me? Stop it!"

But Freddy kept on pacing, waiting...

No, not tonight. Mateo wanted to make it three nights in a row without a casualty.

"One more night. Just one more night..."

Outside in the back garden, on her way to take fresh towels and linens to the *ohana*, Lizzie stood quietly at his door, listening. He'd excused himself to take a nap while she'd stayed on the beach to read. Now this.

It hadn't happened in the rehab center, but something here was triggering it. Perhaps getting close to someone again? Close to her?

She thought about going in and waking him up. Then decided against it. If he was working out his demons in his sleep, he needed to. Besides, he was here as a friend, not a patient, and she had to take off her doctor persona or this would never work.

But it worried her. Because she knew the end of the story. Mateo's best friend had been killed in the raid that had injured him. Mateo had been pulled from the carnage and taken to the hospital, resisting help because he'd wanted to go back to save his friend. Except his best friend couldn't be saved.

While she wasn't a neurologist, she wondered if some deep, buried grief over that was contributing to his condition. Certainly the head injury was. But not being able to save his friend...? She understood that profoundly. Because in the end she hadn't been able to save her father. It was a guilt that consumed her every day.

"Sleep well?" she asked, watching Mateo come through the door. Cargo shorts, T-shirt, mussed hair. She liked dark hair. Actually, she had never really thought about what she liked in terms of the physical aspects of a man, but she knew she liked the physical aspects of Mateo. Strong, muscled...

"Bed's comfortable, but I don't feel rested. Guess I've got more sleep to catch up on than I thought."

Sleep without nightmares, she thought.

"Well, the folks at Makalapua weren't happy to find out where you are. Apparently, you got out of their transportation at the end of the circular drive, when the driver stopped to enter the main road, and then disappeared."

"Transportation? Is that what they call it?"

"Makalapua owns a limo for transporting patients and families when necessary."

"And it also owns an ambulance, Lizzie. *That* was my transportation. Ordered by my doctor. They came in with a gurney, strapped me down to it, and shoved me in the back of the ambulance. I was leaving as a *patient*. Not a guest. And I'm tired of being a patient."

Lizzie sat down on the rattan armchair in her living room and gripped the armrests. "An ambulance? I don't believe—"

"I may have amnesia," he interrupted, "but I still remember what a gurney and an ambulance are. Oh, and in case you didn't hear, I was to be escorted straight onto a military medical plane and met at the airport in California—probably with a gurney and an ambulance there, too."

"Did you get violent? Is that why they did it?"

"Mad as hell, but not violent." He sat down on the two-cushion sofa across from her but kept to the edge of it. "I'm guessing a couple of them are mad as hell right now."

"They only want to help you, Mateo."

They only want to help you.

We only want to help you.

I only want to help you.

Words she'd said over and over for years. Before, they'd sounded perfectly fine. Now, they sounded deceitful.

"Well, restraining me rather than giving me a sedative was preferable, but they were sending me to the place I specifically asked not to be sent."

"You're still Army, Mateo. On inactive duty. That means your commanders make the call and—"

"It's out of my hands." He shook his head in frustration. "I'm theirs until they cut me loose."

"Something like that. And you knew that's how it would be when you went in. When the military and veterans' hospitals didn't work for you, you were given a chance to recover outside the normal system. So, from what I'm seeing, they really were trying to help."

And now he was in no system but, instead in her *ohana*.

"Look, let me see if I can work something out with Janis. Maybe we can get you transferred somewhere else. Maybe another private hospital."

"Or maybe I should just go grab my things and wander on down the beach. The weather's nice. A lot of people move from their homes to the beaches during the hottest weather. Maybe someone will take pity on me and give me a meal every now and then."

"You're not going to live on the beach, Mateo. And I'm not sending you off on some journey to search for something you might not even remember when you find it."

Visions of her dad getting out and wandering around alone were the essence of her nightmares. And she'd even had a live-in caregiver who hadn't always been able to keep track of him.

"So for now you stay here, and we'll see what we can figure out."

"But the military…they know where I am?" he asked.

"Of course they do. I called them because you're not free of your obligation and they had to know. Like I've told you before, I play by the rules. But they're not going to come and take you away from here, Mateo. At least not yet. All they wanted was to know where you were and what you were doing. I told them you were going into outpatient care in a few days."

"That's what you think I'm going to do?"

"That's what I *know* you're going to do if you want to stay here. Janis approved it and, for the record, it's your last chance. After this the Army takes you back, and they'll be the only ones with a say in what happens."

Finally, he relaxed back into the sofa. "These last weeks it's like someone's always doing something to me, and most of the time not even consulting me before they do it. You're the first one who's ever told me beforehand what would happen, and I appreciate that."

"So…you mentioned your mother doesn't know about your current condition? Why is that? Is there some way she could take over medical responsibility for you until you're through this?"

He shook his head adamantly. "She has advanced diabetes. Arthritis. Partially blind. The less she knows, the better off she is. Like I said before, I do call her every day, and as soon as I'm free to travel I'll go to see her. But I don't want the stress of knowing what I'm going through anywhere near her. She deserves a better life than she's ever had before and I'm not going to deprive her of that."

"Which makes you a very good son."

She recalled how, in her dad's decline, she'd tried to keep so many things away from him—things that would cause him stress. So she certainly understood what Mateo was doing, and even admired him for that. It wasn't easy. She knew that.

"I remember when my mother became a citizen in the US. She'd studied for weeks, worked hard to learn the history, the language, and I think the day she was sworn in was one of the proudest days of her life. Making a new life isn't easy, and she did it for me."

"And you?"

"I was too young to realize all the sacrifices she was making to give me a better life. I don't think I appreciated it the way I should. And my mother... I don't want her worrying about me. It's the least I can do. And she's happy back in Mexico, living near her sister, proud of her son the...the doctor." He nearly choked on the words.

She thought about the life her dad had made for her. That had never been easy either, but it had always been good. And he'd put aside many opportunities because he'd chosen to be a father first.

"Anyway, what's next, Mateo? What do you want to happen or expect to happen?"

He chuckled, but bitterly. "Look, Lizzie. I don't know what I'm doing, and I'm sure that's obvious. But I'm not going to impose, and I'm not going to expect you to be my doctor while I'm here."

"Like I *could* be your doctor," she said. "That would

require ethical considerations I don't want to think about. Doctor brings patient home for special treatment? Nope, not me. I can be your friend, even a medical colleague, but not your doctor. So, my friend, I want to take a walk down to The Shack and ask them why they thought it was appropriate to tell someone where I live."

"Then what?" he asked.

"Then guilt them into free shrimp burgers. They're *so* good. But no beer. And no dancing on the table."

"In my defense, it was only a couple feet off the ground."

"You have no defense, Mateo. Absolutely none. And if I catch you up on a table, and I don't care how high it is…" She pointed to the chaise on the lanai. "*That's* as far as you'll go. I might toss you a pillow and a plate of food every now and then, but if you dance on a table I'm done."

Mateo laughed. "You know, from the first moment I saw you walk by my hospital room I knew you were a real softie. Your threats don't scare me, Lizzie. You haven't got it in you to make me sleep out there."

Unfortunately, that was true. Something about Mateo caused her usual resolve to simply melt away.

It wasn't like him to think only in the moment. At least, he didn't *think* it was like him. He'd looked at his calendar and seen that he'd made notes about plans well into the future. Some things still months away. That was certainly a personality trait he didn't remember—especially now, when he was basically on the edge of living rough and not particularly worried about it.

Was that because he knew he could count on Lizzie as his backup?

Mateo looked at his half-eaten shrimp burger and wondered if he even liked shrimp. Had he been allergic his throat would have swollen shut by now. He might even be dead. But he wasn't, and his throat was fine.

Subconsciously, he raised his hand to his throat and rubbed it.

"You OK?" Lizzie asked him.

She was sitting across from him at a high-top for two, looking like an Irish lassie who simply fitted in here. Red hair wild. Brown eyes sparkling with gold flecks that were highlighted by the glow of the citronella candle on their table. The brightest, widest smile he'd ever seen.

"Just wondering if I have allergies."

"According to your military records, you don't."

"You really know more about me than I know about myself, don't you?" he asked. Realizing she had access to his life while he didn't felt strange.

"You do understand why I don't just tell you everything I know, don't you?"

"So you won't fill my impressionable mind with fake notions of who I am. I know it would be easy… false memories and all that. But sitting here with a stranger who knows me inside and out, while only a couple of hours ago I was homeless without a plan is… disconcerting."

Lizzie reached across the table and squeezed his hand. "I'll bet it is. But if you ever settle down you'll work through some of it. Maybe even more than you expect."

He studied her hand for a moment—porcelain-smooth skin, a little on the pale side compared to most of the people at The Shack. Nice hand. Gentle.

"Now that you're not restricted by any kind of medical ethics with me, tell me how much I can expect to return. Or how much will never return. Can you do that much for me?"

She pulled her hand back. "There's no formula for that, Mateo. No way to predict. I'd like to be able to give you a definitive answer, but the brain can't be predicted. You may be where you're always going to be now, or you may improve. Losing pieces of yourself—or, as I call it, living in a fog—has got to be difficult. I see it, and I understand it, but I can't relate to it."

He smiled. "Wish I couldn't relate to it either. Look, I appreciate you taking me in for a couple of days. I really do need some time to figure out what comes next. But you're not responsible for me, Lizzie. Just be patient for a little while, and on my end of it I promise no more dancing on the table or anything else. I'll be cooperative. Tell me what to do and I'll do it."

He meant it, too. It was time to figure out his life, and it was nice having a friend on his side to help him. A friend who was patient and caring the way Lizzie was.

"Why didn't you do that at the hospital?"

"Four walls, a bed, and a window to the world. That's all it was, and it scared me, Lizzie. Still does when I think that's all my life might be about."

"So you refuse traditional help, do everything you can to distance yourself from it, in order to—what? I want to know, Mateo. If I hadn't lived within walking distance of the hospital, or if a couple of the people who work here hadn't known where I live, what would you have done? Because so far all you've done is walk away. From Germany, from the veterans' facility in Boston, then in California, and from the hospital here. From—"

She shut up and took a bite of her burger.

"From *everything*, Mateo," she said, once she'd swallowed. "And it all adds up to you walking away from yourself."

"You were going to say fiancée, weren't you?"

"You remember her?"

"Vaguely. Must have been a short relationship, because she didn't leave much behind in my head. Except, maybe… She didn't want to live with someone in my condition, did she?"

"Actually, I don't know the whole story. It was in your chart, but since you weren't my patient I didn't read it. The only things I know about you are what I heard at the weekly patient review meetings."

"That's right. By the book, Lizzie."

"You think that's a problem?"

"I think in today's medical world it's an asset. There are too many people getting involved in aspects of a patient's care who shouldn't."

Suddenly he could feel the tiredness coming on. And the headache. Dull to blinding in sixty seconds. So, rather than pursuing this conversation, he stood abruptly, tossed a few dollars on the table—enough to cover both meals and a tip—then walked away. He wanted to get out of there before the full force of the headache made him queasy, caused him to stagger.

Once away from The Shack, Mateo headed toward the beach, then sat down on the sand, shut his eyes, and tried to clear his head.

Right now, he didn't care about what Lizzie was holding back. All he cared about was the pain level rising in him and how to control it.

And that didn't come easy these days. Not easy at all.

* * *

She wasn't going to interrupt him, sitting alone out there on the sand. Mateo was entitled to his moods and his mood swings and it wasn't her place to hover over him. If he needed her help, he'd ask. Or not.

It was almost an hour later when he returned to the house. When she looked in Mateo's eyes she saw how lost he was, but she also saw the depth of the man. He was in there—just locked away.

"Look, I'm going out for a night swim, then I'm going to sit on the lanai for a while to relax. You're welcome to come, or you're welcome to stay here and read a book, watch a movie—whatever you want to do."

"You don't have to feel responsible for me, Lizzie. I can take care of myself."

"I was just being polite. You look tired, and I thought a swim might make you feel better."

He looked more than tired. He looked weary. Beaten down. He looked like a man who was fighting with everything he had to get back on the right path. It worried her, even though she had no right to be worried. Still, she couldn't help herself. There was something about Mateo that simply pulled at her.

"And I was just being honest. I don't want you disrupting your life for me."

She smiled. "To be honest, I hadn't intended on doing that. I just thought it would be a nice way to end the evening."

With that she went upstairs, changed into her swimsuit—a modest one-piece, black, no frills, nothing revealing—and went straight to the beach alone, leaving Mateo watching some blathering documentary on her TV.

Too bad, she thought as she dipped her toe in the surf. He might have enjoyed this. And she might have enjoyed doing this with him.

She was stunning, even though she was trying to hide it in that swimsuit. But her kind of beauty couldn't be hidden. Not the outside beauty, and not the inside beauty.

This was a huge imposition, him living in her home. He knew that. But so much of him wanted to get to know her and, while ending up here really hadn't been his intention, when good fortune had smiled on him he hadn't had it in him to turn his back on it.

He moved along the beach from where Lizzie had entered the water. He wanted to join her, but he didn't want to impose. Yet he'd wandered down here, not sure what he was hoping for. Another invitation? Perhaps nothing?

In all honesty he had no right to think anything or want anything, in his condition. But watching Lizzie... It gave him hope he hadn't felt before. Maybe something in him would change. Or something would reset and at least allow him to look forward.

Unfortunately, Lizzie coming into his life now was too soon. He could see himself with her, but not yet.

Sighing, Mateo shut his eyes. All he could see was Lizzie. Her face. The way she looked at him. Sadness. Compassion. She had the power to change a man. The power to change *him*. And maybe that was good. He didn't know, but it felt right. Felt like he was ready.

She'd been on his mind constantly, and he'd thought of little else other than Lizzie from that first moment in the hospital, when she'd walked into his room, sat down in the chair opposite him and hadn't said a word. Not one single word. She had smiled as she'd watched him, but she hadn't talked, and it had got to the point that it had been so distracting, even annoying, that he'd been the one to break the silence.

"Why are you doing that?" he'd asked her.

"Sometimes you learn more from observing than talking," she'd told him.

"And what did you learn from observing me?" he'd asked.

"That you're not going to be easy for your doctors."

Mateo chuckled. Prophetic words. He hadn't been. Still wasn't. And she'd known that simply by observing him.

"There's a shorter way back to the house," Lizzie said, sitting down beside him on the rock where he'd been sitting for the past half hour.

"I didn't hear you coming." He scooted over to give her room.

"But I saw you sitting here. I used to sit here back when my dad was getting bad. I was looking for answers, and even though there were none I always went away with a sense of calm. Back then, calm was good."

"This whole area is nice. Not sure I found any calm here, but the view is amazing." He slid his hand across the rock until it was just skimming hers. "The only places I've ever lived were congested…loud."

"Sounds like a tough way to live life," Lizzie commented.

"There are a lot of tough ways to live life, Lizzie. Some we choose, some we don't." He stood. "Anyway, it's been a long, unexpected day, and I'm ready to see if I can get some more sleep. So…" He looked at her, then shrugged. "Care to have me walk you home?"

Lizzie smiled, then stood and took his arm. "I always did love a gallant man. Just never knew they existed outside of fairy-tale books."

"Well, consider me a poor and humble prince who's at your beck and call." He gave her a low-sweeping bow then extended his arm to her.

"Poor?" she asked, as they made their way along the path. "I saw your financials when you were admitted. You're not wealthy, but you're certainly not poor."

"Then maybe poor of spirit?"

Lizzie laughed. "Somehow I doubt that. I think you're a man with an abundance of spirit. It's just that your spirit is in hiding right now."

Mateo was testing her like he'd done in the hospital with everyone else he'd encountered. It was the same, but different, because now he was living in the real world, which called for real coping skills instead of avoidance.

He'd get the hang of it. She was sure of that. But what he *wouldn't* get the hang of was using her as his enabler. Once she'd enabled her dad too much for too long. In doing that she'd denied the obvious—that the next corner he turned would be worse than the one before. And the one after that worse again.

Well, not with Mateo. He was testing new legs, so to speak. Taking new steps. Learning new things to fill in the gaps. As much as she wanted to make it her battle, it wasn't. For Mateo to get better, find his new direction, he had to take those steps by himself, fight his way through to something that fit.

She could be on the sidelines, watching, maybe holding out a supporting hand. But it was his destiny to control. She had to keep telling herself that. His destiny, not hers.

But it wasn't easy walking into her house by herself, going up the steps to bed alone. No, none of it was easy. In the morning, though, depending on what Mateo did or didn't do tonight, she'd decide what she would do. Or would not do.

CHAPTER FOUR

THE SMELL WAS HEAVENLY. Coffee and… Was something baking? Lizzie wanted to bask in bed a while longer, simply to enjoy the rich variety of aromas drifting up to her, and she could do that. Nothing was stopping her. She was on holiday, after all. She could bask, lounge, sleep, do anything she wanted.

But the clock on her phone showed it was just a few minutes until eleven, which meant she'd spent most of the morning doing that already. It was amazing how good it felt—especially with her bad sleeping habits. Never more than an hour or two at a time. Sometimes missing sleep altogether for a day or more.

Also, she wanted to see Mateo. No particular reason. She simply wanted to see him and ask what he planned for the day.

So a quick shower and Lizzie was on her way downstairs, where he was waiting for her at the bottom, holding out a coffee mug.

"There was no cream, and you don't strike me as the type who'd go in for gratuitous sugar, so it's black. But I did find a papaya tree outside and I picked a ripe one, juiced it, and added a bit to your coffee."

"You remember what a papaya is?" She was not only pleased, she was surprised.

"My mother used to make them into a salsa to use on fish tacos. And papaya cake. That was the best."

"I'll bet it was," she said, taking a sip and letting it glide down her throat. "What else can you cook?"

He smiled. "Well, those fish tacos I just mentioned. Although I try to eat on the healthy side. Tacos, enchiladas, tamales, burritos…they might be food for the gods, but when you work out every day the way I used to do they're also food for the waistline, and it's never been my desire to see mine grow." He patted his belly. "So far, so good. Oh, and I baked muffins, if you're interested. Healthy ones. No sugar, no butter."

"Then you really *are* a cook."

"Let's just say that I'm pretty sure I know my way around a kitchen. Not sure about anything gourmet, but the muffins were easy enough and the coffee was self-defense. One of the nurses in Afghanistan made coffee and it was horrible. I'd been there three days when I decided to take it over myself. Either that or no coffee, because it was eating away my stomach lining."

Lizzie laughed. "Was she that bad or were you just that gullible?"

Chuckling, he shook his head. "I may have known the answer to that at one time. But, since I don't now, I'd like to say she was bad and leave it at that."

Did he know how much he'd just revealed to her? It had come so easily now, after she'd spent so much time asking him questions he wouldn't or couldn't answer. Then suddenly…*this*. She wasn't going to get too excited, but she did hope it was a step forward. Hoped in a non-medical way, of course.

"So, what's on your agenda for today?' she asked, fully expecting him to draw a blank on that.

But the bright look coming over his face told her otherwise.

"Clothes. What I have on…that's it. Hand-me-downs left behind at the hospital. And shoes."

"Then we go shopping," she said, smiling.

He chuckled. "I think I'm one of those men who hates shopping."

"Amnesia doesn't cut it with me, Mateo. You need clothes—we get you clothes. And I love to shop, so prepare yourself. I could turn this into an all-day outing."

Mateo moaned. "My mother loves shopping and when I was young, I was forced to walk behind her, carrying her handbag. It was humiliating, especially to a little boy who was bullied and called a mama's boy, but it worked out because I worked out and got strong, which scared away the bullies." He smiled. "I wasn't really a fighter, but nobody ever knew that."

"Well, I won't ask you to carry my handbag unless you really want to."

Mateo moaned again. "Can't we just do it online?"

"What? And miss the fun of it?" Lizzie took another sip of the coffee and arched her eyebrows in surprise. "This is really good. I'm glad you remembered, because you can make it every morning you're here."

"Actually, I didn't remember the coffee. I remembered my mom and her love of everything papaya. This was just a lucky guess."

"So, Dr. Mateo Sanchez, skilled general surgeon…"

"*Former* general surgeon."

"I'll get on to that later. Maybe ask Janis to sit down hard on Dr. Jenkins and come up with a better treatment plan for you. Anyway, surgeon, chef, devoted son… what else?"

"Not much technology sense."

"With the technology sense of a *nene*."

"What's a *nene*?" he asked.

"A goose."

She didn't know if a few memories really were slipping back or if these were things he'd simply kept to himself. Maybe to maintain some control? But she wasn't a shrink and, whatever the case was, she wouldn't ask.

"The official Hawaiian bird, actually."

"Seriously, with all the pretty little colorful birds everywhere, Hawaii chose a goose?"

She turned and strolled out to the lanai, where one of those "colorful birds"—a beautiful yellow-green *amakihi*—was sipping nectar from one of the nectar stations her dad had built. He'd had such a way with the birds, and with flowers. It was all still there—the colors, the care he'd taken… It was the first thing she went to look at every single morning of her life.

"The goose is a worthy bird," she said, stepping away from where the *amakihi* was feeding, so as not to disturb it. "They've been here half a million years, and they don't damage their habitat, so they've earned their place." She studied the muffin he was holding out for her. "I'm assuming papaya?"

"I was taught to take advantage of what you're given and be grateful for it."

"As long as you didn't climb the tree to get it, I'm good. But if you did…"

Mateo chuckled. "It was on the ground. Trust me. I may not remember a lot of things, but I do remember that head injuries and climbing up papaya trees don't mix. So, about my clothes…"

The headache wasn't bad, but it was too early to feel this tired. All he wanted to do was sit out on the lanai and doze, even though he'd been the one to suggest clothes-shopping. Too much, too soon. Making the coffee hadn't been bad, but baking the muffins had done him in.

He had to show her he was better, because if he didn't she'd pack him off to a hospital somewhere. There was nothing in him that wanted to go. In fact, even though he'd worked in a hospital, being turned into a hospital patient filled him with a fear that, when he thought about it, nearly paralyzed him.

He wanted to know why, but the answer didn't come to him when he tried to find that piece of himself. In fact, the more he visualized himself as a patient, the more he sweated and came close to an anxiety attack.

There were so many mysteries to his life still locked away that when he let it happen the frustration of it all led to a bad temper. But bad temper didn't solve his problems. So why go there? Why not detour around that roadblock? Because perhaps, at the end of the road, something better might be waiting for him.

It made sense. Now all he had to do was convince his logical mind to follow through. And that was the tough part. Because the other part of his mind still wanted to kick and rebel.

But not so much since Lizzie.

"It's not too far. If you're up for a walk, it's about a mile."

She was dressed in a Hawaiian wrap-skirt, midi-length, yellow with a white floral print. Her shirt was a strappy white tank top that left a bit of her belly exposed. No bra. Hair tucked into a floppy straw hat with a few wild tendrils escaping, oversize sunglasses, and sandals.

Normally when she wasn't on duty she slouched around in terry shorts and an oversize T-shirt—*with* a bra. Going out with Mateo, for some uncharted reason, she wanted to look better. Funny how looking better made her feel better. Today she was feeling great. Something that hadn't happened very much recently.

"In fact, there are several shops, so you'll have a choice of clothing."

He stood, gave her an appreciative stare, and slipped into his sandals. "So what kind of clothing are we talking about?" he asked, as his gaze stopped on her exposed belly.

"Whatever you like. Do you remember the way you used to dress?"

She did like the three-day stubble on him, and hoped it wouldn't go once he'd fixed himself up.

"I remember scrubs. A couple of suits… Don't know if I used to hate them then, but the thought of wearing a suit now…" He faked a gigantic cringe. "Pretty sure I slept in the buff."

"Too much information," Lizzie said, fighting back a grin—and a vision of Mateo in the buff.

As a doctor, she'd seen a lot of him, but not all. As a woman, her fantasies went well beyond—and that was dangerous.

Mateo and her on the beach. On a blanket. Him rubbing sunscreen on her back, her shoulders, her thighs…

Definitely dangerous territory, since she hadn't

sorted out what kind of man, if any, she wanted in her future. "You've been in the Army for a while. You weren't sleeping in the buff there."

He laughed. "Well, maybe if I didn't in the past, it's something I might start doing in the future."

"Beach shorts. Tropical print, lightweight, somewhat baggy, stopping just at the tops of your knees. And a sleeveless T-shirt. Maybe some cargo shorts and a few cotton floral print button-up shirts. Also a pair of long khaki pants, with a white, breezy cotton shirt."

"And here I was, picturing myself more as a surf bum."

"Do you surf?" she asked, her mind still stuck on beach shorts and sleeveless T-shirts.

"Don't have a clue. Do you want to teach me?"

"Your last doctor advised you to stay away from activities like that for at least four months. It hasn't been four months."

"Then it's a good thing my last doctor no longer has a say, and my new friend just might be willing to show me some basic, non-threatening surfing moves. *If* she surfs."

"She does—and she's very good at it." She hadn't done nearly as much of it as she would have liked, owing to her dad's condition, alongside her hyper zest for work. But the thought of surfing with Mateo—well, at least bodyboarding—caused a little flush of excitement. "And if she decides to take you out, she's in complete control."

"I never thought she wouldn't be." He smiled. "Anyway, my look is your decision. Except red. I won't wear red."

"Why not? With your dark skin color..."

He shook his head. "Too much like blood. I've seen more of that than I care to. Worn too much of that on me. No red."

"Red's overdone," she said, hiking her oversize canvas bag up to her shoulder. "But blue...*that's* a color."

"So is yellow," he said, smiling. "On you."

"Then you're the type of guy who notices these things about a woman, because in my experience—"

"What experience?" he interrupted.

"Well, in my case not much lately."

Not for years, to be honest. But Mateo didn't need to be burdened with her problems when he had enough of his own to wrestle with.

"You know what they say about all work and no play?" he quipped lightly.

"You're right about that," she returned.

"No, seriously. What *is* it they say?" His eyebrows knit into a frown.

"You don't remember?" she asked, highly suspicious of the twinkle in his eyes.

Was this the real Mateo coming out, or one he was inventing just for her? She'd seen that in patients before—turning into the person they believed she wanted to see. The patient with excruciating headaches who refused to admit to them just to maintain a certain image. The patient with Parkinson's disease who denied his symptoms as a way of denying the disease.

People showed what they wanted—either to deny to themselves or put on a brave front for someone else—and she couldn't help but wonder if that was what Mateo was doing...showing her a side of himself he believed she wanted or needed to see. Maybe to maintain the roof over his head for a while? Maybe because he wanted to impress her?

Whatever was going on, she liked that spark, and hoped it was genuine.

He chuckled. "Of course I do. I was just wondering if you did, since you practically admitted you don't play. But you're not dull, Lizzie. Maybe not bursting with as much *joie de vivre* as you could be, or maybe should be, but definitely not dull."

"Well, dull is in the eye of the beholder, I suppose. I've never thought of myself as particularly effervescent, though."

That was the truth. She was hard-working, serious, dedicated, and passionate about her career, but when it came to the personal aspects of her life, there'd never been much there. Not enough time. Or real interest.

"Then maybe you're not seeing what I'm seeing."

"Or maybe you don't know what you're seeing because you've forgotten what effervescence looks like in a person."

She motioned him to follow her off the lanai and then to the road in the front of the house. The hospital, and her home, were just a little way outside La'ie, on the north end of the island. It was out of the way, but bursting with life.

A lot of people at the hospital commuted up from Honolulu, or one of the larger cities to the south, like Kane'ohe, but she liked this area—liked the relative smallness of it, loved the people. Even though she'd left huge and disproportionate New York City for this, she couldn't imagine living anywhere else now.

Could she return to big city living? If she had to.

Would she want to, though? Not a chance. Living in paradise had spoiled her.

"So, what we're going to see will be surf shops for the most part. There are a couple of shops that specialize in other things—clothes that are more traditional, shoes, those sorts of things. And then there are the food vendors. All I can say is…*heaven*."

"Where every day is a holiday?"

"It can be, if that's what you want. Oh, and just so you know, I need to run into the hospital and sign some papers. You're welcome to come in with me, or wait outside if the old familiar surroundings make you uncomfortable."

"Snakes make me uncomfortable. And bullets. And I don't think I'm especially fond of clingy women, but I could be wrong about that one. Oh, and cats."

"You don't like cats?" she asked.

"Actually, I love cats. Love their independence and attitude. But I'm allergic."

"I've always wanted a cat. Or a dog. But we moved around too much, and my dad didn't think it would be practical, taking an animal with us. I had a goldfish once. His name was Gus. Had to give him to a friend when we moved from Virginia to Germany."

"Because your dad was a surgeon. Career Army?"

"Yep—I was seeing the world at a very young age."

"And enjoying it?"

"Most of the time. Unless he had to leave me behind when he was in a combat zone. Even so, he gave me everything I needed and wanted."

Except a mother. Somewhere along the way her dad had decided he didn't have enough time or energy for another marriage, and Lizzie had often wondered if, in the end, having someone with him besides her might have helped him hang on to reality a little longer.

"It must have been tough on your dad, raising a daughter and maintaining his military career."

"It was what it was, and we managed," Lizzie said, as they walked along the narrow road, while people on bikes and scooters passed by on both sides of them. "When you never have a person in your life—like I didn't have my mother—you get used to it and make it work. My dad and I did."

"What happened to your mother?"

"She lost interest in the life we lived, then in my dad, and left us when I was about five. Died a couple years after that."

"So she never had a chance to make amends?"

"She could have. But she didn't want to."

"And your dad…?"

"He wasn't interested in trying before Alzheimer's hit. Then afterwards he didn't remember her at all."

"It couldn't have been easy on you, taking care of your dad the way you did."

"It wasn't—but I gave him the care he gave me when I was a child. I couldn't just…send him away somewhere."

"He isn't the reason you're here?"

"Actually, he is. They have an excellent treatment program at the hospital and I think it gave him more than anybody might have expected. But he lived at home because he loved it there, and I didn't have the heart to take that away from him. Especially his garden. When he was losing so many things in his life, his flowers still made him happy. It's nice, looking out every day, seeing a little bit of my dad still there. Somehow it makes the end seem easier. But don't get me wrong. I miss him. We had a tough life together, which was no one's fault, but he always tried. He just wasn't single father material, I suppose you could say. And…and now I look at his flowers and wonder if we both could have tried a little harder. Of course, Alzheimer's stepped in before we had much of a chance to do anything."

"How long has he been gone?"

As they walked down the path to the hospital Mateo took hold of her hand and she didn't pull away. It was nice feeling his touch. Having someone there who cared…at least for a little while. His hand was soft, and she could almost imagine it caressing her skin, giving her goosebumps.

Maybe she'd give *him* a few goosebumps as she ran her hand over his tight six-pack abs…

Nice dream.

"A year, now. One less brilliant surgeon in the world."

She noticed Mateo was starting to lag behind, so she slowed her pace to match his, but when she did he slowed down even more. This doctor clearly wasn't comfortable returning to the hospital, even if he was no longer a patient there.

"Do you need to take a break?" she asked, coming to a stop on the narrow road that led to the hospital's front door. It was lined with a rainbow of flowers and green, with draping wisps of vine hanging from the trees.

She'd always loved this path. It had welcomed her the day she'd first arrived, and every day since then. And this was part of her dilemma. To stay or to leave? Admittedly, she wasn't as restless as she'd been only a few weeks before, but her choice still wasn't clear. In other words, she didn't know what she wanted. She'd spent a lifetime living the life her dad had wanted for her, and now it was her turn to choose. But what?

Truly, she didn't know.

"No," Mateo said. "I'm fine. Just not excited to be back here." He took his place against a large lava rock, leaned casually back on it, and folded his arms across his chest. "You go do what you need to do, and I'll wait here."

He pointed to the little shop just down the road. The front was totally open to the air, and several clothing racks spilled out onto the walkway.

"Or wander down there and pick out the most hideous clothes you can imagine."

"I'll be about ten minutes," she said, heading to the front door, walking along the path and crossing over the circular drive that led straight to the welcome sign: *Welina.* Greetings to you. It was a friendly place to some. But to some, not so much.

"I didn't know you'd be stopping by," Janis said, approaching the entrance to greet Lizzie.

"In the neighborhood." She glanced back over her shoulder to make sure Mateo was still there. "Looking for clothes for my…whatever he is."

"Speaking of which—how's he doing? We were worried until you called. But the thing that really concerns me is that he's living with you, Lizzie. That's not a good idea. Dependencies form. It may be difficult to get rid of him when the time comes."

"It was either that or the beach. And he was totally emphatic about not coming back here or going to the veterans' facility in California. So…" She shrugged. "What was I supposed to do? He's not exactly ready to be out in the world on his own, yet."

She took another hasty glance and saw Mateo talking to a handful of strangers who were huddled around him. He did have that kind of personality—the kind that drew people in. He was making good use of that now.

"He's not supposed to be living with one of his doctors," Randy Jenkins said, approaching Lizzie and Janis.

"I'm not his doctor—never have been, never will be. And, not that it's any of your business, he's in the *ohana*, not in the house," Lizzie said, almost defensively.

"Do what you want," Randy said. "He's not a patient here, and right now he's on his own. So be his friend. I'm sure he needs that."

"Randy's right. It's your choice, Lizzie. But don't get too involved. I don't want to see you getting hurt."

"Hurt?"

"You know…feelings that aren't reciprocated. You're vulnerable right now, just like he is, and I don't want that playing against you."

"He's not like you think he is," she insisted.

"Or maybe he's not like *you* think he is," Janis countered. "Just be careful. That's all I'm saying. That, and put a leash on his desire to practice medicine. Because if people associate the two of you as medical partners and he makes a mistake, or forgets something…"

"What?" Lizzie spun around and, sure enough, Mateo was examining the wrist of a young boy who couldn't have been more than seven or eight. "Look, courier those papers over later and I'll sign them. Right now I think I've got to stop a doctor from practicing medicine."

"Easier said than done," Janis warned. "It's in his blood."

That was going to be a huge problem—teaching an

old dog new tricks. Or completely rewiring the old dog until he was an entirely new one. Also, staying detached. That, perhaps, was going to be the hardest part, because Mateo was charming and she was not above being charmed, no matter how much she denied it to herself.

Why? Because she was lonely. Because he was attractive. Especially because he was attractive. Oh, and the charm that just oozed from his pores. She didn't know if that was really him, or a new Mateo he was trying on for size. But she liked it. Too much.

CHAPTER FIVE

IT WASN'T LIKE he'd *meant* to practice medicine on a street corner, but he hadn't been able to help himself. The memory of the career that had been taken away from him kept poking at him, reminding him of who he'd used to be as opposed to who he was now. Nothing. That was who he was. Nothing. No one. A man without a memory living with a woman he barely knew.

"It's not broken," he told the little boy's mother. "Just sprained. It wouldn't hurt to go get an X-ray, but you could save yourself time and money by making a sling and keeping it immobile for a couple of weeks."

He was referring to a child who'd fallen and hurt his wrist. There was enough of the surgeon in him left that he could tell the difference between a sprain and a break. And while he shouldn't have been making the diagnosis, it had just happened. Child in pain, mother worried sick, him reaching out to help. It was not only the life he wanted, but the life he needed. If he wasn't a doctor, then who was he?

Someone from his own past, he decided as he rose to greet Lizzie—who, judging by the expression on her face, wasn't too happy with what he'd just done.

Lizzie.

He liked her.

She leaned a little too heavily toward the no-nonsense side, but he'd caught a few fleeting smiles and laughs, which only emphasized just how much she kept hidden.

"I suppose you're going to tell me I shouldn't be practicing medicine," he said, even before she'd reached him.

"You shouldn't. And without medical supplies?" she asked.

"With a hospital only a few feet away I assumed I was safe. And you know what they say: once a doctor, always a doctor."

"Well, don't tempt Fate, Mateo. You're standing on hospital property and you're lucky Janis is feeling tolerant. Just watch where you're dispensing bandages. OK?"

"Much ado about nothing," he said, grinning at her as he purposely moved to the middle of the street.

"Why did you join the military?" she asked as they headed down the road to a little shop with a rack of brightly floral shirts on display. Typical casual wear that never failed to draw the tourists.

"Honestly? I don't know. Something drew me. Just don't know what it was." Mateo sighed as they stopped to look through the floral shirts. "Like so many other things. It's trapped in my mind. I can almost feel it there. But it won't surface."

"Give it time," Lizzie said, pulling out a blue floral print, then holding it up for Mateo.

"Well, time is something I certainly have a lot of, isn't it?" He shook his head at the print and she put it back. "I think my tastes run more toward T-shirts. At least I can't picture myself in something like that."

"How about you try it on, then decide?" Lizzie suggested, pulling down another one. This time it was a seafoam-green with white hibiscus flowers.

This wasn't working. Whatever the cause, he was getting anxious. Too many colors, too much stimulation. Too many people watching. At least it felt like they were. All eyes on him. Wounds. Blood. Expectations. So many of them. And he was supposed to save them all. But he couldn't. And they kept coming and coming…

"Mateo?" Lizzie said, giving his arm a gentle shake. "Where did you go?"

He blinked hard, then looked at her, not quite sure at first what was going on. Then it came back to him. It was simply another one of those bad recalls. They happened when he was awake. The nightmares came when he slept.

"To a place I'd rather not visit again."

He was wiped out. No activity for so long and now even the little things bothered him. Maybe it was emotional fatigue? Whatever the case, he wanted to be left alone. Wanted time to himself to think, to see if he could bring anything back. To forget there were so many things he no longer remembered.

"Do you mind if I go take a walk on the beach?"

"Are you OK going by yourself?" she asked.

"I'm perfectly capable of taking a walk by myself," he snapped, then instantly regretted it. "Look, things build up in me. Sometimes it feels like I'm a tea kettle just ready to go off. I didn't mean to…"

She laid a comforting hand on his arm and it sent chills all the way up and down his spine. "Pressure relief," she said. "It's common."

"How do you do it, Lizzie? How do you work with

people like me, day in and day out, and not get burned out? Because from what I'm seeing there may never be a satisfying result in my future. Multiply that by all the patients you've cared for who are just like me, or worse… I'm surprised you don't have your own pressure relief to deal with."

"I do, actually."

She took hold of his arm and they headed off down the road toward the beach, strolling casually, like long-time lovers who knew each other's moves intimately.

"Some doctors find it in tobacco, drugs or alcohol. But I'm a little more passive. I like to watch the sunset. Or swim. And if I'm really angsty… I surf. I grew up—well…pretty much alone. Had to learn at a very young age to take care of myself. Because if I didn't, no one else would. Don't get me wrong. My dad did his best. It's just that so much of the time there wasn't enough left of him to *be* my dad. So my pressure relief? A lot depends on where I am. We lived in a snowy part of Germany for a while and I learned to ski. We spent time in Texas and I learned to ride a horse with the best of them. On Okinawa I learned to cook seafood. It all worked out."

They stopped just short of the beach, where she let go of him.

"And medical school?" he asked.

"It seemed like a good choice. And I was ready to get out on my own. See a different world than the one he gave me…do something different than what I'd always done, which was to make the best of any situation I landed in."

"Had to be tough."

"Not all the time. I like working at Makalapua Pointe Hospital."

"But you don't love it?"

"To be honest, I'm not sure what I love. Most days it's my work, but some days it's just being lazy on the beach."

"Am I hearing mixed emotions?"

"Not mixed so much as changing. I love being a doctor. That's the easy part. But the rest of it… Well, that's to be determined later."

"It happens a lot. It's called career burnout."

"I'm just tired right now. Once I've been away a little while I'll be anxious to go back."

"What if you're not?' he asked.

"Then I'll figure it out when the time comes. My dad burned out before his Alzheimer's. Just decided one day he was done. He'd already served a full career in the Army and he was in general surgical practice. It bothered him for a while, but he was happy in his new life. I'm tired, but not burnt out the way he was."

"And my being here isn't helping you rest, is it?"

"Actually, it's nice having someone around. I'm glad you're staying with me for a while. It makes my day… interesting."

Mateo chuckled. "I've been told I've done a lot of things, but making someone's day interesting…can't say I've ever heard that one. But seriously, Lizzie. If I get in the way tell me to go, and I will."

She stepped away from Mateo. "I'll see you later," she said, reaching out, giving his hand a squeeze. "Unless you decide to go somewhere else."

"Why would you say that?" he asked, wondering if

she really wanted to get rid of him and if her hospital-
ity had been offered on little more than a frayed thread.

Maybe he should go. Find a little place to call his
own. Open a surf shop. Forget that he'd ever been a
surgeon and content himself with whatever life brought
his way.

Except…that wasn't him. He wasn't sure exactly who
he was. But he was sure who he *wasn't*.

"Do you want me to leave, Lizzie? Be honest with
me. Should I go?"

Lizzie shook her head. "When I invited you I meant
it. Besides, where would you go?"

"That's a question for the ages, isn't it?"

He had enough money to get him through for a while.
Or he could strike out on his own and hope that something good came of it. But truth be told the appeal of
being alone was overrated—much the way Lizzie had
claimed. And facing the world with only part of you
intact was a scary proposition. He wasn't ready to try
that. Not just yet.

"One day at a time," his mother used to tell him,
because that was the way they'd been forced to live. If
she'd had dreams beyond that he'd never known what
they were.

Did he have dreams beyond his stint in the military? Surely he must have. Or maybe he was like his
mother—one day at a time. And now one day at a time
with Lizzie.

He liked that. Probably more than he should and
more than he had a right to. For now, though, it offered
him something he no longer had—an identity. From
that he would grow.

But in what direction?

* * *

It wasn't like she didn't trust him to find his way back. That part of Mateo was perfectly fine, and if he wanted to return here he would. Simple as that. She was distracted, though. And worried. It had been several hours and there was still no sign of him. Naturally that had made her think of her dad—that day he'd wandered away and hadn't been found.

That was the nightmare that still caused her to wake up sweating and shaking, thinking of him out there alone, sitting in the underbrush near Kapu Falls, waiting for death to take him. Maybe it had been his choice— maybe that had simply been the way it ended for him. And now she was worried about Mateo. Probably needlessly. But all the same she couldn't settle until he was back.

"It's a nice offer," she said now to Kahawai, one of the wealthy property owners in the area.

He was a proper old man, with polished manners and a politeness that far exceeded anything she'd ever seen in another person. He'd come over to her house and brought cake. It was the way of the people here when one of their own was in trouble, and somehow he'd found out about Mateo. So they were eating cake and discussing business to keep her distracted—which wasn't working. Also, Kahawai had been trying to make her a serious offer for weeks.

"But I like where I am, and doing what I'm doing."

Even to her own ears her words didn't sound convincing.

Kahawai was offering to set up a small medical clinic for her to run. Something the immediate area lacked.

"It would be a good opportunity," he said, slicing

her a second, huge piece of cake. "For the community and for you."

They were sipping banana coladas on her lanai— non-alcoholic drinks made from bananas, pineapples, and a splash of Hawaiian fruit syrup. She'd done this with her dad in the beginning, until being sedentary had made him nervous. Then they'd strolled the beach, gone wading, or picked up seashells.

"But I've never practiced general medicine in a small clinic," she said. "I've always had a hospital and hospital resources to fall back on."

That was her excuse for turning down his offer, her reason for not moving on. And, while this was something she and her dad had talked about doing someday, the thought of doing it on her own was daunting. She wasn't sure she trusted herself enough. Not now, anyway.

"Well, I'd never been a property owner," said Kahawai. "But look at what I have now. Good fortune and my uncle's wealth smiled on me."

Lizzie glanced down the beach to see if she could spot Mateo, but it was practically deserted, as it always was at this time of the day. The locals had all gone home, and tourists tended not to know about this spot. That and the fact that it was all privately owned, which meant no trespassing.

"He'll be back in his own time," Kahawai said. "Maybe he wanders the beach like you do, night after night, trying to find yourself. This doctor with no memory...does he mean something to you?"

"He has a memory," she defended, almost too quickly. "He just doesn't have... Let's just say that he's suffered some trauma and now he's trying to come to terms with it."

"And he's living with you until he's cured?"

"He's staying in my *ohana* until he knows what he wants to do. Big difference."

Kahawai grinned as he stood, preparing to leave. "Well, whatever the case. My offer stands. And if your roommate would like to work with you I'll have a place for him as well. I understand he was a great surgeon in his day."

"Good news travels fast around here, doesn't it?" Lizzie said, trying not to give in to the anxiousness awakening in her.

"We're like family, Lizzie. When you decide you want to be part of that family there'll be a place for you."

He carried his glass into the kitchen and exited through the front door, leaving Lizzie alone on the lanai, watching for Matco.

What if he had decided to move on? Had he taken his things? What few things he had?

Suddenly the impulse hit her to head off to the beach and look for him. But, racing past the *ohana*, she found him standing on the doorstep, simply watching the night drop down on the beach.

"Looks like you're in a hurry to get somewhere," he commented, moving over to allow her room enough to stand there with him.

She squeezed in next to him, determined not to tell him what she was up to. She was his landlord, not his keeper, and she had to keep reminding herself of that.

"Just out for a walk," she said, enjoying the feel of being pressed next to him.

"A walk with a vengeance. You looked like a lady

with a purpose." He slid his arm around her waist, and she readjusted to allow it.

"Just in a hurry."

"You and nobody else. That's what I've been observing—the way people take things at their own pace. They don't seem so caught up in modern life here."

"That's all I'm *ever* caught up in," she said.

"Did you learn that from your dad?"

"Maybe. I was always trying to keep up with him."

"Did you ever succeed...before his illness?"

Lizzie shook her head. "He was a tough man. When he had time for me, if I didn't take it he'd move on in the blink of an eye."

"And that's how you want to be? Like your dad?"

Lizzie laughed. "To be honest, I want to be just the opposite of what he was. I want to have a life *around* my work. He wanted nothing *but* work. Sometimes, if I catch myself doing or saying something he might have, I pull back...do just the opposite."

"And that's your problem now. You want to walk totally away from him and you don't know how."

"You should have been a shrink, Mateo." She leaned her head against his shoulder. "You have...depth."

"That surprises you?"

"Well, you haven't exactly been forthcoming about who you really are, have you?"

"It's easier to stay safe that way. I learned that when I was young, trying to make it through school with good grades rather than a bad reputation. Then again in medical school, where brown skin wasn't exactly the norm."

"Did that bother you much?" she asked.

"When I was young, yes. But most kids suffer at

the hands of other kids one way or another. When I started discovering who I was…" He chuckled. "Well, let's just say that I know who I am, but in totally different terms now."

"It's almost funny how a man with amnesia may know more about himself than I know about myself."

She should leave now. Get away from him while she could. Because as intimacy wove around them she was becoming fully aware that Mateo was the man who might make a difference in her life—if she allowed it. But her legs were too weak to support her body and too shaky to move her away from there. And the humid night, even with the cool spritz coming from the air-conditioning in the *ohana*, surrounded her, held her in place…which allowed his kiss in.

Just like the way Lizzie felt, Mateo's kiss was unsteady at first. Tentative, with a masterful edge just waiting to break through. But he held back. Allowed time to pull her into his arms, tight enough so he could smell the faint scent of gardenias in her hair but loose enough to let her respond to his touch. Her arm, caressed by his, burned, and yet she shivered.

"Are you cold?" he asked, his breath warm on her neck.

Lizzie instinctively tilted her head to look up at him. He was tall, much taller than her, and his shoulders were broad…something she'd tried hard not to observe at the hospital in anything other than a professional way. But now her profession didn't stand between them, and she admired what she saw the way any woman would admire a beautiful man.

"Just…unaccustomed…" she replied, her voice barely above a whisper.

She thought briefly about the colors of the evening sky—the golds and oranges, all the colors that took on a different meaning tonight, other than simply being the colors of another night alone on the beach. Stars by the thousands were twinkling. And she was gazing out on the empty sea, her empty life, her empty world.

All full now—if only for a moment.

Mateo shifted just enough to catch her off-balance and push her against the door frame. In a heartbeat he grabbed her and held her tighter, his dark eyes staring intently into hers. Just a breath between them with no place to hide.

"To what?" he asked. "What are you unaccustomed to?"

"You…me…us. All of this. I've held myself back from it."

"Why?"

"Because there was nothing I wanted to become accustomed to. Nothing…no one who mattered. And being like that has become a habit. I'm always too tied up with…other things."

"Maybe this will break your habit," he said.

His voice was deep and intense. So much so, his meaning was clear. And when their lips met his hold on her tightened even more. He was pulling her into him, pressing himself into her.

It wasn't like she wanted to be somewhere else. She didn't. This moment—right here, right now—that was all there was. *Her* moment. And as her eager mouth fused to his she forgot who they were, where they were, or why they were. None of that mattered now. Nothing mattered but the tip of his tongue brushing her lips and the way she welcomed the urgent thrusting that sent even more shivers racing through her body.

* * *

Mateo had expected some heat just from being so close to her. Something mildly pleasant from almost touching. Then actually touching. But the sizzle, the pure magnetic draw of her—that was what caught him off guard. And not just the way she responded to him, but the way he responded to her. Like he'd never kissed a woman before.

The moment his lips touched hers, ever so briefly, and he cupped her neck with his hand, she arched backward, allowing him more of her. And as his thumb caressed the silken flesh of her throat, and she quivered hard against him, he pulled her even tighter to him, to close the gap, to feel the contours of her.

Damn, but her lips were soft. Too soft. And he fought to call back every bit of reason that was escaping him.

But before reason took over, he pressed his lips hard to hers, and felt the twining of her leg with his calf. A tiny, pleading sound was liberated from her throat—and that was when he lost his control. His cool. His will to keep this impersonal. That was when Mateo bent his head and seized that sound, drawing it between his lips and holding it there, for fear that once he backed away it would be gone, and they would return to normal.

His emotions were too close to the surface now. Too naked. Too close to revealing parts of him he didn't even know in himself. Which scared him.

So rather than thinking about it, rather than letting his pure, raw emotions take over, he kissed her with everything inside him—fear for the future, desire for someone he didn't know, desperation for what would become of him once Lizzie was out of his life.

Because she *would* be out of his life. There may have

been mere millimeters between them now, but those millimeters would soon turn into worlds. And those different worlds would separate them.

The thought of that pulled him back.

"Well, that's one thing you certainly haven't forgotten," Lizzie said, brushing her fingers across her red swollen lips.

"It's a natural response to you, Lizzie. Surely you've seen it building?"

"Sometimes I miss the obvious. Partly because I want to and partly because I don't put myself out there."

"How is it with me?"

She raised her fingertips to her lips. "Nice. Very, very nice."

He'd almost hoped she would say something like they couldn't do it again, or it had been terrible. But the smile on her face told him otherwise. Which wasn't good because already he wanted more, when there was no more to give. Or to have.

He was sitting on the lanai, sipping a fruit juice, watching the darkness surround him. It was a good place for him to be, because she was too confused to make much sense of their situation. In fact, broiling a *mahi-mahi*, a simple task, was proving to be almost more than she could handle right now.

"So, reason it out," she said aloud as she chopped the mangoes, cilantro, green onions, and bell peppers to top the fish. "He kissed you, or you kissed him. Either way, it was a kiss."

Perhaps the only kiss she'd ever had that was worth remembering.

"He enjoyed it...you enjoyed it."

Truer words never spoken. But was there anything beyond what they had already? She didn't know, and she was pretty sure he didn't either.

Lizzie drew in a heavy sigh. Her last relationship, which had been her marriage to Brad, was a disaster of epic proportions, and even though it was so far in the past, she wasn't sure she was ready for something else. She'd been played—expecting everything, getting nothing. Maybe she'd even let herself be played, believing what she wanted to believe, seeing what she wanted to see.

Because in the end their collapse had come as no real surprise to her. There'd been hints. His self-imposed curfew. The texts he'd sent when he'd thought she wouldn't notice. Other women. Another life.

"Mateo isn't married," she argued with herself.

But even if she were to get involved, the one thing that frightened her was his lack of memory. Would she always have to be on guard for him, like she'd been for her dad? Always nervous when he was late getting home? Or when she couldn't find him in the house?

She'd lived that life once and honestly didn't know if she had it in her to do it again. The circumstances might be different, but she saw so much sameness. Or maybe that was what she wanted to see. Something to keep her at a safe distance, because she honestly didn't know where she was going.

What would happen if he found himself again and he wasn't the man she thought he was? She'd certainly been in the dark about her husband, and perhaps that was what scared her most. She was falling for this Mateo, but there might be another one waiting to emerge. Having fallen in love with one man who'd turned out to be someone else…she wasn't going near that again.

"And the moral of that story," she said to her salsa, "is don't get involved."

She glanced out the sliding glass door, only to catch herself wondering how much that kiss had changed things. Or if it had changed things between them at all. They were, quite simply, house-owner and house-guest. End of story. At least, she hoped so.

"Doc Lizzie!" someone yelled into her kitchen window. "Come quick. I think he's dead."

That snapped Lizzie from her doldrums and she grabbed her medical bag, clicked on her outside flood-lights, and ran out the lanai door to follow the college-age man down to the beach, where one of his buddies, who'd had a little too much to drink, was lying uncon-scious in the sand.

Immediately she dropped to her knees on the left side of him, and saw Mateo drop to his knees on the right and lay his fingers on the man's neck to check for a pulse. He tried a couple different places as Lizzie inflated the blood pressure cuff, then shook his head grimly.

"Nothing," he said, taking hold of the man's wrist to check for a pulse there.

When Lizzie looked over at him for an answer, he shook his head again.

"I can't get a blood pressure on him, either." She looked up at the young man's buddy. "What happened?"

"We were surfing. Real good tides at night around here. And he fell off his board. Don't know what hap-pened after that. Maybe it hit him…"

"Is he drunk?" Mateo asked.

"We've had a few beers. Nothing serious."

"That's what they all say," Lizzie said to Mateo. "A few beers and a surfboard can get you dead." She said that for the benefit of the young man's buddy. "What's his name?"

"Teddy. Teddy Chandler."

"Teddy, can you hear me?" Mateo yelled, giving the young man a hard thumb in the middle of his chest.

A sternum-rub, as it was called, was a technique used for assessing the consciousness level of a person who wasn't responding to normal interactions such as voice commands. In Teddy's case there was no reaction.

"Call for an ambulance," Mateo shouted, while Lizzie put her ear almost all the way down on Teddy's mouth to see if there was any discernible breathing.

When she could find nothing, she checked for a pulse again. Like before, it wasn't there. So she commenced CPR, placing the heel of one hand on the center of Teddy's chest at the nipple line.

As she positioned herself to start the compressions, Mateo took an IV set-up from her medical bag and inserted it into Teddy's vein—right arm, just below the bend. He attached a saline bag to it, but nothing else.

"Epinephrine could cause severe brain damage," he said, more to himself than Lizzie.

"You remembered that?"

"I remember some of the newer studies stating epi is contraindicated in cardiac arrest."

Lizzie stopped her chest compressions long enough to assess Teddy for breath sounds, but still he wasn't breathing.

Mateo opened Teddy's airway by tilting his head back and lifting his chin. Then he pinched the man's nose closed, took a normal breath, and covered his victim's mouth with his own, giving him two one-second breaths, hoping to see the natural rise and fall of his chest.

Still nothing was happening.

He gave two more breaths, followed by Lizzie, who administered thirty chest compressions. Then they repeated it all.

The second set of compressions caused Teddy to vomit and spit out seawater, and then he sputtered to life, blinking hard, and reeking of far more than a few beers.

"Can I go home now?" the young man muttered, trying to sit up even as Mateo forced him back onto the sand.

"The only place you're going is to the hospital," Lizzie told him. "In a saltwater near-drowning water is pulled out of the bloodstream, and then it pools in the lungs, where it's thicker than normal blood, and can cause heart damage since your heart isn't used to pumping hard enough to circulate the thickened blood."

"In other words," Mateo chimed in, "you may have messed up your heart, so you need to have it checked out."

"Will it hurt?" Teddy asked.

Mateo looked across at Lizzie and smiled. "Probably. But that's what happens when you drink too much and then think you can conquer the surf. It doesn't happen that way, Teddy. Worldwide, one person drowns every two minutes, and while half of those are children, the half that *aren't* children are largely made up of men who take risks. Drinking and surfing is a risk—you got lucky that your buddy knew where to go to fetch a doctor. Normally it doesn't turn out that well."

Lizzie stood and brushed sand from her knees. Mateo was impressive. Besides that, he was a very good doctor, and for the first time she wondered if there might still be a place in medicine for him. What he'd done and what he'd remembered... Heroic didn't even begin to describe it.

Surely there was a place for him?

Someplace better than where he was now?

Someplace where she wouldn't be so tempted by him?

And, make no mistake. Mateo tempted her in ways no man ever had before.

"It's you they need out there, Doc. Not some other medic. This is Freddy. You've got to go. Got to go... Got to go..."

The soldier faded from view then reappeared in an ambulance, motioning for Mateo.

"Hurry up. Hurry up."

"But I need to be here," Mateo protested. "Incoming."

"Go," his nurse was telling him.

She was pointing at the door where, just outside, the ambulance awaited.

"Go, Doctor. It's your duty. This is Freddy."

But the faces in the hall were blurring together. And the soldiers with those blurred faces were all pointing at the door.

"Go!" they were screaming as he dropped to his knees, shut his eyes, and held his hands over his ears. "Go, Mateo!"

He opened his eyes and he was alone. Just him in the makeshift hospital. And the ambulance. No one to drive him. But the voices—they were still in his head.

"Go!" Mateo screamed, then bolted up in bed, sweaty and shaken.

He knew he had to go, but he didn't know where. Dear God, he didn't know where.

Lizzie could hear him scream through her open window. This was his battle to win, not hers. But she desperately wanted to help him through it. Except she couldn't. These nightmares he was having were taking him on a journey he had to walk alone. The answers he needed were there. But they were his to find, not hers to reveal.

She believed that now, as much as she ever had. Still, as she went to her own bed she was shaken. And silent tears slid down her cheeks. She wanted to fight his battles, do away with his demons. But in the end that would only make her feel useful—it would do nothing to help Mateo.

As she laid her head on her pillow and shut her eyes all she could see was an image of someone drowning. Mateo. He was walking into the water and she was the only one there to pull him out. But she couldn't.

That was her nightmare for the rest of the night. He was drowning and she couldn't get to him, the same way she hadn't been able to get to her dad when he was dying. She was letting them down, letting them both down. And she didn't know how to fix it.

CHAPTER SIX

"You OK?" Mateo asked.

He was concerned about Lizzie. She hadn't said a word in over an hour. Sitting there in the sand, staring at the water, she seemed almost like a statue. A beautiful statue, maybe of a goddess watching over the sea.

"I cleaned up the mess from last night's burnt mahi-mahi and salvaged the salsa to put over something else. But I'm not sure what, since you don't keep a lot of groceries in your pantry."

"Because I rarely eat at home. When Dad was in better shape he loved to cook, but then when I took over we ate very simply. If I couldn't fix it in under thirty minutes, we went out. At least until he couldn't do that anymore. Then, with everything he needed from me in the evenings, I usually just brought something home."

"Did you have someone helping you?"

"I had a couple different people who were available when I wasn't here. One was a student nurse, the other a retired physical therapist. They were good with Dad, but he always wanted me, and sometimes he'd get so belligerent I'd have to leave work to come take care of him." She shook her head. "My father was a lieutenant colonel in the Army, and toward the end he didn't even know his own name."

"I didn't either," he said. "Not for several days. I can't imagine how it would be to lose yourself entirely. Even with just pieces of me gone, I get frustrated. And that's nothing compared to what your dad went through. I'm sorry for that, Lizzie. I suppose we tend to think we're invincible, but the scariest thing that happened to me was waking up in Germany when the last thing I remembered was performing a surgery in a desert outpost hospital. Nobody would tell me what was going on, and I certainly didn't have the capacity at that point to figure it out."

He sat down in the sand next to her, handed her a glass of fresh fruit juice, and took her hand.

"I felt so…alone. I imagine that's how your dad felt when he knew he was losing his memory. It's not an easy thing to face."

She scooted closer and grasped his hand a little tighter. "He wasn't cooperative, either."

Mateo laughed. "Either? Which implies what?"

"You haven't been cooperative. So much so, you got kicked out. And now you're homeless. And, while I'm beginning to see what I believe is the real you, you're still not trying to get better. There's outpatient therapy and private counseling available. It's just a few steps from your door. And yet you've never ventured down there to see if there's anything for you. It's disappointing, Mateo. It's like you enjoy being a step out of time."

"Lucky you took me in, then, isn't it?"

"Is it? I mean, sometimes you act like this is a real relationship. That kiss, for instance. Was it the start of something? Was it meant to be manipulative? What *was* it, Mateo? I spilled my guts to you about how unsure I am and got nothing back. Why is that?"

"Did you ever consider that it might have simply been a kiss? That I'm attracted to you and it just happened?"

"See—that's the problem. You're happy taking the easy way out in the things you do, the things you say. When you walked away from your treatment program did you even stop to think what you were doing? I mean, no one wants to stay in hospital, but if you've got no place else to go—"

"When I was in Afghanistan a lot of widowed women with children came to the hospital," he said, remembering how they would show up out of desperation and hope someone there had a solution for them. "The best we could do was a meal, sometimes a blanket, and the few provisions we could scrounge. It was heartbreaking, seeing all those people with no place to go."

"But that's you," Lizzie said.

"That was me before that particular memory returned. If all these images had been coming back, I might have made a different choice. But I didn't, so here I am. What can I say? I made a mistake. Made several of them. And, at the risk of repeating them, it's easier just to keep myself…isolated."

"Because that's what you think you deserve?"

"I can't answer that because I don't *know* what I deserve or don't deserve."

"That's something best left up to you to figure out. It's a fine line, Mateo. You're doing so much better than anyone might have expected, but you've still got a long way to go. And I'm not going to be the one to tip you in any direction."

"I know. The rest of it's up to me. But I haven't quit, Lizzie. I just don't respond well to pushing."

"Because you've always been in charge and suddenly you're not?"

"That probably explains part of it. But the rest… I know it's not me. At least, I hope it's not." He shrugged. "I'm not very happy with myself, but I need to know why I do and say what I do before I can fix it."

"If you're not sure of the problem, how can you fix it?"

"Maybe I can't. I don't know. But the one thing I do know is that kiss…it was real. As real as any kiss I've ever had. And I meant to do it, Lizzie. You know, to seize the moment?"

"Am I just a moment?" she asked.

He shook his head. "You've never been just a moment since the first time I set eyes on you. Want to know what I thought at the time?"

"I'm not sure."

Mateo chuckled. "I'll tell you anyway. You'd hurried up and down the hall several times that morning, always in a such a rush. But then one time you poked your head in my door and said, 'Hello.' Then you were gone. I thought you had the most kissable lips I'd ever seen. You were there maybe two seconds, but in those two seconds I knew you were somebody I wanted to know better. And kiss."

"Seriously? You wanted to kiss me?"

"I'll swear on a stack of hibiscus seeds that's what I wanted to do."

Lizzie reached up and brushed her fingers lightly over her lips. "I suppose I should be flattered."

"Not flattered. But hopefully in the mood for another one someday."

"Time will tell," she said, when she'd really intended to say no. But why limit her options? Especially since she *was* attracted to him? So, time *would* tell, wouldn't it?

Mateo put his arm around Lizzie's shoulder and the two of them stood at the water's edge, looking out on the ocean. It was nearly a perfect night. The skies were clear, the waters calm.

"When I was a kid, sometimes we'd go to Lake Chapala or even the Manzanillo coastline to swim. I was too young to realize we were too poor to stay in any of the nice hotels or eat in the nice restaurants the way most of the people were. To me, it was a treat just getting to go. So we'd pile in the car—my mother, my aunt, my grandmother, and her sister—take along packed food, and have the best day playing in the water. Then one time one of the kids from a hotel called me a *pobre niño*. Loosely translated that means poor kid. I didn't understand what he meant, or what he was implying, but I knew it wasn't good. After that we quit going and my mother never explained why. But I don't think she wanted me touched by that kind of ugliness. Then we moved to California and it was all forgotten. But the look of horror on her face that day... It broke my heart and I didn't even know why."

"Kids can be cruel," she said.

"Not just kids. It's in all of us, I think. But most people are aware of how their words can hurt and don't use them maliciously. On nights like this...perfect nights... I think back to how my little piece of perfection was ruined by a couple of words, and I wonder if the kid who used them against me even remembers."

"But they made you stronger, didn't they?"

"Only because I allowed them to. When you're five, though, all you see is something that's been taken away from you when it wasn't your fault."

"Which is why you became a doctor?"

"Actually, we lived in a small flat behind a doctor's office. He let me go in and read some of his books. Most of them I didn't understand, but by the time I was nine I knew that being a doctor was my calling. When he retired he gave me all those medical references, which were horribly outdated, but I loved reading them. I almost got myself kicked out of school for taking one or two of them to class rather than my textbooks. And you?"

"It was all I knew. I was talking serious medicine with my dad when I wasn't much more than a toddler, and by the time I was old enough to choose a career path medicine seemed like the logical choice. I knew it, I loved it, and most of all I knew what was involved. So there was never any doubt."

"Well, I went through the fireman, cowboy, and astronaut phases, but somehow I always tied them into medicine." He chuckled. "For a while I pictured myself making house calls on horseback."

"I have a friend—a nurse practitioner—who makes calls in the mountains in the east, where it's totally underdeveloped. She goes by horse because the roads are impassable."

"Well, then, bring on the cowboy hat and turn me loose."

Mateo looked out on the ocean again and watched a

small child who was trying to swim toward the shore. She seemed to be alone, fighting the water, and his instinct kicked in.

Without a word, he suddenly dashed out, dived beneath the waves, and got to the child just as she was about to go under. Pulling her close to his chest, he held her for a moment until her cries quieted and the realization that she was safe set in, then he brought her back to shore, where several people had gathered, watching the rescue.

Lizzie spread out a blanket for the little girl, but stepped back when Mateo laid her there and did a quick check to make sure she wasn't injured. By the time he was finished the beach patrol had pulled up with the girl's mother, who was crying as she dropped to her knees next to her daughter.

"She's fine," Mateo assured the woman, who'd bundled her daughter into her arms. "I'm a doctor and I did a quick check. She's more shaken than anything. But you're free to take her to the hospital…"

The woman wiped away her tears and looked at Mateo. "No, I believe you."

"What happened?" he asked gently.

"She wandered off. I think she loses track of where she is and just…" The woman batted back tears. "Susie is autistic. She's smart. But sometimes she doesn't pay attention. And if I turn my back…"

"I understand," he said, laying a reassuring hand on the woman's arm.

"Sometimes she just gets away from me. She's full of life and thinks she can do anything, but…" The woman scooped up her daughter and followed the beach patrol officer back to his car. Before she left, she turned back to Mateo. "So many people are critical when something like this happens. I appreciate your kindness, Doctor. More than you know."

Mateo stood there for a moment after they drove off, then turned to face Lizzie, who'd come up behind him and now stood there quietly, holding on to his arm.

"Just when you think your problem is the worst in the world, you run into someone who has something going on that's far worse. I used to see that in surgery. Back when I was a resident, sometimes I'd get a little depressed that I wasn't assigned to one of the bright, shiny new medical hospitals—and then I'd get this patient whose life was hanging by a thread. It always made me realize how lucky my lot in life really was."

"I didn't even see her, Mateo. We were looking at the very same thing and I didn't see her."

"I wasn't sure I did, either. It was a gut reaction."

Lizzie blew out a long sigh. "Well, whatever it was, I think I just saw a miracle happen."

He chuckled. "Not a miracle, Lizzie. That was me in my element. Me the way I was and the way I want to be again."

"Do you ever wonder what your life might have been like if you'd chosen to do something different?" she asked. "Like me. I had a music scholarship—I could be playing in some world-class symphony orchestra now. But here I am, and I'm not always happy about it."

"Because…?"

Lizzie shook her head. "I don't know. That's the thing. I always wanted to be like my dad, but in the end he wasn't the man I knew. Of course I wasn't the woman *I* knew by then, either."

"As far as I know I always wanted to do what I do…

did. My mother worked hard to get me through school. She even gave up living near her family to relocate to another country, so I'd have a better chance at achieving my dream. But there was that summer I worked on a ranch in Arizona. I was twelve, maybe thirteen. My mother took a job feeding the ranch hands while the real cook was off on maternity leave. By the end of the summer I was convinced my destiny was to be a cowboy, not a doctor. But then, on my very last day, I fell off a horse, broke my arm, and went back to my original plan. I think my mother was glad of that, because she hadn't worked so hard only to see her son herding cattle and mending fences. Not that there's anything wrong with that. But it's not me. Of course, being a surgeon isn't me anymore, either."

"But there's a place for you, Mateo. I'm not sure where it is, or what it is, but skills like yours would be wasted mending fences. Maybe I can help? As a friend?"

"Well, if you find that place, let me know. I'm getting tired trying to figure it out. And so far the road just keeps getting longer and longer, with no guarantees at the end of it. I mean, what's the point of involving you, or anybody else, when nothing about my outcome can be predicted? What could you do to help me, Lizzie? Be specific. What can really be done to help me? Especially when I'm still in a place where when I wake up half the time I have to re-orient myself? What day is it? What time? Where am I?"

"What I can do is make sure you're not going wherever it is you're going alone. The choices must be yours, Mateo. But I can be the support you need."

"Why would you want to tie your life to mine that

way? You've already been through something similar once. Why go back for more?"

To give herself another chance?

To go back and find an outcome that wasn't like her dad's?

She hadn't told him the full story yet, but he'd gathered enough to know that she blamed herself for his death. So was this Lizzie's need to find another path the way he was trying to do?

"Because I can," she said simply.

He tilted her chin up and stared into her eyes. So much beauty there, yet so much sadness. Would it even be fair of him, pulling her into his problems when what he could see told him she had enough of her own?

"My previous doctors didn't get me. They were excited when they discovered I still knew how to peel a banana, when what I really wanted to know was how to perform a carotid endarterectomy. You know, the big things—like how to clear the carotid artery of a blockage, how large an incision I should make in the sternocleidomastoid muscle. I know the result could be a stroke, depending on the percentage of blockage, but I can't run through the procedure in my mind without stumbling. What kind of scalpel did I prefer? Or clamp? What kind of impact would the procedure have on my patient's quality of life? It's all there..." He tapped his head. "But not in the way it's supposed to be—which makes me doubt so many other things in my life, including my decision to leave the veterans' facility and come here, only to be so uncooperative that I get kicked out. That's not me. I know that. And yet when I see what I do..."

He shook his head.

"And then to draw you into the middle of it just because you're willing to be there with me… So much of me wants that, Lizzie. But I don't have the right to take over your life that way. I know I'm a problem. I know I do exactly the opposite of what I need to be doing. And to put all that stress on your shoulders, just because I want you at my side…"

"We all hobble through life with one problem or another, Mateo. I think there's something here for you. Not me, per se. But something else. I'd like to be like you are—the one who spots the little girl in the water and saves her before anybody else even knows she's there. And I can help you because what you're going through is impossible to face alone. I'm sure of that. And I do like you, in spite of yourself."

She expected a kiss, and maybe he did too, but instead he reached up, ran his thumb down the side of her cheek to her neck, and then placed the first of his kisses. Butterfly kisses that made her toes curl.

Everything inside her told her to back away, but she was fighting all that was feminine inside her that compelled her harder into his arms, revealing more of her neck to him. And as he took what she was offering her lips parted with a sharp intake of breath.

The sound of her shallow, rapid breathing as he kissed her caused her to desire more. And as if he'd read her mind, he cupped the back of her neck and kissed her deeply, gently, and so quietly she had to open her eyes to make sure he was still there.

He was, and the look in his eyes told Lizzie that he was desperate to explore. As desperate as she was. Which for the first time didn't scare her. Nothing about Mateo did. And that was the problem. The barriers keeping her away from this man had failed, and she wasn't sure she wanted to put them back in place.

No, that was wrong. She was sure she *didn't* want to put them back in place. And again, in another first, she didn't really care.

"You won't get anyplace close to where you want to be if you're alone."

"I've always been alone."

"Not really. You have a mother. I do understand why you don't want to burden her with this. But she knows things you want to know, and maybe reaching out would be good for both of you."

It was breakfast time again, and she was sitting on the beach, eating a bowl of fruit. She'd spent the night in her room; he'd stayed in the *ohana*. But whose choice had it been to remain circumspect? She wasn't sure, to be honest. Maybe it had been mutual. A natural pulling back of feelings for fear they were getting in too deep too quickly.

Well, it sounded good, anyway. But waking up alone hadn't felt so good. So maybe they were just about the moment and nothing else. All she knew was that she'd felt a cold, hard lump in her stomach when he'd walked her to her door and then, without so much as a kiss to the cheek, gone around to the *ohana*.

He shook his head. "I don't want people that close to me."

"Even me?" she asked.

"I don't know. When I'm with you, that's all I want. When I'm not, I'm cursing myself for being so stupid letting you in."

"You sure do know how to flatter a girl," she said, trying not to sound as grumpy as she felt.

"No offense intended."

"As I'm beginning to learn. But here's the thing, Mateo. There's an offer on the table from last night and the answer is simple. Yes or no? Do you want me standing with you? And this time, please don't dodge the question."

He searched her face for his answer, and all he saw was genuine honesty. This was a big step, though. He'd been wandering alone for a long time, and to invite somebody in scared and excited him at the same time. Because he didn't want to walk away from Lizzie. She made him feel…hopeful.

Swallowing hard, Mateo said, "Yes," in a voice that was barely more than a whisper.

"Then that's where I'll stand."

"Until you get too involved for your own good."

Lizzie bent over and brushed the sand off her legs. "That's for you to figure out, Mateo, if and when it happens. Anyway, I'm going down to The Shack to have some juice and forget everything else for a while. You're invited to join me, or you can stay here and eat whatever you care to fix. Your choice."

"Well, with such a gracious invitation on the table how could I refuse?"

He wasn't in the mood for crowds this early in the day. In fact, he'd hoped to spend some quiet time on the beach with Lizzie, listening to the far-off strains of the waves lapping the shore and watching a ship make its lazy way through one of the channels.

There was so much clutter in his head. So many

things darting in and out. And he didn't know which were real and which were not.

Lizzie was real, though. As real as any woman he'd ever met. And their kiss the night before had been about the *realest* kiss he'd ever had. It could have led to more. Maybe it should have done.

But Lizzie was surrounded by barriers that were surrounded by their own barriers and more barriers after that. He couldn't see her letting them down—not for him, not for anyone. Couldn't see her ever giving in to the moment, even though she almost had during their kiss.

"The beach is no place to be alone on a beautiful morning like this, so maybe I'll tag along. Unless you choose to be alone," he said, hoping that wouldn't be the case.

"Does anyone ever really choose to be alone?" Lizzie asked. "Or is that a decision forced on them by circumstances?"

"Guess it depends on the person and what he or she really wants from life. Sometimes I'm in the mood to be solitary, sometimes I'm not."

"But given the choice between the two?"

"Can I choose to be flexible?"

Lizzie laughed. "You can choose anything you like, Mateo. It's your life."

"Not lately it hasn't been."

"Well, it's up to you to fix that, isn't it?"

"You really put a lot of faith in me to do the right thing, don't you?"

When they arrived at The Shack the place was busy, as always, so she chose to sit on a log under a banyan tree.

"You were a surgeon. I'm guessing a whole lot of people put their faith in you to do the right thing. You, too. You *did* put faith in yourself, didn't you?"

"I did. But it went with the job. I owed the people in my care the best I could give them."

"Plus all the military pressures on top of that. Sometimes I think that's what made my dad too old too soon. He never knew how to relax, even when he had time off."

"Do you relax very often?" Mateo asked. "Apart from your vacations, do you ever make time to do something for yourself? Something you enjoy?"

"I surf. Not as much as I'd like, like I said before, but I do get out there on my board once a week, or more, if I can fit it in. So, what do *you* do?"

"Long in the past I played guitar in a little band. I also painted... Nothing fine. Don't have that kind of skill. But I did murals on the sides of buildings. Urban art is what they call it now, and I really enjoyed it. I've always wondered if any of my work is still out there or if some other urban artist has come along and painted over it."

"You should go see," Lizzie said. "Maybe even create something new."

She flagged down the server, who was hustling his way through the growing crowd.

"I'll keep it simple," she told him. "Portuguese sausages and white rice, *lilikoi* juice and *malasadas*. They're like a fried doughnut," she explained to Mateo.

The server looked to Mateo for his order. "I'll have the same," he said, and then to Lizzie, "I'm trusting your judgment on this."

"Hope that extends to things other than breakfast," she said.

* * *

"Well, you didn't go wrong on breakfast," Mateo said, positioning himself under the banyan tree so that, like Lizzie, he could sit and watch the ocean as morning turned into noon.

"You have to watch the portions, though. The food is good and the portions are huge. I usually take enough back with me for another meal or two."

She settled in next to Mateo, too full to move, too early in the day to feel so relaxed. But she was, and it felt good.

"So, tell me about moving to the States," she asked. "Was it traumatic? Because even as many times as I moved with my dad, it just seemed routine."

"After we moved to the States, when I didn't speak a word of English, I would hang around this little grocery store for hours—listening to conversations, trying to pick up the language. And I'd ask questions of anybody who paid the least little bit of attention to me. My school classes were taught in English, so I was getting the education I really needed at the store. In fact, I was there so much the owner gave me a job, sweeping the floors and stocking the shelves. He paid me very little, but he taught me to speak English and speak it properly. It's not easy when the first words you can understand and can speak are the names of various vegetables, but to this day I can pronounce rutabaga better than anyone."

"Have you ever eaten one?" she asked lightly.

"Hell, no. Those things are nasty." He faked a huge cringe.

"Well, finally we agree on something."

"We could agree on something else if you like," he said.

"And what would that be?" she asked.

"That today's a perfect day to walk along the shore, maybe even go wading, but not alone."

"You're a man of vast differences, Mateo. So, tell me... How is taking a walk with you going to make a difference for me?"

"You're tough, Lizzie," he said, taking hold of her hand and helping her off the ground, so she could take her glass back to the bar for a refill of the *lilikoi* juice. "But so am I—and that's what I want to talk about."

And talk quickly, before he backed out. Because his plan was a hard-set plan that she might like or might hate. He wanted to do this immediately, before negative energy zapped him of this little burst of courage. Now or never.

And that worried him, because his life nowadays was closer to the never...

She loved to walk along the shoreline at any time of the day or night. It was a quiet place, a peaceful place. Sometimes, after her dad was asleep, she'd used to slip away for a few minutes and go stand on the shore, or maybe walk into the water until it was up to her knees and simply take in the beauty of the night.

It had been the only time she'd felt in control. During the day, as often as not, her job had kept her off-balance, due to so many different and difficult demands. And as evenings went, the routine had never changed. She'd sit with her dad in the garden for a while as he fussed with the flowers—something he did even when his memory was practically gone. Then she'd fix his dinner, get him ready for bed, and finally tuck him in.

Most nights she'd sit in the hall on the floor outside

his door for an hour, hoping he was sleeping. Sometimes he was, sometimes he wasn't. Those were the nights he'd get up and wander, and she'd go after him, and then they'd start the whole evening routine over, because he wouldn't remember he'd already done it once and demand to do it again. Including eating dinner.

Some people had told her locking him in his room would be for his own good. But he was her dad and he hadn't deserved that. She could have hired someone to sit with him at night, but so much of her life had already been disrupted, and she hadn't wanted more of it going by the wayside. So she'd done whatever the circumstances had called for. She'd sat outside his door... sometimes slept outside his door.

Slipping out and going to the water's edge had been a rare and guilty pleasure, because even though she'd gone there to relax one eye had always been on the house.

"So why the walk?" she asked Mateo, as they came to a stop and he bent to slip off her sandals.

"Want to go wading with me?"

The truth was, she did. But after kissing him she was afraid that anything even remotely resembling something romantic would bring about consequences far greater than she knew.

She was attracted to him. But she was also afraid of involvement. There'd never been a relationship in her life that had gone the way she'd thought it would, and while she was well able to wade in shallow water, nothing about Mateo signaled shallow water at all.

"What if I don't want to?" she asked, half hoping he would drag her into the water.

Something like that would be new to her, and being

captured by Mateo… Yes, she liked the idea of that. Captured, carried, conquered… All pure fantasy, of course. But nice when it involved Mateo.

"I'm strong enough to carry you."

"You have a twenty-five-pound lifting restriction for a while yet," she answered, wondering why she was protesting so adamantly when part of her really wanted it.

"You're not my doctor, remember? You're just the person I'm living with presently. And telling the person I'm living with that they have a lifting restriction—well…it's something I'd never do. So, in theory, that's information you don't have."

Despite her attempt to stay serious, Lizzie laughed. "I wish I knew what kind of personality you used to have, because I like this one."

"And if it turns out to be the other one? Or one we haven't met at all? Then what?" He kicked off his shoes and headed toward her. "Tell me, Lizzie. Then what?"

"Then we deal with what we're given."

"But what if all my personalities are just part of me, and when you piece them together it turns me into who I really am?"

"Maybe I already like who I'm seeing."

"Seriously?"

"I don't judge people, Mateo. I accept them as they are. Or in some cases don't accept them."

"And you accept me as I am? Even though I'm not sure that person can really be defined yet?"

"Oh, I think there's a lot of definition stacking up. You're just not ready to deal with it yet."

"You know what they say: to everything there is a season…"

"The fine art of procrastination. It can become habitual, Mateo. Just saying…'"

She smiled, then headed toward the water, but Mateo beat her to it, grabbing hold of her hand and pulling her all the way in.

"No procrastination in this," he said, as her head bobbed above the water. "I wanted to do it and I did it."

She splashed water in his face, then started to pull away from him, but he caught her by the hand and held her there, the water just barely touching her shoulders.

"I want to find myself, Lizzie, and I can't do it alone. But it scares me to think how deep I could drag you in."

"Only as deep as I want to go, Mateo. You can't pull me any harder than I let you."

"I was just looking for a place to stay for a few nights, and now this is beginning to sound like a commitment."

"Nothing wrong with commitments. We make them and live with them every day. Should I get out of bed this morning? Coffee or tea with my breakfast? The blue shirt or the white one? Should I let a virtual stranger stay in my *ohana* or let him wander around lost and hope he makes it? We make our choices and those turn into commitments. No, I'm not getting out of bed this morning. I'm committed to staying in bed. And I want to wear the blue shirt while I'm drinking my coffee. Commitment, commitment."

"What about the man sleeping in your *ohana*? Commitment there, as well?"

"Yes, but I haven't figured out what kind."

She wasn't sure she wanted to figure it out. Her dad had always accused her of being too tenderhearted, like that was a bad thing. But it was part of her…the part that opened her up to getting hurt. Like marrying the wrong man because he told her the right story. So her commitment to Mateo—it had to be what worked for him, but also what worked for her. Problem was, she didn't know what worked for her anymore.

"So, let's start this commitment with you doing the cooking while I clean up after you. And you can tend the flowers since I don't have a green thumb."

"And this is part of your treatment plan?"

"It's called retraining yourself to be disciplined. It's where you start, and I'll add things as I see fit."

"It's also called being your slave."

"That, too," she said, smiling. "Also, what about cars? Are you a good mechanic?"

That one stumped him for a moment, and he frowned. Then he shut his eyes. It was interesting watching him search for a memory, and in her experience, when something triggered someone as her simple question had triggered Mateo, there was usually a morsel there. So she stood thigh-high in the surf and watched the outward signs of his inward battle for a couple of minutes before he finally sighed, then smiled.

"I had a…a… Damn, it was a 1957 Bel-Air. Convertible. Red."

He shut his eyes again and didn't open them as he struggled to find more of the memory. She could see there was more coming back to him, and he was smiling as it returned, which excited her.

"A classic?" she asked, to prompt him back into the moment.

"It was. I found it in an old storage warehouse in pieces. The owner said I could have it."

Suddenly, he opened his eyes and looked at her.

"I remember this, Lizzie. Remember it like it just happened. The deal was I locked up for him... Old Man McMichaels—we called him Mick. I made a deal with Mick to lock up for him every night so he could get home early to his wife and kids. If I wanted to lock myself in and work on the car that was OK with him. And if I sold the car he got half. Except I didn't sell the car. It's... I think it's still in his warehouse. Or could be. He said he'd keep it for me until I came back for it. It runs perfectly. At least it did. And it's the only car I've ever had."

He looked at her and a puzzled expression came over him.

"I didn't remember that before, Lizzie. Why is that something I would have forgotten?

"Even the experts can't explain the workings of the brain. And keep in mind that the farther away you get from your accident and surgery, the better you'll do."

"It does work in mysterious ways," he said. "Sometimes when I was a field surgeon I'd see a brain injury so bad I didn't think there was any hope for recovery, and then recovery was almost instantaneous. Then other times..."

He shut his eyes again. Then shook his head.

"He wanted an aspirin. That's why he'd come in that day. Had a headache. Asked for an aspirin. Died before I could give it to him." He opened his eyes and stared at her for a moment. "I hated brain trauma. Hated what I could see, hated what I couldn't."

"Did you have many patients with brain injuries?"

"Too many," he said. "I'm a... I *was* a general surgeon. I had no business doing neurosurgery. But sometimes it couldn't be helped, if we couldn't get a neurosurgeon in for whatever reason." He sighed heavily. "And look where I ended up. Life can sure play some messed-up tricks, can't it?"

Turning slowly, he looked directly into her eyes.

"But you already know that, don't you?"

"Meaning?"

"Your father. Brilliant surgeon, the way you tell it. Then…" He shrugged. "Did he know, Lizzie? Did he know what was happening to him?"

"At first. And he fought back—a lot like the way you do. With stubbornness and resistance. But as his illness progressed, and more of him got lost, the knowledge of what was happening to him went away as well, taking all those years of bravery and the good things he'd done. That was the worst part, I think. Watching this giant of a man lose the things that had made him a giant. He earned those memories and he deserved to have them. But there was nothing I could do except tell him about the things he'd done. And to him they were just stories. Something that kept him entertained for a little while. But even that stage didn't last long, so after that went away I showed him pictures. They meant nothing to him, though. He didn't even recognize himself."

She swatted back a tear sliding down her face.

"It isn't fair, Mateo. Not to him, not to you, not to anybody. Losing yourself like that…" She shook her head. "But you've got hope. My dad had none and there was nothing I could do about that, even though I tried."

"Did you ever resent him for what you had to do?"

"Sometimes…a little. I think it's natural when the demands become more and more. But in a real sense… no. It wasn't his fault."

"And you: the healer who couldn't fix the person

you loved the most." He pulled her into his arms and held her there as the water lapped around them. "I'm sorry you had to go through that, Lizzie. It can't have been easy, and there's nothing else to say except I wish it could have been different for you."

"Like you said, life can sure play some messed-up tricks."

"Why here? Why did you bring him here? Was it just because of the flowers?"

"It was so that a practitioner by the name of Malana Palakiko could treat him. She's a holistic practitioner who uses light therapy, acupuncture, and natural herbs. Traditional medicine had run its course and I'm...open-minded. She has a little clinic a few miles from here, and since nothing else was working... She's one of the best when it comes to treating various forms of dementia. And, while she can't cure Alzheimer's, she does make her patients feel better, and she's had some good results in prolonging the inevitable. Dad loved seeing her. The thing was, even while I knew there wasn't any good outcome, I wanted to make his life as good as it could be as he was fading away, and I think Malana did that. She was so...kind. Patient. Understanding."

"And his doctors at the hospital?"

"When a case is hopeless, sometimes their efforts are as much for the loved one as for the patient."

"Was it that way for you?"

"Maybe. I just wanted to do everything I could. He would have expected that from me. But so much of his treatment...I think it was designed to make *me* feel better, like I was really doing something good for him. What *was* good for him, though, was sitting in the garden and tending his flowers. I didn't see that at first. I was so busy pushing him into treatments that weren't working." She laid her head against his chest. "I could have done better for him."

"Something tells me you're being too hard on yourself."

"Or not hard enough. I knew he was going to be a huge responsibility and I was willing to make sacrifices. What I wasn't willing to do was find support for myself—and it's out there. I'm not the only one to have done what I did, and if I'd just listened—" Her voice broke and she quit talking.

"Is that why you want to help me, Lizzie? To make up for what you feel you didn't do for your dad?"

That thought had never occurred to her, and she was so startled by it she stepped away from Mateo. "Is that what you think?"

"I'm not sure what I think, to be honest. I know your intention isn't malicious, but..."

"But it might be self-serving?"

"People aren't often as generous and kind as you are. In my experience, there's always a motive. People helped me along because I was a boy with brown skin who had an unlimited future ahead of me. Give me an extra shove and you can claim some of that feel-good motive for yourself."

"That's not me, Mateo. People in my life didn't have motives. In fact, I was hardly ever noticed. As for trying to have a feel-good moment at your expense..." She shook her head vehemently. "I don't know what it takes to gain your trust, but I don't come bundled in motives. My life is a lot simpler than that."

"There's nothing simple about you, Lizzie. Nothing at all. Maybe that's why I'm falling...why I like you so much. You're complicated, yet guileless, and the two put together are an interesting mix."

"How interesting?" she asked.

"Very interesting," he replied as he pulled her back to him and lowered his head to kiss her. "Maybe the most interesting person I've ever met—even if I'm not sure how many people I've met and which ones I considered interesting."

"If you intend on kissing me now's the time, Mateo. Unless you'd rather keep on talking and talking and talking..."

Even in the near darkness of the evening he could see her sadness. Or maybe it was more that he could feel it. He understood the melancholia that came with the darkening of the day. Remembered it from Afghanistan, listening to the moans and cries in the night coming from his ward. People in so much pain and fear and he couldn't fix them. Some who would never go home. Some who would.

And now there was his own irrational fear of the dark. During the day he could be as belligerent as hell, and blowing off his anger that way worked. But when it turned dark his belligerence disappeared, to be replaced by melancholia and fear. And some of those moans and some of those cries in the night had been his.

And probably Lizzie's as well. Strangely, that hurt him maybe even more than his own pain did—knowing that something far deeper than she would let him know about was pulling her in.

"Care for a swim?" he asked, for the lack of anything better to say.

"I'm always in the mood for a swim," she said.

After the kiss they'd returned to the house and changed into beach clothes, and taken a towel along with them. Now he grabbed her up off the towel and carried her to the water—where he dropped her.

He didn't set her down gently. Didn't even give her the option to go wading. Against her lame protests he carried her out until he was waist-deep, then dropped her. She went under for a second, and when she popped back up she grabbed his hand and pulled him down with her.

"You could be risking my life," he said, laughing.

Her response was to splash him, then dive back under before he could retaliate. But he was strong in the water. As he dived down he grabbed her by the arm and pulled her back up to the surface, then splashed her the way she'd done him.

"Apparently I have some skill at this," he said, then dove back under.

This time when he surfaced he was about twenty yards away from where they'd been before, and he didn't see her.

"Lizzie?" he called, turning around in circles and looking for signs of her. "This isn't funny, Lizzie. Where are you?"

Her answer was to grab him by the ankle and pull him under, then get away before he had time to resurface. Except he'd already anticipated she'd do something like that, so he got himself all the way down to the sandy ocean floor, then grabbed her ankle and pulled her down on top of him. *Fully* on top of him.

He held her there for a moment, before he realized he was enjoying not only the playtime but the feel of his body against hers entirely too much. So he pointed up, then released her, and followed her to the surface. Both came up spitting out water and laughing.

"Just wait until I get you on a bodyboard," she warned him, and she shoved back the hair from her face enough to see that he was staring at her. Up close and personal. Staring with such an intent look that it gave her shivers that were visible to him.

He hadn't meant to. But she was so beautiful he couldn't help himself. Whether or not she was a woman he would have chosen before, he had no clue. But if he were able to choose now, the only woman in his mind was Lizzie.

That was the problem. There might be other things in his mind that would dictate different choices. And even if there weren't she didn't deserve his problems. As a friend, he appreciated her willingness to help. But as anything else...

"Don't know if I've ever been surfing, or bodyboarding, but the sooner the better," he growled, trying to take those other things off his mind.

And then he dove down and headed underwater for the beach, carrying with him feelings for Lizzie that were far deeper than anything he'd intended.

Was he falling in love? Despite his attempts to talk himself out of it, and all the rationalizations that he didn't want or need that in his life—especially now—was that what was happening to him?

Lizzie headed to the shore as well, wondering when fifteen feet had turned into such a long journey. But it was, and by the time she'd managed to make it to shore Mateo was already standing there in ankle-deep water, dripping wet and looking sexier than any man had a right to—in the dark, in the light, or any other shading of the day.

What am I doing? she asked herself as she stood and walked back to the sand, taking care to keep her eyes averted. *And why am I doing it?*

Because she was attracted to him, pure and simple. She was an adult. There was nothing stopping her. Except common sense. And right now, try as she might, she couldn't dredge it up.

So as she walked past him she turned her head to avoid temptation, and words she hadn't intended to say slipped out. "You look good in the water."

"I wasn't sure you'd noticed."

"Oh, I notice. But I don't always react."

"Sounds very military to me."

"It probably is. My dad always told me to keep my emotions inside, said that people didn't want to see them. When I did, he called me his brave little soldier, and that was high praise coming from a man who didn't believe in coddling anyone."

"So when you said you'd noticed me..."

"The way any woman would notice a good-looking man. I'm only human, Mateo. Maybe a bit more reserved than you're used to, but I'm normal in all the ways that count." She reached over and brushed his cheek with her hand. "This living arrangement could get difficult because of that. But there are worse things in life than being attracted to a good-looking man."

"Or woman," he replied.

"So if we know it's there between us it becomes easier. At least, it should."

After only a few days, Lizzie was already starting to like having someone there with her. Or was it Mateo she liked having there? Either way, this past year had been so lonely, and having a little noise around the house other than her own was nice. Especially after that kiss...

"Are you sure that's true?" he asked, walking alongside her, but at a safe distance. "Admit an attraction and then hope it can be held at an arm's length?"

"I'm not sure how we're supposed to work. More than that, I'm not sure I know how I *want* us to work. Friends, partners, lov—"

She didn't finish the sentence because this was becoming too deep, and she didn't want a volley of emotions going back and forth between them. Especially when there was every possibility that her feelings were turning into more than she'd expected. He was easy to like, she was discovering. More than that, if she allowed herself to admit it, he would also be easy to love—even with parts of him missing.

But could she go through that again? That was the question she needed to figure out before she took the wrong step. Because she did know what it was like living with someone who was fragmented. It was difficult, sad, tedious, and moments of joy were so few and far between.

But that had been her dad. Not Mateo. Which led her to an even bigger question. Could she separate the two? There were similarities in their problems, although not that many. And Mateo was caring and warm while her dad had not been. Still, she'd loved her dad because he'd tried to do better. Yet in her mind the similarities were still large. And that was what scared her.

Would there ever be a time when Mateo occupied all her thoughts, as well as her whole heart, and didn't get squeezed out?

"Like I said before, Lizzie, you can tell me to leave anytime. No explanation necessary."

"I know I can." But she wanted him there. Liked having him there. He balanced her out while she went through her own ups and downs and never judged or asked questions. "That's not what I want."

"Meaning you like having me here?"

"I do, Mateo. It's sort of out of character for me, but yes, I like having you here."

He smiled as he watched her make her way to the front door. She wasn't easy. In fact in a lot of ways, she was difficult. But he liked being here with her, too. In fact, he could see that feeling growing the longer he stayed. She wasn't orthodox, she wasn't predictable, but Lizzie was the real deal, and he was attracted to that asset almost as much as he was to her *other* assets.

"Time will tell," he said aloud, as he walked around to the *ohana*. Time and, he hoped, a few more pieces of his memory.

"You need to go up there, Doc. He's bad and he'll stand a better chance with you."

"I'm not supposed to do this."

Sweat was dripping off his brow, yet he was chilled to the bone. Looking up, he saw the two medics up there working frantically. And they were looking down at him, expecting him to trade places.

"You got an IV in?" he yelled up to them, but his voice didn't carry over the sound of the gunfire that was much closer than he cared to admit. "IV!" he shouted. "Get an IV in him."

They had the equipment with them, and it would be

easier for them to use it than for him to carry up more than he had to.

"Get the IV in him, then I'll come up."

Which meant one of them would come down, since the watchtower platform was too small to hold three people, let alone four.

"IV!" he shouted again, indicating the vein in his left forearm.

Finally one of them leaned over and shouted. "Don't come up, Doc. Too risky. We'll get him down to you, then you can—"

As he was shouting a shot rang out, hitting the soldier in what appeared to be his chest.

"What do we do, Doc?" one of the men on the ground asked. "Tell me what to do!"

Then suddenly they were dying.

They were all dying.

"I don't know!" Mateo screamed. "I don't know."

When he looked up again it was Freddy hanging over the edge. Freddy with his chest ripped open. His friend. His only friend out here.

As he screamed, he woke up in a puddle of sweat. The bedsheets were drenched and his hands were shaking. His memory was returning, and he wasn't sure he wanted it to. What had happened that night…none of it was good. None of it.

Sighing, Mateo left the bed and walked to the window, opened it, and looked out at the stars for a little while.

It wasn't going to leave him. Other things had. Too many things. But this? This was hanging on in huge chunks, tormenting him.

Some memories weren't meant to be remembered and this was one of them. But it was coming back. Damn it. It was coming back.

His screams carried through the night and she couldn't run fast enough to get to him.

"Mateo," she choked, barely slowing as she ran through the front door and up the stairs to his room.

He was standing at the window. Staring out. Not moving. Barely breathing.

"Tell me what to do."

He turned slowly to face her. "They all died, Lizzie. Every one of them, including Freddy. And I was the only one who—" His voice broke, and he sank to the floor. "There was nothing I could do to help any of them."

Lizzie sat on the floor next to him, putting her arm around his shoulder even though he was stiff and resistant. "I'm ready to listen if you're ready to talk."

"But there's nothing to say. I took a risk. Went up the tower when I should have waited. Drew enemy fire and got every one of my ground support killed."

There were so many things she wanted to say—most of them trite. But he didn't need that. So instead she pulled him a little closer and sat quietly, waiting for him to speak again.

It was nearly five minutes before he did.

"Nobody came for a couple of days. The whole area was under heavy fire and they had no idea that one of the casualties was alive. So I lay there, going in and out of consciousness, and I have no idea when I was rescued or what happened after that. The next thing I remember is waking up in Germany. I'd had surgery—I remember that. But I didn't remember my name. Not for days. Or maybe weeks. Then I was sent Stateside, and you know the rest. Belligerent patient. Refuses to help himself."

"Survivor's remorse?" she asked.

"Probably."

Now it was beginning to make sense to her. Mateo was beginning to make sense to her. He didn't want to get better because somewhere, buried deep, he believed he should have died with his men. This wasn't about his memory loss, or his hatred of being a patient. It was about the very essence of a man who carried a burden he didn't deserve.

"Why now?" she asked. "What's bringing all this back now?"

She feared it was something she was doing, or not doing, and she wanted to know.

"Maybe because I feel safe here. The truth is, it's never clear why something surfaces when it does. That's something they've been telling me since Germany. No one really knows why something happens when it does."

"I like the explanation that you feel safe."

"So do I," he said.

CHAPTER SEVEN

BEFORE MATEO, BREAKFAST had always been quick. If she ate it, she never lingered. Most often she grabbed a coffee on the way to work and didn't think about food until her belly told her she was hungry. If it didn't, as often as not she didn't eat.

But this morning she felt like making breakfast for Mateo the way he'd done for her these past mornings. It was simple. Nothing like his elaborate spread. Fresh fruit, toast. And in the casualness of the moment she felt relaxed. Relaxed enough to ask his opinion.

So, over her second cup of coffee, she told him about her opportunity to move from the hospital to a private practice as a primary care provider. She knew it was something her dad would have dismissed as stupid before she'd have been able to get all the words out. He'd actually told her so before his Alzheimer's got so bad.

"Kahawai is really pressuring me. He wants me to buy out his uncle's small practice, possibly expand it, and treat the people who live in the area. He's put me on a deadline now. Says he's going after you if I don't accept."

"Are you happy at the hospital?"

"I'm not *un*happy. It's just that there are so many

memories here I'm not sure I want to stay. Not sure I want to go, either."

"Do you have other options?" he asked.

"A few. None that excite me, though. Maybe I'm too picky—or maybe I'm in a place where I shouldn't be making major life decisions yet. Whatever the case, I won't be doing anything without good reason. So, are you up for a bodyboarding lesson today?"

"The best possible scenario is that once I paddle out into the water it all comes back to me and I remember all the medals I won as a world-class surfer."

Lizzie laughed. "I don't recall your name being on any medal list. Which championship was it?"

"See, that's where amnesia comes in handy. All I have to do is say I don't remember, and people won't press for more information. They'll just assume I'm what I claim to be."

"Have you ever surfed, Mateo?"

"Not to my knowledge," he said seriously.

"Well, it's too soon after your head surgery to do anything more than paddle on your stomach. And, while I already know the reaction I'm going to get, I think you should wear a helmet."

"A stylish one, I hope?" he said, taking both their coffee cups to the sink, then rinsing them out before they went into the dishwasher. "If all I'm allowed is bodyboarding, I'll accept that. But the helmet's got to be pretty damned cool."

"Because...?" she asked, biting back her smile.

"Because I'm pretty damned cool, and I don't want my reputation ruined by a helmet."

She liked that little bit of stubbornness in him. It was

sexy. But was it really him? And was she always bound to wonder if things were really him?

"Then we'll get you a cool helmet. Pink, purple, neon-green?"

"Black—with stripes. Maybe red stripes. And all the gear to match."

He was really quite funny when he wanted to be, and she enjoyed that, because she needed some lightness in her life. "Whatever you say."

"What if I say that you make me nervous?"

"I'll ask you why, and you'll probably come up with some good lie I'll believe."

"Except I'd never lie to you. Not intentionally."

And just like that the light moment had turned serious.

"I may not be the me who existed before, but no matter who I am I'd never lie to you." He reached out and held her face between his hands. "Your face and especially your eyes are very expressive, Lizzie Peterson. Your eyes would show if you ever lied to me. But you wouldn't do that."

"Are you that sure of me?" she asked, backing away from him. His touch was too real, and it was a reality she didn't want to face.

"What if I said yes? That I trust you more than anyone else I've ever trusted except for my mother?"

"I'm not sure what I've done to earn that, but I'd be flattered."

"Then be prepared to be flattered, because I do." He bent to her ear and whispered, "And I think I always will."

She wanted desperately to ask him what he meant by that, but she was afraid of the answer. She'd said yes to a man once before, then proceeded directly into hell. And, while Mateo was nothing at all like Brad, she wondered about her judgment. Maybe didn't trust it so much. Or perhaps everything stemmed from her need not to be alone.

Whatever the case, she wasn't prepared to give Mateo an answer to the question she was pretty sure was coming. So she backed away from him.

"Give me half an hour, then we'll meet in the garden and go rent a couple of bodyboards. We have one quick stop to make first. I promised Kahawai I'd look at the clinic."

"So you *are* giving it some thought?"

"Maybe a little. I'm not one to shut down my options the way—"

She stopped. Mateo was his own man and he was going to do what he wanted to do. At least until he believed that asking for real help was a good option. If that ever happened.

"The way I am?" he asked. "That's what you were going to say, isn't it?"

"Let's just say we're not alike."

"But opposites attract, don't they?"

And they *were* opposites in so many ways. Yet they were also so much alike.

"Who said anything about attracting? All I did was mention I wanted to go look at the clinic. You're welcome to come, or you can do whatever you want. It's your choice," she said.

In so many ways, everything was his choice. But she wasn't sure he was ready for all the choices that would come his way.

Time would tell, she supposed.

* * *

The clinic was bustling when Lizzie and Mateo entered. The line was long, but nobody seemed put out by the wait. It was staffed by one elderly doctor, who didn't move fast, one medical assistant, and one receptionist. People had brought their lunches and were spread out in the garden outside, eating.

It seemed more like a social gathering place than a medical office, and Mateo liked the feel of that. It wasn't the way he practiced, but he could see Lizzie here, working at a different pace than she normally did, and being happy doing it.

"It's not what I expected," he said, as they made their way through the waiting room to the back, where Doc Akoni looked exhausted as he went from one exam room to the another.

"Two doctors here would be great," he said, assuming Mateo was here to enquire along with Lizzie. "The practice is booming, but I'm too old to keep up with it. My goal is to spend the rest of my years with my wife and do the things we never had time to do before. You know…visit kids and grandkids. Travel… Live out my life in leisure."

"Where do your emergency patients go?" Mateo asked, looking over some of the outdated equipment that was still in use: a breathing machine, an X-ray rig, something that chugged along doing rudimentary blood tests, and a few other gadgets that looked as old as he was.

"There are a couple of hospitals with good emergency care down the coast, if the situation isn't too urgent. And, of course, we can air transport them down to Honolulu when it's necessary."

"How often is that?" Lizzie asked.

"More often than I care for. There are some good clinics in the area, but as far as hospital beds go nothing much around here."

"What about Malakapua Pointe?" asked Mateo.

Lizzie shook her head. "No emergency department. That was never part of the plan."

Doc Akoni escorted his next patient into one of the three exam rooms. "Janis Lawton had her vision for Malakapua when it was being built here," he explained. "And, while we were hoping for some kind of emergency department, she was very specific as to the kind of patient she wanted. Her general care wards and surgeries don't really lend themselves to a broader base of patients with the kinds of injuries and illnesses you see here in this clinic. We're minor. We treat the little things and make referrals for patients who need more than we offer. Nobody comes here expecting open heart surgery, or even an appendectomy."

"Which makes you a country doctor," Mateo said.

He was looking at the little girl who was the next patient in the queue. Her skin was red and blistering. She looked listless and dizzy. And it was clear she was suffering with nausea. Definite signs of sun poisoning.

"Can I help you out with your next patient?"

"You can see all the patients you want. I'm assuming you're the doc everybody's talking about…the one with amnesia?"

"Amnesia in some areas. But many parts of my life are intact—like the part that sees a clear case of sun poisoning."

"You know enough to ask for help if you need it, don't you?" Akoni asked.

Mateo nodded.

"And you can read an X-ray? Because we have a rather outdated machine."

Mateo nodded again.

"Sutures?"

"Yes. I can put in sutures."

"Then it sounds to me like you're good to go. Lab coats are in the back, along with an extra stethoscope. There's one central area for supplies, which I keep locked. We don't dispense medicine because the salesmen prefer to avoid us, meaning no free samples. Also, because we're not a pharmacy, we're not licensed to prescribe. Oh, and don't try to refer patients to…" he nodded sideways at Lizzie "…to *her* hospital. Like I said, they don't do trauma, or any sort of emergency, and there's hell to pay if one of our patients accidentally ends up there. The other places we use are much nicer."

Lizzie raised her eyebrows at his pronouncement. She'd heard him say as much before, but didn't really believe it was that bad. But maybe it was. Maybe it was something she should check into if she went back.

"So, how will you treat her?" she asked Mateo, referring to the child.

"Cool compresses. A lot of fluids. And if that doesn't bring up her hydration level fast enough, an IV. Treat her nausea. Take care of her skin with some kind of medicated moisturizer. And keep her out of the sun for a while. Bed rest for a couple of days if she comes down with a fever or chills, which is likely. Then ibuprofen for that. It's all pretty basic. Nothing to worry about that general care won't take care of."

"You're good," Lizzie commented, genuinely impressed.

"So, for now," said Doc Akoni, "if you need to prescribe any real treatment, and not simply apply a bandage, why don't you run it by me first? Or Lizzie, if she cares to stay. All things considered, I don't think you need close supervision at this level of care, but just to be safe…"

"Not a problem," Mateo said. "It's just like going through my residency again."

"Well, be patient. Things will change," said Doc Akoni.

Mateo nodded, then took the child by her hand and led her toward the exam room, motioning for her mother to follow.

"I could use someone like you around here," said Doc Akoni, on his way into exam room one.

"Even with my condition?" Mateo asked, looking at the old-fashioned whiteboard hanging on the reception area wall, where patients signed their names as they came through the door.

"Even with your condition. If you didn't lose your general skills, this could all be yours."

"Not sure I'm ready to run a clinic on my own. Even one as basic as this."

"Things change, son. You never know who might be standing right behind you, eager to help. All I'm saying is, don't discount yourself. You've got everything you need to do this job, if you set yourself free to do it."

Mateo glanced at Lizzie, who was busy talking to a woman who was obviously well along in her pregnancy. "Mind if I hang around here for a little while and help?" he asked her. "Maybe put the bodyboarding off until later this afternoon?"

He nodded down toward the woman's swollen ankles, and Lizzie acknowledged his discovery with a wink.

"I think helping out would be a good way to spend the morning. Maybe I'll stay and put in a few hours as well. And the first thing… Would you mind consulting with me, Dr. Sanchez? My patient is nearing her thirtieth week, and the edema in her feet and ankles is indeed what's bothering her. Since I haven't worked a maternity case in years…"

Mateo looked at the woman's name on the whiteboard, then found a paper file in a rickety old filing cabinet. He studied it for a moment, then nodded. "Why don't you make Leilani comfortable in exam room two, since it's open? I'll be in shortly."

"You OK?" Lizzie whispered as she passed by him on her way into exam two. "Can you handle maternity? I know it's a little more than first aid, but…"

"I did it when I was overseas. A lot of the women who lived there depended on us."

"Then you're the man for the job."

"Only if you oversee what I'm doing. I'm not ready to fly solo with anything more than a cut or a bruise."

"Or CPR," she reminded him as she entered the exam room.

That was true. And so many things had come back to him—like why Leilani had swollen ankles. It wasn't part of the scope of a surgeon's responsibility, but he knew. It was coming back to him. All the pregnant women he'd treated in Afghanistan. The complications…the normal but uncomfortable things. It made him nervous and excited at the same time.

Lizzie wasn't sure what Mateo was thinking, and she hadn't intended working here for any part of the day, but Mateo's eyes sparkled with happiness and excitement.

That didn't mean he was finding himself, but it could mean he was finding a new place. But here? In this clinic? Or maybe just in the general practice of medicine?

He certainly was good. Quick. Alert. In tune with the details of his patient. It was the first time he'd showed any kind of hope, and she was glad for that. Glad for him. Actually, she felt so excited that if she were twenty years younger, she might be jumping up and down like an eager child.

Twenty minutes after his examination of Leilani, Mateo said, "Everything looks good. Your blood pressure is normal, baby is the right size, and you look like a first-time mom with a glow."

"What about my swollen feet?" she asked.

"Right…" he said, nodding. "It's called edema, and it's normal—especially in the evening and during warmer weather. It happens in about seventy-five percent of all pregnancies, and once it starts you're stuck with it until you deliver."

"Why?" she asked, and her attention was focused solely on Mateo, not Lizzie, who stood off in the corner, observing.

"Well, it happens when your body fluids increase to nurture both you and your baby. That results in increased blood flow and pressure on your expanding uterus, which is what causes the swelling. Look for it to happen in your hands, as well."

"Then it's really normal?" the young woman asked.

"Perfectly—as long as it's kept under control. However, if it becomes excessive, and comes along with a couple of other things, like increased blood pressure or rapid weight gain, that could indicate a problem, and you'll have to let your doctor know about it."

"Is there anything I can do about it? Maybe take a pill, or something?"

"I think the natural things you can do are better. Such as trying not to stay in one position for a long period of time. Also, elevate your legs when you're sitting. And I always recommend sleeping on your side—your left side—because it helps your kidneys eliminate waste, which reduces swelling. Then, there are other things that might help. Pregnancy-appropriate exercising. Avoiding tight socks or stockings. Drinking lots of water—around ten glasses a day. That helps eliminate the waste in your system that causes the swelling. And comfy shoes. If they feel good, wear them—and skip the vanity shoes. And, last but not least, cut out excess salt. It causes you to retain water, which is exactly what you don't want."

"It sounds so simple," Leilani said, heading toward the exam room door.

"It is—and it will only last a few more months." Mateo smiled as he escorted Leilani through to the waiting room. "Just use common sense and you'll be fine. But if you think something's not right call a doctor—or a nurse practitioner, if that's who you're using."

"I'm not using anybody," she said. "Doc Akoni confirmed my pregnancy at the beginning, but now when I come here and see so many people waiting I don't stay, because I have to get back to my job. Today I got lucky. You're here and the line is going faster."

"You need regular care," Mateo told her. "For your own health as well as your baby's."

"I'll get it closer to the time."

With that, Leilani disappeared through the door and hurried on her way.

"She doesn't get any regular care," he said to Lizzie, who was standing in the hallway, still watching him.

"A lot of people don't. I saw it when I traveled with my dad. See it here, too. Too many complaints...not enough doctors to go around."

She was proud of the way he had handled himself, and he couldn't have been more spot-on in his examination and in answering Leilani's questions if he'd been an obstetrician.

What Mateo had was a real gift. He remembered things she'd forgotten. Sleeping on your left side—she wasn't sure that was something she'd ever known about pregnancy. She admired what he was doing, looking at something that was new to him, and safe.

Admiring him personally was not so safe. But one was spilling over into the other and she wasn't sure she knew how to stop it.

Or if she even wanted to.

When the morning was over, and the queue was cut down by more than half, thanks to Lizzie and Mateo pitching in, they decided to postpone their bodyboarding and spend the rest of the afternoon relaxing.

Mateo was glad of that. His headache was back— probably from overexertion. It had been a good long time since he'd worked, and he'd discovered he wasn't in the same good shape he'd used to be when...

Mateo shut his eyes for a moment and fractured pieces of his makeshift military surgery came back to him. Nothing was concrete. Nothing really rang a bell.

Except an older nurse sitting at the triage desk… Was she knitting?

"Something wrong?" Lizzie asked as his eyes shot back open.

"Her name was Mary. She knitted…for a grandchild, I think. She was my surgical nurse. Damned good nurse. Knew more than pretty much all the rest of us put together."

"That's just coming back to you?"

He nodded as they took a seat at The Shack, on a lava rock wall surrounding an almond tree. "She was this amazing bundle of energy we all respected. Short, a little round, gray hair, and she could out-move any one of us."

"That's a good sign, Mateo."

"But triggered by what?"

"Something familiar—like working in a congested medical environment this morning. Or something someone said or did. Or maybe one of the patients you treated reminded you of another patient somewhere else? I mean, I don't know enough about triggers to talk about them, but maybe it's just time. Remember: to everything there is a season…?"

They stopped talking as the server brought drinks—lemonade for Lizzie and something Mateo had called "the usual."

"They know you well enough here to bring you a drink without you telling them what you want? I'm impressed."

"It's a mix of fruit juices—whatever's on hand except banana. It overwhelms everything else, so they don't include it."

"And the bartender just happens to remember that?" she asked.

"He was in the clinic earlier. Suffered a pulled muscle in his neck in a minor injury on the beach breakwaters. I just happened to mention what I liked, and I guess he remembered. Care for a sip?" he asked, holding out his tall hurricane glass to her.

"Should I be jealous that you've made friends here already and the only people I know work at the hospital?"

She took the glass and he felt the soft skin of her hand caress his, maybe linger a second or two longer than it should. Their eyes met, again lingering a bit longer than he'd expected. But he wasn't complaining. Being here with Lizzie like this made him realize there was no place else he wanted to be.

Would she ever consider him something more than a friend? Or just a reminder of what had happened to her father? Those were the questions on his mind right now, and he wanted to ask her, but he wouldn't for fear of her answer.

If she said no, that he could never fit into her life in a different way than he already did, that would devastate him. And if she could never look at him without being reminded of her dad's illness... Well, that would be the last piece of sharp-edged glass dropping to the floor...

"Nothing to be jealous of. I've always made friends easily. When I was a kid I could charm just about anybody to get anything I wanted."

"I never really had time to make friends. Just when we were finally settled in one place, it was time to move on. And now... I haven't changed much, to be honest. It's easier being alone. I can make my life exactly what I want it to be without interference."

"I've never really been alone. Growing up, I was social. Then in college and medical school…let's just say I liked to party. After that, the Army wasn't exactly a place where anyone got to be alone."

"My dad was very 'social,' as you call it. But that never happened to me. He always said I wasn't outgoing enough, and as it turns out he was right. I have my work, though."

"And that's enough?"

Lizzie sighed, then took a sip of her lemonade. "Was today enough for *you*, Mateo?"

"It was different—but I can't really judge it in terms of being enough or not enough. I enjoyed the work, enjoyed getting back to medicine for a little while, even if it wasn't in a surgical capacity."

Lizzie was mellow this evening. No particular reason why, but the feeling had been dragging at her most of the day and now she was ready to give in to it. Let it take her wherever it wanted to.

Mateo had gone with a couple of people he'd met at The Shack to a private yacht party, and even though he'd asked her to come along she hadn't been in the mood. Instead she'd stopped by the hospital, to have a chat with Janis, but had decided not to go in once she'd got there.

She and Janis lived the same life. They worked. In twenty years, when she reached the age Janis was now, she could see herself being the one with the tiki cup collection, serving tropical drinks to colleagues who dropped by her office. Tonight, that had just hit too close to home, and she'd decided she didn't want to see it, so instead she'd gone home, turned on some soft music and was now reading the latest volume of *Topics in Primary Care.*

The first article that caught her attention was about newly approved disease-modifying therapies for multiple sclerosis. It was an expanding field that was resulting in some exciting outcomes. Next she read about Trigeminal Nerve Stimulation for ADHD in children, but wasn't sure that kind of electrical stimulation was anything she wanted to try. Finally, when she got to an article about initiatives in the management of non-motor symptoms in Parkinson disease, her eyes practically crossed.

But she was too tired to go upstairs to bed. So she shut her eyes and allowed herself five minutes to rest there before undertaking the stairs.

It was warm indoors. The fan overhead was spinning, but still moisture dampened the front of Lizzie's floral green Hawaiian wrap-dress—her favorite for lounging. She stretched out on the chaise, revealing long, tanned legs underneath the dress, then arched back, hoping to catch a little more of the breeze from the fan.

Five minutes led to ten, which led to twenty, which led to an hour—and all she got for spending the extra time lounging was such a vivid image of Mateo she didn't want to interrupt it.

Perspiration was beading between her breasts now, and it wasn't all about the heat.

"Looks like you're having a restless night," he said, from outside the open lanai door.

"Medical journals make me restless," she said, tugging her dress back into place and assuming a more conversational position. "I didn't think you'd be back this early."

"Parties are boring when you don't know anybody there." He stepped inside but kept his distance, going no farther than just barely in the door. "The people seemed nice enough, but I decided I'd rather come back here and spend the rest of the evening with you."

He gave her legs an obvious stare, then moved a few more steps into the room.

"I thought maybe we could go swimming. No one's down on the beach and it's a lot cooler outside than it is in here. Care to go?" He walked over to her and held out his hand.

She was sure he was staring at her breasts. Her dress did nothing but make them more prominent than they already were. He'd caught her looking a way no one was meant to see, and there was nothing to do about it but ignore the fact that she was barely dressed and either go with him or go to bed.

And while going to bed had seemed appealing an hour ago, she was over that now, and her mind was forming a vision of her and Mateo on the beach.

Bold move...but Mateo made her feel bold. And needy. And ready to try something that would make sure she didn't end up serving drinks in pink ceramic pineapples to anybody who happened to be passing by.

So she took his hand, stood, and followed as he led her out the lanai door, not missing the fact that he was dressed in long cargos and a white dress shirt, and hadn't changed into swimwear.

"We didn't turn on the floodlights," she said, as they headed toward the beach.

"Do we need the light?" he asked, stopping and turning to face her. "There's a big moon out tonight, and that should be enough."

The world seemed dreamlike as she stood there, anticipating something…anything. But it was clear from his lack of movement that the next move was up to her to make—if there were to be a move. So, without speaking, she started to undo the buttons on his shirt. One at a time, as her fingers trembled.

This was uncharted territory for her…seduction. The slow headiness of it. Before, with Brad, it had been an act of urgency on his part and she'd been merely a participant. But this was her seduction, and Mateo made it obvious that to keep going or to stop was for her to decide.

He was watching as she continued to unbutton his shirt, making her way down his chest, taking care to brush her fingers over his skin on her journey. Lizzie liked it that he watched her. It made her feel wanted in a way no man had ever wanted her. So with each button, and each deliberate brush of her fingers to his skin, she went one step more, leaning in to kiss what her fingers had just caressed, and listening to him moan as she did so.

"You know you're killing me," he whispered, as she tugged his shirt off his broad shoulders and dropped it on the ground.

"You know that's what I intend to do," she said, smiling softly at him as his hands reached down and gently caressed her back, her arms, her shoulders.

Then he pulled her up and hard to his chest, letting their heated bodies press together.

"My turn," he said, reciprocating button for button, caress for caress, kiss for kiss, and then likewise pulling her shirt off her shoulders and dropping it on top of his, leaving them pressed together skin to skin.

He was looking into her face. "Did you know this was the first thing I thought about when I met you? You were standing there, arms folded across your chest like you always do, assessing me. And my assessment of you, before I even thought about you as a doctor, was that you completed paradise. I'd taken the standard tour and none of it had made a difference, but then there was you…"

"And *my* first thought was that you were going to be trouble."

"Were you right?"

"In more ways than I counted on."

She let him lead her farther down the path to the beach, and to the edge of the water. That was where they stopped, and she removed his cargos and let him stand there in his boxers.

Would this be the thing that ended them? One more step into the water with Mateo and there would be no turning back. Perhaps somewhere in the deepest part of her she'd known this was inevitable. But what she didn't know was what would come next.

This was where the everyday Lizzie would have stopped. Yet this was where the Lizzie who wanted to come out of her shell would begin. Which was she?

As it turned out, Mateo answered that question with his first kiss. It was soft and delicate, just barely there. Lizzie responded with a second kiss—it was more demanding than she'd expected. Harder than she'd known she *could* kiss.

And that was her answer as she took that next step into the water. Then the next and the next. Even though she couldn't have Mateo in the truest sense, she wanted him *now*, and for the first time in her life Lizzie gave in to what she wanted.

In the ocean.

In the moonlight.

In Mateo's embrace.

CHAPTER EIGHT

As THE MORNING light peeked in through the blinds Lizzie opened her eyes and stretched, then turned on her side, expecting to see Mateo there. But he was gone.

After their lovemaking in the ocean they'd returned to the house, running bold and naked, not much caring if they were caught, then showered off the sand and spent the rest of the night exploring, then cuddling, and doing all those things that had finally caused her to sleep in his arms, more peaceful and contented than she'd felt in a long, long time.

No promises had been made. In fact, few words had been spoken. There had been no need. Between them, the emotion had been so raw that words hadn't had any place. They'd both known what this was about: a growing need. Still, waking up with him still there would have been nice, and she was disappointed that last night hadn't extended into the morning.

Dressing, then heading downstairs, Lizzie half expected to see Mateo in the kitchen, or maybe on the lanai, but he was in neither place. He'd been there, though. Coffee was made, and there were fresh muffins sitting out, waiting for her.

So she indulged, and by the time she'd finished

Mateo was there, standing by the sliding door to the lanai, smiling. He was holding a couple of bodyboards under his arm.

"Are you sure you got the right size?" she asked.

"The girl in the surf shop measured me—twice."

"I'll bet she did," Lizzie said, as she did a mental check to make sure.

The board had to come to about mid-chest, and that was where her eyes fixed for much longer than they should have. But what a chest to fix on...

Having Lizzie stare at him like that was nice, especially after last night. But in the full light of day it made him nervous. It also made him keenly aware that he couldn't have what was within his reach. No delusions, no forgetting anything. She deserved what he couldn't give her—a fully functioning man, not just the shell of someone who didn't know who he was, let alone how he was going to work out the rest of his life.

"You do realize that 'bodyboard' has another meaning, don't you?" he said. "It's used in radiation therapy and it allows the intestinal tract to drop out of the treatment field?"

"You really are full of yourself, aren't you?" she asked, laughing.

"It was just something I remembered when I was buying these. Too bad what came back to me wasn't more useful."

"Well, if that's what you want to use your bodyboard for it's up to you. I prefer to use mine in the water, paddling over the waves..."

"Capsizing?" he asked.

"You always turn toward the negative, don't you?"

He shrugged. "Maybe capsizing is a memory."

"Or maybe it's your way of trying to convince me to let you start with a kneeling board, or even a full surfboard. Which I won't do because you've had brain surgery. In case *that* has slipped your mind."

"Wish it would," he said, resisting the urge to reach up and feel the tiny area where the doctor had drilled. "And it wasn't exactly brain surgery. It's classified as a minimally invasive procedure."

"Like I don't know that?"

"Like there's a huge difference between having part of your skull removed and having a tiny hole drilled."

He knew the procedure like he knew the back of his hand—not because he'd had to remove that many subdural hematomas, but because he'd read up on the procedure dozens of times after it was over. It was so simple—drilling a burr hole the size of a dime, inserting a catheter and letting a clot-buster drug drip in. Over several days the clot disappeared, and there was no need for a more substantial procedure, like a craniotomy, where the skull was cut open and the clot was manually removed.

That was the procedure he'd done too many times, and how he wished he'd known more about the other procedure when he was in the field. But it was still new, and in field surgery the tried and true was always the go-to. He'd been in the hospital in Germany when the procedure had been used on him.

Mateo blinked hard to rid himself of the image of what they'd done to him. It was a reminder of too many things he'd known and done as a battlefield surgeon. Things he'd never be able to do again.

"Nope. Can't forget that. It's caused me to part my hair differently."

"Well, if it's of any consequence, the post-surgical notes I read said your procedure was textbook-perfect."

"Not a comforting thought, Lizzie," he said. "Someone tapping into your brain."

"Because you don't like thinking of yourself as a patient? Or because brain surgery, no matter how minimal, scares the bejeebies out of you, like it does most people?"

"One from Column A and one from Column B, please. Being that close to what could easily have been deadly isn't what I care to have come into my mind. It always does, though. And I know I shouldn't complain, since I was one of the lucky ones, but that doesn't make it any easier."

"Did it ever occur to you that if you start your real recovery by accepting the fact that you were a patient, which makes you the vulnerable one, it might take you to the next step, where you'll start dealing with the emotional aspects of vulnerability? And after that... who knows? But your recovery, Mateo, could take a long time."

"Well, it seems I've got plenty of that," he quipped.

"And in the meantime?"

He shrugged. "Take it a day at a time, I suppose. I mean, what else can I do? And don't suggest anything to do with the hospital, because you know how I feel about that."

"I'm not sure you're aware, but I do listen to the things you say and watch the things you do, and you're not helpless. In fact, you function very well. Like yesterday at the clinic. No mistakes—not even any hesitation. Take note of yourself, Mateo. The answers are there. And if they don't come, then start with something that will make new memories. People do it every day."

"But I'm not 'people,' Lizzie. I'm me, and I'm impatient to get on with my life."

"Then *do* it, Mateo. Starting today—right now—look at everything as new. You've got a clean slate. That's a beginning."

"You know, there are times when I really hate your optimism."

She laughed. "Me, too. But I'm stuck with it. And as long as you're stuck with me…"

His lips curved into a suggestive smile. "And how long would that be?" he asked.

"Let's start with a month and see how that works."

"A month? With benefits?"

"Everything's negotiable."

Finally, his full-out smile returned. "Is it? Then tell me what you want to take to the bargaining table to open negotiations, and I'll make sure I'm there with whatever you want."

"I'll just bet you will be," she said, swooshing past him and heading toward the beach. Smiling a smile Mateo couldn't see.

She was magnificent, riding the waves. So much beauty and poise skimming over the surface of the water. And in the instant when she disappeared into the wave on her belly, and then emerged standing, balancing herself, she looked like Aphrodite, the goddess of love, or one of the Greek goddesses of the sea.

This was the most uninhibited he'd seen her. It was as though when she became one with the wave she ascended to another place—somewhere ethereal, somewhere that freed her from whatever it was that kept her bound otherwise.

"You ready for your big adventure?" she called as she came walking toward him, her tight black swimsuit emphasizing curves he knew he shouldn't be observing and her wild red hair slicked back, exposing the entirety of her perfect face.

Lizzie dropped her surfboard next to where Mateo was sitting and watching, and picked up one of the bodyboards.

"It's fun in its own right," she said, holding out her empty hand to pull him up.

But he didn't want to move. He'd spent the last hour watching perfection, and that seemed infinitely more interesting than him being out there, flopping around on a bodyboard.

"Truthfully? I'm good, sitting here watching you."

Lizzie dropped down on the huge, multi-colored beach towel with him, grabbed a bottle of water from the small cooler they'd brought, then smiled.

"Because you're a coward?" she taunted.

And her smile was so infectious he caught it in an instant and smiled back.

"Because you're having a good time, and I don't want to interrupt that for what may be some pretty pathetic attempts to keep my belly flat on a board."

Her eyes roamed down to his belly, then back to his face. "Your belly will be fine," she said.

But it wasn't his belly he was concerned about. Other parts were reacting. All the man parts, as he would expect. And most especially his heart.

Was it beating too quickly? Was his breathing coming a little too shallow and fast? It felt that way, and he wasn't even thinking of her in terms of anything that could cause that. It was simply a natural reaction. A primal urge, he wanted to tell himself. Even though he knew it was more than that.

"What about the rest of me?" he asked.

"Do as I say and you won't have any problems. First, for a beginner, it's best to choose a calm spot, where the waves aren't so high. Maybe a couple of feet, but no more than that."

Mateo scooted a little closer to Lizzie, not so much that she would notice, but *he* certainly did.

"Then wax the board. It should already be waxed, but I prefer waxing myself since it's essential to getting a good grip."

"The whole board?" he asked, even though his mind was more on applying sunscreen to her entire body.

"No. Just the top and bottom third, and the edges."

"For a good grip?" he asked.

He was wishing this was more than a simple body-boarding lesson. Not that he would or could take it anywhere. But something about Lizzie caused him to realize how much he'd missed these past years, and how much he'd forgotten. Smooth skin against his. The touch of delicate fingers. Soft kisses turning wild.

He was putting last night on mental replay and wondering how he was going to manage for the next month. Thinking like this wasn't doing him any good, but he was sure enjoying it. Especially since the object of his attraction—and maybe more—was Lizzie.

He'd never cared much for red hair before; he did remember that. But *her* red hair ignited him. And getting involved with another doctor... That had definitely been off his list, since he knew the ins and outs of that intimately. But he was no longer a doctor, and even if he were it wouldn't matter. Not with Lizzie sitting beside him and their thighs brushing together.

"For staying afloat. Oh, you didn't get yourself a rash guard. Some people like them, because they reduce chafing from the board itself, but maybe that won't bother you."

It wouldn't. Especially if she treated any rash he might get.

"Personally, I like the contact with the board. It gives me a better feel for what I'm doing."

"And the swim fins? The girl at the beach shop said I had to have them."

"Definitely, yes. They'll help you paddle out farther, so you can catch better waves. Oh, and the leash…it attaches to your wrist."

"Seems like an awful lot of trouble just to catch a wave."

"It is—but there's no sensation like it in the world, no matter if you're vertical or horizontal. So, did she sell you a helmet? Black with red stripes?"

"She did."

"And…?"

"And I'll wear it, Lizzie. OK? I'll wear the damned helmet."

He might have argued more with her, but she was so into the moment and he didn't want to break that. She looked beautiful—her eyes sparkling, a slight blush to her cheeks. This was Lizzie in her element, and he was enjoying being there with her even if he didn't so much as get the bottoms of his feet wet.

"Excellent. So, gear up and let's do it. Wade out until

you're knee-deep, then put your belly to the board and keep your hips in contact with the tail of the board."

"And my hands?"

He knew where he wanted to put them, but what *he* wanted and what *she* wanted were two different things. Still, he could almost feel her hands skimming down the side of his body, like they had done the night before…

"Top corners of the board. Make sure you keep your fins under water, then paddle out—one-handed or two, doesn't make a difference—until you see the wave you want to catch. For starters, we're going to catch some smaller ones."

This was getting serious. He needed to get his mind back on what he was about to do, otherwise his amateur performance would turn into a clown show because he'd missed one or two vital steps. Of course, mouth-to-mouth from Lizzie sounded pretty good, if that was what it came down to. Especially now that he knew the secrets of her mouth…

"When you do see a wave, point your board toward the beach and start to kick and paddle. The wave will do the rest."

"Sounds simple enough," he said, looking down the beach at all kinds of people surfing and bodyboarding.

He'd been an adventurer. He remembered that. Remembered scaling rock walls, paragliding, even some dangerous sledding in there. Straight downhill, hoping to avoid the trees and the other sledders. But this? It scared him. Not because of the risk, but because he was, like she'd told him, vulnerable. He didn't know if his adventurous side would come back or if he'd turn into one of those people he could see from where he was, who paddled out and simply sat there on the board, too afraid to move.

"You don't have to do this," Lizzie said.

"I do," he replied, taking off his blue floral print shirt. "In more ways than you know."

To prove it to himself and—more—to prove it to her. That was important…showing Lizzie that side of him—the side that wasn't a patient, that wasn't vulnerable, that wasn't so damned disagreeable. It mattered more than he'd thought it could.

Finally, after another mental bout with himself, he slipped the fins on his feet, grabbed his board, and walked to the water's edge. Lizzie was right there next to him, and he found some strength in having her there. But he hadn't always been this way. That much he remembered.

"It's a simple thing," he said. "I've done much more dangerous things than this. Yet I'm not sure I'm ready to take the next step."

"It's not easy, facing your fears," she said, giving his arm a reassuring squeeze, followed by a tender kiss to his cheek. "Especially when you might not even know what they are until they pop up out of nowhere."

"What scares you?" he asked, looking out over the wide expanse of water.

"Lots of things. Making a medical mistake with one of my patients. That may be my biggest fear, because people rely on me, and if I do something to let them down, or even worse…" She shut her eyes briefly, then shook her head. "Horseback riding. Got thrown when I was a little girl and broke some bones in my back. It wasn't a huge trauma, but to this day I've never been back on a horse. Oh, and spiders. You haven't heard a good scream until you've heard me scream when I find a spider on me—or even near me. And some of the spiders here on Oahu are enormous. Like the cane spider."

She gestured, indicating something larger than a dinner plate, which was an obvious exaggeration, and just saying the word caused her to shiver.

It was a cute display, and something he hadn't expected from her. His version of Lizzie taking on the world had just knocked itself down a peg and he liked seeing that side of her. It made him realize that she had her own vulnerabilities, and that he wouldn't be standing out there alone on that sandbar he could see in the distance, holding on to his own bag of insecurities.

Mateo chuckled. "Well, I'll protect you from spiders if you protect me from myself."

"Do you *need* to be protected from yourself?" she asked.

He took a step into the water, then paused. "If I knew the answer to that I'd tell you."

Then he gathered up every bit of courage inside him and marched out until he was submerged to mid-chest. Lizzie followed him and immediately mounted her board, then waited for Mateo to do the same.

"This isn't too bad," he said, once he was belly-down on the board.

"Paddle around for a few minutes. Get used to the feel of it. Sometimes it's nice to just float for a while and let your mind wander."

"Do you do that?"

"Not so much now," she said, paddling over until her board was next to his. "I did when my dad was alive. He was…difficult. Sometimes it felt like I was failing him even though the doctor in me knew what was happening to him."

She paused for a moment, then continued.

"For me, the ocean has curative powers. When I was a little girl, traveling around with my dad, there were several times we lived near a beach. I think that's where I found my balance."

"So Hawaii was a logical place to come?"

"Actually, I lived here before, when I was a teenager. Dad was getting older, and thinking about retirement in a few years, so he transferred to one of the military hospitals here. It was the first time I ever had much of him in my life—which is one of the reasons I came back when he was diagnosed. Some of my best memories were here, and I remembered how much he'd loved it here as well."

"I'm from a little village in Mexico. The people there were poor. My mother was poor, too, and there wasn't enough work for her. Yet she got a sponsor in California, from one of the humanitarian groups, so we came to the States legally and she achieved her dream—which was to see me succeed."

"And now?" Lizzie asked.

"When I'm ready to travel I'm going back. My mother has the right to know what's happened, since she was a large part of my motivation. It's not going to be easy to tell her, though.

Lizzie laid her hand on his arm and squeezed. "So often the right things aren't. But she'll be glad to know that you're safe, and basically in good shape."

"Maybe you'd like to come with me?"

"I might… Mexico is one place I've never been."

The almost-promise made his heart skip a beat. But

taking Lizzie home to meet his mother would be no small deal. The people in the village would throw parties, and sing and dance halfway through the night. There would be piles of food, amazing drinks—and all because Margarita's boy was bringing a woman home. Lizzie would love it, he thought.

"If you go with me, prepare yourself for the biggest party you've ever been to—all in your honor."

"*My* honor?"

"They're a friendly bunch of people. What can I say?"

He wasn't about to tell her that taking her to meet his mother would be as good as a wedding announcement. They weren't ready for that yet. There were still issues to be resolved.

"So, you want to go catch a wave with me now?"

He took in a deep breath. "The waves really are calming, aren't they?"

"And they're calling my name. Mind if I…?"

"Do your thing, Lizzie. I'll be right behind you." Enjoying a view he was pretty sure he wanted to enjoy for the rest of his life.

In preparation to catch a good wave she paddled out a little farther, and found the perfect one that carried her almost all the way back to the shore. It seemed so natural for her. And for him? Well…he paddled out, like she did, found his wave, aimed his board, and rode the wave as best he could, weaving and bobbing in and out of the water until he almost hit shore.

"Wasn't as graceful as you," he said, spitting out a mouthful of saltwater as he stood and grabbed his board. "But that was fun. Thank you."

Lizzie smiled at him. "All part of the service offered to my houseguests. Want to go again?"

"How about I sit here and watch *you* go again?"

"Whatever you want," she said, turning and walking back into the water.

Mateo shut his eyes as the headache overtook him again. It had come and gone for days now, but this one was excruciating, pounding harder and harder, until suddenly everything around him was spinning. The sky, the sand, the water. Himself.

He turned to look for Lizzie, who was just emerging from the water, and waved her over.

"Migraine," he said as she approached.

The brightness of the sun was bothering him. And a wave of nausea pounded him so hard he fell backwards into the sand.

"Not good, Lizzie," he managed to gasp as she dropped to her knees next to him. "Not good at all."

"Has this happened before?" she asked as she felt for his pulse.

"Yes, but not as bad."

"And you didn't bother mentioning it?"

"It's a headache. Everybody gets them."

She pulled back his eyelids and studied his eyes for a moment, wishing she had her medical bag. His pupillary response was sluggish, and the size from right to left varied, but not by much. It was clear something was wrong, but she couldn't risk leaving him here like this to go get her medical bag.

He grasped her hand. "I think I might be in trouble here," he said, holding on tight.

"I need to get you to the hospital so we can get a scan to see what's going on."

"For a freaking migraine?" he snapped, then clearly instantly regretted his tone of voice. "Just let me stay here and I'll be better in a few minutes."

"Unless it's not a simple migraine. I mean, I don't think it's a stroke, nor is some kind of neuro inflammation at the top of my list, but it could be another clot. Most definitely you've got some changes in brain activity that underlie the chronic pain you've been having, and my best guess—which is all I have at the moment— is that it's connected to your earlier brain trauma. So I can leave you here in the sand and hope it doesn't advance to another level, like a stroke, or I can get you to the hospital to see what's really going on. Your choice, Mateo."

"You know…that's the thing I most dislike about doctors. They take it to the limit."

"How do you mean?"

"It's a migraine. I've diagnosed them and treated them. But you're thinking way beyond that, aren't you?"

"That's why they pay me the big bucks. I'm very good at thinking way beyond what's normal or necessary."

He laughed, then moaned and grabbed his head. "Look, Lizzie. I appreciate the concern, but it's a stinking headache. That's all."

"I hope you're right about that, but in case you're not are you sure you want me to walk away and leave you with an unconfirmed diagnosis?"

She moved closer to him, took his hand, and bent down to kiss him on the lips.

Just before the kiss, she whispered, "I really don't want to lose you, Mateo, and it's not because I'm a doctor who hates losing patients. It's because I'm a woman who doesn't want to lose the man she's falling in love with."

She still needed to figure out how that would play out, as none of her feelings of trepidation had changed. But that was a discussion for another day. Right now, all she wanted was to get Mateo better.

"And if you make the wrong decision and I walk away…it would break my heart. I don't want that happening and I don't deserve it."

That much was true.

That she loved him was also true.

"Get me to the hospital and give me the scan," he said, trying to open his eyes, but failing, as if the sun nauseated him. "Do whatever you think needs to be done."

Blowing out a sigh of relief, Lizzie made the call, then sat there holding his hand while they waited.

One thing was sure. A life with Mateo wouldn't always be smooth. But it would always be good. And she hoped they could get to that point. Because after Mateo there wouldn't be anybody else. For all his stubborn ways, he was the only one she wanted.

When the time was right, she'd tell him. But there were issues to work out before any kind of commitment could be made, and those issues scared her. Neither of them came to this relationship unscathed. Two wounded people… Could that work?

"Are you going to hold my hand when they send me through that long tube of extreme claustrophobia?" he asked.

They were in the changing room and he was expected to put on one of those hideous gowns.

"Seriously? You're claustrophobic?"

"Maybe a little."

She tied him modestly into the green and blue gown he hated so much, then gave him a blanket to spread over his lap as they wheeled him down the hall—*in a wheelchair*—for his tests.

"I always tell my patients the best thing for that is a shot of vodka—*after* the procedure."

"Hate the stuff," he said, reaching out to take Lizzie's hand once they were in the waiting room.

"Sex works, too," she whispered. "Depending on the diagnosis."

"*Now* we're getting somewhere."

Lizzie was worried and trying to hide it. He could see her struggle. She wasn't very good at hiding her expressions from him.

"It's going to be a migraine, pure and simple. You do know that, don't you?"

"No, I don't." Lizzie sat next to Mateo, holding his hand as the technicians prepared him for a CT scan. "Look, this isn't going to take long, then if nothing shows we can go home and you can spend the rest of the day sleeping. Now, I'm going to run down to Janis's office for a minute and have a quick chat with her, if you don't mind?"

"Go," he whispered, as if the sound of his own voice hurt him.

"Two minutes—tops," she said, bending over the hard, flat CT table to give him a kiss. "I'll be right back."

She hated leaving him there, but there was nothing else she could do. She needed distance, and a couple of minutes to sort out her feelings. And some reassurance.

"You've got it bad, don't you?" said Janis, joining Lizzie, who was leaning on the wall outside the CT room.

"Depends on your definition of 'bad,'" Lizzie said. "Do I have feelings for him? Yes. What kind of feelings? Not the kind I should be having. Oh, and he didn't want to have this CT," she said.

"Did it occur to you that the man is so scared he doesn't know what he's doing? I mean, to look at him you'd never guess that, but Mateo is…*different*. He's a healer who can no longer heal. He has no home, no place to go, no plans for his future. If I were in his shoes, I'd be scared, too."

"I think he wanted to die."

"He wants to live, Lizzie. He just doesn't know how. If he had a death wish he wouldn't have showed up on your doorstep. To Mateo, you offer hope. And loving him the way I'm pretty sure you do is an added bonus he didn't count on. So give the guy some slack. Back off when he needs it, and stay close when that's what he wants."

Janis's words rang in her head as she made her way back to Mateo. It wasn't just Mateo who was resistant, though. Or scared.

"So, you ready to get this done?" she asked, as the tech wheeled him into the room and helped him take his position on the CT bed. "Ten minutes and it'll all be over."

"Or starting again," he said.

Lizzie swallowed hard. "If that's how it turns out we'll work through it. I'm not going anywhere, Mateo. So if you start over this time you start with someone in your corner."

She bent down to kiss him, but he caught her off-guard and pulled her almost on top of him, gave her the kiss of a lifetime.

"That was…nice," she said, pulling back from him. "But maybe not appropriate here."

He grinned up at her. "That's just me being true to character."

"Has anyone ever told you you're incorrigible?"

"Has anyone ever *not* told me I'm incorrigible?"

"Dr. Peterson?" blared a voice from the microphone in the next room. "We need to get on with this test. Dr. Sanchez isn't our only patient."

"But way to go," Janis added through the same microphone.

"Now look what you've done," Lizzie said to Mateo as she left the room, fanning herself.

Rather than join her colleagues in the control room, she went to her office to wait, dropped down on the sofa, and shut her eyes until Janis came to talk to her.

"It's a small hemorrhage. Same place as before."

"Because we went bodyboarding?" Lizzie asked, as tears tickled the backs of her eyes.

"I'd say the first injury simply caused a weak spot. I think this would have happened no matter what he was doing."

"I wasn't cautious enough—just like I wasn't cautious enough with my dad." Finally the tears overflowed, and she batted at them with the back of her hand. "Have you admitted him?"

"We're in the process. Then we're going to fix him—hopefully for good this time."

"With a drip?"

"Clot-busters save lives. And I think there's a lot of life in Mateo that needs saving. And guiding."

"Not my responsibility," Lizzie said.

"When you love somebody the way you do Mateo, *everything* about him is your responsibility. It changes your world, Lizzie. Nothing's the same anymore. But because Mateo is a sick man, you're the one who must step up and assume more than responsibility. You need to step up and accept his love—because he does love you."

"We have a long way to go before either of us can do anything. But I suppose now's as good a time as any to get started."

"*After* the procedure, please. This is Mateo I've got to deal with, and you know how he can be."

She did—and that was a large part of why she loved him. To her, Mateo was nearly perfect. Sure, there were some flaws. But they were such a small part of him, while his kindness and compassion embraced most of him.

Maybe Janis didn't see that, but *she* did, and that was all that really mattered.

Janis took off her surgical mask and threw it in the trash on her way out to see Lizzie. "It's done. He's sleeping peacefully. I need a tropical drink. Care to join me on my lanai?"

"Could I have a raincheck?" Lizzie asked. "I think I'd like to go sit in his room for a while."

"He's mumbling nonsense," Janis warned her. "Something about letting it happen. I'm assuming that means you?"

"I hope it does," she said, then headed off to Mateo.

"Janis says everything went well," she said, sitting down next to his bed. "You've got a catheter in your head, which will stay there several days, but the clot was small and likely just a residual from your initial injury."

He opened his eyes to look at her, managed a lazy smile, then went back to sleep. But he held on to her hand for dear life, and she vowed to stay right there with him until the anesthesia wore off and they were bringing him that green slime they commonly referred to as gelatin.

She recalled his first day there, when he'd asked her to please put on the first page of his chart that he loathed and detested green gelatin—or any gelatin, for that matter. And cottage cheese.

She'd never quite gotten around to doing that.

Lizzie laughed, even though nothing in her felt like laughing.

"Toward the end, Mateo," she said, even though he wasn't awake, "my dad only ate things with bright colors. I suppose he thought the color had something to do with the taste. But when they brought him his tray, if it didn't have something red or yellow or purple on it he wouldn't eat it."

She looked up, watched his heart monitor for a minute, and noticed how perfect his rhythm was. He was a strong man. This would only be a minor setback for him.

"Oh, you're back in your old room. Thought you'd appreciate being here…for old times' sake." She gave his hand a squeeze. "And your old hospital gowns are ready for you, too."

"Do you ever stop talking?" he asked, even though he didn't open his eyes.

"Does it bother you?" she asked, glad to hear his voice sounding so clear.

"No. It lets me know I'm alive and have something to look forward to."

"What?" she asked breathlessly, thinking of all the things he might say. Hoping *she* topped his list.

"Green gelatin."

"Funny thing is, I didn't even know it was happening. It kind of crept up on me, a little at a time."

She was sitting on the lanai with Janis, sipping something fruity from an original brown tiki cup. Janis was sipping something fruity from her favorite pink pineapple. It was late into evening now, and Mateo was still sleeping like a baby while she was trying to figure out the next step.

"I gave his case back to Randy," Janis informed her. "He's not as tolerant as you, so if you know what's good for your boyfriend you'll warn him to shape up or he'll be kicked out of here one more time."

Her boyfriend. Lizzie liked the sound of that.

What would come of it? She didn't know.

But right now that didn't matter.

She had a brick wall to scale before she could do anything.

His head hurt like a son of a gun, and to make matters worse there were five containers of green slime on his bedside table. Just looking at them jiggling at him made him feel nauseated. So did the hospital gown and the no-slide booties someone had slipped on his feet.

"This isn't the way life is meant to be lived," he said to Lizzie as she entered his room.

"They told me you were awake and in your usual good humor." She gave him a quick kiss, then sat down on the edge of the bed. "Has Janis been in to see you yet?"

"Nobody's been in to see me except the green gelatin fairy and you."

"Well, the news is good. The clot was small. It probably resulted from a weak suture put in on the first surgery. And your recovery can be done at my house, if that's what you want."

"What I want is for you to listen to me, and then tell me if I'm right or wrong."

"About what?"

"Your feelings for me. You're in love with me—or I hope you're in love with me—but it scares you because of what happened to your father. You're not sure you can get involved with someone with memory loss again."

"That's very perceptive," she said.

"But is it true, Lizzie?"

"Some of it is. You aren't the same as he was, but sometimes when I see that lost look in your eyes…"

"Have you seen it lately?"

She paused for a minute to think about it. "Not really."

"Your dad's illness wasn't your fault, Lizzie."

He reached for her hand, then pulled her closer to him until they were almost lying side by side.

"I know that. But…"

She bit down on her lip, willing herself not to cry.

"It was a really hectic day. He wanted to go for a walk and I didn't have time. I didn't let his caregivers do it because it was about the only way Dad and I were connecting, and I didn't want to be cheated of that. I promised him we'd go later…like he understood what I was saying. About an hour later I got the call to say that Dad had wandered off. It wasn't the first time, but he always headed toward the ocean, and I was so afraid… Well, we searched the shore for hours and there was no sign of him. The search continued for five days. *Five days*, Mateo. He was out there lost and alone for five days. And then the rescuers found him. He'd gone to Kapu Falls, which was one of his favorite places. He'd actually planted a flower garden there."

"Nobody went there to look?"

"Actually, they did. But Dad had crawled into some underbrush and apparently gone to sleep. At least that was what the coroner said. And he stayed in that same spot for five days. Maybe because that's where he wanted to die, or maybe he was simply waiting for me to come take him home. We'll never know."

She clenched her fists and shut her eyes.

"That's the nightmare I live with every day. And there are so many what-ifs. What if I hadn't gone to work? What if we'd taken the walk he wanted to take? What if the caregiver hadn't turned her back? What if I had one more lock put on all the doors?"

"It's impossible to predict outcomes all the time, Lizzie. Sometimes you're right, but as often as not you're wrong."

"Exactly, Mateo. You can't always predict outcomes."

"Meaning?"

"Meaning that at some point you've got to get on with your life or it will bury you. I was being buried. Not sure what I wanted to do. Yet the answer was always there. I was the one who had to open my eyes and see it, though."

"And the answer?"

"You, me…a beachside clinic. You can't operate anymore, and that may be a reality for the rest of your life. I think you've probably figured out that I've lost the heart for working in a hospital. I want a simpler life, and life's too short not to go after what you want."

"You said you and me in that clinic?"

"The reality is, for now, you'll have to be supervised. I can't predict the future, and I'm not even sure I would if I could. But you're a good doctor and you deserve to be back in medicine. Maybe it's not the way you want, but it's what you can have. And perhaps that's all we really need…what we can have. I think we could build a life around that, if you want to."

"Me as patient, you as caregiver?"

"No. That's not at all what I want."

"Then, as your equal. Someone you don't have to watch day and night. Or at work."

"Why are you twisting this, Mateo? I thought…" She shook her head. "Have I been wrong about this all long?"

"You took in a homeless guy, Lizzie. What's there to twist in that?"

"I thought I took in someone who wanted more from life. Was I wrong?"

She was battling gallantly against the tears that wanted to fall. To finally admit her feelings, then have them slapped back in her face…she couldn't even begin to describe the pain.

"No, you weren't wrong. But I've given it a lot of thought, and…" He paused, drew in a deep breath, then let it out again, agonizingly slow. "And I don't see how it could work with us. I don't want to be taken care of, like you took care of your dad, and I'm sure that's not what you want either. But I'm afraid it's inevitable. Also, I don't want to be watched for the rest of my life, with you wondering if it's the real me when I make a little slip-up. It's got nothing to do with the way I feel for you and everything to do with breathing room."

"I haven't been giving you *breathing room*?"

"You have. As much as I can handle right now. But in the future…"

"You don't have to say it, Mateo. What I saw as the beginning of something that might last was merely a port in the storm for you. But I'm glad I put myself out there for you—because it proved to me that I can do it. It was my choice, and it had nothing to do with my dad." She got up from the bed. "I'll have your things brought to the hospital, Mateo."

"This isn't what I want, Lizzie. I want to figure out how we can be together—not apart."

"What you want, Mateo, is a life that doesn't come with the complications we both have. That's what I wanted at first as well. But we don't always get what we want, do we? Oh, and as for falling in love—it shouldn't be about figuring out how to do it. It should be about how you can't live without the other person. How loving the other person makes you a better person. I'm sorry it didn't work that way for you, because it did for me."

He started to get out of bed, but he was connected to too many wires and tubes, and the instant he tried to stand every single one of the alarms went off.

"I do love you," he said as she headed for the door. "It's just that—"

"And that's where it ends, Mateo. After you tell someone you love them there should be no more words.

No qualifiers. But you have a qualifier, and that says it all. I'm sorry this didn't work, because I love you, too."

With that, she was gone.

And he was stuck in a lousy hospital bed, with a tray full of green gelatin which he wanted to throw at the wall.

But he didn't. That was the Mateo who had existed *before* Lizzie. The one who existed after her merely shoved the bedside tray away, slunk down in bed, and pulled the sheets up to his neck.

CHAPTER NINE

Eight weeks later

MORNINGS WERE NOT her friend. Especially now, when she spent every one of them being sick and looking puffy. It was part of the process, her doctor had told her, but that meant nothing when she was sprawled on the bathroom floor, glad for the cool feel of the tile underneath her.

"Come on, Lizzie!" Janis yelled through the door. "It's perfectly natural. If you spend your entire pregnancy this way, by the time the baby gets here you're going to be a basket case."

"Babies!" she yelled back. "Not baby. When he got me, he got me good."

Janis opened the door a crack and peeked in. "You're not even dressed."

"Not getting dressed today."

"So what do I tell your patients?"

"That pregnancy and doctoring don't mix."

Janis pushed the door the rest of the way open and went in. She sat down next to Lizzie, who still wasn't budging.

"Someone should have told me," she moaned.

"Ever hear about using protection?"

"We did. It didn't work—*obviously*." Lizzie rolled over on her back but still didn't get up. "See how big I am and I'm only two months in. Do you really think I'm in any shape to see patients? I mean, I'm wearing a *muumuu*, Janis. A freaking muumuu."

"Get used to it. The bigger you get, the more you'll come to appreciate your muumuu. Oh, and if you want another, I hear there's a mighty handsome man working in a surf shop a couple blocks over from the hospital. In case you didn't know, he stayed here, Lizzie. He's working hard with a PTSD counselor, as well as sticking to Randy's cognitive behavior program. I'll bet he'd like to see you."

"He knows where I live." Lizzie wrestled herself to a sitting position and leaned against the wall.

"Doesn't he have a right to know about the babies?" Janis asked.

"He does—and he will. But he's so deep into his treatment programs now I wonder if I should wait, rather than throw him another curve ball he has to deal with."

"Have your feelings for him changed?" Janis asked her.

Lizzie patted her belly. "No. In fact, they're growing deeper every day."

"And you expect to work things out sprawled here on the floor in a muumuu?"

"There's a lot to work out," Lizzie said, finally ready to get up.

"Do you know who you sound like?" Janis asked, pushing herself up and heading toward the door.

"No. Who?"

"Mateo. Do you remember when he was full of excuses, not doing anything to help himself, and everybody was getting frustrated with him?"

Lizzie thought about it as she pushed herself off the floor. "I didn't accept his excuses, did I?"

Janis gave her a knowing wink, then left.

And Lizzie put on some regular clothes and decided a walk was in order.

Funny how that walk took her right by a surf shop, where the clerk inside was keeping a whole line of people entertained with stories of his days as a surfer. Like he'd ever even *been* on a real surfboard.

It was such a funny sight, Lizzie laughed…probably for the first time in weeks. This was the father of her babies—the man she loved despite his faulty memories.

Lizzie waved at Mateo when he finally spotted her in the crowd, then waited until he made his way through the crowd to smile at him.

"Looks like you've found your calling," she said, fighting back a laugh. "Talking about your exploits from your days as a surfer?"

"Give the people what they want," he said, taking her by the arm and leading her out of the crowd. "I've wanted to see you. To talk to you about that day. I was overwhelmed, Lizzie. I hope you realize that?"

"You could have come around to apologize," she said, as they sat down on a bench under a banyan tree.

"I did. Every day. Who do you think has been tending your dad's flower garden?"

"I never saw you. And as for the garden… I just…" She shrugged. "I didn't give it any thought."

"Which is why it was getting weedy, and droopy from a lack of watering. I know I hurt you, Lizzie. And

I'm sorry for that. But for a while I couldn't live with myself, let alone draw somebody else into my mess. I needed time…and space."

"And?"

"And I've been doing everything I can so that when I finally came back to you, hat in hand if that's how I had to do it, you'd see the differences in me. I wasn't good enough for you then. Maybe not even now. But I'm working on it. Trying new things where old things I've forgotten used to be."

"Like working in a surf shop?"

"If that's what it takes. I know there's a lot I won't get back, and I'm trying hard to come to terms with that. Some days are better than others. Occasionally I get so damned frustrated that all I want to do is go someplace and turn myself into somebody else. Like my surfer persona."

"But you stayed?"

"Because I have to. Because I fell in love with the most wonderful, stubborn, and opinionated woman I've ever known, and to walk away from that would be the worst thing I could ever do in my life. I'm trying hard to fix myself for *me*, Lizzie. But it's also for you. For a future where you won't have to worry about me every minute of every day. For the time when I leave the house and you won't have to pace the lanai and wonder what's happening to me. You deserve that, Lizzie. We both do. But I'm the one who has to fix that. And I'm trying." He brushed her cheek with the back of his hand. "I stayed because I want to prove myself to you. Prove that I'm everything you need and want."

"You have been, Mateo. Every day since I met you. I mean, it hasn't been easy, and I've some adjusting to do myself, but living all these weeks without you…it's been miserable. I've been miserable. And that's not how I want to be. Especially now, because I need an *equal*, Mateo. I mean, we can't predict the future, but we can live for what we have today, and that's what I need. I thought so at first, anyway. But then my need changed into something I wanted more than anything I'd ever wanted in my life, and I didn't see you getting involved in that. In fact, you pushed me away."

"Because I'm not sure yet who I am, and I still get frustrated when I can't pull up a memory. I'm working hard at dealing with myself, but that still adds up to a lifetime of misery for you, and I don't want that."

"Not misery, Mateo. Not if you love someone enough. The way I love you. What I finally realized was that your belligerence is only your way of trying to hang on to the pieces of you that you remember. You're fighting back."

"And I'm scared, Lizzie. Scared to death. But having you there made things better. And my memory of that night in Afghanistan…" He pointed to his head, "I do remember it now. Every bloody detail. How my friends tried to rescue me and died. How I lost my best friend. How I laid there for two days before anybody found me. It's not a pretty thing to recall, but it's my memory, which means it's part of me. And I've found other parts as well. Some good, some not so good. For better or worse, all of it me, though. And as these bits and pieces are returning, they give me something to hold on to. You give me more, though, and I want to earn my way back into your life. Unless I blew it too badly to fix."

"You didn't blow anything, Mateo. I think we were

always just two people fighting to get through to each other. Sometimes succeeding, sometimes not." She took hold of his hand and laid it on her belly. "And sometimes going farther than any expectation either of us had."

"Seriously?" he asked. "You're…?"

"Eight weeks along. Healthy and grumpy. Having some battles with my hormones."

"Do you know if it's a boy or a girl?"

"Could be one of each…"

"I did all that?" he said, his pride obvious.

"It took two of us, Mateo. I did have a part in this."

He laughed out loud. "And here I was thinking that being alone, while it isn't good, isn't as bad as I thought it was. I'm assuming you want me involved?"

"I'm wearing muumuus, Mateo. And eating everything in the house. Does that sound like a person who doesn't want her baby daddy involved? Someone has to save me from myself—especially since for breakfast this morning I ate a whole mango pie."

"The whole thing?"

She nodded. "Would have eaten another one if I'd had it."

"Sounds to me like you're going to need that muumuu."

"Not as much as I need you. Will you come home, Mateo? The babies and I need you there. And, more than that, I want you there."

In answer, he pulled her into his arms and kissed her, while across the street Janis sat at an outside café with Randy, watching the whole thing.

"Looks to me like we're about to lose one of our doctors," she said. "I think our Lizzie is about to become otherwise occupied."

EPILOGUE

As WEDDINGS WENT, Lizzie and Mateo's was a small, private affair. Janis stood up for Lizzie and Randy stood for Mateo. They were in the flower garden, surrounded by all the beautiful flowers her dad had planted. Definitely paradise in so many ways.

For the ceremony Lizzie held Robert, named for her dad, while Mateo held Margarita, named for his mother. The twins were six months old now, just getting to the age where they had their own opinions—which were sometimes a bit vocal.

"I think Robert needs changing," Lizzie said.

"And Margarita seems like she's hungry," her soon-to-be husband responded. "Maybe we should take care of that before the ceremony begins, so we're not interrupted part-way through."

"Especially since we've waited so long for this."

She looked back at the small crowd gathering, and at Janis passing out tiki cups full of whatever her concoction of the day was. No one was left without a tiki.

"I think Janis has everything under control for a few minutes."

Lizzie and Mateo dashed into the house to take care of the twins, who'd become the center of so many lives since, for now, they went to work every day with Mateo. Not to the surf shop, but to the clinic they'd bought. He and Lizzie worked there full-time, loving the life, loving the work.

The clinic was busier than ever, with more and more patients coming through the door every day. The addition of a nursery was a blessing, as Mateo refused to be separated from his family, and now Dr. Lizzie Peterson-soon-to-be-Sanchez was a part of that.

Lizzie still had a way to go in not taking on the blame for her dad's death, but Mateo was always there to help her through the rough spots. And she was always there when his memory lapses gave way to frustration.

"He's going to be here today, you know," Matco said. "Since we're marrying in his garden."

"Sometimes it's like I feel him here, looking after his flowers. He would be happy knowing you're the one doing that now."

She brushed a tear from her eyes and looked over at Mateo, who had a spit-up towel slung over his shoulder and was holding a baby who was happily indulging in a bottle.

"Guess I should feed Robert, too," she said, tossing another spit-up towel over her own shoulder and giving him his own bottle.

And that was how they walked down the path to the trellis where they would take their wedding vows. A family of four. Everything Lizzie had never known she wanted. Everything she would ever need.

One husband, two children, and paradise.

The perfect life.

* * * * *

HEALED BY THEIR UNEXPECTED FAMILY

KARIN BAINE

MILLS & BOON

For Georgia and Jordan xx

CHAPTER ONE

'So, you're the woman I'm about to impregnate? Nice to see you again.'

'Hello, Mr Garrett.' Kayla O'Connell shook hands with the man her brother, Liam, and his husband, Tom, had set her up with for this baby-making exercise.

So much for this remaining nothing more than a business transaction when one firm handshake, one touch from him was enough to make her weak at the knees. She would rather not have him involved in this at all. It would have been easier to do it with a stranger. Meeting Jamie at her brother's wedding had been sufficient to rattle her.

'Oh, Kayla, I would've thought we were on first-name terms by now. Jamie's fine.'

Even though his slow, sexy smile had her transfixed, that smooth charm he possessed always made her nervous. It reminded her of her parents and the façade they'd used to put on for the rest of the world to hide the multitude of sins committed behind closed doors. He was easy on the eye, but he knew it, and took way too much enjoyment in the fact she blushed every time he came near her.

However, since he was Tom's big brother there was no way of avoiding him. 'Thanks for coming, Jamie.'

'You know I'd do anything you asked. All you have to do is give me the word.' He held her gaze a second longer than necessary, sending shivers all over her body at the underlying suggestion. What scared her more than Jamie's blatant flirting with her was her reaction to it. But rather than admonishing him for his suggestive comments, she had to use all her strength not to give into the temptation he embodied.

'We're not doing this for me. It's for our brothers and that's who we should be focusing on.' Kayla couldn't take her eyes off him as he sat down in the chair opposite, loosened his navy and silver striped tie and undid the top button on his shirt, revealing that small patch of skin at his throat. The picture in her mind took on a whole new explicit nature, transporting the scene into a bedroom rather than a busy London café.

Clearly, her body had gone into panic mode about this surrogacy idea if she was fantasising about the father-to-be. Who, in ordinary circumstances, she would've run a mile from. Lately, she'd gone for safe guys, who never really lit her fire but she knew would never hurt her. Self-preservation after abusive parents and an ex-boyfriend who'd thought he could control her. Thank goodness she'd had her brother's support in helping her realise Paul had gradually been taking over, manipulating her into doing what he wanted and leaving her scared to question him.

It had been a blow to realise she'd reverted back to that submissive behaviour she'd employed to keep her parents happy rather than face the consequences. Trust wasn't something she gave easily, and Paul had taken what was left from her.

It was no wonder her relationships since hadn't lasted, because she couldn't bring herself to fully invest in them in case history repeated itself. She'd been content being single and not having to worry about anyone except herself. Kayla would go as far as to say she'd never get into another relationship again and certainly had no inclination towards starting a family of her own. That was why being around Jamie was so difficult. She might be attracted to him, but she also knew he was the type of man capable of breaking hearts. His brother had told her as much.

'Of course, but that doesn't mean we can't enjoy each other's company too, does it?' He reached across the table to take her hand and stroked his thumb across her fingers. She could only watch, dumbstruck, knowing she couldn't give an answer without incriminating herself.

A shuffling by the table alerted her to someone else bewitched by her companion. The young girl carrying over his coffee hovered long after she'd set the cup down, openly staring at him.

'Thank you.' He turned on a full-watt grin that sent the waitress scurrying away again with a giggle. Jamie had that cheeky glint in his brown eyes Kayla was sure made most women swoon, although she knew he wasn't the settling-down type either. That was one of the reasons he'd apparently agreed to do this. Kayla directed her thoughts back to the surrogacy, since that was the reason they were actually here.

'So, I know you're a respected GP in your practice, a partner. Tom told me you raised him after your parents both died, and you've said yourself you don't want anything to do with this baby when it arrives.' It wasn't important how hot his skin felt against hers or that he'd ignored every other woman at the wedding, trying to capture her attention. For these purposes, all she needed to know was that he had brains as well as good looks and that he wouldn't be hanging around driving her to distraction once his part of the deal was over.

'That's not as brutal as it seems on the surface. I'm happy to help the newly-weds start a family but I'm not interested in being a father myself. I don't mind being the fun uncle, though. Do you have a problem with that?' He cocked his head to one side, eyebrow raised as he tried to rile her. She wasn't going to rise to it. Even if he was making sexy eyes at her, causing her to tingle in all sorts of places. Yes, she did have a problem with it.

Perhaps this had been a bad idea, but she'd thought they should at least discuss what they expected from this arrangement. In Jamie's case, apparently that was nothing. He was primarily going to be the sperm donor. Perhaps with the odd appearance for birthdays and family get-togethers.

She couldn't criticise when that was as involved as she wished to be in the baby's life too. In her case, a loving auntie who was free to come and go as she chose. She was the surrogate, an incubator only for this baby, because any idea of family beyond her brother terrified the life out of her. Their parents' tyranny had made her realise the damage a person could do to a child and she didn't want that level of responsibility. Liam and Tom were two of the nicest men on earth and a child would be lucky to have them as parents.

'Not at all. I was just checking.' She sipped her herbal

tea and wished the others would hurry up and join them to ease the tension.

She tried to forget their first meeting and how flustered she'd been around him. A matter he'd taken great satisfaction in and flirted with her outrageously until she'd demanded he stop. He obviously wasn't used to women saying no to him, her request amusing him all the more. The truth was she'd been afraid of reacting to his advances when her body had been on fire for him after just a few suggestive comments. He wasn't her type. Actually, she didn't have a type because there wasn't a man alive she was willing to trust.

Of course, their brothers had been blissfully unaware of their sizzling chemistry, so wrapped up in the happiness of their big day. When they'd proposed Jamie as the sperm donor for the surrogate baby she had agreed to carry for them, she'd been unable to find it in her to object to the idea.

'I never thought my little brother would be the first to get married and have a family.' He shook his head, the affection for his sibling shining brightly in his smile.

'It was a lovely wedding.' The grooms had spared no expense in sharing their happy day with their friends. They'd taken their vows in the Royal Observatory in Greenwich. Toasted with champagne in the courtyard over the Meridian Line, where the east and west hemispheres met. Later, they'd had their meal in the Octagon Room under the stars. Those still standing had gone on to party in a nearby hotel, and booked rooms for the night. The whole day had been magical.

'Amazing. I had concerns it might be a bit…cheesy but I suppose some might have called it romantic.' He leaned across the table as he said it, reminding her of the telescope viewing she'd done with Jamie right there beside her. With him so close she'd been oblivious to anyone else in the room.

As the grooms' family, they'd spent the majority of the day in close proximity but that was the moment she'd become *aware* of him. By that time of the evening, his perfectly groomed hair had had its curl back and he'd had a shadow of a beard bristling over his once clean-shaven jaw. He'd shed his tux jacket and untied his bow tie so it hung loosely around his neck. It wouldn't have taken much to tug on the ends and pull him in for a kiss. One she'd known would be hot when he'd been giving her his undivided attention all day. Thank goodness that had been the moment Tom and Liam had announced they were moving the party to the hotel and saved her from herself.

'The food was good too.'

'The first dance was my particular highlight.' Clearly, he wasn't going to let her forget their more intimate moments of the day.

That first dance, when Jamie had swept her up on the dance floor at the happy couple's insistence they join them, had indeed been memorable. Those three or four minutes in his arms, their bodies pressed close together swaying in time to the music, had been heavenly. When he'd whispered in her ear, asked if she wanted to come up to his room, she'd almost agreed. Her hormones would've followed him across the dance floor and into his bed, but her head and her wounded heart wouldn't allow it. That was when she'd known she'd had to stop his flirting with her and once the song had ended, she'd made sure to keep her distance from him. Until now.

'It was good to see Tom and Liam so in love. They're going to make great parents.'

Jamie sighed, perhaps resigning himself to the fact she didn't want to be reminded of the chemistry they'd experienced that night. Something which apparently hadn't dissipated since they'd last seen each other.

'Tell me, Kayla, what is it you're hoping to achieve by offering yourself up as a surrogate? You're a midwife, aren't you? Surely this isn't a situation you would usually encourage?' He lounged back in his chair, crossed his long legs at the ankles and made himself comfortable whilst he turned the spotlight back on her. It was a safer topic of conversation for her than the wedding night.

'I'm a doula now. I left my position as a midwife so I could give more support to my expectant mothers. It's none of my business what the story behind their pregnancy is but it is my job to be supportive of their choices. I just want parents and babies to be happy. The same goes in this instance too.' She would move in with the guys for the duration of the pregnancy, to keep them involved throughout, then hand over the baby so they could start their happy little family. Something she and Liam had missed out on their entire lives.

'Do you have a problem with that?' Her brother's sexuality was a touchy subject for her and she was very protective of him despite being the younger of the two.

It had been their parents' reaction to him coming out as gay which had finally given her the push to leave that toxic environment with him and move to London from their small village in Northern Ireland. They'd spent their entire childhoods cowed in fear of their disciplinarian parents, but it was when their mother and father had disowned their own son she'd seen them for the monsters they really were.

Jamie set his coffee cup back on the table and held his hands up. 'Not at all.'

'Good. Then we're both on the same page.' This baby was going to share the traits of both its parents and she wanted to be certain there weren't some dodgy conscience-free genes about to be introduced.

'I wouldn't do this for just anybody. It's not as though I make weekly deposits down at the local sperm bank and get off on the fact there could be dozens of Jamie Juniors running around out there. Tom asked me to do this because he can't and with me as the donor it means he still has a biological connection with the baby. The same way Liam has because you're the egg donor.'

'I have my own reasons for agreeing.' Liam deserved to have some happiness and though she hadn't been able to do anything in the past to help, she was in a position to do it now. It was information Jamie didn't need to know. Her past was none of his business.

'Oh? You're not doing it simply out of the goodness of your heart, then? Like me?' He was making fun of her because she was taking this seriously. She wished he would. It would make her feel better to know the father of this baby was sensible, reliable and stable. Even if he wasn't going to be an active participant.

'If you just wanted to have a kid, you should've taken me up on my offer at the hotel.' The man winking at her, and setting her body aflame with desire, didn't fit in with the profile supplied by those who knew him better than her.

From the glowing accounts she'd heard before they'd met, she'd expected a deadly serious, old-beyond-his-years father figure, who'd raised Tom as his own son and was giving him away at the wedding. She'd known he wasn't keen on long-term relationships, but she'd put that down to his busy work schedule. After getting to know him she wondered if there was anything more to him than a rakish playboy who thought nothing of propositioning her. Either way, she'd be having words with her brother about his suitability for this role.

'Don't think it hasn't crossed my mind.' The truth slipped out before she could catch it. She took another sip of her tea to keep her from saying anything else to feed his widening grin.

It wasn't that she'd never been in the company of a handsome man before, or had one come on to her. She'd been getting better at handling herself in those situations because she was sick of pretending to be someone she wasn't. Her early years had been spent trying to be the perfect daughter to prevent angering her parents. The hangover of that learned behaviour as an adult had seen her enter into a disastrous relationship where she'd spent most of it trying, and failing, to meet her partner's expectations. She was done trying and didn't need the drama of having another man in her life. If only all her other body parts agreed with her brain.

'Well now, wouldn't it make more sense to cut out all the intrusive medical procedures and do things the old-fashioned way?'

Now her head was filled with explicit images of Jamie naked except for the tangled sheets they were entwined in. That longing that she'd convinced herself had been a one-off the last time they'd met began again inside her.

With those brown eyes sparkling with mischief and

promise, she was tempted to take him up on the offer. Neither of them wanted some grand love affair but it was obvious they had a connection that would make sparks fly.

'I suspect sense wouldn't be playing a big part in that scenario. More like lust.' One of them had to be honest about this attraction they were dancing around. Pretending that this talk of a secret liaison was for their brothers' benefit wasn't fooling anyone.

She swallowed hard and tried to pull herself together. When this pre-conception meeting had been first suggested, she'd sworn not to let him literally charm the pants totally off her this time. Now she was swearing at herself for getting caught under his spell again.

'Would that really be so bad?' His dark gaze rendered her immobile now that he'd made her so hot she'd melted into her chair.

'There's no guarantee we'd conceive that way.' She was scrabbling for excuses now when her head was full of the possibilities available to her with him. The alternative conception method Jamie was suggesting sounded so much more enjoyable than the one planned that she was afraid she was going to take him up on it.

'It doesn't have to be a one-time offer. I'm prepared to put the hard work in to make this happen.' His voice dropped so low she could feel it deep in the pit of her stomach, and lower...

'I, uh...' She had no words. Her brain was mush, her mouth dry. It had been a while since she'd shared a bed with anyone. Longer still since she'd had this level of passion stirred up inside her.

Despite all the promises she'd made to herself about staying away from men, and this one in particular, all she could think about was grabbing him by the hand and finding the nearest hotel room. At this stage she wasn't even thinking of a baby, only her own pleasure. That wasn't part of the deal.

Jamie couldn't believe she was considering his outrageous proposal, or that he'd made it. There was something about Kayla that intrigued him and made him want to push her buttons. When he'd first spotted her at the wedding, he'd known this was the sister Liam had spoken about fondly. The pretty blonde in the off-the-shoulder, gypsy-style floral dress had to be the woman he'd heard loved animals too much to eat them and enjoyed nothing more than meditating and clearing something called chakras. From a distance, she'd seemed so calm and serene and totally in character with the Kayla who'd been described to him. Until she'd spoken to him. Then the carefree, laid-back, spiritual doula he'd heard about had changed into a tightly wound spitfire.

Only around him though, he'd noted. From a distance he'd watched her charm everyone else with her easy-going nature and was amused by her reaction when he was around. Her pale skin flushed a dramatic scarlet when he spoke to her and she couldn't get away from him quickly enough. He might have taken offence if it weren't for the surreptitious glances he noticed she kept shooting his way. Her interest in him seemed to mark a change in his behaviour too. Ordinarily he wasn't quite so…abrasive.

Now she appeared more open to the idea of a fling his juices were flowing. When the air between them was still so charged with sexual awareness in the middle of a coffee shop, he knew they could set the sheets on fire together.

'You know, my place isn't far from here and my car's just outside…' he tossed out as he finished his coffee. It was madness, yet that flash of lust he'd seen when he'd mentioned the idea was unmistakable and irresistible. As was the subconscious licking of her lips and toying with her unruly blond hair. All signs she was interested in him. Along with the fact she was yet to tell him where to get off thinking she was the type of woman who'd agree to some afternoon hanky-panky with someone she hardly knew.

'Jamie, I…uh—'

He was expecting her to turn him down, but she set down her cup with trembling hands and was beginning to lift her handbag from the floor as if she was getting ready to go with him. Jamie unhooked his jacket from the back of the chair and dug for his car keys in the pocket. This was the most spontaneous, reckless thing he'd ever done. That included volunteering to be a sperm donor for his infertile brother.

'I'm so glad we caught you two!'

At the sound of Liam's loud Northern Irish voice, they jumped apart. As though they'd literally been caught in the act. Chance would have been a fine thing.

'Actually, we were just leaving.' He held out a hand to help Kayla up but as she glanced between the two men Jamie knew the moment had passed. For now.

'You can't go yet. I've only got here and Tom's on his way. We want to catch up on all the gossip and tell you what's happening at the clinic.' Liam pulled out a chair and invited himself to join them. The couple had been heavily involved in a project out in Vietnam setting up facilities for medical care in impoverished areas of Central Vietnam and it would be rude of them not to stay and listen to their latest news.

Kayla couldn't even meet his eye now, so Jamie had no choice but to sit back down and quell the excitement that had been escalating until his brother-in-law crashed their party.

Tom arrived shortly after. 'Sorry I'm late. The trains are a nightmare as usual. Got held up leaving Victoria Station because of a signal failure or something. What have I missed?'

He gave Jamie a half-hug and kissed Kayla on the cheek before pulling over another chair from a nearby table and squeezing in beside his husband.

'Nothing. Unfortunately,' he mumbled. It was difficult not to sound ticked off when these two had killed the mood and left Kayla glaring at him for saying so.

'Good. Kayla thought we should meet up to discuss any qualms anyone had about the process. Is there anything we should know about?' Tom's question was met only with silence.

They hadn't got around to listing the pros and cons about the baby idea when they'd been busy flirting up a storm. Kayla didn't strike him as the type who'd stay silent if she had a problem and, since he'd been on board from day one, Jamie didn't see the point in making them sweat.

'Nope. We're ready and willing to get our baby-making on. Where do we sign?' His answer clearly delighted the two men, who grasped each other's hands.

'Kayla? You're the one who'll be doing all the hard

work. Now you've had a chance to talk it over with Jamie, are you happy for us to push ahead?' Even Liam sounded nervous about his sister continuing with her commitment and he didn't know Jamie had just propositioned her.

Any hint of sexual attraction towards him seemed to have evaporated since she was still frowning at him for his earlier indiscreet remark. 'Jamie has made it clear he's not the sort of person interested in committing to this beyond his ability to fill a plastic cup. I think you should get that down in writing in case he changes his mind again.'

Wow. He hoped it was sexual frustration causing her to lash out too. If she really believed he was the unreliable, flaky type who'd mess his brother around, she knew nothing about him at all. He'd spent his whole adult life raising and providing for his kid brother. That was why he'd no intention of marrying or having kids of his own any time soon. Now Tom was married and starting a family, Jamie was free of responsibility. He no longer had a dependant to think of with every decision he made, and he didn't think it was selfish of him to want a little quality time for himself.

He couldn't be sure if she'd formed her disapproval of him at the wedding or this afternoon when he'd made a pass at her and hadn't followed through, but it was no longer important. Once he'd done his part behind closed doors he'd walk away with a clear conscience and wouldn't have to set eyes on her again.

If she was as sensitive as she appeared, he'd be better off letting her despise her. There was no point in getting involved with someone who'd read more into a fling than he was willing to give. Jamie had been there, done that, and wasn't in a hurry to repeat the experience. The same could be said about his attitude to fatherhood.

CHAPTER TWO

IT HAD BEEN three months since that dreaded phone call from Jamie, but she could still hear it.

'I'm sorry, Kayla, there's been an accident. Tom, Liam...they didn't make it.'

Her world had fallen apart with those words at a time when she should have been enjoying her pregnancy. She'd conceived on the first attempt, thanks to the assistance at the fertility clinic and not an afternoon of passion with Jamie. With their brothers' well-timed intervention that day, she'd taken back control of her senses and avoided any further one-to-one dealings with Jamie.

The guys had gone over to Vietnam to tie up loose ends on the project they'd been working on out there. As Tom was an architect, and Liam a builder, they'd used their skills to build a medical centre for an impoverished area they'd visited on their holidays a few years ago. This was supposed to have been their babymoon, their last trip before they settled down into family life. Heavy rainfall had caused flooding, resulting in a landslide in the area where they'd been staying. Liam and Tom had been swept away to their deaths.

It was only a matter of weeks before this baby was

due and she had no idea how she was going to do everything on her own.

'Kayla. Let me in.'

Oh, yes, and Jamie had suddenly turned into a stalker, showing up all the time and trying to convince her he was out to win Father of the Year. It was a complete turnaround from his visits earlier in the pregnancy when he'd been more interested in catching up with his brother than acknowledging the baby. The way she'd preferred it. Life was difficult enough for her trying to come to terms with the fact she was about to become a mum without having to deal with him and those unwanted feelings he kept stirring up inside her.

'I don't care if you are the father of this baby. You're practically a stranger and I have no intention of letting you interfere in my life.' Kayla slammed the door and promptly burst into tears. This was all such a mess.

She rubbed her hand over her huge belly. 'I'm so sorry, little one. We all wanted better for you.'

He or she should have had happily married parents with a life mapped out. Not an unlovable mother and a playboy father who'd never wanted the responsibility of a baby, handing it over to those better suited to the parenting role. She'd let this child down before it had even been born. How the hell was she going to provide the upbringing it deserved? It wasn't as though she had good role models to follow. She was going into this blind.

Another veil of tears fell, soaking the delicate silk scarf around her neck; Liam had bought it for her last birthday. Her brother had known she'd adore it because of the motif. The dragonfly was her personal totem and a powerful symbol of change and light in many cultures.

In this case Liam said it represented the start of their new life and the rebirth of their family.

Now it was a reminder of everything she'd lost.

She slipped the scarf off her neck and draped it around the photograph of Liam and Tom on their wedding day. Happiness radiated from their smiles as they gazed at each other, so full of hope for their future together. Only to have it so cruelly snatched away from them a short time later.

'I have as much right as you to be here.' Jamie's voice carried down the hall to interrupt her grief and cause her temper to flare again. His constant presence was preventing her from focusing on more important matters. Such as the prospect of becoming a single parent.

'How did you get in?' She watched helplessly as he stalked into the living room as though he owned the place.

He swung the house key around his finger on the hand-stitched felt key ring she'd made with Tom's name on it as a moving-in present. 'This is my house too, remember? You're not the only one who lost a brother and it's about time you stopped avoiding me. We have a lot to discuss.'

Their brothers had left everything to the two of them in their wills, making it impossible for Kayla to avoid him unless she sold up, and there was enough upheaval without having to move to a new house as well. It was a pity the wills hadn't been updated since the surrogacy arrangement. Then they might have had some idea of what it was they were expected to do.

Jamie threw himself onto the settee and she worried he was ensconced for the night. There was no other choice for her but to join him. Although it took her slightly longer to ease herself and her bump into a chair.

'I thought you'd made it abundantly clear from the start you didn't want anything to do with this baby.' She wished that were still the case. He had a choice where she didn't. No matter what happened, she had to give birth and be a mother to this baby.

'That was when I thought I was going to be nothing but a sperm donor to make my brother's dream of being a father come true. I wanted Tom to be happy. No matter how unconventional, I wanted to see his dream of having a family come true. Now he's gone this baby will need someone to look out for it.'

'I'm looking out for it. I *am* the mother.' He wasn't the only one who'd done this with the intention of making the couple happy. This wasn't the time to be searching for accolades. Jamie had provided his little swimmers because Tom's hadn't been doing the job they were supposed to, but she'd been the one who'd gone through the intrusive medically assisted insemination process.

It was she who'd carried the baby all this time. She was the one whose body would never be the same again.

'In case you've forgotten, I'm the father.'

'I haven't forgotten. I'm giving you the opportunity to walk away. As you'd planned from the start.' She didn't want to parent on her own, but it was preferable to a lifetime of being tied to this man.

Kayla had moved to London with Liam nearly fifteen years ago to escape the control of their parents and she wasn't going to tie herself to a man she hardly knew now. That hadn't ended well the last time she'd been conned into it. She'd been left broken-hearted and homeless when she'd rebelled against Paul's dominance in their relationship.

It wasn't that long since she'd lost her brother. She was vulnerable, and she wasn't going to let anyone take advantage of that.

Jamie stood up. He was imposing at his full height, which had to be a good foot taller than her five-foot-three-inch frame. Especially when he was dressed in his GP's sharp suit and tie and she was in her ever-expanding maternity leggings and voluminous, stretch jersey, dark grey bump-coverer.

He strode towards her with such purpose her mouth suddenly went dry.

Then he leaned down and whispered, 'Not going to happen.'

The ebb and flow of a shiver brought the tiny hairs on her arms to attention as his breath warmed her cheek. He gave her scant time to linger on her body's reaction and walked away again towards the kitchen.

When she managed to compose herself enough to follow him she wished she hadn't. Her sense of incredulity and temper rose further with every cupboard he opened, showing no respect for the fact this had been her home for the better part of a year. He might have inherited a share through tragic circumstances, but his lack of good manners and bold self-entitlement were not aiding their already strained relationship.

'Don't you have any proper food in this place?' He was rummaging in the fridge, turning his nose up at the contents as he inspected them.

'I only have *proper* food. It's much healthier than that processed junk you probably favour.' Liam and Tom had shared her healthy approach to food, but Jamie didn't look as though he could be sustained by lettuce and carrots alone.

'Give me a dirty, big burger any day,' he grumbled, confirming the belief he was a man who enjoyed the red-meat-fuelled lifestyle of his caveman ancestors.

Although lean, Jamie was solid muscle and sinew. She could see that by the way his tailored shirt clung to his torso, and his thighs stretched the fabric of his tight-fitting black trousers. This was someone who needed protein to fuel his workout. He'd be more inclined towards swimming rather than being a gym bunny, she decided. Mainly because she could imagine him gliding through the water with those powerful limbs, showing off that streamlined body in nothing but a tight-fitting pair of swim trunks.

'I said, we're going to have to do a grocery shop or I'll starve to death here.'

Kayla blinked away her glistening-wet, semi-naked fantasy to centre on the fully dressed version of Jamie, whose mouth was twitching as he tried not to laugh. It was then she realised she'd been staring, and it hadn't gone unnoticed. She blamed the sudden heat consuming her body on the rise of her blood pressure at having an unwanted visitor going through her things. Not due to any thoughts of Tom's big brother with his wet hair curling at the nape of his neck or water sluicing over his naked body.

'You—you don't live here. My cupboards are none of your business,' she blustered, slamming shut all the doors he'd opened during his plundering.

'Well, here's the thing, Kayla. It was one thing being the biological father only and Tom taking responsibility for raising this child. Now he's not here, the baton passes to me and I'm afraid I'm not going to sit back and let your hippy-dippy ways dictate my baby's life.' He folded his arms and rested his backside against her worktop as casual as he liked.

Meanwhile, she was sure she was about to combust into flames. His baby. Calling her hippy-dippy. He'd wiped out her credibility as a mother in one insult. She didn't think being a vegetarian and using meditation as a form of stress relief justified anyone making fun of her. It was her way of taking back her life and being at peace with herself.

Kayla opened her mouth, then closed it again before she said something very unladylike. Once the moment passed she called upon her rational self to counter his ill-judged argument.

'First of all—' her voice was louder than she'd intended so she dialled it back before he accused her of being hysterical '—this baby is not a baton. It is a human being that has been growing inside me. Therefore, I think it's safe to say you're not going to *let* me do anything. I'm its mother.'

'And I'm its father.'

The man was infuriating beyond words.

Count to ten, Kayla, and don't even think about launching that frying pan at his head, even if it is within arm's reach.

Jamie levered himself off the worktop and walked towards her. Kayla immediately backed away. She didn't enjoy confrontation. Usually, she did her best to avoid it when raised voices and tempers brought back memories of a childhood best forgotten.

Unfortunately, Jamie brought out the worst in her and vice versa. In all the time she'd known Tom he'd never shown anything but adoration for his older brother. He'd talked about him in such glowing terms Kayla had expected him to be a saint. From her perspective he was purely an annoyance.

Especially when they both knew she'd been prepared to walk out of that coffee shop and engage in some sordid afternoon shenanigans if their brothers hadn't turned up that day. She didn't like him knowing he was a weakness where she was concerned in case he used it to get the upper hand.

'Look, Kayla, I'm not here to fight with you. I just want to make sure you and the baby are healthy. This is the last link I have to Tom and the only family I have left.' It was a heartfelt plea, but there was no way she was giving him room to start dictating to her. She'd had enough of that growing up.

'So, what are you going to do? Draw up a contract and a diet plan according to what you deem a suitable lifestyle? We're not in some weird relationship where I'm happy to submit to your dominant will. I'm not that kind of girl.'

'Wow.'

'What's wrong? Have you never had a woman talk back to you before?' With his looks and his status as a partner in his GP practice, no doubt he was used to people doing his bidding with no questions asked.

The rumble as he laughed did things to her insides she wasn't prepared for. 'No. It's just interesting that's where your mind went.'

'Liam and Tom might have left you half of this house, but you have absolutely no claim on my body.' Her mind chose to interpret those words differently than they were intended. Forbidden images of Jamie's mouth and hands possessing her sprang from nowhere, causing chaos within.

This pregnancy brought more problems than heartburn and weight gain. Especially when these feelings were so rare she didn't think she'd experienced them even with her exes. A problem that had ended all her relationships and made her consider this surrogacy in the first place.

Sex wasn't something she'd been able to fully enjoy when she couldn't find it in herself to give control of her body completely to someone else. The same could be said about love.

Now a few arrogant words from a man who had a knack for getting under her skin were already wreaking havoc on her insides again.

One thing was for sure, she had to find some way to get Jamie out of her life so she and the baby could live the life Tom and Liam would now never be a part of.

'Technically, whilst you're pregnant with my child, I do have an interest in your body.' Jamie couldn't help himself. There was more than a hint of truth in those words and not solely for the baby she was carrying.

Small and curvy even before she got pregnant, Kayla physically wasn't his usual type. Her honey-blond hair fell in messy natural ringlets around her shoulders, as chaotic as her rolled-through-a-jumble-sale fashion sense. The layers of mismatched vintage clothes she favoured, most people would have consigned to the dustbin.

Personality wise there was a major clash between them, as this current exchange would attest to. She was hard work, a pain in the backside he could do without.

Yet, since losing Tom and Liam, he hadn't been able to keep away from her. He knew it was more than their shared grief but hoped his sudden interest in her would end once the baby was born. Anything else would have disaster written all over it. Her shudder of obvious disgust at his comment was proof of that.

'My body is absolutely none of your business.' She folded her arms across her blossoming cleavage and Jamie tried to avert his stare.

'Ditto. So, I'll thank you to stop looking at me as though I'm a piece of meat.' By the way she'd been ogling him earlier he'd say her pregnancy hormones were running riot. It was a reminder of that day in the café when they'd come close to succumbing to temptation. Thank goodness they hadn't, when things were complicated enough between them.

'I was not!' Her reddening cheeks gave her away.

'Let's get one thing straight here, Kayla.' He flicked the kettle on and lifted a mug down from the cupboard. 'My only interest is in the baby you're carrying.'

'Mine too.' Composure regained, she walked right up to him. Close enough for him to drink in her floral scent. It was likely something she made herself from daisies and buttercups under the light of a full moon.

Kayla opened the cupboard above his head, lifted out a handmade, slightly wonky, blue-glazed earthenware mug and set it down on the counter.

'I assume you have a birth plan in place? I don't imagine the event is something either of our brothers would have left to chance.' Even if Kayla seemed the sort of person to let nature take its course. There was a very bohemian quality to her. As though she'd be more at home in some hippy commune living off the earth and communing with nature than working nine-to-five and living in a suburban semi.

'I'm having a natural birth. At home.'

He should have known.

'Not happening.'

'Excuse me? It was what your brother, Liam, and I wanted. You can't just swan in here—'

'And what? Want what's best for my baby? Which is to be born in a hospital where the best medical care is at hand should anything go wrong?'

Kayla couldn't believe what she was hearing. They had planned as peaceful a welcome into the world as they could provide. Now, Jamie was storming in demanding as much noise, disruption and upheaval that came with hospital births in comparison. No way was she having that. The days of letting anyone walk over her were long gone.

'In case you're not aware, I was a qualified midwife before I became a doula. I know the difference it can make to mum and baby when a birth is at home, surrounded by familiar faces, enveloped in love rather than machines and overworked staff. That's why I changed careers.'

It had been difficult for her to adhere to the rules laid out by the hospital management when births didn't run to their specific timetable or targets. She realised quickly after qualifying she'd much rather devote herself to one family at a time than be on a conveyor belt moving from one mother to the next without making any real personal connection.

'Then you know there are potential risks with any

pregnancy. Complications during a home birth can't be dealt with as effectively as they could be at the hospital.'

'I'm qualified to make those kinds of decisions that might warrant a hospital transfer.' It didn't happen often, but in emergencies she would encourage medical intervention where it was needed. The welfare of baby and mother were always top priority.

'Tell me, are you planning on giving birth naked and alone in a field?' There was that patronising tone she'd come to know well when involved in a heated discussion with another medical professional on the subject.

'You might not agree with my methods but please don't mock them.'

'It's hard not to,' he muttered, reinforcing the idea that a calm, peaceful birth wasn't going to be possible anywhere with him around.

'What is so wrong in wanting to be in the comfort of my own home, listening to the music of my choice and letting nature take its course?' There'd been too much upset already during this pregnancy and the least she could do now was give this baby a smooth transition from the warm cocoon of her body into its new environment.

'It's selfish,' he answered without taking time to think about what it meant to anyone other than him.

'No, it's simply an alternative to a hospital birth. Women have been doing it for centuries. I think I'll manage.'

'What? You're going to deliver the baby yourself? I'm sorry, but this is crazy. I've already lost my brother. I'm not prepared to jeopardise my baby for the sake of your whim to raise a flower-child. I don't think the sixties were all they were cracked up to be, you know.

There was a higher mortality rate back then, likely for this very reason.'

Breathe in. Breathe out. Don't punch things.

Kayla hadn't realised dinosaurs still roamed the earth masquerading as pretty doctors, but Jamie was living proof.

'There are such things as friends. I know that concept might not be familiar to you if this is how you speak to everyone you meet. I have my own doula to assist with labour as well as a community midwife.'

'Great. It's reassuring to know there'll be two of you howling at the moon and stinking the place out with incense.'

She didn't know where he plucked these ideas about home births from. He was a GP, for heaven's sake. She was sure he'd dealt with them in his time. This seemed more personal to her. As though he simply disapproved of her and her life choices when, really, he knew nothing about her.

All his talk so far surrounded his wishes for his baby, relegating her to the role of incubator who shouldn't have any opinion of her own.

'I really don't care what you think, Jamie. This is my safe space. My body. My baby. My birth plan. You won't be here anyway, so it won't affect you.' At this rate the baby would be cutting its first teeth by the time she told him it had arrived.

There was no way she was having him anywhere near her, stressing her out during the most important, and unexpected, phase of her life as she transitioned into motherhood. Given the chance he'd probably be shouting instructions like her old PE teacher, calling her a slacker and pushing her until she was sure her lungs would explode. That wasn't the atmosphere she was striving for on this occasion.

'Who says I won't be here?'

'This is my first baby and I've still got a few weeks until my due date. The chances are slim you'll be in the vicinity when I go into labour.' She certainly wasn't going to tell him.

Jamie Garrett hovering over her every decision was the last thing on her wish list. It was the worst possible scenario after losing the men she'd thought were raising this child.

'I'm going to increase those odds.'

'How?' She was compelled to ask, though she did so with a sigh. He was exhausting and as soon as she got shot of him she'd do a bit of meditation to clear her chakras from the negativity he left in his wake. She might even listen to the CD of whale music the boys had given her as a joke present. It would be her way of sticking two fingers up at the biological father-to-be who'd be horrified at the very idea.

'I'm moving in.' The self-satisfied smirk strengthened the impact of the bombshell.

She'd been wrong. This was the worst possible scenario and she was powerless to do anything about it.

CHAPTER THREE

'This isn't how it was supposed to be. Liam and Tom were going to be the parents. Once I gave birth, my part was done. It certainly wasn't intended to be a dictatorship run by you.' Kayla promptly burst into tears and Jamie's elation at getting the upper hand instantly gave way to something more sympathetic.

He hadn't come here to antagonise her. Since Tom's death, all he'd wanted was to be part of his baby's life and to be a dad. The flirty nature of their relationship had to change in the wake of their loss. He'd changed, knowing he had new responsibilities to meet, and Kayla was a part of that new chapter. Upsetting her further wasn't going to do anyone any good.

'Why don't you sit down?' He pulled over one of the high-back stools from the breakfast bar. Now that pigheadedness had left her he could see how vulnerable she was. It must be hard for that little body of hers to be carrying that bump along with the hopes and dreams of both their brothers.

'Stop telling me what to do!' she yelled at him, her face scarlet as she vented her fury. Tears soon followed the outburst as her sobs ricocheted around the kitchen walls before hitting Jamie square in the chest. So much for wanting the best for mother and baby. He'd added more stress on top of already losing her brother.

Jamie backed away, crouched down with his hands raised in surrender as though pacifying a dangerous animal before it could attack. 'I was only trying to make you more comfortable. I don't want the baby to be in any danger because you're all worked up.'

He didn't suppose she had a blood-pressure cuff tucked away with her bongo drums and crystals in her birthing accessories. In this instance he might well make a dash out to his car where he had one in his bag for emergencies. He'd like to check her blood pressure. That was if she'd consent to him being close without hitting him with something.

'Shut up. Shut up. Shut up!' Her voice gradually grew louder until she was verging on the edge of hysteria. Kayla stomped her foot on the floor with that final instruction.

Jamie could only watch in horror as a trickle of liquid soaked her trousers and splashed on the tiled floor.

'Okay. Don't panic, but I think your waters have just broken.' He dared to venture into her personal space, put an arm around her shoulders and guided her towards the living room.

'It's too early.' She was clearly in shock since she permitted him to lead her.

'Not really. The baby's viable at this stage. No need to panic. Now, do you have something I can put down to protect the sofa?'

She was waddling even more than usual, but she didn't put up any further protest. 'There are towels in the wooden chest in the corner.' There was a dazed quality to her voice he wasn't sure was preferable to the ranting she'd been doing only moments earlier.

The area she directed him to was separate from the rest of the furnishings in the room. A circle of primary-coloured over-sized cushions on the floor had been carefully arranged. It had the appearance of a giant, gaudy bird nest, but this wasn't the time for him to make any further mocking comments. He ignored the questions burning to be asked, the jokes begging to be made, to retrieve a couple of faded grey towels from the chest.

'I'll phone ahead to the labour ward and let them know you're coming in. My car's outside. I can drive you to hospital.' He covered the seat cushions as best he could to enable her to sit down until he brought the car around to the front door.

'How many times do I have to tell you I want a home birth? Cherry is my doula. Phone her and my midwife. Their numbers are in the birth plan in my bag.' She directed him back to the weird cushion nest where her labour bag was sitting waiting for this very moment.

'I'll phone them for you but as you're not full term I'd prefer to get you to hospital.' He was doing his best not to be confrontational but when they held such conflicting views on the subject he knew he was fighting a losing battle.

'This is your fault. You've ruined everything. I'm not letting you take this away from me too.' Kayla let out an anguished cry and doubled over, clutching her belly.

'Contraction?' He crouched down in front of her, timing it with his watch.

She nodded, her face contorted with pain, and Jamie wished he could swap places with her. All he could do was hold her hand and wait until the pain subsided. He didn't care that she'd almost cut off his circulation she was squeezing him so hard.

It was his fault. He'd been so determined to be part of this he'd trodden all over Kayla's feelings to the point of starting her labour. When all she'd wanted was a peaceful birth.

'I'll phone Cherry, so she can come and sit with you, and I'll let the midwife know labour's started.' It was the least he could do.

'You'll stay with me until she comes, right?'

He made a move to get the numbers from the file, only for Kayla to grab his hand again. It was the first indication that she wanted his help, though he knew it was only through her fear of the unknown. He wanted to be here for her, holding her and providing the support he'd so far failed to give her.

'If it's all right with you I'll be staying until the baby's born.' That way he could make his own observations and decisions about how the labour was progressing. If he had any inkling at all anything was wrong, he'd be straight on the phone to the hospital.

'I don't want you interfering any more than you already have, Jamie. Get Cherry here.'

'How about a compromise? I'll stay, at a distance, but the first sign of anything untoward and we're back to civilisation for help.'

'Fine. Just get Cherry.' Another sob erupted, followed by a further contraction. This baby was apparently in a hurry to meet its parents.

Kayla tried her best to think away the pain, to focus on the beautiful baby she would have at the end of this. To no avail. She'd been through innumerable labours and births, but panic had set in when she'd experienced that first vice-like pain for herself. She wasn't ready to become a mother.

'I'm surprised none of my patients ever slapped me when I told them to breathe through this. It's easier said than done.' With the next wave of agony, she attempted to channel it into Jamie via his fingers. He deserved to share in every aspect of this labour if he was so keen.

'I guess you don't want me telling you you're a good girl, then?' His grin soon changed to a grimace as she tightened her grip. She trusted there was sufficient venom in her stare to prevent him from making further patronising comments even in jest.

The sound of the doorbell saved his fingers from being completely mangled but did leave her temporarily without an outlet for her pain. It was worse being alone for the few seconds it took him to answer the door. That brief time, sitting on her own in the quiet room with her baby on the way, confronted her with the truth she had to do this without Liam and Tom's support. Heaven help her, she needed someone with her for this. Even if it had to be Jamie.

'Hey, honey. Is it that time already?' A waft of gardenias announced Cherry's arrival and was enough to set off a new rainfall down Kayla's face.

'Contractions are already four minutes apart. The midwife is on her way.' It was Jamie who provided the details Cherry needed to help organise the labour. Strange, when he'd made it clear he didn't agree with her methods, but he was here, supporting her decisions after all.

Cherry came to sit beside her on the couch. 'Goodness. We'd better get you organised. Jamie—'

'Dr Garrett,' he corrected her. It was likely his attempt to assert some authority in a situation where he knew he had none.

Cherry, like Kayla, wasn't someone easily intimidated. 'I'm sure Kayla has told you we want to create an informal atmosphere here. If you don't mind, I'll stick to Jamie. Now, if you could go and make us all a cup of tea, I'll help Kayla change out of these wet clothes.'

Everything in his tense jaw said he did mind. Nevertheless, he did leave the room for them to have their privacy.

'The father, I take it?' Her best friend, doula, and all-round good egg, Cherry, helped her to strip off.

'Not the one I'd planned on having around but he's insisting on it.'

'That's not a bad thing when you don't have Liam and Tom around any more. I mean, Debbie and I are here for you, but, you know, he's family.' Between them they managed to redress Kyla in the cotton nightdress she'd left by her pregnancy pad for labour. Although, if she felt the desire to do this naked at a later stage she'd still be shedding her outward skin, regardless if Jamie was here or not. Giving birth was not a time to worry about inhibitions.

'You and Debbie are more family than Jamie. I hardly know him.'

'Give him a chance, Kay. You two are in this together. Besides, he's kinda hot. I'm surprised you two didn't just conceive the old-fashioned way. I'm sure it would've been a hell of a lot more fun.'

'Cherry!' She didn't share the fact it had nearly happened because any attraction had been rendered irrelevant. It was clear they couldn't be in a room together without rowing. Sharing a bed would've caused fireworks. That was probably why she couldn't get the idea out of her head.

'What? I can still enjoy looking at a pretty package even if it's not quite to my taste.'

'I think your wife might have something to say about that.' Her best friends were happily married but Kayla still experienced an irrational possessiveness over a man who wasn't hers and never likely to be.

'Debbie would be on my side.'

'He's the total opposite to his brother. Jamie is rude, annoying…rude, and a dinosaur.'

'At least one of those statements is false. Would a dinosaur father a baby for his gay brother and his husband? I think not.'

Ugh. She was being too logical at a time Kayla was well within her rights to detest the father of her baby. She'd seen her share of women cursing the men who'd made them go through the pain of childbirth and she was no exception. Even if it was for a different reason. He wasn't Liam or Tom.

'Whose side are you on anyway? I thought a doula was supposed to keep me calm and agree with whatever I say?'

'Not quite.'

'Aagh!' That intrusive cramping squeezed her body tight and stole away any thoughts on anything other than the pain.

'That's it. Deep breaths. In and out. Remember this is all for a reason. Your body is doing the most important job in the world for you and getting ready to deliver this baby.'

Kayla closed her eyes and visualised the tiny wonder she was going through all of this for and the joy she should feel at finally holding it in her arms. Not the terror that had her in its grip at the thought of what the future held for them both. She held Cherry's hand until the contraction eased.

'Sorry, Kay. From now on I'll have my doula hat on and forget dishing out advice as your sassy best friend.'

'Don't let her disappear altogether. Your kind of truth is exactly why I wanted you with me for this.' Tears began to well again at all the plans she'd made with the proud fathers-to-be.

Tom and Liam had been just as excited as her about the prospect of the birth and having Cherry there too had seemed like the icing on the cake. One big happy family. Now Cherry was the only thing left from those plans.

'Tea's ready, or whatever passes for tea in this house.' Jamie returned, eyeing the cups on the tray with some suspicion. No doubt he'd prefer strong builder's tea full of caffeine, milk and sugar to her herbal alternatives. Too bad.

'There's no room for your negativity here, Jamie. This birth is going to be a positive experience and that extends to accepting how I take my tea.' She helped herself to a raspberry tea and waited to see how he'd react to his.

'That's right, and you need to rest between these contractions, Kayla. Sip some of your tea and close your eyes for a while. You'll need all your strength.' Cherry plumped the cushions around her back and Kayla did as suggested.

Experience watching her own patients told her labour could be a long and difficult road. The reward was always worth it in the end, but it took a toll on the mothers all the same. The unpredictable nature of labour meant any breaks should be taken advantage of when possible.

Another contraction hit and stole away any idea of relaxation. They seemed to be coming thick and fast and she couldn't believe she'd worried that everyone would be sitting around the house waiting for labour to start. It was well and truly under way.

She could see Jamie frowning behind Cherry. 'They're only three minutes apart now. Where is this midwife?'

'She probably thought she had a little more time to get here since it's Kayla's first baby. I'm sure she's on her way.' Cherry's calm response prevented Kayla from panicking more than she already was. It was natural to be afraid of the impending birth, but she didn't need the extra stress of doing it without her midwife.

'So is the baby.' His tone was accusatory, and, she suspected, directed at her.

'I'll give her another ring. Jamie, could you sit here with Kayla until I get back?' Neither protested at Cherry's request. He simply came to her side where he needed to be.

'Are you comfortable?'

'What do you think?' She'd never been more uncomfortable in her whole life.

He ignored her death stare and her barking response. 'I mean, can I help you get into a better position?'

Okay, maybe he wasn't a complete nuisance. He could have his uses.

'My back is killing me. I don't know how women do this for hours, sometimes days on end. I want it over already.'

'At this rate you might just have your wish. Why don't we try you leaning over this and see if we can find you some relief?' He pulled over the maroon velvet ottoman she kept her knitting in. Kayla noted he was using 'we' now. He'd committed to this birth with her and to be honest she was glad. She had a friend and support in Cherry, but if the midwife didn't get here, she might need his medical expertise. He wouldn't let harm come to this baby that had become so precious to him and therefore had to take care of her too until it arrived.

The pressure was already starting to build again, and she wanted to sob. Regardless that this was a happy event, she was tired and in pain already. She needed her big brother to hold her hand and tell her everything was going to be all right, the way he'd done her entire life.

Jamie helped heave her up from her position on the floor until she was on her knees, forearms resting on top of the ottoman. 'We're going to time this one.'

Kayla rocked her body, attempting to relieve the pain, resting her weight on her arms. The firm pressure at the base of her spine helped ease it and she realised it was Jamie, rubbing her back without her having to ask.

This one lasted longer than the others. Kayla heard a low moaning in the distance before she realised it was coming from deep inside her gut. She felt, and sounded, like a heifer about to give birth to its calf.

'That's it, Kayla. This one's nearly over.' The reassurance was as far from patronising as Jamie could get. He was encouraging her, cheering her on and telling her she could do this when she was full of doubt.

When there was a pause, he helped her back into a sitting position. She closed her eyes and waited for sleep. Jamie's hand brushed the damp strands of her hair away from her brow. The cool touch of his skin against hers was a relief in itself and she held his hand there for maximum effect.

'You like that, huh?'

She didn't have to open her eyes to know he was smirking, knowing that he'd been needed here after all.

'Uh-huh.'

'I'll get you a cold compress when Cherry comes back.'

On cue, she heard her say her goodbyes over the phone as she walked into the room. 'Kayla—'

At the sound of uncertainty in the usually unflappable Cherry, Kayla snapped her eyes open, immediately on her guard.

Cherry approached from the opposite side to Jamie and patted her shoulder. 'I don't want you to worry, but the midwife's been in an accident on the way over. She's fine but she's going to be a while longer.'

Concentrate on the breathing. One, two, three...

Jamie dropped her hand and got to his feet. She watched him pace the room with growing unease, rubbing his temple and doing his best not to explode at her.

Four, five, six...

'What happens now?'

'She's phoned an ambulance for you and explained what's happened. It all depends how quickly they can get here.' That deathly pale colour didn't suit Cherry at all. It wasn't her fault this had happened any more than it was Kayla's. No one could have predicted this. Except for Jamie.

'I could still drive you there. If that's what you want?' The pleading was there in his eyes for her to go with him. To make some effort to get help in case something went wrong with the birth. She understood why, but his peace of mind wasn't going to come before hers.

'No. I'm having my baby at home.' She kept her voice as calm and measured as she could, to let him know she was making this decision with a clear head. Despite having no pain relief or a midwife, she was still going to do this her way.

Instead of arguing with her, he turned to Cherry. 'Have you delivered a baby before?'

'No, I've seen plenty but it's not my job to get in the way of midwives or doctors doing theirs.'

'Doulas are there to support the mums, not intervene in any medical procedures. Generally, they're not qualified for that.' Kayla was but only because she'd worked as a midwife beforehand.

'I want to make sure we know what we're taking on here if the ambulance doesn't arrive before the baby does.' Unlike Jamie, Kayla didn't want to think about that, but it was a scenario they had to consider.

'All signs have pointed towards a healthy baby thus far. There's no reason why this shouldn't be a straightforward birth without complications.' If there had been any problems during the pregnancy she would've been the first to put herself in the hands of the doctors. Her wishes wouldn't come at any cost.

'Let's hope so.' His sarcastic, 'It's only life or death,' follow-up comment hung unsaid in the air between them.

'What about you, Jamie? Have you ever delivered a baby?' Thank goodness Cherry was here to provide a buffer between them and some common sense. In case any of them had forgotten in the heat of the moment, he was a qualified doctor.

'A long time ago and it was an emergency. No one's choice. Especially mine.' He could continue to argue if he wished but this was still happening. Her belly began to tighten, her body gearing up for another round of fun.

'You're a doctor, I'm a midwife. I'm sure we'll... manage.' She ended on a gasp, her breath stolen by the strength of the contraction.

'Good. This surge is powerful. It's a sign we're getting close.' It was the kind of positive language she used as a doula too, but not even Cherry's well-intentioned words could stop the sobs accompanying the now relentless stage of the birthing process.

She clung onto the fingers wrapped around hers but was dismayed to find they were Cherry's, not Jamie's. He was on his way out of the door, making her heart sink into the soles of her bare feet. If he left her now there was no chance they would ever work together as parents to this baby. Co-parenting required commitment and respect. Not stamping of feet until they got their own way. That went for her too. She might not have been ecstatic about his involvement, but he had earned his place here. If he still wanted it.

That dull ache at the base of her spine was becoming unbearable now. The groan she emitted was cathartic, but it was only when Cherry helped her into a position on all fours she found any relief.

'Where did Jamie go? I need him.' Everything around her shifted out of focus as she entered some sort of trance state, giving herself over to mother nature.

Her fevered forehead cooled with the application of a wet flannel placed against her burning skin.

'I thought you'd gone,' she managed, in between deep

breaths, and hoped she wasn't hallucinating Jamie's return to her side.

He furrowed his forehead into a frown. 'You want to give birth here so here is where I'll be.'

He seemed irritated she would think anything less of him, but he'd surprised her by compromising for her benefit so soon. She'd feel safer knowing he was on hand to help if no one else got here on time. Not that she had much time to dwell on anything but herself for very long.

'I can't do this any more,' she wept, wanting to collapse into a deep sleep and wake up when it was all over. Better still, to wake up and find the whole surrogacy idea had been a dream.

'You can't go back now. Don't worry, it won't be long.' He was saying and doing all the right things. It made a change from their constant battle to be top dog. Jamie was all right when he wasn't trying to take over all the time.

'Let's get her back against the cushions.' He even did as Cherry bade him and helped manoeuvre her when there was a reprieve from the contractions.

'I'll take this away again. I don't think it's helping much now.' He removed the not so cold flannel and rested his palm on her forehead instead.

'That's nice. You're nice.' The slight pressure along with his cool touch was equally welcome.

He brushed her hair away from her face again and repeated the soothing action until he'd nearly convinced her sleep was possible. Her body wasn't long in reminding her that it wasn't.

A strong pulling sensation tugged between her legs,

along with the urge to get into a squatting position. 'Give me a hand to get up, please.'

'Do you want to push?' Jamie moved front and centre, getting ready to deliver this baby who didn't seem to care who was, or wasn't, present for the arrival.

'Kayla doesn't want to traumatise the baby by forcing it out. The birth is to happen naturally.' Cherry was only repeating what her client had told her, but on this occasion, Jamie was right. Her body was telling her to push.

'I think it's happening whether I like it or not.'

'On the next contraction I want you to bear down. I'm going to have to push your nightdress up out of the way, okay?'

It wasn't as though she could give birth without him seeing her, so she nodded. He was a doctor and it seemed ridiculous for her to start feeling shy now. Then the pain reminded her she didn't care about anything other than getting this over with.

'We can get through this.' The other member of the cheer squad continued to rub her back, showing her support whatever decision Kayla made.

Both shouted their encouragement as she entered the final stage of her labour quicker than anyone had anticipated.

'Hold on to my shoulders and hurt me as much as you need to.' He made her smile with the sincere offer.

'I'll hold you to that.'

'It's a one-time deal. Only to be redeemed during labour,' he said with a smile, which disappeared with her own as she cried out again.

'Where is that ambulance?' He rolled up his shirt sleeves as she pushed down on his broad shoulders, using him as leverage to encourage the baby out. In any other circumstances a father delivering his own baby should've been a wonderful bonding experience, but this wasn't a normal set-up. With Jamie here, it made her feel less alone in her unexpected induction into parenthood.

'Close your eyes and see your baby emerging into this new world.' Cherry's voice was the calm in the storm, keeping her grounded when she wanted to scream.

'The baby's crowning. I can see the head. You're doing great, Kayla. Our baby's nearly here.'

Our baby. That nugget barely registered amid her fugue, but it was an important reminder all the same. This was Jamie's child too. No matter how unconventional the conception.

There was such a buzz in the room as they anticipated the moment they were all here for, Kayla dug deep for another burst of energy to push through the pain.

'Kayla, I need you to hold off on pushing for a while. Cherry, can you come and give me a hand?'

'Jamie? What's wrong?' She struggled to sit up. The atmosphere changed as Cherry and Jamie exchanged concerned glances. It was a surge of nausea that rose in her this time through fear she'd made a mistake by having the baby at home after all.

'The umbilical cord is caught around the baby's neck. I just need you to slow this down until I can untangle it.'

She'd probably seen and dealt with more occurrences of this than Jamie but that didn't stop her from visualising her baby suffocating.

'Panting breaths now, Kayla. There's no need to panic. Jamie's got this.'

The short, panting breaths Cherry coached her

through helped stave off that urge to push, giving Jamie time to work so baby's oxygen supply wasn't cut off to the brain. This was his baby too and he wouldn't let anything happen to it when he'd fought so hard to be here with her.

'That's it, Kayla. The cord's free now. When the next contraction comes, baby will be here.' It was the pride with which Jamie delivered the news that gave her the confidence that everything was going to be all right after all.

Jamie couldn't quite believe he was here doing this. Delivering his own baby. None of this was what he'd expected to happen when he'd signed on to help his brother have a baby with his husband. Yet he wouldn't want to be anywhere other than here right now, helping Kayla as she gave birth to their son.

'It's a boy.' His cry echoed hers as he caught the slippery bundle in his hands and all the emotion surrounding the moment and the lead up to it came pouring out. He'd lost his brother, but Tom had left Jamie with this precious gift.

'Is he okay?' The panic in Kayla's voice was understandable. His blood had frozen in his veins when he'd seen that cord threatening the life of this baby before it had even begun.

He passed the baby to Cherry, so she could hand him to his mother for that all-important skin-to-skin contact.

'He's beautiful. Congratulations, Mummy and Daddy.'

Jamie was exhausted and all he'd done was catch this determined mite. It was Kayla who'd done all the hard work. Yet her eyes were bright against her flushed pink skin as she murmured a loving hello to her firstborn. He'd never seen anything so beautiful.

'You did a fantastic job, Kayla.' The gentle kiss he placed on her cheek seemed only natural as he leaned across to coo over the baby with her.

'You too,' she said, giving him a shy smile before quickly looking away again.

Hopefully this was the beginning of the thaw between them that was needed so they could move forward as parents.

The repeated thumping on the door broke through the intimate family portrait as the outside begged to be let in.

'That could be the paramedics. I'll get it.' Cherry went to open the door and left them alone with their baby for the first time.

'I think he's got your lungs,' Jamie teased as baby Garrett voiced his displeasure at great volume.

'Hmm, well, he's definitely got his daddy's temper.' She teased him right back, comparing him to the red-faced, bawling tot cradled in her arms.

He didn't care when the casual use of the *D* word had hit him harder than her intended insult. Jamie was a daddy, now and for the rest of his life. Parenting was something he swore he'd never do again. It was a privileged position he had now only because his brother had lost his life.

His desire to live the rest of his life without responsibility for another life was no longer an option. The question now was to what extent he'd continue to play a part in his son's upbringing.

CHAPTER FOUR

'DAD, WOULD YOU like to cut the cord?'

It was one thing being a stand-in parent for his little brother, or a biological father who'd been ready to walk away from any responsibility. To hear someone give him that title and make him face the reality of deciding to raise this child was a whole new ball game. Jamie didn't know the first thing about looking after a baby other than what he'd read in medical books. He looked to Kayla for guidance before he answered the paramedic. It was down to her to make that call.

'I think you've earned that right, don't you?' She was glowing with happiness as she swaddled the baby in the colourful crocheted blanket he'd seen in the wooden chest along with the towels. He wasn't sure he had earned the right. Where Kayla looked natural as a mother, doubts and uncertainty suddenly clouded his judgement about his new position as a parent. With the playboy reputation Kayla had awarded him because of his inability to commit, he wasn't sure he'd make a good role model.

The judgement on his character did seem a little unfair. From the outside it might appear as though he was a love 'em and leave 'em kind of guy. However, his attitude towards relationships wasn't entirely as heartless as it might appear. He and Tom had suffered because of their parents' obvious mistake in having children. Their father had been selfish and not a man who should ever have considered having a family. It hadn't changed him. He hadn't suddenly stopped being an adrenaline junkie who preferred his own company in the outdoors because he had two young boys at home. Jamie had always been afraid of inheriting that selfish attitude and blighting some other youngster's childhood.

Oh, he'd raised Tom as best he could, but he was his brother and he'd had no choice. There was nothing to say he'd make a good father. Especially when his behaviour since Tom had moved out hadn't been conducive to family life. He wasn't as naïve as to think a child could suddenly change him from a carefree bachelor into a doting dad. It wasn't as though he'd been contemplating settling down into family life with a significant other. This was purely down to tragic circumstances beyond his control.

Although, he was thankful he'd been here during the birth for all manner of reasons. Not only because he'd provided the medical support at a time of potential danger but because it might have changed Kayla's opinion about him. He wanted her to see him as someone she could go on this journey with, not merely as an obstacle in her path. If he was going to do this, he would need her help to guide him on the journey.

'I'm so glad you guys turned up,' he joked with the male paramedic who passed him the scissors, entrusting him to cut the cord between mother and baby. Now he was out in the world it was down to Jamie and Kayla to protect him. A thought that did nothing to quell those rising fears about his suitability as a father to this child.

'Looks as though you did pretty well without us.' There was a slap on the back to accompany the compliment, but it was Kayla, not Jamie, who was the real star. She'd stuck to her guns and because of her tenacity neither she nor the baby were experiencing any after-effects from the pain relief routinely offered in hospital. He couldn't say he could have held out so long without begging for drugs to alleviate the obvious pain of childbirth.

The high-stakes delivery had made him sweat enough to need a shower, though he'd kept his worry from Kayla. She'd needed him to be strong and confident about what he was doing, even if it hadn't been the whole truth at the time. Panicking her could have jeopardised the baby's life when his oxygen had already been restricted. He knew how differently things could've turned out if he hadn't been able to untangle that cord.

'We're just going to give mother and son a check-over before we go.' The paramedic gave him a heads-up that they needed some space to work but Jamie was only too glad to hand over the duty of care to someone else.

'Sure. I think I'll step outside for some air while you're doing that.' Jamie left them to do their checks and walked out through the front door, which was still lying open.

Kayla had Cherry with her for moral support, so he hoped she wouldn't notice his absence. Up until everything had gone pear-shaped she might have welcomed it. He'd rather not have had to step in and take the place of her midwife, but he hoped it would change her mind about the kind of man she thought he was.

He set foot onto the pavement out front and the cool air woke him up to reality. A stumble over his own feet sent him reaching for support. He backed up against the wall, the world spinning around him.

He slid down until his backside was resting on the ground, his legs flat out before him. Some of that gas and air Kayla had been keen to do without would be the ticket for him right about now. It was easy to see why men were eager for a stiff drink after their baby was born. Especially if they'd had to deliver it themselves.

A few deep breaths later and the fear of passing out began to leave him. It wasn't so much the actual birth that had taken a toll but the emotional impact of the situation. He was a dad. He had a son. Kayla was going to be okay. There were so many good things to celebrate, yet everything was tinged with sadness that Tom and Liam weren't here to be part of it.

Jamie didn't realise he'd been crying until the tears dripped off the end of his chin and splashed onto the ground.

'He's perfect.' Kayla couldn't stop staring at her son. For the first time in her life she felt as though she'd really accomplished something. She'd made this perfect little human being. Not on her own, of course—Jamie had played a vital part both before, and during, the birth. There was a lot to thank him for. He'd provided excellent medical backup when she'd needed it and been a great accompaniment to Cherry with moral support. He was obviously more than a pretty face and a smart mouth after all.

At this moment, the baby was her whole world. He was her only family and the last link she had to Liam. She only wished he could have been here to meet him.

'Is it too early to discuss a name yet?' Cherry helped the baby to latch on for that first important breastfeed to give him the best start in life.

'I think I'll talk to Jamie first.' It was the least she could do to involve him in that decision, even if she would claim the final say on the matter. Naming the child was the first of the big decisions she'd have to make. Something he'd have to live with for ever. It wasn't a responsibility she took lightly when everything she did as a parent now could have repercussions later. Her parents' every action had impacted negatively on her and she didn't want the same for him.

Tom and Liam had agreed on waiting until the baby was born to name him.

'Until we see what he looks like,' Liam had insisted. They hadn't even wanted to know the sex beforehand, wishing to be *surprised*.

Now there was a part of her that wished they had been able to enjoy the excitement of knowing they'd have a son. If they had chosen a name she would have been able to honour those wishes now. As it was she didn't even know what surname he should have.

Although they'd joined their surnames when they'd married, O'Connell-Garrett might be too much of a mouthful to inflict on a child. There was also a fear that by giving him Jamie's surname he'd think he had more rights now than being simply the sperm donor. It was a minefield.

'We're going to head off now. You're both doing great but, remember, any problems at all and get down to the hospital.' The paramedics packed up their gear and, though she'd declined their suggestion of a check-up at the hospital, Kayla was glad they'd been here to deliver the placenta and give the baby the all-clear.

'Thank you so much for coming out. You'll excuse me if I don't see you to the door.' She was a little tender and her legs were wobbly, making walking anywhere a chore she wasn't ready to undertake yet. For tonight she expected to set up camp in her pillow fort.

'We'll probably see you again in a few years' time.'

It took a moment for her to get the joke but the thought of going through this a second time was the last thing on her mind.

'No chance.' She hadn't intended this to happen first time around. At least, not with her as the primary parent.

'That's what they all say.' The female paramedic all but pushed her jovial colleague out of the door and rolled her eyes in apology at Kayla.

With the outsiders gone, and only Cherry and the new arrival keeping her company, the house was slowly getting back to feeling like home. Even if there was a new, demanding male who was going to monopolise her time and thoughts for the rest of her life.

'Where's Jamie?' Surely, he hadn't run out on them already? He'd been an integral part of the birth and she expected him to be here. She needed someone who understood the loss she'd suffered and the mixed emotions she was experiencing now their baby was here. Jamie was the only one who could relate, and she was desperate to know if he was feeling the same confusion and fear about suddenly becoming a parent.

'I'm sure he'll be back. Now, I'm not confident baby's

getting anything. We might need to shift position a bit.'
As Cherry plumped the cushions around her and tried to
find a better position, the baby stopped sucking and let
out a yell, clearly displeased he wasn't getting enough
milk. His face was screwed up into a red ball of fury.
His shrill wails tugged at the very core of her brand-
new mothering instinct and she immediately wanted to
pacify him. He was in such a temper his gummy mouth
was too busy bawling to attempt a second time.

'Who's making all that noise in here?' The sight of
Jamie walking in lifted her heart and her spirits.

'I can't get him to latch on properly.' The smallest
act she couldn't do for her child somehow felt like a
failure. What if she couldn't do this any better than her
own mother and father and screwed his life up too as
a result? The guilt would suffocate her if she thought
she'd inflict the same pain on another human being as
her parents had done to her and Liam both physically
and mentally.

'You know yourself it can take time. Don't worry,
Kayla. He's not going to starve.' When she was doing
Cherry's job she told mothers the same thing, but it
was such a blow not to be able to mother him properly
straight away. Breastfeeding was a natural thing and it
shouldn't have been a problem for her. Not when she
coached other women on how to do it successfully.

'Tell him that.' No amount of cooing or cradling
would settle him. Every cry was a dagger in her womb.

'May I?' Jamie stepped over to take the baby whilst
she covered herself up again.

'Go for it.' He couldn't do a worse job as a father
than she was currently doing as a mother.

He very gently reached out to take the screaming

infant and tucked him into the crook of his arm. It was then Kayla saw the telltale red-rimmed eyes. He'd been crying. Perhaps he'd just realised what he'd got himself into as well. Although, it was a shock to discover there was anything serious going on beyond his sarcasm and the constant teasing. She hadn't even seen him cry at the memorial service for their brothers when she'd hardly been able to stand, she'd been so overcome with the loss and grief.

Jamie had taken care of planning that day, greeted the mourners and organised the caterers as though on autopilot. She'd doubted he could've loved his brother as much as she'd loved hers when he'd been able to carry on as though his life hadn't just crumbled around him.

Seeing him now, she wondered if he hadn't simply been strong for her sake. He'd gone outside to cry tonight where she couldn't see him. She'd never know if the tears had been through pride, grief or relief at the circumstances in which their son had entered the world. It was a sign there were layers to Jamie beyond the cocky façade. Unless he was simply feeling sorry for himself, having realised exactly what he'd committed himself to.

'You have to give your mummy a break. It's been a long day, and this is all new to us.'

If there was anything more adorable than a big man cooing at a tiny baby in his arms, she'd yet to see it.

As if he were stunned by the phenomenon himself, the young master's yells subsided to a whine. Typical. He was going to be a daddy's boy to a man whose obligation was supposed to have ended when he'd deposited his seed into a plastic cup.

All the raving Tom had done about his brother raising him might have been justified. If Jamie was a natural father, what did that make her? Where did it leave her? Perhaps there were things she could learn from him after all.

'Is there anything you'd like me to help you with, Kayla?' Cherry peered at her with concerned eyes.

If Jamie hadn't been here she might have broken down and admitted her fears about not being able to breastfeed. Since he seemed to have mastered his part already, she was reluctant to do so. She was the one with the hands-on experience with babies. Now she was worried all that practical knowledge and learning meant nothing when she hadn't had a great parenting role model from the start. It wasn't in her genes.

'I might need some help getting settled for the night.' Post-birth doulas were often used as practical support as well as a shoulder to cry on when needed but things such as housekeeping no longer seemed important in the wider picture.

'What about sleeping arrangements?'

'I…um… I—we haven't discussed that. Jamie had just arrived when I went into labour.' Since his concern had been centred around the labour and subsequent birth, the subject of his moving in hadn't risen again.

Jamie stifled a laugh. 'I think Cherry was talking about you and the baby.'

'Oh.' She was sure she'd turned the same colour as her frustrated, hungry baby.

Jamie made her flush further by adding, 'Yes. It's way too early to think about that yet,' with a wink.

Teasing a delirious, exhausted new mum wasn't something she was a fan of and so she didn't respond to him directly. 'Cherry, if you could give me a hand upstairs I think I'd like to sleep in my own bed. I'll keep the baby in with me for the night.'

She didn't have a partner to worry that co-sleeping would interfere in their relationship as some couples found.

'We could run you a nice bath first if Jamie doesn't mind babysitting?'

'Not at all. You deserve a relaxing soak.' The proud daddy continued pacing the living room, rocking his son in his arms as though he'd been born to do it.

Meanwhile, Kayla didn't believe she deserved anything more than an 'I told you so' after her plans for a peaceful home birth had nearly gone so disastrously wrong.

'Are you sure? He might need a nappy change.' That first one was always a sticky, dirty job and her wicked side wanted to leave him on his own to cope with it and expose a weakness. They'd been parents for five minutes and already she'd made it into a competition. One he was winning by a mile.

'I can manage. Go.' He shooed them away and got to work setting out the changing mat and terry-towelling nappies she had waiting to be christened. She didn't even mind missing this first milestone at home if it meant there was something less for her to fail at.

Kayla stepped gingerly into the bath, closed her eyes and slid down under the bubbles. Bliss.

'Do you think I can stay here until he starts university?'

'You might be a tad wrinkly by then.' Cherry passed her a flannel and busied herself organising some old towels for her to dry off with when she did eventually get out.

'I don't think anyone would notice.' She threw the flannel over her face and blocked out the world.

'What gives, Kay? You were so happy when I put that baby in your arms. Now you're acting as though you don't want him anywhere near you. This is me speaking as your friend who wants to help, not your doula.'

It was ridiculous to be jealous of Jamie, but he was unfazed by this life-changing event when she was just so overwhelmed and underwhelming when it came to actual parenting.

'Jamie is so much better at this.' She pouted beneath her cotton face mask.

'Based on what? That the baby stopped crying when he saw him for the first time? Damn, that man could stop traffic. I don't blame him.'

Kayla snatched the flannel away to give Cherry the full effect of her death stare. 'You're not helping.'

'It's natural to be tired and emotional. Giving birth is a big deal. As for the feeding, you have to persevere. You know all this.' Cherry soaped her hair with shampoo, the gentle massage as she rinsed reminding Kayla of Jamie's tending during labour.

'At the minute it seems impossible.'

'We'll get you settled into bed, then I'll bring the baby up and you can try again.'

The bath had helped her to relax but when Cherry helped her into bed all Kayla wanted to do was sleep. The renewed cries from downstairs reminded her that was going to be a thing of the past.

In the end Cherry didn't have to go anywhere. Jamie knocked on the bedroom door, the baby's increasing frustration over his mother's failure to feed him suffi-ciently echoing through the house.

'Come in.' She propped herself up on the pillows and hoped she looked more presentable in a clean nightshirt than when he'd last seen her.

'Hey. Sorry, but I think he's looking to be fed again.' With an apology, Jamie stepped into her bedroom and handed the baby over.

It seemed absurd in the circumstances that this should be the first time he'd set foot in here when they'd conceived this child together. However, if he was the only capable parent around here she might ask him to stick around for a while longer.

The baby grizzled against her, sending her anxiety levels into the roof.

'I'll leave you to it.' Jamie backed out of the room and it was on the tip of her tongue to ask him to stay. Even though he couldn't help her with this, his presence kept her grounded. He was the closest thing around she had to family now. Apart from this baby they'd created between them.

'Okay, let's see if we can get this little one sorted out.' With some assistance, Cherry got them into a nurs-ing position. His hungry mouth latched onto Kayla and she gasped at the first sharp pain. Any discomfort she experienced soon faded into insignificance when he began to feed in earnest.

'He's doing it!' She watched his angry face even out into contentment as he suckled.

'You did it.' Cherry's praise wasn't necessary to make her feel as though she'd achieved something, but it was nice to have someone witness and acknowledge the progress. Doing this one thing right helped her believe that there was a possibility of being a better parent than the ones she'd been born to.

'Knock knock.' Jamie returned carrying a tray and nudged the door open.

'He's feeding.' Kayla couldn't wait to share the news to prove she was capable of doing this job as mother as well as he was doing his as a father so far. It hadn't escaped her notice the baby had been cleaned, changed and smelled of those delicate baby products she'd lined up for his first bath. All without Jamie mentioning he'd done it or expecting some sort of accolade most men expected for doing the smallest of tasks. This was someone used to simply getting on with things.

'Well done, both of you. I thought you might need some sustenance yourself.' He set the tray down on the other side of the bed and handed a cup of herbal tea to Cherry. There was another for Kayla along with a plate of toast and jam. She'd never been so grateful for a snack in her whole life.

'That's very thoughtful, Jamie. Thank you.' She'd have to wait for the baby to finish feeding before she'd get to enjoy it.

'I'll take him, so you can eat.' Anticipating her dilemma, he threw a muslin square over his shoulder and transferred the baby, who was in a milk stupor.

'It looks as though you have everything under control here. Is there anything you'd like me to do? Do you want me to stay the night, Kayla? Jamie?'

It would be easy to say yes and keep her friend here as long as possible. To have her at hand the second she had another wobble in confidence. Although it wasn't going to help her acclimatise into her new role if she had someone doing everything for her.

Kayla did a lot of work with parents after birth to continue providing support whether it was doing household chores or minding baby while they napped. However, she didn't want Jamie to think she couldn't manage. She owed it to Liam, Tom and the baby to be the mother he needed. They'd never wanted strangers involved in raising this child. Now she was the only one left she didn't intend to renege on that. Even if it meant doing it alone.

'I don't think that will be necessary.' It was Jamie who rebuffed Cherry's offer before she had a chance to do it more subtly.

'Kayla?'

Doulas, although not wishing to cause any unrest between parents, were employed primarily for the mum's benefit. Therefore, it came as no surprise when Cherry deferred to her for confirmation she was in agreement.

'I think I'll be fine for tonight. I'm sure the midwife will be calling around tomorrow to check on us too. If I need anything I can phone you.' She'd keep her phone by the bedside just in case. Cherry and Debbie lived only ten minutes away should she find herself overwhelmed by the prospect of motherhood once she was left alone.

'We'll be fine. Thank you, Cherry.'

'We?' If Jamie thought making some tea and toast was all it took to allow him to bulldoze his way into her life, he was mistaken. Any decisions concerning the baby, or the running of the house, were hers to make alone until he proved she could trust him enough to include him.

'I'm not about to go and leave you here on your own. You've just given birth and you're exhausted. Plus, there's the whole "being the dad" thing. I'd like to spend some time with my son, if that's okay with you?' Jamie thought they'd been making progress up until now. He was doing his best to show her it would be better for her to let him play his part and do this together.

That wasn't to say it was easy for him. He might have raised Tom, but he'd done so after he'd been weaned and potty-trained. The poo-nami he'd dealt with downstairs had made him feel mildly queasy but what kind of dad would he be if he couldn't even change a nappy without supervision?

Mind you, Kayla seemed more impressed by the snack. If such a small act, or thought for her welfare, had become such a big deal it was no wonder she had trust issues. There was no doubt in his mind that Liam and Tom would've looked after her, but now there was no one. With them gone he didn't want her to retreat into isolation. Neither of their brothers would have forgiven him if he walked out on her when she needed him most. He'd simply have to work harder on bonding with her as well as their son.

'I—uh—'

'That sounds great, Dad. You can be on hand for the practical things Kayla needs through the night. Call me, Mama K.' It was beginning to feel as though he had an ally in Cherry when she was pushing for him to be included too. Perhaps he'd been too quick in disparaging her role when Kayla took more notice of her doula than her baby's daddy.

'Mama K' wasn't as peppy as the new nickname suggested as she merely grunted her reluctant acceptance.

'I'll see you out, Cherry. You and junior stay where

you are.' He ignored Kayla's scowl, knowing Cherry would have agreed with him on the matter anyway.

It was a picture he'd never known he'd wanted to see but suddenly the image of the mother of his child cradling their son in bed was everything. Regardless that Kayla didn't want anything to do with him, that natural instinct to protect them had already kicked in.

It was probably for the best that they'd never made it into bed that afternoon at the coffee shop. Now he'd seen her give birth to his child they had a special bond. One that couldn't be forgotten about in favour of any desire he might have harboured towards her. He could never bed her now and relegate her to the list of women he'd hope to never cross paths with again in case it developed into something serious. This already was serious. Kayla and the baby were his world now. There was no way he was going to complicate that by letting attraction get in the way of this new family dynamic. He was a dad now and the best thing he could do for his son was be better than his own. That entailed putting aside his own wants and needs to focus on those of his son.

'If there's anything at all you need, don't hesitate to get in touch. I know she's stubborn but hang in there. She needs you more than she'll ever admit to.' With a hug and a kiss on the cheek at the door, Cherry disappeared into the darkness, leaving Jamie as backup for the night.

He trudged back up the stairs, bone-weary but with adrenaline still pumping through him after being called into action. If he was confused about his thoughts and feelings around the birth, he could only imagine what Kayla was going through too. Not that she would ever share it with him, he supposed. Something they'd have to rectify if there was any hope he could give her the support she needed to raise this child between them.

The two were asleep when he crept back into the bedroom. He kicked off his shoes and eased himself onto the mattress with the baby lying between his parents.

'What are you doing?' Kayla snapped her eyes open at once.

'I'm just lying down. I can watch the baby if you want to get some rest.' He thought about the fact he'd crawled into bed beside her without an invitation. Being the baby's father didn't give him the right to do that and he could tell by the dark look Kayla was shooting his way that was what she was thinking too.

'I can go if you'd prefer?' He sat up again before his head managed to touch the pillow.

She hesitated but not for long. 'No. Stay.'

'Thanks.' He rolled over onto his side and rested his head on the inside of his arm, so he could watch his son sleep. Kayla was doing the same.

'I think he has your colouring,' he said, marvelling at the tiny blond eyelashes resting against his pale skin and the tuft of golden hair on his scalp.

'You think?'

'Definitely.'

She smiled at that. Both Kayla and Liam were fair whilst he and Tom were darker. He used to joke with the two men that they looked like an angel and a demon when they stood together.

As much as Jamie would be pleased if their boy resembled his mother more, he hoped to see some resemblance to his own family. A reminder he wasn't alone in the world.

'I hope, somehow, we can see a bit of Liam and Tom

in him too. Does that sound stupid?' It seemed Kayla was on the same page as she reached out and lifted the baby's hand on one finger.

'Not at all. That's what I was thinking too. Maybe he'll have that touch of red in his hair I used to tease Tom about.'

'Or Liam's cheeky charm. That one could talk his way out of anything.'

'We'll keep them alive no matter what,' he promised, knowing how important that was to both of them. This child would grow up knowing how amazing his uncles were even though he'd never get to meet them.

'We can't keep calling him "the baby" for ever. It's important he has a name and an identity.'

'What? You're not going for James Junior? JJ for short.'

She shot him down with one of those looks that could wither a rose from a hundred yards. 'No.'

'Seriously though, do you think we should name him after our brothers? William Thomas?'

Kayla wrinkled her nose. 'I don't think it would be fair on him. It would be kind of weird too, calling out my brother's name when he's not here.'

'Good point.' It would probably rip their hearts out to have an everyday reminder of their loss and it wasn't the baby's fault. He shouldn't have to feel guilty he was here when they weren't. Something which surely would have to be explained when he was at an age to understand the circumstances in which he'd been brought into the world.

'What about something they liked?'

'I'm not calling my son Rioja.' They'd both loved

to party in their younger days but had settled down in preparation for a parenthood they'd never got to enjoy.

'I was thinking more along the lines of musicals or films.'

'They were both sci-fi geeks. Didn't they meet at that convention?'

'Yeah. They did love their cosplay. I can only imagine the outfits they'd have made for this little one.' That shadow seemed to move in again, clouding over the sunshine that had come into their lives. He supposed it was always going to be this way. Every joy they found in their son was going to be tinged with grief. Unless they could somehow marry the two and be reminded of the fun times they'd had with the guys.

'What about Luke? I vaguely remember a late-night conversation when they were discussing possible baby names. I think that was one of the ones they'd favoured for a boy.'

'Luke.' Kayla sounded the name on her tongue whilst studying the sleeping babe between them. 'It suits him.'

Her approval of his brainwave made him feel as though he was contributing. He'd take that victory and leave the question over the surname for another day.

'Baby Luke it is, then. When he's old enough we'll do a photo shoot in costume together. We'll make it fun and honour Tom and Liam in our own way.'

'If you think I'm wearing a skintight bodysuit purporting to be some sort of body armour you've got another think coming!'

He hadn't considered that, but now that was all that was on his mind. It would be a boyhood dream come true to have a girlfriend dress up in a superhero outfit. Jamie stopped himself from saying something along those lines and ruining his chance of being part of this family for good. When had he started seeing Kayla in a different light from simply being the oven for his brother's surrogate baby, anyway? Probably around the time they'd first met, and she'd treated him with such unexplained disdain. He'd always enjoyed the company of feisty women when that passion often carried on into the bedroom. Where they were now. With their baby.

'I'll wear the bodysuit, then, and really give us something to laugh about.'

He succeeded in doing just that when she chuckled. 'I'll look forward to it.'

She stopped laughing at his expense and looked so deep into his eyes the mood changed between them again to something more charged. 'Thanks, Jamie.'

'For what?' As far as he could see she was the one who'd done the hard work.

'For being here. Despite my attempts to get rid of you. I'm glad you didn't listen to me.'

'Stubborn, is what Cherry called you.'

'I stand up for what I believe in. I don't think there's anything wrong with that.' She sniffed, not finding any humour in her friend's description.

'Not at all, but not everyone is out to hurt you either. Some of us simply want what's best for you.'

'That may be true…on this occasion. It doesn't mean you'll get away with it in future.' The warning was there for him not to try and walk over her wishes again in future. He knew better than that, but he wouldn't apologise for stepping in when he deemed it necessary. Like tonight.

'Noted and understood.'

For a while they lay in silence listening to the soft

snores of their sleeping son. Jamie was overcome with a surge of gratitude and admiration for the woman whose bed he was sharing. He watched her fight sleep, her eyes fluttering open and closed until they finally shut tight. She was bound to be exhausted and he wasn't going to leave her here to parent alone when there were two of them to share the workload. It was the least he could do in return for the son she'd given him, for the family she'd created with him and for honouring his brother. Best of all, she'd permitted him to be part of her life. An honour he wouldn't take for granted.

He reached out and brushed his knuckles across her cheek, barely touching her warm skin.

'Thank you, Kayla.' He leaned across, careful not to disturb Luke, and placed a kiss where his fingers had touched her cheek. She let out a little moan and snuggled deeper into her pillow with a smile.

For a man who'd sworn off taking on more responsibility in his personal life, he couldn't think of anywhere else he'd rather be than in bed with Kayla and his newborn son.

CHAPTER FIVE

KAYLA WAS HALFWAY between sleep and consciousness. She knew she had to open her eyes, face the day along with her new responsibilities, but sheer exhaustion kept dragging her further down into the bed. She was so delirious she'd even imagined Jamie kissing her last night. It had been so vivid she could still feel the gossamer-light touch of his mouth on her skin.

The show of affection, even in her imagination, had been welcome. It had gone some way to assuaging her fears she was a rubbish mum when she'd spent most of the night feeding, or trying to feed, Luke. Her full, aching breasts were a reminder of why she had to wake.

Those mothering instincts forced her to peel her eyes open. Only to find the other side of the bed empty. She scrabbled to sit up, scouring the room for evidence of her baby.

'Luke? Jamie?' He'd stayed with her through the night, leaving her to feed in private but there for nappy changes and tea-making. Invaluable, but that didn't give him just cause to take her baby away without her consent.

Barefoot, she padded along the landing calling his

name, a rising panic fluttering in her chest overshadowing any other physical discomfort.

Jamie had been insistent about being a dad to this baby. What if he'd waited until she'd fallen asleep and taken Luke?

She picked up her pace and started down the stairs. 'Jamie? Have you got my baby?'

He ducked his head out around the living-room door. 'He's in here, sleeping.'

Not even a finger placed on his lips could stop the rage inside Kayla unleashing in a verbal torrent. 'How dare you? How could you scare me like that? You had no right to take him without my say-so.'

Her whole body was shaking as she faced him, standing halfway down the stairs. She should never have gone to sleep and left him with the baby. Luke was her responsibility and Jamie couldn't sneak in and take that from her when he wanted.

Jamie stared back at her, mouth agape, apparently unable to give her an explanation. In her current mood she didn't care how cute he looked with his half-flattened hair, wrinkled shirt and morning stubble. Since she was the mother, she was the one who'd take care of this child on their brothers' behalf.

'I've told you once already to get out of my house. Don't make me say it again.'

Her threat shocked him back to life.

'Kayla, calm down. I only moved him so you could get a better sleep. You were up half the night feeding him.' He didn't reference his own lack of sleep, which was apparent by the dark circles under his eyes, but that didn't make her any more susceptible to his obvious charms.

'That's my job. To feed him.' At the same time she heard the baby wake with a shrill cry, she felt the dampness on the front of her nightdress as her milk came in. Nature proving the point on her behalf. It was impossible for her to deny her responsibility to this child she'd brought into the world.

'I'm not disputing that.' Jamie sighed as she pushed past him at the bottom of the staircase on her way to retrieve her son.

'You don't have to do this on your own, Kayla.'

'I do.' Liam wasn't here any more, and she'd have to get used to that. He'd been her lifeline through childhood, taking punishments on her behalf and deflecting their parents' negative attention from her when needed. If it weren't for him loving her she might have believed she deserved every bad thing that had ever happened to her.

It was him who'd talked her into going to London in the first place, subsidised her through her midwife training and sympathised when the job wasn't what she'd expected. Liam had been the one to get her out of her toxic relationship with Paul and convince her to start the career she wanted as a doula. Now he was gone she'd have to learn to stand on her own two feet. Apart from Luke, she was alone in the world. For his sake she had to be strong and stop relying on someone who was no longer there.

She lifted Luke out of his basket and undid the front of her nightgown to feed him. Jamie turned away. She knew she could've been more discreet while breastfeeding but this was her home. She shouldn't have to cover up. If he didn't like it, he could leave.

Rather than do that, he stormed across the living-room floor and flopped into an armchair. 'Why does everything have to be a battle between us? You're the most infuriating woman I've ever met.'

'Probably because I won't let you get your own way.' She stroked the top of Luke's head, watching with satisfaction as he fed greedily. It seemed between them they'd figured this thing out.

'This isn't an either-or scenario. We are both his parents and should be working together. I thought we were trying to make this a partnership?' He leaned forward, resting his arms on his knees, his head hanging low. In fact, he looked as defeated as she'd felt not so long ago. If it hadn't been for him giving her a hand in the small hours of the morning she probably wouldn't have slept at all. All he'd been guilty of was doing his best to alleviate some of her burden.

Despite her resistance he was still here. Either he was trying to wear her down to take over when she was at her lowest ebb, or he was being honest about his motives—he simply wanted to be a father to Luke. Something that she didn't have the right to deny either him or her son.

'It's Liam and Tom who should've been here, working together to raise him. When they died, I accepted that I'd have to parent alone. You were never part of the equation, Jamie. By your own choice.'

'Something I've told you is no longer an option for me. I can't walk away from my son. We're going to have to come to an agreement.'

The hairs on the back of Kayla's neck stood up on end at the hint there could be a fight for custody brewing.

'What is it you want, Jamie?' There was no point

dancing around the subject and wasting time. She couldn't dispute the fact he was the father and had rights over his son.

'I want to move in with you. At least until he's settled into some sort of routine.'

That was it? As much as she didn't want him barging into her life, a temporary housemate would be preferable to being dragged through the courts for access.

'What about work?'

'I'm entitled to paternity leave and I have some holidays to take if necessary. I'll make arrangements with the partners at the clinic.'

'If I agree, it doesn't mean you're entitled to try and take over in here.' She wanted to make that very clear.

'That's not what I want. If one of your clients' husbands said he wanted to help out more, what would you suggest?'

He'd found her Achilles heel, using her own advice against her. There was one way to take advantage of support being offered to new mums, but it involved handing over one of her main jobs as Luke's mother.

'To make sure mum's getting plenty of rest.'

'What could we do to increase the opportunity of rest for you in this situation?'

At the moment she was nothing more than a milk factory for her offspring. It seemed by the time he'd finished a feed it was time for the next one. There was no way of telling if he was getting enough at a time. They couldn't keep on in this fashion for ever. The lack of sleep alone would have her crying over his crib every night beating herself up for failing to keep him satisfied. There was nothing to lose and everything to be gained by dispensing the same advice here as she gave to her clients.

'I could express some milk and you could do some of the feeds.' She conceded defeat and prayed he wouldn't take advantage now he had one foot in the door.

Jamie was going to move in and co-parent with her. Only time would tell if she was doing the right thing in letting that happen. It could be that she'd just invited someone else into her life who'd quash her free will by trying to impose his upon her.

It had been four weeks since Luke's arrival and Jamie had moved in. His life was as upside down as he'd known it would be upon stepping up as a father. It wasn't as though he hadn't known what he was in for after going through this once before with his little brother. As at that time, he hadn't planned for his life to take that route now either. He hadn't even anticipated staying with Kayla this long. Hell, most of his relationships hadn't lasted this length of time. Apart from the one with Natalie, which had proved he was just as selfish as his father, not taking anyone's feelings into consideration except his own.

However, Kayla had needed him, someone, to share the load with. Sleepless nights and what seemed like a constantly hungry baby had taken a toll and though they were living in the same house they were like zombies barely registering their surroundings at times.

He might have found it easier if they were married and children were something they'd committed to together as husband and wife. If he'd planned his life around having a young family. It was difficult when your world was turned upside down in a heartbeat.

Babies weren't something you could return like unwanted gifts.

Now his son was here, of course Jamie wanted him, loved him, and would do anything for him. That didn't mean it was easy. Especially when he was continually trying to prove to Kayla his worth too. It was stress upon layer of stress, but he knew it had to be the same for her too.

She hadn't asked for him to be parachuted into her life either but now they needed to make the most of the situation they were in. Together.

Something she was struggling with, along with trusting him. The concessions she'd made thus far he knew were only because she was exhausted. He was determined to show her he wasn't the man she'd believed he was when they'd first met. Not any more.

'There you go, buster. All clean again.' He picked up from the changing mat the wriggly bundle who was smelling a lot sweeter than he'd done five minutes ago.

Cherry came out of Kayla's room at the same time he left the nursery.

'Hey. Is everything all right?' He was every bit the anxious partner as well as the doting dad. With Luke content and snuggling into his neck, he wished he could do more for Kayla too. The neck snuggling was optional.

'I think she's more like her old self. I'm hoping she's moving past the baby blues, but we'll keep an eye on her.' She wasn't telling him anything he hadn't noticed himself. Kayla had been weepy, which wasn't unusual for new mums with hormones going haywire. Also grieving for her brother, with no other family around to support her. Except for him, who she wasn't overjoyed about having around.

Add to her very emotional circumstances a fussy feeding baby, it was no wonder motherhood hadn't been full of rainbows and unicorns for her so far. It would be easy for a parent to throw their hands up and say they'd had enough, walk away without a backward glance. He thought of his own father, who'd never enjoyed the ups or downs of family life, and realised it said a lot about the strength of a person to hang in there even when parenthood seemed overwhelming. She might not see it now, but he knew Kayla was tougher than his military-trained father. That made her the best mother Luke could want.

'I've taken over doing some of the night feeds, but I think she's a bit resentful of that.' By getting her to express milk so he could bottle-feed Luke, it should've eased some of the pressure on her, but it wasn't working out that way. He'd asked Cherry to come over and have a chat with Kayla since she didn't seem to want to open up to him.

'It's common for new mums to think they've somehow failed by letting a partner help with the feeding. The best thing you can do is to persevere and maybe get her out of the house if you can. Try and get some normality back. I'll pop by for visits when I can too.'

Jamie led her out of the house, her words swirling around his head as he sought an answer as to how best to serve Kayla. The trouble was this wasn't *normal* for either of them. They were learning how to be a family as they went along.

It would take doing something together, something

beneficial to their arrangement, for them to bond. He'd have to think like Kayla to figure out what that might be.

'A baby massage class? Seriously?' If Jamie had suggested they went down to the register office and got married Kayla couldn't have been more surprised.

'I thought it might be good for Luke, and us. It's supposed to help bonding and attachment, as well as a host of other benefits.' He handed her a computer printout as evidence of his covert research.

'I know all about it. I'm just surprised you do. I didn't think you were on board with that sort of *hippy-dippy nonsense*.' Jamie was surprising her more every day. Not least because he was still here, changing nappies, cooking meals and giving bottle feeds when required. They were the actions of a man who simply wanted to do his bit.

Yet, she couldn't bring herself to trust his motives and be thankful for him being here. To her, it represented her failure as a mother. Luke wasn't settling with the bottle-feeding either.

'It can't do any harm, can it? It will get us out of the house for a while at least.' As he was already strapping Luke into his car seat for the journey, he wasn't leaving her much of a say in the matter.

'My company's that bad, is it?' She hadn't been herself since Luke's birth, but she wasn't likely to be ever again. From now on her every decision, her entire life, revolved around this new arrival.

'No, but we need to introduce this little one to the outside world some time. This is our chance to do some family bonding.'

Family. It was a word, a concept, capable of striking

fear and longing into her heart at the same time. She would've loved to have had a family of her own, but her childhood experience had turned it into something to be wary about. It was more than biology, it was that feeling of belonging, love and support she'd had with Liam and Tom.

She didn't know if the significance of the word was the same for Jamie or if it was merely a throwaway comment.

Instead of dwelling on it, she chose to focus on the bonding aspect of the classes he'd joined on their behalf. 'They do say that the one-to-one time during baby massage helps parents recognise their baby's needs. I'm willing to try anything which will make me a better mother.'

It was an insight into her vulnerability she hadn't intended to share but one he'd surely seen for himself recently.

Jamie stopped packing the changing bag with baby essentials to look at her. 'What on earth would make you say such a thing?'

Kayla fussed around Luke, making sure he was well covered before they transferred him out into Jamie's car.

'Let's face it, the breastfeeding hasn't exactly been a resounding success.' If it had been she wouldn't have conceded so easily to the idea of him moving in.

Jamie let the bag fall from his shoulder and walked over to her. She didn't want to make a big deal of this with him and wished she'd kept it to herself in case he used it as ammunition against her later. He rested his hands on her shoulders, the importance of touch reaching home when the gentle pressure was a reminder someone was there for her. Even if it wasn't the brother she'd shared so much with. The only person who'd ever truly loved her.

'You are an amazing mum. Don't ever think different. You've fought for everything you believed best for Luke.'

'That hasn't always worked out either, has it?' She thought of the home birth, which could've gone so wrong, and the breastfeeding, which had. The shame was so great she couldn't look him in the eye. She was a fraud who'd made out she was the expert when, really, she had no clue when it came to raising her own baby.

'Hey.' He cupped her face in his hands and forced her to look at him. The concern for her, the sincerity she saw in his eyes, were unexpected. Perhaps she'd expected him to gloat, or, as she'd seen with other partners, pretend there was nothing wrong.

In that moment she wanted him to hug her, kiss her softly and reassure her everything was going to be all right. The way she'd been imagining him doing in her dreams these past weeks.

'That's enough of that talk. Where's my ballsy earth mother who'd walk over hot coals before letting anything defeat her?'

It was kind of nice that was how he saw her. Dared she say it, even complimentary?

'She's here somewhere. Under layers of baby sick and mum tum.' To say she wasn't at her best was an understatement. She was always telling her new mums not to be so hard on themselves and not to worry about stretch marks and weight gain when they'd just produced another human. It was different when you saw the changes in your own body.

In the scheme of things her appearance was the least

of her worries, but she wasn't herself any more. She was aware of that every time she glanced in a mirror. It didn't help her self-esteem knowing Jamie was witness to her gradual decay. His comment highlighted the fact he'd noticed the changes himself. How could he not?

'Kayla, Kayla, Kayla. What am I going to do with you?'

It was a rhetorical question but, when he was still touching her, her mind went to some interesting places regarding what she wanted him to do with her.

A quiver of desire shook her body and for a split second she thought she saw a flicker of interest cross his face too. Then Luke squawked a reminder that he was there, and reality hit home. How could anyone be interested in a woman with unwashed hair wearing yesterday's dirty clothes?

She pulled away, suddenly self-conscious and feeling foolish. Hormones. They could be blamed for everything. Along with the amount of time she was spending with him. He was right. They did need to get out of the house.

'Ignore me. That's what you should do.' She lifted the baby carrier with an *Oof*. Her tiny son was heavier than he appeared.

'That's not something easily done,' he muttered under his breath as he reached out and took the weight from her. 'You shouldn't be straining yourself. No arguments.'

She didn't dare when he swung the baby so easily with one muscular arm. They needed a crowded-room intervention before she started having fantasies about all his other body parts too. Her permanent state of exhaustion lately had curtailed her less than platonic thoughts about him. When she was awake, at least. Her dreams, on the other hand, had become so X-rated it was difficult to separate them from reality. More so when he was parading around her house half naked in the mornings.

'I guess it's time for master Luke to make his introduction into the big wide world. Baby massage, here we come.'

This was about her son, their bond and doing whatever she could to make him happy. It was not a turning point in her relationship with Jamie simply because it was his idea. Or because her body was reminding her there was more to her than being a mum. She was a hot-blooded woman too.

CHAPTER SIX

'WELCOME, EVERYONE. As you may or may not be aware, baby massage is an ancient tradition. It's not simply a new trend the hipsters have latched onto.' As the instructor, Jocelyn, addressed the class, Kayla gave Jamie the side-eye. She knew he'd only done this for her, not because he believed it would be of any use to them.

He kept his gaze straight ahead, but the corner of his mouth tilted up in amusement.

'We're here to promote health and security in our babies. Massage has been known to aid sleep, circulate and alleviate digestive conditions. Best of all, it provides a relaxing experience for baby and parent, reducing stress. So, if you'd like to get started you can lay baby down and lay them on the towels you've hopefully brought with you.'

'Here goes nothing.' Jamie took a couple of towels from the changing bag and spread them out on the wooden floor, leaving Kayla to remove Luke's bumblebee-embellished sleep suit. The room was sufficiently warm she didn't have concerns he'd be too cold.

'Please don't worry if baby needs to be fed or changed during the class. They're our priority here so do what you have to to make them comfortable without judgement.' The woman taking the class did her best to calm the fears of any anxious parents and Kayla was glad she wasn't the only one who might be out of her depth here.

'He's been fed, winded and changed but I can't guarantee he'll enjoy this.' She was surprised to find she was the more sceptical one about what this was going to do other than stress her out if she wasn't doing it right.

'We've got nothing to lose.' Jamie shrugged, and she prayed he was right.

'Okay, mums and dads, we're going to start with the legs. Using a little of the oil you have, I want you to wrap your hands around baby's thigh and, with one hand at a time, pull down in a "milking" motion.' Now that did sound weird even to Kayla's ears.

Her raised eyebrow was mirrored by Jamie's, with added smirk. Nevertheless, she performed the massage on both of Luke's legs.

'Good. Now moving on to the feet, gently rotate each one this way and that. With your thumb I want you to stroke the top of the foot right down to the toes. Then, trace circles over the soles of the feet. Finally, we're going to take each toe between our finger and thumb and stroke those too.'

Luke was slippery beneath Kayla's fingers, but he seemed content lying there as she caressed him. She could hear some babies complaining and the instructor encouraged the mums to cuddle them until they settled back down again. There was a small burgeon of pride that they were doing okay compared to a few of the others present.

Jamie was kneeling beside them on the wooden floor, observing and whispering encouragement to her and

Luke. It didn't seem fair to leave him on the periphery when he was the father, and this had been his idea.

'Why don't you do his arms?' she suggested as they were asked to repeat the process.

'Are you sure?' He confirmed she was happy in him participating before he shuffled over on his knees and squeezed a few drops of oil onto his hands. As he massaged their son's dainty arms Kayla was aware of the size of him in comparison. Those large hands enveloping the tiny limbs, capable of doing so much damage, were nothing but tender and loving. Her stress levels were reducing by the second watching him soothe their baby.

So much so, she let him carry on with the chest massage they were given instructions for too.

'Stroke your hands out over baby's chest. With a flat palm at the top of his chest, stroke gently downwards.'

Kayla was mesmerised by Jamie's rhythmic actions and his concentration. This wasn't a demonstration to impress her, or a bid to fool her into thinking he was someone he wasn't. This was a father caring for his baby. She'd seen much of it these last weeks, as well as his kindness towards her. The issue of their baby's surname and his father's details on the birth certificate had yet to be addressed but every day she spent with him earned him a more permanent place in his son's life.

'Jamie, I think—' Her attempt to broach the subject was interrupted as their baby took direct aim at Jamie's chest with a forceful stream of urine.

'Luke! Really?' There wasn't much Jamie could do other than stem the flow with a hastily positioned towel, but his once white T-shirt was already stained with baby pee.

'It proves he's definitely relaxed,' she pointed out in between peals of laughter.

'Glad to see you two are enjoying it.' His wide smile said he was being genuine, and the incident hadn't bothered him at all.

Although, Kayla wouldn't have minded if he'd felt the need to strip off too. Living together had provided numerous opportunities for her to view him *sans* shirt. The sight of a toned male torso wasn't something she'd thought she needed in her life until it had become the highlight of her morning. Such a contrast to the barely-made-it-out-of-bed-today look she offered in return.

She tossed him a pack of baby wipes and a clean towel. 'Dry yourself off and I'll take over with our little piddler.'

'I swear you two planned this behind my back.' He dabbed at the stain on his shirt, giving them a mock scolding. It was clear Jamie was going to be a pushover when it came to their son for real. She wasn't sure she'd be any better when she adored him so much.

'We wouldn't do anything to embarrass Daddy, would we, Luke?' It was the first time she'd assigned him the title out loud and the world hadn't ended. Accepting Jamie as Luke's father was the right thing to do. More than that, it was good to know she had someone to share all this with. She wasn't alone after all.

As she turned Luke over to massage his back, there was a gentle pressure on hers as Jamie rested his hand on her. 'You don't know how much it means to hear you say that.'

That delicious tingle of awareness that accompanied his touch reached up to tickle the back of her neck.

'I've been thinking about making it official. It's

about time we registered Luke's birth, don't you think?' She scooped up the now sleepy source of their amusement and love and faced his father.

'I would absolutely love that.' Jamie's eyes were sparkling with bright tears, the move as significant to him as it was to her.

There was no going back now. Once he was named on the birth certificate Jamie would be part of Luke's life for ever. And hers.

Jamie was on cloud nine as they left the class. Despite his son christening his new T-shirt. The class had gone better than he'd ever expected when it had prompted Kayla into a conversation about the birth certificate. When she'd first called him 'Daddy' when talking to Luke, he'd have sworn his heart stopped momentarily at the shock. This was getting real. He'd achieved what he'd set out to do and ensured his place in Luke's upbringing. With that came a lifetime duty to take care of his son.

He'd been so hell-bent on getting Kayla to accept him as Luke's father and cement a place in his life, he wondered if he'd really considered the implications. Once his name was on the birth certificate it was official. He was a dad. The consequences of not being a good enough parent were something he'd lived with his entire life because of the selfish actions of his father. He wouldn't intentionally do anything to hurt Luke but the onus on him to be a better father than his own weighed heavily on his heart.

That carefree existence he'd anticipated once Tom had become independent was now a thing of the past. He hadn't thought much about his own future beyond making up for his lost youth. Now the only one available to him was here with Kayla and Luke. He hoped it was enough for him. That he was enough for them.

'What's all the noise?' Kayla drew his attention away from self-pity back to the cacophony of sound out in the hallway liable to undo their hard work in getting Luke to sleep.

'It's probably the next class. Baby yoga. I looked into that too, but we'll have to wait until Luke's older and you've had your six-week check-up.' He'd researched lots of classes before he'd settled on baby massage. It had been hard work finding something to suit them that was also something he was willing to participate in. When Kayla was up to it she might join some of those singing classes where they all sat in a circle singing nursery rhymes to oblivious infants, but he wasn't that much of a happy-clappy chappie. At least not in public.

'You'd be willing to do yoga with us?' Her incredulity at the prospect after he'd demonstrated he was prepared to do almost anything for them hurt feelings he wasn't aware he had. Here he was committing the rest of his life to looking after his son, yet Kayla clearly still didn't trust him to stick around. After a month of her getting to know him, seeing him doing his best for this family, he expected her to think better of him. Otherwise what was the point of him being here?

'Sure. I'll order up some yoga pants specially,' he said, with a lot less enthusiasm than he'd had when he'd started this quest for a family-bonding activity.

'Now that I'd like to see.' Her interest in seeing him in the unforgiving tight fabric stopped him from wallowing too much.

'You would?' His spirits lifted further as she blushed

ferociously, realising what she'd said. Perhaps she had been paying him more attention than she'd led him to believe.

'I'm joking. Is it getting hot in here? Maybe we should get out of this stuffy room.' The more she bustled around Luke, collecting his belongings and pretending she hadn't encouraged Jamie to parade around in skintight pants, the funnier he found it.

'Maybe we should stay. I could strip down to my boxers and you could watch me do the downward dog, if that's what you're into.' It seemed so long ago when he'd teased her at the wedding, but now he remembered why he'd enjoyed it so much. He made her flustered and to him that suggested she wasn't impervious to that attraction he'd felt towards her since day one. Perhaps, subconsciously, that was part of the reason he'd agreed to participate in the surrogacy when it cemented a connection between them they might have otherwise avoided.

She tutted but didn't outright dismiss the idea.

By the time they were ready to leave, the rest of their class had already gone, and the new attendees were filing in. It was a much more animated and vocal group who replaced their sedate gathering. Mostly down to the age of the younger participants, who were mobile and giving their parents the runaround.

'I think the object of this class might be to tire the kids out, along with all that well-being and inner-calmness stuff.' The chaos of temper tantrums and crawling, falling little ones was a scary insight into what the future held for them. He could see the same realisation in Kayla's wide eyes as she watched it unfold around them too.

'Fingers crossed it works, for the sake of their poor

mothers.' It was obvious her focus was on the harassed parents chasing their offspring and trying to get them to sit on the mats provided for the session.

Jamie noticed there were several using reins, with one end tethered to the child and the other around the mother's wrist so they didn't wander too far. He thought they'd be better using one of those retractable dog leads instead. Then the rug rats could be reeled in at the touch of a button. He didn't share that thought with Kayla in case she deemed it inappropriate and saw the joke as a gauge of his parenting skills.

'At least we only have one to contend with.' His eye had been drawn to the twins in the corner who had hared off in different directions as soon as they'd come through the double doors. Little blond heads bobbed up and down as one jumped on the yoga mats whilst the other picked something up off the floor.

'Lena, sweetheart, what have you got in your mouth? Let Mummy see.' Lena's mother edged cautiously towards her daughter as though approaching a skittish fawn, then launched herself like a lioness to wrestle the unidentified object from her cub's mouth.

'Goodness. You'd need eyes in the back of your head to manage those two.' Kayla followed their escapades, her head turning left and right as though she were at a tennis match.

'Yeah. Maybe I should go and see if she needs a hand.' If he and Kayla were finding aspects of parenthood hard to handle, he could only imagine what it was like to have two toddlers and apparently no one to help out. He was sure the rewards outweighed the parenting trials, as he was finding out for himself, but that didn't mean a person couldn't use a hand sometimes.

He set the baby carrier beside Kayla and headed towards the mother to offer his assistance, hoping she wouldn't be as offended as the mother of his son tended to be when he wanted to help.

It was on his mind whether or not to introduce himself as a GP or a parent when there was a loud thud from the far side of the room.

'Billy!'

'Jamie!'

Both mum and Kayla drew his attention to the hurdling tot who'd been temporarily left unsupervised.

They all ran towards the child, who was lying motionless on the floor. Jamie winced as he realised that thud had been his head hitting the hard wood. It had been loud enough to stop all the other chatter in the room as everyone else looked on in horror.

'Billy? Someone help me. He's not breathing.' The distraught mother was kneeling over her unconscious child, with the other one caught under her arm. She attempted to lift him up and Jamie was quick to step in.

'Stop! Don't move him. Let me assess him first.' He could see the fear flicker in the mother's eyes and she was frozen, unsure of what to do.

'Jamie's a doctor. He knows what he's doing.' Kayla gently encouraged the mother to come away and let him get on with examining her son.

'Billy? Can you hear me? My name's Jamie. I'm a doctor. I need you to open your eyes for me.' There was no response. He was careful in tilting the child's head back and lifting his chin in case there was a neck injury but opening his airways took priority. There was no chest movement and no sign, or sound, of him breathing. He turned to the women standing close by. 'I'm going to have to perform CPR.'

He didn't have time to react to the anguished cries of the mother, but Kayla had that in hand as she reassured her everything would be okay.

'Everyone, I think it would be best if you all go outside. We don't want to upset the other children.' She addressed the room too whilst Jamie started rescue breaths.

Jamie pinched Billy's nose closed between his finger and thumb and opened his mouth a fraction. With a deep breath, he placed his lips around the child's, making a tight seal. He blew and watched the little chest rise. When he broke the seal, he watched the chest fall again as it would if the child were breathing normally. Jamie took another breath and repeated the process.

He heard Jocelyn, the instructor, shoo everyone out of the door and footsteps as she walked over to the scene.

'I've phoned for an ambulance. Let me take these little ones out of your way so you can focus on Billy.' There was no objection from Kayla or the other mother as she walked away carrying Luke and holding Lena's hand.

'This isn't working.' The five rescue breaths hadn't done anything to get him breathing on his own again.

Unprompted, Kayla knelt down beside him and began chest compressions. Positioning herself above the baby, and with her arm straight, she placed the heel of her hand on the lower part of the breastbone. Making sure the pressure wasn't applied over the ribs, she pushed down.

They exchanged glances. No words were needed for

him to know she was thinking the same thing as him. They needed to save this child's life. It could easily have been their own baby. Would they be so calm then and able to provide the same medical assistance?

Jamie had known from the second he'd become a father it wasn't only his personal life that would be affected, it was going to influence his work too. He would relate better to every overwrought parent who came to him worried about their own health or that of their children. Each child he treated now he was going to compare to his own son and what he would do in the same circumstances. Being a father would make him a better man and a better doctor all because of Luke. A child he wouldn't have if not for Kayla and their brothers.

'No sign of life,' Kayla confirmed as she ended the round of compressions and he got ready to perform more rescue breaths.

'Let me know if you want me to take over.' He knew how exhausting it could be to continue CPR until an ambulance arrived; he'd had to do it several times over the course of his career. There was no telling what experience of this situation Kayla had. It was easy to think her work as a midwife and a doula only involved delivering babies. Whilst childbirth in this day and age wasn't as risky as it had been in previous decades, there could still be serious complications. All of which Kayla had demonstrated she could cope with, given this life-or-death situation she was handling so professionally.

On a personal note, it was nice to have that physical and mental support. He was so used to doing things on his own—from raising Tom, grieving for him and even down to working out of his own office in the clinic—it was a wonderful new experience.

A partner wasn't something he'd ever really considered. He figured another person in his life would simply entail more responsibility, more demands on his time. Kayla was beginning to show him there were benefits to having someone to share these moments with. It reminded him he wasn't alone and gave them a common bond they could chat about together later. Letting another person into his life might not be as bad as he'd always imagined. He wanted to make Kayla feel the same way when it came to raising Luke.

Despite this new revelation, Jamie was still aware of Billy's mother sobbing nearby, Kayla counting with every compression, and, more importantly, the sirens outside in the distance.

'Checking for signs of life present.' He called it before they repeated the process, praying they could get him breathing on his own rather than simply keeping his heart circulating blood around his body.

As they sat back Jamie tried to block out the white noise around him and listened for any gasping, watched for any movement. Slowly, Billy's chest began to rise and fall by itself. He checked his pulse and the sense of relief to feel it beating faintly against his fingers made him choke on the emotions of a new dad saving the life of someone else's baby.

'He's breathing!' Kayla spotted the signs too and quickly passed the information on to the anxious mother.

Between them Jamie and Kayla turned Billy onto his side, into the recovery position, and continued to monitor his breathing in case they had to administer further CPR.

'Mummy's here, sweetheart.' The mum sat down beside the child and stroked his forehead, tears streaming down her face. Kayla put her arm around the woman's shoulders and squeezed. Jamie could see she was crying too. He wasn't far from it himself. Later, when the shock kicked in and he was nursing his own son to sleep, reality would probably hit home. At least on this occasion he had someone who'd gone through it with him to talk it over and process what had happened.

'The paramedics will take over from here and get him to the hospital for a check-up,' he managed to croak out, his throat dry and aching from trying to hold it together.

'I'm sure he's going to be fine. Jamie and I will call the hospital later and find out how you're all doing.'

'I can't thank you enough. I dread to think what would've happened if you hadn't—' The woman's voice cracked as she contemplated the consequences.

'We *were* here and he's breathing on his own again. Everything's going to be all right.' Jamie didn't have to spend too long convincing her as the paramedics came rushing in to tend to their tiny patient.

He and Kayla got to their feet and let the crew take over once they'd passed on the relevant information concerning Billy's condition. They were both in a hurry to get out to their own son to check up on him, but it was fair to say they were both a tad unsteady on their feet now the adrenaline was subsiding and shock was setting in. All the other parents had left, with only the class instructor remaining, holding Lena's hand and carrying Luke in the other.

'I thought it would be best to send everyone home.'

'Good call. There's no point in getting the other kids distressed. I doubt anyone would want to go ahead after that anyway.' There was no way people would manage to be serene and do a yoga class after that. It was going to take quite a while for him to calm down and get his heart rate under control.

'Billy's going to be okay. We got him breathing on his own but they're going to take him in the ambulance to the hospital just in case.' Kayla swung Luke up into her arms and snuggled into him. Jamie would wait his turn, but he wanted that physical contact with his son too for reassurance he was safe.

'Oh, thank goodness.' Their temporary babysitter clutched at her chest. 'I have first-aid training myself but I'm glad we had professional medics present to save him.'

The ambulance crew came past with Billy's mother following close behind. 'Thanks, everyone, for all your help. I'll take Lena with me to the hospital. Their dad's going to meet me there.'

'Take care,' Kayla called after them as Lena tottered off hand in hand with her mother, clutching the lollipop that Jocelyn must have given her to pacify her during all the drama. At least the twins would have two parents at the hospital to share the responsibilities. He guessed childcare was something he and Kayla were going to have to figure out around their work schedules. Although, she'd probably be taking as much maternity leave as she could for now.

'I think I'll go and make us all a strong, sugary cup of tea. We need it.' Jocelyn got no argument from him but as Kayla was about to voice her objection, he stepped in.

'Caffeine and sugar for the shock. Doctor's orders.' Then they could go home as a family and thank their lucky stars they all had each other.

CHAPTER SEVEN

WHAT KAYLA WAS realising about parenthood was that she had to set aside any impending meltdown and continue with the baby's schedule as normal. Rather than hyperventilating over what they'd been part of at the yoga class, she had to feed Luke, give him his bath and put him down for the night before she could even analyse what had happened.

'That's what I call a mad day,' she said as she dropped down onto the sofa beside Jamie.

'It was intense.' Jamie kicked off his shoes and opened the takeaway cartons sitting on the coffee table in front of them. The healthy-eating plan had taken a back seat these past days as they got used to their new routine. Although Jamie had been cooking for her, and it was tasty, it wasn't her usual menu. It was a stretch too far to expect him to cook tonight too when the events of the day had left them both drained. He'd gone out for Chinese food instead and as she sucked up the noodles in her vegetable chow mein she was glad they'd decided on a takeaway. It gave them some much-needed time out for the rest of the evening.

'And scary. I'm glad Billy's going to be okay. Thanks for phoning the hospital and checking up on him. I don't think I would have slept otherwise.' Even though he'd been breathing on his own, there was always that worry something could happen and his condition could deteriorate. The reassurance could tick one thing off her worry list even if there were other things troubling her.

'Nor me. I think I've got new-dad hormones going on.' Nothing seemed to be affecting his appetite as he helped himself to a huge forkful of unidentified meat in an unnatural red sauce.

'Really? You were so cool today, as though you weren't fazed at all.' The way he'd dealt with the emergency so confidently and efficiently, she'd convinced herself that getting upset about a patient was unprofessional of her. It was Jamie's stoicism that had got her through the incident when she'd been thinking about Luke the whole time they'd been trying to revive Billy.

'Are you kidding me? Life or death isn't something I take a casual attitude towards. I had a job to do—it was simple as that. Remember, it was you who did the chest compressions, and he wouldn't have come back if not for that too.'

'It was a team effort, I suppose. It's just…you seem to be doing so much better as a dad than I am as a mum.'

'How do you figure that one out?' He set his cutlery down and frowned at her, waiting for her to explain herself and expose her weakness.

'You've had experience with Tom and you've dealt with the dirty nappies and feeds better than I have.' It took a lot to admit that to him and open up about how useless she thought she was in comparison. To have him laugh in her face wasn't something she was prepared for.

'Is that what you really think? Listen, I was Tom's

big bro, not his parent. I might've been the one to cook his dinner and take him to school, but I certainly wasn't on call during the baby years. As for the rest, I messed up there too sometimes. I didn't know how to raise a child any more then than I do now. That first night with Luke, man, that was a steep learning curve. I think the world fell out of his backside. His clothes were so badly stained I had to throw them out. I cleaned him up and put a new sleep suit on him so you wouldn't think I was incompetent. It was important to me that you thought I was up to the job.' He ducked his head and looked up at her with those big brown eyes.

It was her turn to laugh, but more out of disbelief that he'd been as out of his depth as she'd been. 'Why have we been torturing ourselves pretending that we know what we're doing?'

'I can only speak for myself here, but I was afraid if I didn't measure up you'd give me my marching orders.'

It wasn't an outlandish notion when she'd been so hostile towards him and resentful of his position in her son's life. 'I'm sorry I made you feel like that. I know what it's like to live under a constant threat.'

She took a sip of her water, her mouth dry at the mere thought of her parents. Jamie deserved an explanation of her behaviour when it had been misdirected at him at what should have been the happiest time of his life. 'My mum and dad were very strict. I don't know if Liam ever discussed them with you?'

He shook his head. 'All Tom told me was that they'd disowned him when he told them he was gay, and he didn't like to talk about them. So I didn't. I figured that kind of people weren't worth wondering about.'

One thing in Jamie's favour was that he didn't have

a homophobic bone in his body. It was refreshing after growing up in a small village where Liam had been constantly gossiped about and shunned when they were younger. 'Trust me, they're not.'

'I take it you're not in contact with them any more? They weren't at the memorial service.'

'As a rule, I don't have anything to do with them. My conscience got the better of me though, and I did phone to let them know about the accident. They made it very clear that they didn't care.' The emotion of that conversation, at least on her part, threatened to spill out again. Her throat was raw as she fought to quell the bitterness back inside. Jamie didn't need to know they'd said their brothers had died because of their 'sinning'.

'I'm so sorry. That must've been a hard call to make.'

'The worst,' she said through a strained smile.

'Do they know about Luke?' It was a reasonable assumption that a child's grandparents would want to be part of his life, but her parents weren't reasonable or kind. Nor were they the kind of people either of them would want in their son's life.

'No. I swore that day I'd never contact them again. Trust me, you wouldn't want them anywhere near Luke. My father ruled with a firm hand, my mother with a cruel tongue. Between them they kept us terrified in case we did anything to upset them. That's why I was so against you being involved. I don't want anyone to have control of me like that ever again. You seemed like a threat to that, barging in and demanding access to your son.'

'I had no idea. I'm so sorry. Losing Tom was like the end of the world and I just wanted something, someone to cling onto. I wanted my family back.' He stared at his hands and Kayla knew he was thinking about his brother and all the things they would no longer do together. She did it herself every time someone mentioned Liam.

'That was why I agreed to the surrogacy. I couldn't see that I would ever find a man I'd completely trust to enter into that kind of serious relationship where I'd want a child with him. I made the mistake of getting involved with someone who took advantage of my history. He manipulated me and changed me into someone I didn't recognise. Someone weak who was desperate to please him with no thought to her own needs. It's been hard for me to trust myself, never mind another man. This was supposed to be the easy way out.'

She'd been naïve. They all had. A baby was a serious commitment and a responsibility for life. He wasn't going to solve all of her issues with her parents and the control they'd exerted over her. It was down to her to move past it all so her son wasn't tainted by her legacy. She didn't want Luke growing up afraid to love, or share his life with someone, because that was what she instilled in him.

'I'm sorry, Kayla, and I can understand that to some extent.' Jamie scooped up some rice along with the bright red concoction, leaving Kayla waiting for him to finish so she could hear how he related to her tragic lack of love life. From everything she'd heard, Jamie Garrett was never short of a woman in his bed. That was part of the reason she was wary of getting into any sort of a relationship with him. Even a platonic one. She hadn't seen the point in setting up a family dynamic if he'd take off the next time a woman caught his eye.

However, he'd shown a commitment to Luke these past days that went beyond mere bragging rights.

She watched him swallow, then take another forkful of food. Unlike him, she couldn't eat another mouthful until she heard the rest of this story explaining what made him him. 'I don't know much about your personal background except that your parents passed away when Tom was young.'

He took the hint to continue and paused with the food halfway to his mouth. 'They weren't bad people. Dad was in the army so we didn't see that much of him. Even when he was on leave he was an outdoorsy kind of guy. You know, he went away on hiking trips a lot. He was a bit of a loner and probably shouldn't have had kids. He had a climbing accident, broke his neck in a fall. Mum died about five years later when Tom was eleven. She had a stroke and never recovered.'

'That's horrible. I'm so sorry. You were all so young.' It sounded as though the family had been blighted by tragedy and now he'd lost Tom too. Life could be so fragile, and unfair. She'd found that out with her brother's death. Even though she didn't have a relationship with her parents, she could understand how great a loss Jamie had suffered to date. It was a testament to him that he'd been able to carry on when they'd been orphaned and assume guardianship of his brother when he'd been barely an adult himself.

'There was never really any time to process each event. After my dad's death I stepped up to be the man of the house, keeping Tom in line and taking care of bills and things. When Mum went it was only natural I took on both parenting roles. Losing Tom has been the toughest time of my life. I'm not sure I'll ever get over it.' He pushed his food away, his appetite apparently leaving, and Kayla knew it was her fault for bringing up painful memories.

'I'm not sure we're supposed to. Death changes the people left behind but I think it's important we carry on and live the life our loved ones never got to have.' She expected Luke was going to make that easier. With a child in her life she had no choice but to carry on for his sake and get up each morning to start afresh. Her mind might take a while to catch up in leaving the past behind, but outwardly she was determined to try.

'I can't help thinking that I wasn't there for Tom when he needed me most. Perhaps I was too giddy about the idea of being a single man free of responsibilities to think about the danger he and Liam were putting themselves in out there. I should've warned them what they were doing was reckless, instead of celebrating my bachelor status. Even though he was a grown man, I don't think I stopped taking care of him until he and Liam got married.'

'There was nothing you could have done, Jamie. They wanted one last adventure before they settled into family life and we wouldn't have begrudged them that. What happened was a tragedy, an accident that no one could have foreseen.' She'd torn herself apart too, wondering if she could've done anything to prevent their deaths, but no amount of guilt or apportioning blame was going to bring them back.

'I was too self-involved. At that time of my life I wasn't taking anyone's feelings, other than my own, into consideration. Including yours. I'm sorry for the way I behaved at the wedding. My ego got a little out of control for a while there, realising I was still attractive to the opposite sex despite my advancing years.'

'You're hardly ancient.' She didn't want to tell him there was no need to apologise when his forthright manner at the wedding had awakened emotions, sensations in her she'd given up on ever having again. Once she'd realised relationships were never going to work out for her, she'd thought she'd shut them off, considered them a waste of energy. Clashing with Jamie at the wedding had made her realise she wasn't dead from the neck down.

Perhaps having her eyes opened to the fact she was still open to a man's attentions had scared her into the surrogacy deal. Knowing once she was pregnant her focus would be completely on the baby and she wouldn't leave herself vulnerable to another doomed romance. That had been her get-out plan. Until their brothers had died and brought Jamie back into her universe, along with that resurfacing chemistry it was getting harder to deny lingering between them.

'Why, thank you.' He smoothed his hair back with his hand, feigning an arrogance she now knew wasn't the real Jamie.

'You're handsome, single, with a medical career. Why wouldn't women find you attractive?' Despite trying to be casual, she felt her cheeks burning with the heat of the admission she was one of those women.

'Wow. So many compliments tonight. You'll make me blush.'

It was Kayla who was blushing furiously as he teased her. She tried to play it cool with a roll of the eyes. 'I'm serious. Are you telling me you haven't had your fair share of advances from smitten women over the years?'

'I didn't say that.'

Was it her imagination or were his cheeks a little pinker than usual? Kayla experienced a twinge of jealousy imagining a string of gorgeous women chatting up the father of her baby. It was possible this living together and raising a child had fostered the idea in her head that they were in some sort of fantasy relationship when, really, circumstances had forced them together. There was no reason she should have any claim on him when he wouldn't be within a hundred miles of her if not for their son.

'Yet you never sought to get married and have a family of your own. Why now?'

'When Tom was growing up I didn't want him to take second place the way we had when our dad was alive. I was dating someone, Natalie, but I didn't have the time or energy to commit long-term. Inevitably she got hurt when she realised marriage wasn't on the cards even though we weren't more than kids ourselves. Since then I've found a brief dalliance here and there avoids the drama. I wasn't a monk, but for a while there I was going through some sort of delayed adolescence. The one I missed out on.'

It was a heartfelt admission on Jamie's part that he had been the playboy she'd suspected, at least for a while. The important question on Kayla's mind now was which Jamie she was currently shacked up with, because there was only one of those characters she was interested in having around.

'So, you're back in parenting mode…but what happens when you do meet the woman of your dreams? Will Luke remain your top priority?' She didn't want her son to suffer for the sake of his father's libido should he lapse back into his Lothario alter ego, or if he started a new family with a woman he truly loved.

'I have no plans for any more children,' he answered with a lopsided smile. 'Even if I did, I can promise you Luke will always be my number one.' He said it with such sincerity and conviction she believed it. Whilst she was glad for Luke's sake he would always have his father, she was heart-sore that there was no mention of her in his priorities. She wasn't his partner in a romantic way but, as co-parent, she would still be part of his life in some form. Whilst it didn't seem relevant to him, she was already coming to terms with having him around. She'd miss him if he suddenly met someone else and relegated his parenting duties to unsupervised weekend visits.

'I'm kinda getting used to having you around,' she confessed, in case he was still in any doubt about that.

'Good.' He held her gaze a fraction too long until the hairs on the back of her neck began to stand to attention, her body flirting with the idea his interest in her might go beyond their mutual offspring after all.

She glanced away first, her imagination doing nothing to make her life any easier. Jamie might not seek to control her, but neither was she going to let emotions or desire dictate her actions.

'I'll take these away—'

'Why don't I tidy these up—?'

They both reached for the discarded takeaway cartons on the table at the same time. Their hands accidentally grabbed one another but it was some time before either let go. Kayla's heart skittered in her chest, barely taking the time to fully form each beat. How desperate it would make her appear for affection if she turned into a Regency era heroine who swooned at the mere touch of a man's hand.

'Be my guest. I think I'll go on to bed. Don't worry about waiting up. I'll take the first shift with Luke and you can get some sleep.' Somewhere that wasn't her bedroom. A place where she wouldn't be sleeping any time soon.

'If you insist. It has been a long day.' He didn't argue the way he usually did, always elevating her need for rest above his. Perhaps he was keen to get away before she did make a scene and embarrass herself.

Kayla didn't hang around to dissect her reaction to him any further. Instead she peeped in on Luke, who was still sleeping soundly, and retrieved her nightdress from under her pillow. She disappeared into the bathroom to change into the strappy, satin nightgown she'd taken to wearing instead of her mumsy nightdress. It was cooler and made her feel more like a woman than a mere baby machine. She almost convinced herself it was nothing to do with how she looked to Jamie as she brushed her hair in the mirror until it shone.

Teeth brushed, and with her recently removed clothes in her arms, she opened the bathroom door and ran straight into Jamie. A bare-chested Jamie, clad only in boxers.

Her carefully folded pile of laundry tumbled to the floor as she came face-to-pecs with his smooth, taut, hypnotic torso.

'Sorry, I didn't realise you were in there.' He seemed genuinely surprised to run into her, but he didn't step back to let her past. His eyes travelled over her bare shoulders, assessing her new look, and when his gaze dipped down into the V of her black chemise Kayla was powerless to disguise her reaction this time. Her nipples hardened into tight buds, swollen against the silky fabric and garnering further attention.

'I'm finished now. It's bedtime. For me, I mean.' By spelling out the sleeping arrangements she'd simply guided him to where her own thoughts were headed.

'Well, goodnight, then.' As though it were a nightly tradition, Jamie dipped his head to place a kiss on her lips. Kayla stood up on her tiptoes, keen to receive it.

Eyes closed, she revelled in the slight brush of his mouth against hers. It reminded her of those gentle kisses of reassurance she'd enjoyed in her dreams, night after night.

'Night,' she said when it ended, forced to open her eyes and come back down to earth.

Jamie didn't move, his eyes still trained on her mouth and the atmosphere between them crackled with awareness and desire. She was frozen to the spot under his hungry eyes and her need for more than those few seconds of his touch. There was a fleeting compulsion to reach out and pull him down for an encore, but she resisted in case it jeopardised their current non-warring status.

She let her hand fall to her side. It would be more useful lifting her discarded clothes from the floor. 'I suppose I should really pick those up,' she said, staring up at his mouth and marvelling at the way it fitted so perfectly around hers.

'Yeah,' he said, 'you really should.' Then he wrapped an arm around her waist and yanked her towards him, knocking her off her feet.

His mouth was hard on hers this time, punishing her for this inconvenient attraction, yet demanding more of her. Kayla heard a satisfied sigh escape her lips as her body melted onto his, leaving him to support them both. The flat of her hand was braced against his chest, so hard and warm beneath her fingertips she shuddered with the solid contact. Jamie's response was to pull her closer, his hand sliding up and down the small of her back and sending darts of desire everywhere he touched.

Kayla clung to his shoulders with both hands to keep her upright as he deepened the kiss. He lashed his tongue around hers, fighting for dominance when she was happy to surrender to his will on this one occasion. Every part of her was aching with need for him, especially when she could feel his body's rock-hard confirmation he wanted her too.

'You've just had a baby,' Jamie rasped, his throat sounding as raw as hers felt holding back emotions she was afraid to unleash in the heat of his kiss.

'Your baby.' It almost seemed unbelievable now when they were just getting to know each other that she'd already borne him a child. If she'd had any hint of this passion available to her they might well have conceived the easy way.

Despite their obvious chemistry, she couldn't completely block out that ingrained instinct telling her to be wary of letting her guard down. Nothing had changed in her head simply because Jamie had kissed her; relationships were still going to be a problem for someone who had difficulty trusting a partner. The one she already had with him as Luke's father wasn't something she could afford to mess up. It was more important for her son to have a dad than it was for her to have some ill-fated affair with the nearest man available to her.

Even if she wasn't still recovering from the birth, she knew this couldn't go any further.

The sound of Luke's cries from across the hall interrupted Jamie's path as he moved his lips across the edge of her jaw. He stopped just before he kissed that sweet spot behind her ear that made her knees buckle with the right man. Physically, Jamie Garrett felt very much like the right man, but no such being could possibly exist for Kayla in real life.

'I should go and feed him.' Her body was for sustaining her baby now, not feeding her need for intimacy.

Jamie took a step back, putting some much-needed distance between them. He fought to get his breathing, and the rest of his body, back under control. It wasn't easy when she was standing in front of him with kiss-swollen lips, the strap of her nightdress falling down to expose her soft, pale skin and looking thoroughly ravished.

The signs had been there for a while that something was fizzing between them. Lingering looks, that personality clash gradually turning into mutual respect, and lying in bed together watching their son sleep had all been building up to that kiss. It hadn't disappointed. That release of finally satisfying his craving was short-lived. Now he'd tasted her full lips, had her soft flesh moulded around his body, he wanted more. All of her. Walking away now was like trying to stuff a cork back into a still-fizzing bottle of champagne, yet he knew he had to. Neither her body nor her soul were ready for that. He wasn't sure he was.

After Natalie he swore he'd never lead another woman on believing there was something more to their relationship than he was willing to give. It was Kayla's strength that drew him. That stubborn streak that said she didn't need him was intoxicating to a commitment-phobe. Yet, getting involved with his son's mother would be the ultimate lifetime commitment. Something he just couldn't give.

'Give me a shout when you want me to take over.' Although Jamie didn't want her to bear the brunt of the childcare and sleepless nights, he might make an exception tonight. He needed time to process what had just happened and why he'd instigated that kiss. The spontaneous passion they'd just submitted to wasn't something easily dismissed or forgotten.

After everything she'd gone through he didn't want to betray the trust Kayla was already putting in him by letting him stay here in the house. He'd never been in the market for a family and although he now had a son, he couldn't promise her for ever. That was what it would take for a woman like Kayla, who'd been taken advantage of too often. She needed support, not someone else using her for what she could give him. Kayla wanted to be the best mother she could for Luke and he didn't want to get in the way of that.

Jamie had been doing things on his own for too long to suddenly have to share his world with someone new. He was just trying to get his head around being a father and all the responsibility and disruption that entailed. There was no way he could be a partner, a boyfriend, or whoever Kayla needed to help her move past those trust issues created by her parents.

Not when he had his own to deal with.

CHAPTER EIGHT

KAYLA YAWNED AND STRETCHED. She actually felt as though she'd had a proper night's sleep. The first since Luke had been born. A glance at the clock told her it was seven-thirty a.m. That was a lie-in as far as she was concerned. He'd slept better too, his body clock seeming to adjust since he'd taken fewer feeds through the night.

It was like waking up on a bright summer's day even though she'd yet to open the curtains. Not only was she rested but, thanks to Jamie, her dreams had been full of stolen kisses and passionate embraces. She was definitely starting the day on a high.

Even though they'd both probably come to realise they'd made a mistake, the memory of that one erotic moment would put her in a good mood for the rest of the day.

He'd been so good to her and Luke, she daredn't jeopardise that by getting carried away by one kiss. It was probably the longest he'd gone without female company of the intimate kind and he'd merely wanted to make sure fatherhood hadn't killed his pulling power. Certainly not with her anyway.

She coupled the lazy smile on her face with another stretch. Jamie must've taken Luke downstairs again so as not disturb her. Now she'd stopped searching for ulterior motives in his every action she could see how thoughtful he was.

Lying on her back, staring at the ceiling, she wondered if she was supposed to lie here until her assistance was required with the baby. Perhaps he intended to surprise her with breakfast in bed. She rolled over onto her side, ready for a second sleep when she heard fidgeting in the room, followed by a baby grizzling.

'Luke?' Sure enough when she peeked over the side of the bed into his Moses basket he was just beginning to stir. 'Time to get up, lazybones. I wonder if Daddy's slept in this morning too?'

Luke gazed up at her with familiar big eyes. 'You look just like your daddy. Don't tell him I said it, but you'll have the girls queuing up at your door when you're older.'

She scooped him up, cherishing this quiet moment, both contented to be where they were. There was only one thing missing from this family scene. 'Why don't we go and see if Daddy's up yet?'

Jamie was always keen to help bath Luke and two pairs of hands were always better than one.

'Jamie? Are you up yet?' With Luke cradled in one arm, she knocked on his bedroom door. When there was no reply she eased the door open, but the bed had already been made and the curtains opened.

'He must be downstairs. We'll sneak down and surprise him.' She rubbed Luke's nose with hers. This was what mornings were for, long lie-ins and playing with their son.

She tiptoed down the stairs, careful to avoid that one step that squeaked near the bottom and might give her away. It was starting to feel like a family home again and she couldn't wait until Luke was old enough for them to play hide and seek properly.

Suddenly, the thought of him being able to play those carefree childhood games that had been unavailable to her under her parents' roof now held so much significance. They'd hated noise. When she and Liam had been permitted to play, they'd had to do so under the threat of violence in case they were too loud. Although her brother had constantly challenged their rules and rebelled against the strict regime, Kayla had always tried to be on her best behaviour, afraid to upset them. It had taken moving to a different country to break that pattern and she didn't want another generation of her family to be tainted by messed-up parents.

Whatever happened with her and Jamie, she wanted her son to be happy, to have fun and, most of all, feel safe in his own home. There was no reason why she couldn't start doing that for him from now. Once they were fed and dressed it was time to go out and have some fun.

'Jamie, why don't we take Luke out for a walk in the pram?' She wandered into the kitchen, convinced his silence would be explained once she found him tucking into breakfast there.

Except the kitchen was empty. There wasn't as much as a dirty dish left as evidence he'd been there. She walked over and touched the kettle. It was cold. This was beginning to feel as if she were living in a mystery novel. Then she saw a note stuck to the fridge using the blue dragonfly magnet Liam had made for her out of polymer clay, holding it in place.

Didn't want to wake you two sleeping beauties!
Gone to work to catch up on some paperwork.
See you later, J

A stone dropped into Kayla's stomach. So much for her happy family day out. Jamie had sneaked back to work without a word. Not even a kiss on the note. As if last night had never happened. Perhaps that was why he'd gone this morning before she'd had a chance to see him. He regretted it.

Kayla knew anything more than being Luke's parents was probably a bad idea, but she didn't regret the kiss when it had been so amazing, so real. If it was going to change things between them she needed to know now for Luke's sake as well as her own. They couldn't provide a safe, loving home for their son if his father kept avoiding his mother over one lust-fuelled misadventure. She didn't want either of them to live with that sort of uncertainty and refused to be emotionally manipulated by anyone again, no matter how unintentional.

'Well, little man, it looks as though it's just you and me. If Daddy doesn't want to spend the day with us, it's his loss.'

'Everything looks great. You have a very strong boy here. Absolutely nothing to worry about, Mrs Hills.' Jamie put the baby's nappy back on as soon as he was able to after giving him a thorough check-over. He knew all too well what could happen when his son had christened most of his shirts during changes.

'Thanks, Doctor.' Ellie, the health visitor at the clinic, lifted the clothes they'd stripped off the baby earlier and attempted to take over.

'It's fine, I can get him dressed. I've had plenty of practice lately.' He didn't have anything else to do anyway. The staff had been shocked to see him this morning and, since there was a locum in situ in his office, he was surplus to requirements. With the baby clinic on this morning he'd volunteered his services to Ellie rather than return home.

He was being a coward, he knew it, but he'd needed to get out of that house and that world he and Kayla had built for themselves there. It wasn't real life. As demonstrated last night with his unprompted make-out session with Kayla. It didn't matter she'd apparently been holding back too, given her equally animalistic response to the kiss. This morning he'd made the decision to come into the surgery and back to some semblance of normality. He and Kayla had been living on top of each other taking care of Luke, and he was worried it was clouding his judgement. They'd become each other's world and that was possibly why they'd suddenly acted on that attraction that had been there since the wedding. Neither of them was in the right place for a serious relationship and that was the only type available to them now they were parents. A fling would make things awkward when it ended, and they still had to make decisions and time together for their son.

'Dr Garrett has just become a father himself,' Ellie explained to her patient, though she was probably just coming to terms with the news herself. He kept his personal life to himself and, although he'd had to tell the partners about his impending fatherhood, the first most people had known was when he'd gone on paternity leave. The circumstances weren't anybody's business and, to be honest, he wouldn't know where to begin explaining it. Although there was bound to be gossip, he hoped his colleagues would respect his privacy.

'Oh, congratulations.'

'Thanks.' If he'd thought coming into work today would help take his mind off those left at home, he'd been very mistaken. Even if he hadn't been cooing over babies this morning, he'd spent most of his time wondering what Kayla and Luke had been doing without him. He hated to miss a moment of his boy's life now Luke was the most important person in his life, and no longer simply a gift he'd given to Tom and Liam. Then there was the note he'd left stuck to the fridge. How long had it taken Kayla to realise he was gone and how had she reacted?

There was a chance she'd be glad to get the house to herself again, but he suspected she would be miffed at the way he'd run out on her. The adult thing would have been to talk over what had happened last night, but he wasn't ready to do that when he hadn't figured out how he felt about it himself yet. He'd enjoyed it, he'd wanted more, but the timing was appalling. If only they'd given in to temptation at the wedding they might have saved themselves all this confusion now wondering 'what if?'.

'I didn't know you were married, Doctor.' Mrs Hills's casual comment was something he knew he'd hear a lot of over the next few days until people took the hint that subject was off limits.

'I'm not.' He handed back possession of her newborn with a fake smile plastered onto his face, ignoring Ellie's look of horror that someone had dared challenge him outright. He didn't want to make anyone uncomfortable, but neither was he going to lie about his circumstances to save anyone else's blushes.

'Sorry. It's none of my business. There aren't many people who do get married these days, I suppose—'

She was frantically rocking her baby and trying to backtrack at the same time, but it was Ellie who stepped in and put an end to the awkward conversation.

'Thanks for your help, Doctor. I'm sure you have other patients to get back to.'

He didn't but it was the excuse he needed to get away from further interrogation. 'No problem. If you need me for anything else, give me a shout.'

He didn't have an office to retreat to today. It wouldn't be very professional of him to barge in and wrest control back from his substitute. Instead, he made his way to the staff room. He couldn't remember the last time he'd managed to drink a full, hot cup of coffee without interruption. Although, as he sat down in the quiet room, feet up, he couldn't help thinking about Kayla and Luke. She wouldn't have time out from parenthood and he didn't want to get used to it himself. Despite his reservations about taking on that responsibility again, he'd slipped back into that role of protector without too much hassle. The nappy changes and the feeding gave him quality bonding time with his son and those blissful moments during Luke's naptime were when he and Kayla got to chill out together.

He'd never lived with anyone other than his brother. That implied a commitment he'd never been willing to give to a woman. Yet, he and Kayla had fallen into a comfortable existence, forming a relationship neither of them had seen coming. He liked being part of a family again, enjoyed her company and loved having someone to talk to at the end of the day.

As Jamie sat alone with his cup of coffee the silence

was overwhelming. Heaven help him, he was missing Kayla and his boy after only a few hours of being parted from them.

Rachel, one of the receptionists, opened the door and reminded him he wasn't so alone after all. 'Dr Garrett, your, um, your son is here to see you.'

Luke certainly hadn't come down here on his own and since the flustered member of staff didn't seem to know how to address his visitor it meant only one thing. Kayla was here too. His day was beginning to look up.

'I hear Dr Garrett is helping with the baby clinic today. That's made my day, I tell you. Very easy on the eye.'

The woman sitting beside Kayla leaned in to share her news, bouncing her curly-haired daughter on her knee. She was clearly looking forward to her appointment and as Kayla glanced around the waiting room all the other mums were chatting excitedly at the prospect too.

'I'm not here for—'

'Don't get me wrong, he's an excellent doctor, has time for everyone, but a little eye candy doesn't hurt every now and then.' Jamie's number-one fan gave her a wink as she was called next for her appointment. Kayla gave a little smile. He'd love to know he was thought of as eye candy amongst the new mums and she couldn't help but feel a swell of pride as well as being territorial. He was her baby's father and she wasn't sure how she felt about other women ogling him. Then again, as far as she knew, she was the only woman in the room he'd kissed.

She was taking a risk by coming here unannounced. Especially when he'd skipped out on her this morning without as much as a goodbye. She'd been in something of a temper when she'd left the house. One that hadn't been improved by trying to manoeuvre a pram onto a bus for the first time. Although it had to have been easier than taking the Tube. She didn't know why she'd headed to the clinic other than a need to confront Jamie about his behaviour this morning.

However, as she'd pushed Luke's pram through St James's park and seen tourists and families making the most of the summer sunshine together, she couldn't help but think he was missing out. He mightn't want to spend time with her but that didn't mean he had to lose that quality time with his son. If he wanted to take Luke for an afternoon in the park she'd happily settle for some respite at home. It wasn't as though he was scheduled to work today anyway; he was simply avoiding her. She'd had no idea he'd be taking the baby clinic, but it meant she blended in with the rest of the crowd waiting to see him. Although the receptionist had looked taken aback when she'd said his son was here.

She was waiting for someone to either call her through or throw her out when the man himself appeared in the waiting room. All the women in the room sat up a little straighter, including her.

'Kayla? Come on through.' He was smiling, looked pleased to see her. Then again, he probably wore that expression for all his patients.

Her last thought as she followed him down the corridor was how disappointed that other woman was going to be when she realised he wasn't going to be there for her appointment.

'I'm sorry to impose on you like this at work.' As she pushed Luke's pram through the clinic, seeing the other mums coming and going who actually had good reason to be here, Kayla realised how selfish she'd been turning up like this. He was a busy man, a doctor in demand, a lot of things to a lot of people, not just her.

'Don't be daft. It's good to see you.' He stopped at one of the doors lining the hall and kissed her on the cheek. Okay, it wasn't a full-on snog but at least he wasn't recoiling from her in disgust. Whatever his reason for coming in here today he did appear genuinely pleased to see them. Although, that might have more to do with the cute passenger in the pram.

'I didn't know you were going back to work. I thought you still had some holidays booked off?' If she'd had any idea it mightn't have been such a shock this morning or seemed like an excuse to put some distance between them. An idea that couldn't be totally dismissed when he ushered her into the room and closed the door as though embarrassed to be seen with her.

'It was a spur-of-the-moment decision. Now, can I get you a drink?' It was then Kayla realised he'd brought her into a communal room rather than his office.

'No, thanks. Luke and I were just out for a stroll and thought we'd pop in and say hello. I can see you're busy, though. We'll see you at home later.' She was reversing back out of the door, convinced he'd brought her in here because he thought there'd be safety in numbers once those extra chairs in the room were filled with other members of staff.

'Don't go. Honestly, I think I'm just in the way here today. Why don't I come with you? Where were you headed?' This turnaround was making her head spin, wondering what could have happened in the few hours since he'd left the house that he actually wanted to spend time with them now.

'We were going to go to the park, maybe go and see the ducks. It's nice outside. I thought we'd make the most of the good weather.' She hadn't planned much beyond calling in to see what had driven him out first thing this morning. Whatever the cause, it seemed to have passed now otherwise he wouldn't be so keen to join them outside in the real world.

'Sounds good. Let me tell them I'm leaving for the day and I'll join you. Have you eaten?'

'We had some breakfast when we woke up, but I guess it'll be lunch time soon. I'm sure Luke will let me know when he's hungry.'

'Why don't we stop and get some food to take with us to the park, then we can really make the most of the afternoon?'

'Sure.' It was an unexpected turn of events but certainly one Kayla wasn't going to turn down. Spending the day kicking back with Jamie and Luke in the park sounded like the tonic she needed.

There was none of that macho nonsense preventing Jamie from being seen pushing a pram. If anything, Kayla thought she might have to wrest it from him to get her turn. He wheeled Luke through the clinic, pride exuding from every pore as he introduced his son to every person who stopped him to take a peek.

She didn't miss the curious looks directed at her from waiting patients and in a fit of pique made sure her hand rested possessively on the handle too. This was her family. Regardless of what did or didn't happen between her and Jamie, they were Luke's parents. Jamie was always going to be his dad and part of her life.

'He's quite the crowd-puller,' Jamie boasted, striding out onto the street, smiling at every passerby. Kayla wasn't going to fuel his ego by pointing out a handsome, eligible doctor with a baby was the main attraction.

'We should get you a puppy, then you'd have the attention of every female, and quite a few males, within a hundred-mile radius.' His failure to introduce her as anyone significant to his admirers prompted an uncharacteristic pang of sadness. It hadn't done anything to quell her fear she was still playing the role of surrogate. The oven for Jamie's bun, which he wanted to share with everyone but her.

He frowned at her, the barb not hitting home. 'I'd never get any work done. Listen, there's a place on the corner that does a nice lunch selection. Why don't you take over here and I'll grab us some takeout?'

'I'd be honoured.' So far, the most she'd been permitted to do was adjust the parasol attached to the pram to prevent the sun from shining in on Luke.

It wasn't that she was jealous of the attention Jamie was giving Luke, or that she was being edged out so Daddy could take over. No, her sudden bout of petulant behaviour had come about because it was clear they were no longer acting as a cohesive couple out in public. Despite everything telling her it wasn't possible, she wanted them to be a team, to be together. When he'd agreed to leave work and come with them he'd given her that fizz of hope in her belly that there was a chance last night's passionate embrace hadn't been a one-off after all.

He met her back out on the pavement holding up a

paper bag in triumph. The sort that said the deli catered for exclusive diets and tastes rather than some nondescript takeaway that served up cold pasties and sandwiches to the masses.

'That's lunch sorted. Now to find somewhere to eat it.' He was so utterly charming and thoughtful it was hard to remain mad at him for long.

He wasn't organising a picnic in the park for Luke's benefit, or to keep his adoring fan club happy. This was entirely for her and him. An afternoon relaxing in the sun like any other couple. Those clouds that had been steadily moving in to spoil her day began to dissipate until her smile was as bright as the sun shining overhead.

They walked on through the park, past families playing ball games, couples stretched out together on the green and dog walkers trying to get their enthusiastic charges under control.

'How about here?' Jamie found a shady spot beneath a huge tree, far enough from the sun worshippers to provide privacy whilst she fed Luke.

'Perfect.' She put the brakes on the pram, and Jamie stripped off his jacket to spread it out on the grass.

'There's really no need to ruin your suit on my account.' Although she appreciated the gesture, she could only imagine the cost of getting grass stains out of the expensive light grey fabric.

'I can't have the mother of my child sitting on wet grass, can I? I'm a gentleman. Now, take a seat and I'll serve lunch.' From anyone else Kayla would've judged the gesture over the top, but she'd seen sufficient similar behaviour to know he was the genuine article.

She lifted Luke out and sat down to feed him with

the thick tree trunk providing excellent support for her back. The tangle of branches above their heads also shielded them from the glare of the afternoon sun.

Jamie lay down beside her, putting the other half of his suit at risk by lying on the grass. He kicked off his shoes and socks, removed his tie and loosened his collar. 'That's better.'

Kayla watched him with amusement at how quickly he'd been able to switch off from work and relax. 'Why don't you make yourself comfortable?'

'If I was going to do that, the shirt and trousers would be off too, and I'd be lying here in just my boxers.' His flirty wink coupled with an image she'd got to know well around the house conspired to raise her temperature so much she might as well have been sitting in direct sunlight.

'Well, we don't want to have to bail Daddy out of jail so I'd advise keeping your clothes on for now.' Kayla adjusted her blouse once Luke had taken his fill, then winded him over her shoulder.

'In that case we should concentrate on filling our bellies. Especially since you have to keep your energy levels up for greedy guts here. I'll take him, and you help yourself.' They did the baby handover so Jamie was in charge of the back rubbing, leaving Kayla the pick of the deli cartons spread out on his jacket.

With the plastic cutlery provided she helped herself to some of the giant couscous jewelled with pomegranate seeds and edamame beans. The tomato and basil pasta salad filled her up quickly so she passed when Jamie offered her a share of his samosa veggie wheat wrap. Bless him, she knew he'd much rather have been tucking into a dirty big burger, but he'd gone out of his way to make this special for her. She washed her lunch down with a mouthful of pure orange juice and flopped back down on the ground.

'I'm stuffed.' That satisfying full feeling in her belly made her want to close her eyes and sleep for a while. She was content lying here with Jamie and Luke in a way she hadn't been for years, if ever.

'I wish I could say the same.' Jamie tossed the empty wrapper from his lunch back into the bag, not looking quite so gratified with his food choice.

'I'm sure there's something else left in the bag.' She dug in again and retrieved a package of apple wedges and toffee dipping sauce for him. 'Someone's got a sweet tooth.'

'I thought we needed something decadent.' He tried to pull off the cellophane, but it wasn't easy when he was cradling Luke in one arm.

'I'll do it,' she said, opening the package and dipping an apple into the sweet, sticky sauce to hold out for him.

He dipped his head, his lips brushing against her fingers as he took the fruit from her. She watched him with fascination as he crunched on the apple. There shouldn't have been anything erotic in the act, especially given their location. Yet, she found it incredibly so, imagining that mouth accepting her as easily as the piece of apple. His tongue licking her sweetness as thoroughly as he cleaned the toffee left on her fingers, sucking each one slowly and deliberately. The whole time he was seducing her with his mouth, his eyes didn't leave hers and she knew he was imagining the same scene playing out in the bedroom. Minus the food and the audience.

'Jamie—' Her throat was as dry as other parts of her were wet.

She was unable to explore what either meant or if he was experiencing the same inner turmoil as the moment was brought to an abrupt halt by a football landing with a direct hit onto their picnic. Leftover couscous and pasta spilled out and sounded the death knell for Jamie's jacket. Luke, who had been in the land of nod, was startled awake by the noise and let out a yell. Jamie was no longer teasing her but on his feet, swearing under his breath. Her peace and contentment had come to an end.

'Sorry.' A red-faced teenage boy appeared, took one look at the mess, grabbed his ball back and ran off towards his mates.

'Be more careful next time,' she yelled after him, aware they could have hit the baby. If she'd been paying more attention to their surroundings rather than fantasising about the father of her child, she might have seen the danger headed their way. She scooped up the devastation left behind and threw it back in the bag with unnecessary force.

'Hey, no harm done.' Jamie reached out a hand to rub the small of her back, soothing her and Luke at the same time. He had that knack of knowing what was worrying her and doing what he could to defuse the tension trying to strangle those moments of serenity. On this occasion she had a right to be annoyed but sometimes uneasiness crept in uninvited at times when she let herself enjoy life. It was a hangover from those days under her parents' rule, waiting for her punishment to be dished out for forgetting her place. Which, according to them, wasn't to feel a second of happiness. Liam, and now Jamie, were the only people ever capable of blocking out those memories to live in the moment.

Like now, when he was reassuring her there was no

lasting damage except to his clothes. Once again providing a calming presence for her, preventing her from spiralling into a 'what if?' scenario that would've kept her on edge for the rest of the night. She took several deep breaths to restore her pulse to its normal rhythm, then Jamie, seeming to sense her need for a cuddle, placed Luke back in her arms. Inhaling the clean, fresh scent of baby powder immersed her back into that world of innocence and a life untouched by cruelty. Her baby deserved better than a parent who couldn't move on from the past when there was so much to appreciate today.

'We're supposed to be relaxing, so come on.' Jamie sprawled out on the grass again and patted the space beside him. She accepted his invitation, placed Luke on the jacket between them, and lay down. Eyes closed, calm restored, it wasn't long before she drifted off into a peaceful slumber.

The sound of chattering children somewhere nearby filtered into Kayla's consciousness and she opened her eyes to check on Luke. There was a slight panic when she found the space next to her empty, but her eyes caught sight of Jamie sleeping nearby, with the baby lying soundly on his chest.

Her heart grew twice its size to accommodate the amount of love she had for the sight of this hunky doctor with their tiny son sleeping in the dappled sunlight. That iconic bond really ought to have been captured, in black and white, to capture the hearts of teenage girls all around the world.

She hadn't heard Luke grizzling but she supposed Jamie had moved him so as not to disturb her. Kayla rolled over onto her side to study his profile up close without that fear of being caught staring at him. There were copper threads woven through his dark, wavy hair she hadn't noticed before. The long dark lashes were a particular feature she liked, framing his beautiful brown eyes, hidden from view for now. He had a strong, straight nose, pointing like an arrow to those full lips she'd dreamed about too often.

Embracing her current live-in-the-moment mantra, she gave into impulse, leaned over and kissed him. The soft caress of his lips against hers was everything she remembered from the last time they'd touched. Then he kissed her back and blew her whole world apart once more.

Jamie was only half sleeping, enjoying the quiet and simply spending time with his favourite people in the world. When he felt that exquisite pressure on his lips he knew it was Kayla by the lemony scent of her hair falling around his face as she kissed him. This was everything he'd been waiting for and he responded with the full strength of his feelings for her with every fibre of his being.

He turned into the kiss, keeping one hand on Luke so he didn't disturb him, sliding the other into Kayla's hair to hold her where he wanted her. Her tentative tongue sought his, but Jamie was no longer holding back, increasing the intensity of the tryst with every taste of her. His mouth was hard against hers now, the rest of his body following suit, and when she moaned against his lips he knew he had to cool it or risk making a public spectacle in the park.

He pulled back, released her from his grasp and opened his eyes. Her heavy-lidded eyes, mussed hair and bruised lips suggested they'd had more than a smooch. It certainly felt like it. His heart was thudding so hard, his breathing laboured, it was no wonder Luke was beginning to stir.

'Wow. Where did that come from?' She pressed her forehead to his, her breathing coming in short gasps.

'You started it,' he said with a laugh, doing his best to lighten the crackling tension between them.

Kayla let out a long, dreamy sigh and shuffled over beside him. That unspoken question about what they did next tried to wriggle in between them, but Jamie refused to let it have room. Not when Kayla was lying with her head tucked under his arm and his son was sleeping on his chest. He didn't want anything as brutal as real life crashing in and ruining this perfect family picture.

CHAPTER NINE

No MATTER HOW much she wanted to, Kayla knew she couldn't spend all day here lying curled up against Jamie, revelling in his solid warmth and smooching like teenagers. There was a nip in the air now that the afternoon sun was beginning to fade, and she wouldn't wish for Luke to catch a cold.

'We should put him back in his pram,' she whispered, although not keen to break the spell keeping them in this lovely daydream together.

'Just. One. More. Kiss.' He peppered her lips with tempting little pecks before drawing her bottom lip into his mouth and teasing her with the tip of his tongue. She literally could do this all day.

Luke started to grizzle and reminded her why she couldn't. Reluctantly, she drew away from Jamie's mind-bending kisses and transferred her attention back to her son. She didn't know how today's progress in their relationship was going to affect them once they were back in more familiar surroundings, but they'd have to face reality sooner or later.

'When you're older we'll be able to play football and feed the ducks like everyone else,' she told Luke as she carried him over to his pram.

'Or, you know, we could give him a brother and sister to keep him occupied while Mummy and Daddy get to kiss in peace.' Jamie rested his hand at the base of her neck as he whispered into her ear, sending her body haywire at both points of contact. She knew he was only joking. One snogging session didn't constitute a marriage proposal and two point four children. Even if they had conceived a child before their first kiss.

'You're only saying that now because we haven't been through the teething stage, potty training, the terrible twos…' Today had been blissful but she wasn't so naïve as to think every day was going to be as easy. They hadn't really been tested yet as parents, never mind as a couple. She hoped that was what they were becoming—she wasn't into kissing men on a whim. With Jamie being the father of her child and her temporary housemate, it was always going to be more complicated than just a kiss here and there. That was why she'd held back for as long as she had despite her growing feelings towards Jamie. Now she'd made that leap of faith in showing him, in trusting him, it was all or nothing for her from now on.

'All things I'm very much looking forward to.' He squeezed her close, making her heart give a giddy skip as a future together flashed before her eyes. One that wasn't as unappealing as it had once seemed.

If things carried on much the way they had been between her and Jamie she couldn't see any reason to be afraid of sharing her life with him. He'd been respectful of her need for independence, yet had helped when she'd needed it, and he was a great dad. As well as a fantastic kisser. She stopped before her imagination conjured images of other things he would be equally skilled in. Some things were worth waiting for and it would be a while before she'd be ready for anything more than they'd shared today.

A matter of weeks ago she'd been adamant she wouldn't let him invade her life or be a part of Luke's. Now as they walked home together she wanted so much more. If she was risking her heart and her whole world to let him in, this had better mean something special to him too.

'Oh, isn't he gorgeous?' Their journey home was brought to a halt by an admiring stranger. If she hadn't been leaning into the pram cooing over Luke the compliment could've been referring to either male currently in Kayla's company.

'Thank you.' She accepted the compliment on their behalf from the middle-aged woman who was now taking a keen interest in Jamie too.

'I'm about to become a grandmother for the first time soon. That's my daughter over there. Ready to pop in a couple of weeks.' The proud gran-to-be pointed to the heavily pregnant woman sitting on a park bench nearby, who gave a weak wave back.

'Is she okay?' It was Jamie who enquired after her health, though it was obvious to Kayla too the woman didn't look well at all. Her face was pale, and she was rubbing the base of her spine with both hands.

'Either she has overdone the walking, or the heat has got to her. I thought she should rest for a while before we head home again.'

Kayla steered the pram over towards the bench. She couldn't in good conscience keep on walking past a pregnant woman in discomfort, and she was sure Jamie wouldn't either. 'Hi. Your mum said you weren't feeling too well. Is there anything we can do for you?'

'I'm fine, thanks. Just some back ache. I'm sure it'll pass.' She offered a strained smile, which wasn't totally convincing.

'There's some water in the bag if you'd like a drink.' Jamie reached into the tray under the pram and pulled out a bottle.

'That would be great. I am a little dehydrated.' She accepted his help much easier and the smile shone a tad brighter as Jamie took a seat beside her on the bench.

'Would you like us to call an ambulance for you?' Kayla pulled out her mobile phone. Dr Garrett's charm, effective as it seemed now, couldn't cure whatever ailed her.

'I don't think that's necessary. I'll be all right in a minute.' She took another swig of water from the bottle.

'I'm a doctor over at the clinic. If you think you could make it that far I could give you a check-over?' Apparently Jamie wasn't going to take her word for it either and Kayla would be happier if they could get her into some sort of medical facility to check on her and the baby.

'Erin, that's not a bad idea, love. Let the doctor see what's what with you and the bub, then we can phone Gary to come and pick us up.' Her mum was kneeling down beside her now, trying to convince her to accept the offer of help.

'A midwife will be able to take a look in case you are in the early stages of labour.' Kayla understood the need to maintain her independence and some control over her body. As she'd found out for herself, it wasn't always wise to be stubborn for the sake of it this late in a pregnancy.

That seemed to jolt Erin into a reality check. 'I can walk. I haven't had any contractions and my waters haven't broken but, goodness knows, I don't want to have my baby in the middle of a public park.'

With assistance from Jamie and her mother, Erin heaved herself up from the bench.

'We can take it slow and you can hold onto the pram for support if you need it.' Kayla relinquished sole command of the pram to make room for her. It was the least she could do in the circumstances.

Once they made it to the clinic Jamie commandeered one of the cubicles in the treatment room for Erin. 'I'll go and see if the midwife is available to see you.'

He rushed off, leaving Erin and her mother in the room and Kayla uncertain of her place in the doorway with the pram. This wasn't the end to the afternoon they'd planned. Whilst she wanted to provide Erin with all the help she needed, she couldn't simply abandon her son in the process.

'Ow.' Erin's face was full of pain as she gripped her belly with both hands. 'My bump is very tight, as though it's being squeezed.'

'You may be in the early stages of labour. Hopefully the midwife can tell you for sure once she gets here.' Erin squirmed in the chair and her mother tried to get her to focus on something other than the pain.

'You're in the best place, love. Isn't it lovely in here? Looks very modern. We might have to think about changing our GP to this nice young doctor.'

A sudden gush of liquid confirmed Kayla's suspicions that Erin was in labour despite her denial.

Since Luke was sleeping soundly, Kayla ventured into the confined room. 'Don't worry, I'm sure we can get someone to clean that up. If you're in labour, you might be more comfortable up on the bed. I'll give you a hand.'

Between them, the women helped Erin onto the bed. She was still clutching her belly, her face scrunched up in pain. This contraction was intense and not letting up. Hopefully the midwife wouldn't mind Kayla getting involved. She wouldn't want to tread on anyone's toes professionally, but she wanted Erin to remain as calm as possible. A first baby was special, and the memory of the birth lasted a lifetime. If she was going to be part of it, she wanted to be sure she'd done everything in her power to make it as painless as possible for the mother.

'Okay, the bad news is the midwife and health visitor are out on their rounds. The good news is that Kayla here is a qualified midwife.' Jamie rushed back to land her right in the middle of the unfolding drama.

'Erin's waters have just broken. You're going to have to call an ambulance. I don't practise any more, remember? I'm a doula now. I support patients more on an emotional basis these days, Erin.' She wanted to be transparent about her professional limitations since she'd left the hospital. Then it was down to Erin whether or not she wanted her to be involved.

'She practically delivered our baby herself.' Of course, Jamie was singing her praises, because it would get him off the hook. He'd already helped deliver one unexpected surprise and clearly wasn't in a hurry to do it again.

'Not exactly,' she tried to protest when he'd done as much to bring Luke safely into the world.

'I just want someone to tell me everything's all right,' Erin cried out. In pregnancy, the unknown simply increased anxiety levels at an already stressful time.

'I'm sure it is. I merely want to make sure everyone's on board with me doing the checks?' Everyone nodded enthusiastically. 'What about Luke?'

'My secretary is on her way to babysit. I'm sure we'll have the whole staff vying for cuddles. He'll be fine.'

With no more excuses available, Kayla went to the wash station to scrub up before she did an examination.

'Dr Garrett, I'd like you to be present too so you can report I've followed all relevant procedures.' He could also provide medical backup if needed. It was his practice after all. She'd only come in to invite him out for lunch.

'I'm going to phone for that ambulance and let the rest of the staff know what's happening in here.'

'There's a real pressure pushing down. It feels weird down there and it hurts real bad.'

'In that case, Erin, I'm going to have to do an internal exam. Is that okay?' As soon as she was given permission she covered Erin's lower half with a modesty sheet and helped her remove her underclothes.

The problem was immediately obvious. 'Okay, Erin. You're fully dilated. I can already see the head.'

Jamie returned as she delivered the news and seemed to realise this baby wasn't hanging on for the ambulance, rushing around to get the necessary equipment organised for the impending birth.

'That's not possible. I'm having my baby in hospital. Gary's going to be with me. I don't have the music I picked out or my delivery bag with me.'

'I know, but Junior is in a hurry to meet his mummy.

This time tomorrow you could be sitting at home with him.' Kayla knew it was a shock. Precipitate labour, or fast labour, didn't give any thought to the nine months the mother had spent planning how her delivery and birth would go.

It was difficult for those mums to adjust to labour and develop a coping strategy when the contractions could involve one long, intense, continuous pain. The important thing was to make sure the baby was delivered safely when there were dangers involved in such rapid births. At least she was in a clinic with medical professionals and hadn't given birth in a public toilet in the park.

There was no time for pain relief or even a need to cut Erin as her son slid out after just a couple of pushes.

Kayla's elation and relief evaporated quickly when she saw the green tinge to the baby's skin. He was having difficulty breathing and his little body was limp. 'I think he's inhaled the meconium.'

'Give him to me. I need an endotracheal tube,' Jamie yelled to the nurses and staff assembled outside the cubicle as the drama unfolded.

Meconium, baby's first faeces passed in the womb, could become trapped in the baby's airways or lungs if inhaled. The severity of meconium aspiration, dependent on the amount inhaled, could lead to long-term complications including lung problems, hearing loss or neurological damage. In some rarer cases it could even lead to death. It was vital they got him breathing.

'What is it? What's wrong with my baby?' Erin was sobbing and clutching her mother's hand as Kayla passed him to Jamie.

She knew that heart-stopping fear of thinking something terrible was threatening your baby's life having gone through it only days ago herself. Although Kayla would want her to know what was happening it was as important to keep her calm as it was to keep her informed.

'He's having a little trouble breathing. We need to clear his airways as much as we can. The ambulance will be here any second. I'm sure the hospital staff are on standby to make sure you get the treatment you need straight away.' He might need to go into a neonatal intensive care unit to be closely watched, but he'd receive antibiotics and oxygen therapy to help him on the road to recovery.

Jamie inserted the flexible plastic tube into the baby's windpipe through his mouth to suction his airways. He continued clearing until there were no visible signs of the meconium in the suctioned fluids, working so calmly and efficiently one would have thought this was his area of expertise.

The paramedics arrived then and took over, administering oxygen as they ushered mother and baby to the waiting ambulance. Kayla and Jamie exchanged relieved smiles across the room strewn with debris from the emergency delivery that had thankfully ended well.

They made a good team. Twice now they'd worked together through possible birth complications. It made her think about the future and the possibilities out there for the two of them. Especially now when she was reminded how much good she could still do as a midwife helping to bring children into the world.

'Oh, you like that, don't you?' As Jamie held his slippery son still in the bath, Kayla scooped water over his scalp and body to rinse off the soap suds. Bath time was fast becoming a highlight as they spent this quality time together with Luke.

'It won't be long before we're reading him bedtime stories too.' There wasn't a sound out of Luke except for contented gurgling as Kayla lifted him out to wrap him in a fluffy towel.

It was a domestic scene he'd never imagined he'd be part of again. Yet it was a much-needed slice of normal life after the fraught afternoon. He imagined it would be the same after a full day treating his patients at the clinic. Something worth coming home for.

'I'll look forward to that. I know I was only supposed to be staying in the interim, but I'd like to be around to do more of this kind of stuff.' He'd resisted the idea of family until he'd nearly lost it all. Thanks to Kayla and Luke, this was a chance to be part of one again. To belong somewhere other than work was as though a whole new world was opening up to him.

'Sure. We don't have to put anything formal in place. I think we're doing okay the way we are.' She kissed him full on the lips as she passed him on the way to the bedroom, but it didn't put his mind fully to rest.

They might have made roads towards a relationship, but it was early days. He wasn't expecting any commitment there yet, but he was keen to know where he stood in terms of being Luke's father.

Once the baby was settled into his night's sleep Jamie dropped a gentle kiss on his forehead. 'Goodnight, son.'

Being able to do that, to say those words, brought a lump to his throat. With every passing day as a dad he found it more difficult to understand his own father's behaviour. Family life had never been enough for him.

Whereas Jamie found pleasure in every moment with his son and wouldn't voluntarily be deprived of a second of it. Sorrow balled in his gut too when he remembered how much his brother had wanted this baby and would never get to experience the joy of fatherhood for himself. It was something Jamie would never take for granted when he knew how privileged he was to have been given this gift.

Today had been a reminder of how precious, and fragile, life was. Neither he, nor Kayla, had been able to save their brothers but if they could prevent one more unnecessary death all the training and hard work had been worth it.

'I wish Tom and Liam could have been here to see this,' he said, uncharacteristically sentimental as he watched his sleeping son.

'Me too,' Kayla said before giving him a much-needed hug.

When she let go, much too quickly for his liking, she went to check the baby monitor was switched on and gave their son one last kiss. "Night, sweetheart.'

Once they'd tiptoed out of the room and closed the door she let out a long sigh as though she was finally allowing herself to relax.

'Come on. I think we're due some down time.' Jamie took her hand and led her down to the living room, sat her down on the sofa and took off her shoes. He kicked off his own before lying lengthways on the settee, bringing her with him so she was lying in his arms.

'This is nice,' she mumbled and snuggled into him. It didn't matter to Jamie how cramped it was with both of them lying here when her body was packed so pleasantly against his.

'We had a busy day. It's nice to be able to come home and do this.' If he had his way he'd be able to do it every day. He didn't want to rush her, but he didn't see the point in wasting time. They wanted to be with each other, to be there for their son.

Tom and Liam's accident had shown him he shouldn't take anything for granted and he wanted to be the best partner for Kayla, the greatest dad to Luke. He believed the best way to achieve that was by moving in with them permanently.

'I'll admit, it wasn't the return to work I'd planned.' She rotated her position until she was face to face with him.

'No, but I'm glad you were there.'

'Likewise.'

'You were great putting Erin's mind at ease that we knew what we were doing, and the baby was going to be all right. It's impressive watching you work.'

She batted his shoulder, deflecting the compliment when he'd been the one who'd saved the baby's life. 'You're just saying that because you think I'm the type of girl who'll swoon if a doctor praises her.'

'And you're not?' He leaned in closer, his eyes trained on her lips as he locked onto his target.

'It depends on the doctor.'

'Kayla, I want you to know I will never tell you something simply because I think it's what you want to hear. I'll always be honest with you.' He couldn't imagine ever feeling the need to lie to Kayla when it was the one thing guaranteed to lose her for ever now she'd started to trust him. After everything she'd been through he was privileged even to be with her here. A position he was not about to abuse.

'I think that's the nicest thing anyone has ever said to me.' She looked up at him, the teasing putting a twinkle in her eye and tilting her lips up towards him.

'Uh-huh. Well, here's another one for you. I've never been as happy as I have been with you and Luke these past days.' Despite her attempts to lighten the mood he wanted her to know he was serious in his commitment.

Jamie understood her need to protect herself and Luke. By swearing off long-term relationships he'd erected those same barriers around his heart. Yet there was no denying they were beginning to crumble. He'd fallen for Kayla and that wasn't going to change simply because he was afraid of being tied down again. That had happened the moment he'd decided to step up and be the father his son needed. If anything, that should have made him warier of getting into a relationship with Luke's mother.

Her eyes misted with tears and he watched her throat bob as she swallowed them back. 'Shut up and kiss me.'

He smiled at her directness and knew it was her way of telling him she felt the same without saying the words. If she didn't reciprocate the sentiment she would've told him rather than force either of them to live a lie.

It was nice to be with someone who told it as it was instead of leaving him to guess what she wanted from him. Kayla was a strong, decisive woman who wouldn't put up with any nonsense or be wishy-washy about being with him. She was an all-or-nothing girl, which suited him because he wanted everything she had to give.

He took possession of her mouth with his, her body sighing against him as they joined together. With his hand splayed on her lower back under her shirt, she quivered at his touch. In turn, she rested her hand on his chest, his heart trying to burst free at the simple contact.

With every kiss, every caress of her lips, his body grew harder, wanting more, yet he was content with what they had here. A kiss between two single adults shouldn't be a big deal, but in some ways it was everything. Jamie had enjoyed one-night stands in the past to relieve sexual tension, but somehow this seemed more intimate. Sex could mean nothing other than a physical release at times, but lying here, kissing the mother of his baby, was a whole new ball game.

They hadn't even taken their clothes off yet and he was picturing their future together as a family. He intended to take things slowly with Kayla from here on in so he didn't ruin things. Something told him once they consummated this relationship it would be for ever. The timing had to be perfect and they had to be together for the right reasons. Not simply down to convenience or confused emotions. He didn't want to ruin what they had, or what they could have, together.

Slowly, frustratingly, he eased back on the intensity of the kiss. Kayla too seemed to realise they couldn't carry on without burning each other out with this sudden flare of passion. She huffed out another sigh and rested her head on his chest.

He stroked her hair until her eyes fluttered shut and her breathing was deep and even. She was exhausted. He was too, trying to work through these new emotions. One thing was for sure. He'd rather be here, wide awake with Kayla in his arms, than go to bed alone. That single life he'd wanted for so long was now a thing of the past. Everything he wanted was right here.

CHAPTER TEN

'I'LL BE HOME as soon as I can get away.' Jamie leaned over the sofa and gave Kayla a peck on the lips.

They'd fallen asleep here last night and he'd almost slept in. Luke too had chosen to have a lie-in this morning. With two of them squashed onto the settee it should've been the most uncomfortable sleep ever, but it had been quite the opposite. Wrapped up in Jamie, she'd had the best slumber she'd had in a long time. Now Jamie was referring to the place as home she was hoping it was the first of many nights together to come.

'Good. I'll be here, waiting.' Not right here, she had to get washed and dressed and sort Luke out, but she would be looking forward to Jamie's return. His kisses were worth hanging around for. He made her feel free again, liberated from her hang-ups. She'd trusted him and, so far, he was doing everything right. He wasn't even pressuring her for more than a kiss and a cuddle when it was evident they both wanted more. Instead of leaving for work, Jamie bent down again to kiss her more thoroughly. Then he deliberately toppled over the couch, careful not to hurt her as he covered her with his body. Her giggling was halted as he kissed her longer and deeper.

'As much as I could do this all day, one of us has work to go to.' If they did much more canoodling they'd end up going further than she was ready for physically or mentally. She didn't want to rush into anything. Since they were already living together and had a child, she thought they could take their time with the physical side of the relationship. She could do without the pressure on her to be anyone but herself. There'd been too much of her life spent being Kayla the perfect daughter, the grieving sister, and overwhelmed mum. She didn't want to dive right into being Kayla the girlfriend and losing her identity all over again. It would be nice just to be herself and not worrying if that was enough.

Jamie groaned and, with one last hard smooch, climbed off her again.

'Later,' he said, his voice huskier than she'd ever heard and sending her insides into raptures. That promise of an extended couch cuddle gave her shivers. When one word and a few kisses had become the most erotic moment of her life, she knew she was investing too much into one man. Her imagination and libido were running away with thoughts about the effect the next stage of their relationship could have on her, but at what cost?

There were more than her feelings to consider. She had a son now. If it all went wrong, and she lost herself again, she couldn't simply start over the way she had the last time. Liam wasn't here to pick her up and put her back together and, as Luke's father, Jamie was always going to be a part of her life. He'd told her his relationship history and hadn't made any promises that he could commit to her any more than he had to any other woman. She had to ask herself if the growing feelings she had for him were worth acting on after all, if heartbreak was inevitable.

'You've had a busy few days, then?' Cherry sat down with two mugs of herbal tea. Although a visitor in the house on this occasion, she'd made the tea, leaving Kayla free to nurse Luke.

She'd filled her in on the events at Jamie's clinic after their walk in the park. Neglecting to share the developments between them on a romantic level.

'Yes. I'd forgotten what that adrenaline rush was like to be involved in those emergency cases. It's so good knowing you've helped a mother and baby during difficult times.' Her role recently had become sedate, more of a counselling basis than being an active participant in the birth. Whilst rewarding in itself, her involvement yesterday had her thinking about where she would do the most good.

The speed with which her relationship with Jamie was moving had also given her pause for thought. She was beginning to think she needed some space from him before things progressed any further.

'Sounds to me as though someone's missing work.' Cherry eyed her over the cup as she sipped, knowing Kayla wasn't one to sit still for long. She might have struggled with motherhood initially but now she was thinking about getting the rest of her life back on track too.

'It's more than that. In some ways, now that I'm a mother myself I want to do something for those who aren't as fortunate as I've been. I mean, I had you and Jamie to support me during a relatively straightforward birth. There are so many people I could help with my qualifications and experience.' Yesterday had given her a taste of what could be achieved if she was in the right place at the right time. Although she was savouring the wonders of motherhood, she couldn't, and didn't want to be at home for ever. There was a big world outside Jamie Garrett and she'd do well to remember that.

Since leaving home she'd always worked to support herself, not relying on anyone else and she wasn't about to start now. Sharing a house and a child with Jamie didn't mean she was going to hand over control of her life in a package with her heart.

'What are you thinking about? Are there big changes afoot?' As ever, she could count on Cherry being supportive, never being critical, or telling her what she should do. In these circumstances she knew her parents would insist she stayed at home devoted to her baby. Hypocritical, but that was who they were. They would never have admitted to being bad parents, only of having bad children.

Mind you, they would have keeled over at the notion of her being an unmarried mother shacked up with the man who got her pregnant. The thought did secretly make her smile and she imagined telling them the circumstances behind Luke's birth to see the looks on their faces. The sort of thing Liam would've done purely to spite their tyrannical doctrine. Except Luke was hers and they had absolutely no right to taint him with their vile ways.

'It did get me thinking about Liam and Tom's project in Vietnam. They worked so hard to fund that community and set up a clinic there. I wondered about going out there to help for a while and get a real idea of what they achieved.' It would bring her closer to them and she could even visit their graves and say her goodbyes properly. She knew they would've approved her plans. Even more so if she brought Luke with her to be a part of it all.

'I'm sure there would always be a need for qualified medical staff. Have you thought about what you would do with Buster, here?' Cherry lifted the end of Luke's bib to wipe away some of the milk he'd brought up when he'd been winded.

'I don't think there'd be a problem taking him with me. I'd still be feeding him myself, so it makes sense.' It wouldn't be a normal working environment where it would be frowned upon to bring her baby with her. Besides, it would encourage other mothers to see him there and realise she knew what she was doing.

'What does Jamie think about that?' It was Cherry's not so subtle way of reminding her there were two parents to consider but she wasn't about to abscond with their baby for ever.

'I haven't told him yet.' Seeing Cherry's raised eyebrow, she added, 'I'm going to tell him tonight.'

'Uh huh. You let me know how that goes.'

'What do you mean?' Kayla found herself getting defensive at Cherry's sarcastic tone.

'I mean, Jamie doesn't strike me as the kind of dad who'll sit back and let you take his son halfway around the world without a say.'

There was that word *let* again. Why did everyone think she needed permission to run her own life?

'Maybe you don't know him the way I do.'

'Yes, I doubt I do. The glow about you these days has nothing to do with post-pregnancy hormones and everything, I suspect, to do with your new housemate.'

If Cherry was trying to avoid an argument and fish for gossip at the same time, she'd hooked herself a whopper.

There was no way Kayla could keep her secret for ever. 'Things have…evolved over these past days.'

'I knew it!' Eyes wide, mouth open, Cherry leaned in, waiting for her to spill the details.

'We've only kissed but I think it could lead to something more serious.' They hadn't discussed what they wanted to come from this new development, but neither of them would want to jeopardise Luke's future for a mere fling.

'That's great. I'm so happy for you and I'm sure Liam and Tom would be too.' The touch of Cherry's hand on hers and the reminder of her brother brought tears to Kayla's eyes.

This situation would've appealed to Liam's warped sense of humour and Tom's romantic nature. They would've taken credit for the matchmaking too. If not for them or Luke, she would never have realised what a great man Jamie was or how great a father he'd make. Except she wanted to take his son, his only family, to the very place that had claimed his brother's life to escape her feelings for him.

'I wouldn't start celebrating just yet. I don't think I'm ready to get into a relationship with someone who has made it very clear he doesn't do commitment. He hasn't even suggested moving in permanently, for goodness' sake.' If he'd shown her any sign she meant anything more than Natalie, or his other past conquests, she might have considered it worth the risk of making a go of things. There was too much to lose based on a case of wishful thinking.

'Don't write him off altogether. Talk things over first.

I know you've been hurt in the past, but this could be the start of a great future together for the two of you.'

'I wish I could believe that, Cherry.' She sighed, but life had taught her not to expect too much. That was exactly what it would be if she believed Jamie would commit to her for ever. Too much.

More than ever, Jamie was grateful he'd gone into general medicine rather than the frantic pace of emergency care. Life as a doctor would never run to nine to five, Monday to Friday shifts, but he did have some down time when he wasn't on call. In hindsight he shouldn't have been in such a rush to get back to work and made the most of his paternity leave to squeeze out every second of quality time with his family. It was too late now. He'd made the knee-jerk decision to go back simply because he'd feared getting too close. Now he realised home with his family was where he wanted to be more than anywhere else.

Perhaps it had taken that short separation for him to realise that. It could've been spending that afternoon with them that reminded him of the important things in his life. Whatever it was that had changed his views from the pitfalls of domesticity to the rewards of having people he cared about around him, there was something to look forward to at the end of every shift.

He used his key to let himself into the house, careful not to make too much noise in case Luke was sleeping and he woke him up.

'Hey,' he said softly as Kayla peeped her head around the doorframe.

'Dinner's ready,' she said with a grin.

'Now that's what I call a welcome home.' He could

get used to this. Especially if he came home to Kayla's kisses and a home-cooked meal every night. He couldn't remember the last time anyone had cooked for him. When he and Tom had lived together he'd done all the cooking and he was used to cooking for one throughout his subsequent bachelor lifestyle. He hadn't minded, but Kayla's gesture tonight showed him how nice it was to have someone think of him, to want to take care of him for a change. It was also an indication that she was getting things under control herself if she'd been able to juggle looking after Luke and making dinner. He certainly hadn't expected it.

'What have I done to deserve this?' Once he'd hung up his coat and walked through to the dining room he could see she'd gone all out for him.

The table was set for two, with heaped bowls of vegetable pasta. He was grateful she'd gone to this trouble for his benefit. In this case, the way to a man's heart was definitely through his stomach. He'd thought he couldn't love her any more than he already did until she'd surprised him with this.

The thought struck him so hard he practically fell into his chair. He loved her, and not in the way he loved the look of this carb-laden meal before him. In the couldn't-stop-thinking-about-her, didn't-know-how-he'd-live-without-her conventional sense. He'd assumed his want of her company had arisen from being around her so much it had become a habit. Now they'd had a little time apart he could see it was much more than that. He wanted to spend every second of every day with her, raising their son, or kissing like teenagers in the first flush of love. Preferably both.

'I thought it would be nice for us to sit down to a

meal together once you got home from work. Luke's getting settled into a routine now and things are becoming more manageable.' She certainly looked happier and he could see she'd taken time with her hair and clothes today. Not that he would've minded if she'd had bedhead and spent the day in her pyjamas. She simply appeared more like the Kayla he'd first met, so together and confident.

'It's great. Thank you. I mean, you didn't have to, but it's much appreciated.' He helped himself to a mouthful of creamy pasta and Jamie knew he'd found heaven here with her and Luke. There was nothing else he could've wanted for and he considered himself a very lucky man indeed.

'I can't guarantee it'll be a regular occurrence once I'm back to work.' Kayla was picking at her dinner whilst he was wolfing his down. Jamie hoped cooking this for him hadn't been a step too far for her.

'Of course. We can always take turns making dinner. I'm just happy to have some company. Usually I'm a dinner-for-one-in-front-of-the-TV sort, so anything else is a bonus.' When Luke was older meal times would become messier as he explored new foods and textures. They'd probably spend their evenings cleaning the evidence of it off the walls.

'I'm glad you're enjoying it.' She gave him an uneasy smile and laid her knife and fork down on her plate side by side. It looked as though she was preparing to tackle something more unsavoury to her palate. If Jamie hadn't almost finished eating he might've lost his appetite too at the thought they were going to have a talk about something more serious than dinner or assigning household chores.

'Okay, what's wrong?' He didn't actually want to know when he was content to carry on as they were. In asking they'd have to confront whatever was ailing her and the family dream might come crashing down around him. Except he'd promised to be honest with her and that didn't involve pretending there was nothing wrong when there was clearly a problem. In return, he'd expect Kayla to be honest with him.

'I'm thinking about returning to work.' She was chewing her bottom lip, but if she thought he was the type of partner to keep her chained to the kitchen she didn't know him at all. Similarly, he'd always known Kayla wouldn't be a housewife for ever. She had too much to give to be wasted on just one man.

'Good for you.' He wanted her to see he was being supportive and not to be afraid of saying whatever was on her mind. It was the only way to make a relationship work and, goodness knew, he wanted this one to last.

'You don't mind?'

'Not at all. Why should I? It's your decision, your life. I'm sure we can make some childcare arrangements for Luke around both of our jobs.' They'd be thorough in their search for suitable help in that area when neither of them would take chances when it came to doing what was best for their son.

'Actually, I was thinking about taking him with me to work.'

He took a minute to consider that extra information. It could work. As a doula, Kayla worked for herself and, although that involved being on call for a patient going into labour, there was nothing stopping her from taking Luke too. It was preferable to leaving him with a stranger in a nursery.

'I'll be here to do my bit too and I can watch him if you get called out through the night.' He didn't want her to shut him out again or disrupt Luke's sleep merely to make a point that she could do everything herself.

'I was considering going back into midwifery.' It wasn't a huge bombshell, given the way she'd become immersed back into that role so suddenly yesterday.

However, he wished she would hit him with everything at once rather than drip-feeding him little titbits.

'How would that work with Luke? Do they have crèches for the hospital staff? Would you have to re-take your qualifications after being away for so long?' It didn't matter to him if she did. He'd support her emotionally and financially until she was exactly where she needed to be to find her vocation.

'Not where I want to practise. I've been looking at helping out in the clinic Tom and Liam set up. Jamie, I want to go to Vietnam and take Luke with me.'

There it was, the devastating truth truck capable of obliterating everything in its path and leaving him with nothing. Kayla was leaving him and taking their son with her.

As she said it, she tried to focus on the excitement of a new adventure instead of the sadness at ending things with Jamie. She wanted to carry on with Liam and Tom's efforts and be someone her son could be proud of when he was older. As well as put some distance between her and Jamie to get her senses back in working order.

'No way in hell.' Jamie's voice was so measured and menacing it sounded so unlike him.

'Excuse me?' A prickling sensation started across

her skin and crept up the back of her neck as she found he was no longer a caring partner supporting her, but a stern authority figure dictating to her. It gave her flashbacks of Paul telling her she wouldn't go out with her friends if she really loved him. Then her father, spittle forming at the corners of his mouth as he went nose to nose to yell at her when she'd expressed an interest in a school disco.

'I'm sorry, Kayla, but there is no way you are taking my son to another country. To the very place where my brother died. I didn't know you could be so cruel.' That hard look she'd seen on his face when she'd broached the subject had now changed into one of pain. He was thinking only of himself by accusing her of such venom. Not of what she wanted or of the good she could do where it would count most.

It said a lot that in the heat of the discussion he only cared about his son being taken away, not that she would be leaving too. Clearly, she'd been reading way too much into those passionate interludes between them.

'If you think so little of me I can see there is no future for us.' It had all been too good to be true. She'd have been better off as that cynical version of herself, combatting his attempts to charm her, when she'd known things would end this way. They always did. Thanks to her parents she attracted people who thought they could rule over her the way they had. Except this time she had Luke to think about. He was her priority and he'd be safer travelling with her than being stuck in a toxic house like the one she'd grown up in. She wasn't going to wait around until the full force of Jamie's dominance made itself known and he tried to impose it on Luke too.

'I live in the real world. One full of everyday dangers for a newborn without asking for more by taking him to a foreign country.'

'Do you honestly think I would risk my son's well-being?' She couldn't believe what she was hearing. He was being ridiculous. It wasn't as though she wouldn't have researched the idea thoroughly before deeming it safe to travel with a baby. No, Jamie was trying to assert his authority over her, and over their son. She wasn't having it.

'That's exactly what you're doing.' He pushed back his chair and got up to pace around the room. Determined not to be intimidated ever again, she copied his move, pulling herself up to her full height to face him.

'Luke is my son. Liam was my brother. This decision is mine to make.' Her independence meant more to her than a possible romance that had been doomed from the start. She'd gone ahead with the surrogacy idea at the time because she'd believed having a child in an actual relationship wasn't going to be possible. There was no joy in finding out she'd been right all along. The biggest mistake she'd made was adding his name to the birth certificate.

'It's not all about you, Kayla. Luke is my son too and, in case you'd forgotten, I also lost a brother. Which is the reason I'm not prepared to let you risk my son's life over there.'

Her hands balled into fists into his use of that word, which conjured up memories of her parents' lists of rules and the consequences she incurred if she broke any of them. Thank goodness Jamie didn't have any real hold over her other than the grip he had around her heart. At least seeing his true colours now should lessen the heartbreak she was facing at losing him.

'If I hadn't already made my mind up about going, your attitude has convinced me why this is a good idea. I need to get away and remember who I am. That's no longer a woman who'll cower every time someone raises their voice at me.'

He actually laughed at that. The dark, hollow sound giving her chills. 'Kayla, I am nothing like your parents. I care. That's why I don't want you going over there.'

She wanted to believe him, and she had, up until a few minutes ago. Now those barriers had shot back up there was no way she was going to let him sweet-talk his way back into her heart and take advantage of her. 'I'm sorry, Jamie, but my mind is made up. We're not going for ever but, make no mistake about it, we are going.'

His face darkened. 'Not if I can help it.'

She didn't like the threat hovering in the tense atmosphere, waiting for the opportunity to strike and hit her where it could do the most damage. 'What do you mean?'

'As Luke's father I have certain rights. I'll fight you on this if I have to.'

The thing she'd dreaded most about their crazy situation had actually come into being. Jamie was going to betray her in the worst possible way. He was going to use that trust she'd shown him in naming him on the birth certificate to try and control what happened to her son.

'You will have to. There is no way on this earth I'm going to give him up. He's all I have in the world.' She hated the sound of her strangled voice as she battled not to cry in front of him. It was a sign of weakness she couldn't afford to show him when he'd probably try and use it against her somehow.

'Be reasonable, Kayla.' He walked towards her, arms outstretched, but she didn't want him to touch her now she realised everything between them had been a lie. All along he'd only wanted access to his son and used her to get it. She'd been so weak, so desperate for someone to love her and fill that void in her life that Liam's death had left, she'd abandoned her senses to believe they could be together as a family. Now she knew the truth she had to fight to save what was left of it. Her and Luke.

'You're the one who's being unreasonable, Jamie. All I want to do is take Luke to the place which meant so much to his uncles, the men who were supposed to raise him. Without them he would never have been born. You didn't even want him, remember?'

'That's not fair. He wasn't a baby then. Since his birth you know I've been there every step of the way for you both.'

'Until now.'

'All I'm asking is that you think about what you're doing to Luke, and to me, by going through with this harebrained scheme.' He was back to being that arrogant know-it-all she'd met at the wedding. This was the true face of Jamie Garrett and the supportive partner had obviously been a ruse to garner her trust. He hadn't shown any interest in hearing her plans or what safety measures she'd have in place to protect Luke out there. As far as he was concerned, his word was law and he wouldn't hear any different. So why should she even give him house room?

'Get out of my house, Jamie.' She didn't often raise

her voice so when she did people took notice. They knew she was serious.

'Pardon me?' He didn't budge.

'I said get out of my house.' She marched down the hall, lifted his bag and his coat, opened the front door and chucked them out onto the path.

'Kayla, please.' He followed her but hovered in the doorway, unwilling to go after his belongings.

'You can collect the rest of your things tomorrow. I'll box them up.' Arms folded, jaw set, she was unyielding in her decision. She needed him gone so she'd no longer be under his influence. So her feelings for him wouldn't eat away at her conscience until she doubted her own decision-making.

'I thought we'd already had the row over the house. It's half mine too.' It was a last-ditch attempt to guilt her into letting him stay but nothing could persuade her to change her mind now. She had too much to lose.

'Yeah? Sue me. When you're talking to your solicitor about custody rights you can bring it up with him. Goodbye, Jamie.' She held the door open wider for him, refusing to back down.

'Kayla...you know I don't want any of this.'

'Goodnight, Jamie.'

He sighed and shook his head before eventually stepping outside. She slammed the door, not wanting to see him stoop to retrieve his things from the ground and so that he couldn't see the tears running in rivers down her cheeks. It was the hardest thing she'd ever had to do and she only found the strength because of her son. She was Luke's mother and, unlike her own parents, would protect him at all costs. Even if it cost her the love of her life.

CHAPTER ELEVEN

'WHERE ARE MRS HENSHAW's blood results? We've been waiting weeks now. It's unacceptable. Get onto the lab.' Jamie was at the clinic early, catching up on the patients the locum had treated in his absence.

'What's wrong with you this morning? Did the little one keep you up all night?' When his secretary didn't immediately rush to follow his instructions he eventually looked up from his computer screen.

'Sorry. What?' If she'd been trying to start a conversation with him he'd missed it. His head was full of thoughts only about Kayla and Luke and how much of a mess he'd made of things last night.

'You're not your usual affable self. I thought perhaps the baby had kept you awake.' She was subtly pointing out he was being a grouch. His personal life was not something his patients, or the staff, should suffer for. The only one to blame was him for his outburst at Kayla last night. As a result, he'd spent the rest of the night, alone in his bed, cursing himself for ruining the best thing that had ever happened to him.

'Er…something like that.' He had to say something to get rid of her before she asked any more questions and it became obvious to her too what an idiot he'd been.

It was natural for Kayla to want to go and see what Liam and Tom had been working towards out in Vietnam. Any sane person would have been proud that she wanted to do more than go sightseeing and intended to put her medical knowledge to use out there. Deep down he knew she'd never put Luke in danger either. He'd panicked the instant she'd suggested the trip, thinking of all the problems that could befall the people he loved most in the world.

Looking back today, he thought it was no wonder she'd thrown him out. He hadn't asked anything about the trip she was planning, focusing only on the negatives. Telling her he'd fight for custody had sealed the fate of their relationship. It had been a stupid thing to say. Done in the heat of the moment before he'd taken the time to think about what he was saying. Jamie wished he could take it back, but he doubted he'd get the chance. He'd be lucky if the rest of his belongings weren't strewn all around the garden by the time he got over to the house tonight.

'Right, then. I guess I'll go and chase up some results.' Perhaps sensing she wasn't going to get any more conversation out of him, his secretary scooped up the paperwork and scurried out of the room to find better company.

'Good idea.' He didn't look up to see her leave. To be honest he'd been so caught up in feeling sorry for himself he'd forgotten she was there. Nothing seemed to hold his attention at present. He'd lost interest in everything because he had nothing without Kayla and Luke.

His hand hovered over the phone sitting on the desk. He wanted to hear her voice, ask how Luke was this morning, and most of all apologise for his overreaction. Except he knew that fear something would happen to them out there wouldn't leave him. There was no guarantee they wouldn't go around in circles disagreeing over her plans. He didn't know how to resolve the situation, only that he wanted to. They had so much together, had a future before them, and he didn't want to throw that away. If only he knew how to keep Kayla happy and Luke safe.

Right now, he'd settle for a conversation without Kayla thinking about the harsh treatment she'd received at the hands of her parents. He knew that was why she'd been so defensive and angry enough to throw him out. She couldn't despise him more than he despised himself for making that comparison a possibility in her eyes. He'd never intentionally hurt her, but he didn't know if it was too late to convince her of that. If he told her he loved her, wanted to be with her for ever, she wouldn't believe him because of the timing. It was down to him to find some way to convince her they had something worth saving and do everything within his power to make that happen.

'I take it things didn't go well?' Cherry was on the phone first thing in the morning. It only took Kayla's sniffling when she answered the phone for her to realise things hadn't gone to plan.

'That's an understatement. Please don't say you told me so.' She'd spent enough time berating herself for being so stupid in trusting Jamie, for falling for him, and making him such an important part of her and Luke's lives in the first place.

'Oh, Kayla, I would never do that. I just didn't want to see you hurt like this.' Thank goodness her friend *couldn't* see her. She'd have taken one look at Kayla's puffy eyes and red nose and tracked Jamie down to give him a piece of her mind. Doulas, and best friends, were very protective of new mums and their somewhat fragile emotions.

'Well, it's done now. Jamie made it clear he's going to fight for custody if I try and take Luke abroad.' As she said the words that sadness that had been sitting heavily on her chest from last night again threatened to suffocate her. It was one thing walking away from her parents, who had never shown her any kind of love, but quite another to leave someone she loved. It was heartbreaking, knowing it was the end for them. Even more so to think it had all been a lie.

She took no pleasure in discovering she'd been right to be wary of getting in too deep. Now she was questioning if he'd ever had feelings for her at all, beyond her being the mother of his child. Although she'd never said it, never admitted it to herself, she'd fallen in love with Jamie. That was why it was hurting so damn much to have lost him. Now she was grieving all over again for a man she loved and a life she'd never have. How difficult it was going to be to still have him in her life as Luke's father and be reminded of everything that had happened between them.

'There's no hope at all?' The sympathy in Cherry's voice was all it took to set Kayla off again, tears falling and her throat constricting, strangling the wail rising from the depths of her soul.

'No,' she croaked. 'Things were said which can never be forgotten.'

'That's a shame. I mean, I knew he wouldn't like the

idea, but I thought you could work it out, talk it through. You two seemed a good fit.'

Life had a horrible way of surprising her when she least suspected it.

'Thank goodness we didn't do anything stupid like get married or I'd be in real trouble. No, it's better to end things now before it gets too complicated.' If she'd agreed to him moving in permanently she would've been forced to see him every day, take him into account in every decision she made. At least this way she could try and forget him and retain some of her independence.

'What about your trip?'

'Oh, don't worry, it's still going ahead. With or without Jamie's consent.' That stubborn streak that had flourished in her since her move to London, away from her parents' influence, stopped her tears in their tracks. She would find a way to take this trip with Luke. Even if she had to steal away in the dead of night. No one was going to stop her from living her own life.

When Cherry heard that she grew more concerned about Kayla's state of mind and she had to talk her out of rushing over. She was done being weak. The one thing she did draw strength from was her son, so as soon as she hung up on Cherry she rushed upstairs to get him.

'Morning, sleepyhead.' She had to rouse Luke for his morning feed. If she let him sleep on he'd be awake all night and, goodness knew, she didn't want to go back to that again.

He didn't really stir even when she lifted him out of his crib. It was so unlike him. Usually he was wriggling about in there, his arms and legs flailing around, eager to get out and start the day. This morning he was just kind of floppy. Call it experience, or plain old motherly instinct, but she knew something was wrong.

'Luke? Come on, wake up, sweetheart.' She tried blowing gently on his face, but he wasn't responding. His chest was rising and falling steadily so she knew he was still breathing. A huge relief when she considered the alternative.

His cheeks were bright red and when she felt his forehead he was burning up. He was too young to be teething and, though it could be something as simple as a virus, running a fever at this age could cause lasting problems. She laid him down on her bed and stripped him down to try and reduce his temperature, but she didn't want to take any chances. If this was anyone else's baby she would've told them not to panic, it probably wasn't anything serious, but to get him checked out with the GP as soon as possible.

Calculating the length of time it would take to get him over to the health centre, she decided she wanted more immediate action. She grabbed her phone from the bedside table and contemplated who to call. It was an emergency to her, but she wasn't convinced a temperature necessitated an ambulance. There was only one person she knew who could help and who would be as concerned for Luke's welfare. She had to swallow her pride and put her son before her wounded heart.

At the sound of Kayla's voice on the phone Jamie had almost broken down and begged for forgiveness there and then. It had been the fear in her voice and the reason for her call that had stopped him. She wasn't extending an olive branch, she was contacting him because their son was ill. He hadn't wasted any time in leaving work and jumping in his car. There was nothing more important to him than Luke's health.

'How is he?' He was breathless when he got to the house. Kayla had come to the door with Luke in her arms. She was pale, apart from the redness around her eyes, and it was all he could do not to reach out and hug her, assure her everything was going to be all right.

'I'm probably being one of those over-anxious mums, but I didn't want to take any chances. He wasn't himself at all this morning and running a temperature.'

'Not at all. Better to be safe than sorry. Thanks for phoning me.' She could've contacted her GP, or turned to Cherry for help, but she'd chosen him. He was thankful that she wasn't letting their disagreement come between him and his son. Hopefully it was an indication that, no matter what their relationship, he would still be part of the family.

'Where would you like me to examine him?' It seemed so odd now to be asking permission to go anywhere in the house when it had become his home up until last night, but he wasn't here as Kayla's estranged partner. He didn't want to upset her any more by asserting his rights to the house and his son. That was a matter that could be resolved at a later date and hopefully through a civilised discussion.

'We can take him upstairs. I'm sorry I dragged you away from work, but I thought you would understand my worry more than anyone.' She gave him a sad smile before leading him up to her bedroom. A place where they'd spent so many nights together ensuring their son had everything he needed.

'Of course I do. As for work, I wasn't supposed to be back until next week, so I think I'm surplus to requirements for the time being. They were glad to get rid of me for a while.' He thought back to earlier, when his secretary had all but accused him of being a pain to be around. Then the relief he'd seen on her face when he'd said he had to leave. He vowed to make it up to her for being so grumpy. Cake seemed to be the required currency to get the staff on side and he made the decision to stop by the bakery on his way to work tomorrow. He couldn't afford to upset all the people in his life.

Once upstairs, Kayla laid Luke on the bed. She'd done the right thing in stripping him down and trying to lower his temperature. Unchecked, a fever could lead to fitting and a possibility of leaving a child brain-damaged. Jamie tried not to think the worst. They were both medical professionals; they weren't going to let their child get into that sort of danger.

'His temperature is still high.'

Kayla leaned over and studied the reading for herself. 'It is lower than it was first thing.'

'Good. I'll check his ears too.' With his otoscope, he shone a light into Luke's ears. 'There's a lot of inflammation there. I think he's got an ear infection.'

'My poor lamb.' Kayla sat on the bed and did her best to console her son, who was protesting against the intrusion.

'I'll nip out and get him some ear drops to try and take that swelling down. He might need some antibiotics too if it doesn't clear up.' All being well, they could get this under control. He knew both of them could relax if Luke's temperature would come down and they could relieve some of his pain. At least there was something he could do in this situation to stop him from feeling so powerless. It was relations between him and Kayla that still needed attending to. He wasn't going to sit back and let resentment steal away what they'd had before he'd opened his big mouth, when they had so much worth saving.

Since the lines of communication had been opened, Jamie hoped Kayla would hear him out on the other matter tearing his guts out. This was his only chance to convince her he was not the monster she believed him to be and he would do everything in his power to prove it.

Kayla had stopped fretting so much since Jamie had dropped everything and rushed over. Not only because he'd gone out and got the medical supplies needed to treat Luke. Despite everything that had been said, all the things she'd accused him of last night, she was glad to have him back here. He'd been the only person she'd wanted to come and treat Luke and reassure her. Underneath it all she knew he was nothing like her parents. She'd been looking for an excuse to push him away because it was easier to do that than to risk her heart. Scarred so deeply by the past, she was afraid there could be no such thing as a happy family for her and didn't want to put herself through the pain of losing everything when it all went wrong. Except in the aftermath of that conversation last night, pain was all she'd felt. There had been no relief in sending Jamie away because he'd challenged her decisions.

'Do you mind if I stay here until I know he's out of the woods?' Jamie had returned from the chemist within record time. Now he'd administered the ear drops and given Luke some liquid paracetamol to help bring his temperature down, all they could do was watch and wait. Kayla was lying right here beside him on the bed until she knew he was all right.

'Not at all.' She knew Jamie was equally anxious. He wouldn't have dropped everything to come here if he weren't.

He glanced at the bed uncertainly as he took off his coat.

'Go ahead. Take off your shoes first, though.' She gave him a little smile to show she didn't mind him lying here with them. After all, it had become commonplace for all three of them to end up in here. It would be churlish now to deny him that closeness to his son.

'Thanks.' He kicked off his shoes, removed his tie and opened the top button of his shirt. It reminded her of that day in the park when they'd been so content, carefree, and unbothered by the world around them.

'I'm not going to change my mind about the trip, Jamie.' It was one thing deferring to him when Luke was sick, but she wanted him to realise it wouldn't change her plans. She wasn't going to allow him to use an ear infection to take the higher moral ground.

'I wouldn't expect anything less.' He was lying on his side grinning at her, back to being his irritating self when she was trying to be serious. They couldn't simply forget the one thing guaranteed to tear them apart even if there was a chance to get back together.

'I mean, if anything, this goes to prove he can get sick anywhere, but we'll have the same medicines available out there as we have here. That's the whole point of the clinic.' Childhood illness was part of life and they weren't going to do Luke any favours by trying to wrap him in cotton wool. Being Jamie Garrett's son didn't mean he should be treated any differently from any other child.

'I know.' The fact he wasn't putting up any argument only succeeded in her strengthening hers.

'You can't tell me how to live my life, Jamie. I've had enough of that.' If he was agreeing with her only to secure a place in Luke's life, she knew he'd eventually break cover. 'I won't have Luke exposed to the sort of parent I was forced to suffer under.'

That did wipe the grin off his face and she braced herself for another altercation with Jamie's Mr Hyde alter ego. He shifted position so he was sitting upright.

'Do you honestly believe I am anything like your parents? That I would prefer to keep you trained to obey my every command rather than have you fighting me on every issue?' His scowl had softened as he tilted his head to question her real perception of him.

She thought back to those times when they'd clashed, the reasons behind it, and the passion it had sparked between them. Most times it had been at her instigation, fighting her feelings for him, yet unable to resist the pull between them. Jamie had always seemed to enjoy it, her quest for independence and spiky defences not putting him off. He'd never asked her to be anything but true to herself.

'No,' she answered quietly.

'No. I love you, Kayla. I love Luke. The only thing I'm guilty of is wanting to keep you safe. I know I went about it the wrong way but there was no deeper, darker motive for the way I acted last night.'

Her head was spinning. His words were going around and around too fast to catch hold of and really explore what he was saying. She closed her eyes, tried to make them slow down.

It was possible she'd sabotaged any chance of a relationship herself by insisting she was going to Vietnam now when there wasn't any real hurry. She'd simply been using it as an excuse to get away and avoid facing the feelings she had for him. Worried he didn't reciprocate them. He'd just said he loved her. It was why she was so afraid to invite him into her life. Loving Jamie was handing over a very big part of herself to him— her heart—and trusting him not to abuse the privilege.

It would be down to her whether or not to give him a second chance. That meant taking a leap of faith and trusting that he only had her and Luke's best interests at heart. There was only one way of testing that and remaining true to herself.

'I—I love you too, Jamie, but I'm still taking that trip. With Luke.' It took all the courage she had to tell him that and show him her weakness, but she couldn't expect honesty from Jamie and not give it in return.

'I thought you might say that. That's why I got these.' He pulled out a cardboard sleeve from his back pocket and handed it to her. When she opened it, there were tickets with their names on them nestled inside.

'What's this?'

'Airline vouchers. For all of us. I didn't know when, or how long you wanted to go for. You can use these whenever you're ready. I hope that's okay?'

'Er…yeah.' She pulled out the ticket with Jamie's name on it. 'You're coming too?'

'If you want me to? I'm never going to stop you doing anything you want to do. I want to be supportive. This can be our first family holiday.'

'I would really love that.' This gesture was everything, proving she didn't need to flee her feelings for him when he loved her and wanted to be by her side come what may.

'Wait. You're actually agreeing with me on something?'

'Yeah. Don't get too used to it. If I think something's worth fighting you on I won't hold back.'

'Oh, I'm counting on it. They do say the making up after is always the best part.' Jamie leaned over their sleeping baby with that devilish look in his eyes that told her she was in trouble. She kind of liked it.

'Really? Then we have some major making up to do.' She leaned over to meet him.

'Am I forgiven, then?'

'Shut up and kiss me, Jamie Garrett.'

'I'll take that as a yes, then,' he muttered against her lips before showing her exactly why she should forgive him. His kisses were worth risking her heart on.

Kayla had everything she needed in this room. Her family. It might not be the one she'd planned for, but she knew Liam and Tom would be proud of them. Luke had two parents who loved him and that was all that mattered. Falling in love was just a bonus.

EPILOGUE

Two weeks later

'FLIGHTS AND ACCOMMODATION are booked. I have work covered until we come back. I know it might be premature since the trip isn't until the end of the year, but I want to make sure everything's in place. Is there anything else we might have forgotten?'

'I don't think so. If we have there's plenty of time to sort it out. Relax, Jamie.' Kayla couldn't help but laugh at his enthusiasm now they were going together as a family to Vietnam.

If she'd had any lingering doubts he was only going to keep her in check and make sure Luke wasn't in any danger, they'd vanished. He was taking his role as medical relief very seriously, liaising with the other staff out at the clinic to see what was needed.

Since he'd surprised her with the vouchers and they'd stopped bickering about the trip, life had been a dream for her. Luke had recovered from his ear infection after a couple of days and she'd asked Jamie to move in permanently to prove the faith she was putting in him as a father and a partner.

He was still sleeping in his own room, but he hadn't

put her under any pressure to share her bed. If anything, it was she who was suffering when they stopped things from going any further than lingering kisses and he retired to the other end of the hallway. She didn't want them to be in separate rooms in Vietnam but wanted them to go out there united in every way.

'I will once we get this one to bed.' Jamie scooped up their son and carried him into the nursery. Luke had settled better in his cot there with more room to move around. Although they'd both been anxious about leaving him to sleep on his own there, baby monitors had been able to reassure them he was fine.

When Jamie came back she knew she would have to make the move because he would never presume to share her bed. After tonight, she hoped that would change.

'You don't have to go.' It didn't come out as confident or as sultry as the invitation had sounded in her head.

'Are you sure?' If his raised eyebrows were anything to go by, he hadn't expected the offer either.

'I'm sure.' She patted the side of the bed he usually lay on when they were here cuddling with Luke.

'I don't want you to feel you have to do anything…' He was sliding onto the covers beside her, close enough she could feel his warm breath on her face.

'I want to. It's been a while though.' Only now, when they were lying here together, was she beginning to worry. Now she'd had a baby, her body wasn't the same. Never mind the addition of stretchmarks, she didn't know if things would *feel* the same down there.

'We'll take it one step at a time.' He followed the promise with one of those long, languid kisses capable of making her forget her own name.

She quivered with anticipation as he slid his hand under her nightdress, up along her thigh before slipping in between her legs. Tentatively, he tested her readiness with his fingers, but she'd never wanted anyone or anything more. As he stroked her she let her head fall back onto the pillow, enjoying the sensation of getting to know her own body again and what she liked.

The sheets rustled, and she opened her eyes to see Jamie moving down the bed.

'What—?'

'Shh.' He quieted her with that mischievous glint in his eye as he nudged her legs apart and his intent became clear.

Kayla was gasping for air before he even touched her. Then he dotted gossamer-light kisses along her inner thigh and she heard herself groaning for more. He parted her with his tongue and the rush of arousal coursing through her left her limp in its wake. His intimate caresses brought her a pleasure she'd never dreamed of, until he began to thrust into her with his tongue and he exceeded those new heights. She was floating on a cloud of ecstasy at his command, in no hurry to wrest back control of her body this time.

There was no holding back as he drove her to the brink of her climax and when she toppled over the edge she fell hard.

When she was able to breathe properly again, think and talk, she realised she was the only one who'd had any relief. 'What about you, Jamie? It's not fair to leave you wanting.'

He kissed the tip of her nose. 'Don't worry about me. There's plenty of time for us to explore each other. A lifetime, if you can put up with me.'

'Sounds like heaven to me.' It wasn't a conventional proposal but, then again, they had never been a conventional family.

Kayla wouldn't have had it any other way.

* * * * *

MILLS & BOON

Coming next month

A FLING TO STEAL HER HEART
Sue MacKay

Raphael let himself into the house and stopped. Paint fumes hit him. A foreign lightness in the hall made him gape. Wow. What a difference. Should've done it years ago. Except there'd been no motivation before. Izzy had changed everything.

She stood at the bottom of the stairs, dressed in over-large paint-spattered overalls with a roller in one hand and a wide grin on her face. A paint smear streaked across her cheek. Cute. Sexy. 'What do you think?'

I think I want to kiss that spot.

His stomach crunched, his blood hummed.

I think I want to kiss your soft lips and taste you.

Forget humming. There was a torrent in his veins. He was over waiting, being patient, giving her time. He had to do something about his feelings for her.

Dragging his eyes away from the sight that had him in melt-down, he looked around at the white with a hint of grey walls, woodwork, ceiling, and felt his mouth lifting into a smile that grew and grew. 'Amazing. Who'd have believed getting rid of that magenta could make such a difference. This hall is twice the size it was when I went to work this morning.'

'That's a relief.' She placed the roller in the clean tray.

'You were worried I wouldn't like it?' He stepped closer, put his keys and phone on the bottom stair and stood there watching the varying emotions flitting through her beautiful old-wood-coloured eyes.

'Not really.' Her teeth nibbling her lip told him otherwise.

He had to force himself not to reach over and place a finger on her lips to stop her action. 'Why wouldn't I? It was me who bought the paint two years ago.'

Izzy shifted her weight from one foot to the other, then lifted her head enough to lock those eyes on his. 'I worried I've over-stepped the mark by doing this without telling you what I was up to.'

Izzy never worried about upsetting him. Carrying on with whatever she thought best was a trademark of their friendship, always had been, and was one of the reasons he adored her. Something was off centre here, and it frustrated him not knowing what that was. 'Relax. I'm more than happy with what you've done. In fact, I'm blown away.' He waved a hand at his new hall. 'This is amazing. It fires me up to get on with doing up the rest of the house.'

He hadn't noticed the tension in her shoulders until they softened, and a smile touched those lips. 'Thank you, Isabella.'

Her eyes widened and she glanced away, came back to lock eyes with him again. The tip of her tongue appeared at the corner of her mouth. 'Phew.'

Raphael could not stop himself. He reached out, placed his hands on her arms and drew her closer. 'Again, thanks. By doing this you've starting turning my house into a home and up until now I hadn't realised how important it is if I'm to continue living here and become ensconced in a London lifestyle, not just working at the hospital every available hour.'

She was shaking under his hands.

His thumbs smoothed circles on her arms. 'Izzy.'

Her breasts rose, stilled, dropped again. 'Rafe.'

Afterwards he didn't remember moving, couldn't recall anything but his mouth on hers at last. Soft. Sweet. Isabella. Strong, tough Izzy. Returning his kiss. Returning his kiss!

Continue reading
A FLING TO STEAL HER HEART
Sue MacKay

Available next month
www.millsandboon.co.uk

COMING SOON!

We really hope you enjoyed reading this book. If you're looking for more romance, be sure to head to the shops when new books are available on

Thursday 20th March

To see which titles are coming soon, please visit
millsandboon.co.uk/nextmonth

LET'S TALK

Romance

For exclusive extracts, competitions
and special offers, find us online:

 facebook.com/millsandboon

🐦 @MillsandBoon

📷 @MillsandBoonUK

Get in touch on 01413 063232

For all the latest titles coming soon, visit

millsandboon.co.uk/nextmonth